# THE PRICE OF PERFECTION

by

## Jaclyn Edmunds

*Happy reading!*

*Best,*

*J. W. Edmunds*

Beaten Track
www.beatentrackpublishing.com

## Beaten Track

First published 2014 by Beaten Track Publishing
Copyright © 2014 Jaclyn Edmunds

A CIP catalogue record for this book
is available from the British Library.

ISBN: 978 1 909192 83 6

Beaten Track Publishing,
Burscough, Lancashire.
www.beatentrackpublishing.com

# Dedication

This book is dedicated to Ellen Zarter. You helped foster a love for the written word, turning it into my solace and passion.

# Acknowledgements

I would like to express my gratitude and love for my parents for their continued support throughout this whole process. Special thanks also go out to Elana Pirtle-Guiney, for never being too shy to offer her opinion. And to Beka Feathers, for reading every revision, ever, and still helping me feel confident and optimistic.

# Chapter 1

Uckfield, early May, 1810

MICHAEL SKIDMORE, the newest Viscount Averly, and his younger brother, Ryder, were lost. While traveling to London from Brighton, a trip they had made several times in the past, they somehow happened upon a small Sussex town that they had never before encountered.

Michael and Ryder, riding their well-bred mounts, were already attracting more attention than Michael would have desired. He turned to see a woman walk out of a small shop, holding the hand of her young son. Both the woman and child stared at them, jaws identically slackened. Michael grimaced. Apparently strangers were not welcomed with excessive fanfare in…Good Lord! Did that small sign refer to this village as Uckfield? Michael should have pressed more firmly to take that other fork. Ryder had an abysmal sense of direction.

An inn and tavern on the far end of town beckoned the two travelers. Michael glanced back up the dirt road that had led him there. A short distance away, a butcher, still grasping his cleaver, stared belligerently at the two strangers from the doorway of his shop. The brothers hastily dismounted and snatched up their belongings. The rest of their things would follow them into London, once their Brighton home was fully closed for the Season.

Michael's hope that the stares would cease inside The Griffin was soon proven optimistic. The entire tavern fell silent upon their entrance. Here was not a place where Michael would flaunt his new title.

After questioning the innkeeper, Michael was directed to a merchant who often traveled to Uckfield to visit his son. The gentleman told him where to find the nearest crossing over the River Ouse. By the time Michael had the directions he sought, it was too late in the evening to continue on to London.

As he and Ryder settled into their small room at the inn, Michael hoped fervently that his valet in London knew a way to wash the inn's unsavory smell from his coat and breeches. If it could be arranged with the innkeeper, he had every intention of having dinner sent to his room.

When Ryder learned of his brother's intention to avoid the inn's taproom, he shook his head in dismay. Unlike Michael, he wanted to take advantage of their misfortune and enjoy the evening. Although Ryder absolutely respected his brother, he often wondered how he might convince Michael to add some excitement to his life. It seemed as if Michael became stodgier and stodgier as time went on. And so, as Michael stretched out on his bed, hands tucked behind his head, Ryder descended the stairs to join the less agreeable inhabitants of Uckfield, Sussex.

---

The news of two particularly distinguished gentlemen traveling through the small town of Uckfield had not yet reached Miss Charlotte Henwood. She likely would not have cared to hear the gossip in the first place. Instead, she rose the following day and prepared to enjoy a vigorous morning ride. After all, she had a great many things to consider.

One thing was certain: Mr. Charles Trivett's courtship was not proving to be as exciting as the sensation novels implied. They had enjoyed a ride together the morning before. However, both the ride and the conversation had proven painfully sedate.

Charlotte wished she could be satisfied with Charles. His twin sisters, Caroline and Eleanor, were Charlotte's closest friends in Uckfield. Now that the twins were in London preparing for their first Season, Charlotte needed to find something else to occupy her. No doubt at his family's suggestion, Charles had begun to call on her regularly.

In every way that mattered to the residents of Uckfield, the man was perfect for her. Charles' father was the most prosperous landholder for miles, as well as the magistrate. Although Charlotte was not exactly wealthy, her father held a title. In addition to Charles' excellent prospects, he was quite handsome. The light blond hair and blue eyes that he shared with his sisters would properly complement her darker features. With the thick black hair and warm brown eyes she had inherited from her Italian mother, Charlotte would never be considered fashionably attractive. Nevertheless, her high cheekbones, dark lashes, and full lips lent her an exotic air. Everything was shaping up to a perfect match.

Charlotte had tried so very hard to fill yesterday's ride with interesting conversation. When she had enquired as to how Charles usually spent his days, he had replied, "Learning how to manage the accounts, I suppose."

"Is there a certain writer you enjoy, or sport you play? A hobby?" she had asked, her tone turning somewhat desperate. Charles had merely smiled, vacantly. She was beginning to notice that most of his smiles were a touch vacant.

Hopefully, a vigorous ride today would help her mull over her concerns. She had worn her better riding habit the day before. However, once home, she had jumped off her mare to land straight into a mud puddle. She should not have been surprised. It had rained every night for the past week.

Today was cloudy, but rain-free, and a bit chillier than was typical for the time of year. Charlotte was actually quite pleased that she had been forced to wear her warmer—albeit more worn—wool habit. When she had first bought it, the habit had been a vibrant violet, but now it was a faded gray. Perhaps the residents of Uckfield would not recognize her as easily, dressed as she was. The vicar and his wife often commented to her father on her tendency to ride at a full gallop across the countryside. Her papa cared little, but Charlotte hated to bother him over something so inconsequential.

Choosing to live dangerously, she also left her hair loosely tied behind her back, wanting to feel the wind catch and toss it about. Charles had told her the previous day that he would be trapped inside, going over the household accounts all day. She and Esmerelda, her mare, were ready to fly.

To be safe, Charlotte rode to the side of town opposite her father's and the vicar's home. She seldom traveled to this end of Uckfield. The vicar and his wife often warned her away from The Griffin and the inn's uncouth patrons. Charlotte's feminine sensibilities were apparently too weak to withstand exposure to such unsuitable behavior. Were women even allowed inside The Griffin? She remembered the vicar's wife speaking badly of a woman who, after being fired from the vicar's employ, had been forced to find a position there. So clearly some women could be found inside the place, but apparently not women like Charlotte.

Had her father ever been inside? Or the vicar? How else would he know what kind of men spent their time there? Charlotte smiled to herself as she envisioned the rigidly proper vicar sharing a table with a highwayman or thief.

As Esmerelda carried her rider away from town, Charlotte couldn't help but turn around to catch a glimpse of the notorious inn and tavern. Had she been facing forward, all would likely have gone well. But when her mare slid in a patch of mud, Charlotte was in the perfect position to slip off and land unpleasantly on her backside. In the mud. The unpleasant jolt of her landing left her stunned for a moment. Her first thought was that it was a very good thing she wore her second-best riding habit.

A distant shout drew her attention to a man riding toward her, dark brown hair waving in the wind. How perfect. An audience would only make her fall more pleasant and memorable. The stranger quickly dismounted to catch Esmerelda's reins. As Charlotte lay inelegantly on the ground, she noticed that he appeared quite tall—much taller than Charles Trivett.

"Are you all right?" He turned to her as he soothingly stroked Esmerelda's nose.

Should all men's breeches be that fantastically tight? Yes, she decided, they certainly should. Charles did not fill his breeches out in such an impressive manner. Perhaps if his were tailored better? This gentleman's brown breeches and sage coat were clearly well-made. Perhaps he could recommend a tailor.

Oh dear, she still hadn't spoken. No one had ever taught her the appropriate subjects to discuss while lying in a puddle. "Erm, well, I think I'm going to bruise." Well done, Charlotte. Very clever.

Michael took in the woman lying on the muddy ground. She hadn't seemed to fall incredibly hard, so he had concerned himself more with her mare at first. The mare had clearly been preparing to flee. He should have paid more attention to the girl. She was absolutely lovely. Her gleaming hair was dark as sin, if untidily tossed by the wind and her fall. And now that she spoke his gaze was drawn to her lips. They were so very full, and appeared enticingly soft. Such lips were perfectly designed for...things he should not be considering at the moment.

Charlotte's eyes met those of her rescuer. "Oh my." She needed a closer look to discover if they were blue or green. And his jaw was so solid and masculine; she wanted to lightly run her finger from his ear to his arrogant square chin, just to see how firm it felt.

As she tried to stand, she discovered that her backside was even sorer than she had thought. She quickly sank into the mud. "I believe I have injured my, erm..." It was a bit late to remember that ladies did not discuss their rear ends. "Well, I need a moment before I try standing."

"Can I help you return to your home or family?" Michael decided that the horses were not going to bolt, so he approached the young woman, holding out his hand to her. "I would be happy to assist you in wherever you need to go, Miss…"

"I'm Charlotte. So sorry. Erm, and you are?" Could she be any less ridiculous, lying here on the ground while making conversation? The Trivett twins would know just how to behave when encountering such a handsome gentleman. Then again, they had the advantage of an overbearing mother who had drummed the rules of etiquette and social interaction into her daughters since birth. Charlotte's mother had passed on when she was four, leaving her father in charge of her rearing. Her dear papa had taught her history and philosophy, but not propriety or comportment.

Oh dear, wasn't she supposed to have provided him with her last name? How completely uncouth! Before she could supply it, he spoke.

"Michael Skidmore, at your service." Michael had not yet had opportunity to present himself as Viscount Averly and did not intend to do so in this small town. Honestly, Michael doubted the residents of Uckfield knew how to treat a viscount. Not that he, himself, was entirely certain how a viscount ought to be treated. His relationship to the direct Averly line was so distant he had never expected to inherit the title.

This country miss, with her hair tumbling in disarray in her face and her muddied habit, likely would panic to discover a titled lord was assisting her after her fall. He repeated his earlier question, "May I escort you home?"

Once standing, Charlotte admitted that her rump was going to have an unpleasant bruise later on. "Thank you for your offer, Mr. Skidmore, but I live a way beyond the other side of town and I'd really rather not walk there quite yet." No doubt the vicar would also criticize her for allowing this stranger to escort her home. This gentleman clearly did not belong in Uckfield.

"Perhaps we could rest for a while in a place where the seats are not composed of mud and grass? I don't doubt you'll be more comfortable indoors somewhere."

Charlotte couldn't help but smile in relief. By now the mud had completely saturated her drawers, which was not the most pleasant experience. "That would be absolutely wonderful."

So, Charlotte came to be leaning heavily on the arm of a handsome stranger as she walked slowly back into town, both their horses led by their reigns behind them. She turned to get a better look at his profile.

Now that she had a closer view, she saw that his eyes were a clear green in the center, with a darker forest green ringing the outside. Charlotte couldn't recall ever seeing more beautiful eyes. He seemed to be only a few years older than she, perhaps five-and-twenty. Goodness, he had a freckle on the outer edge of his lower lip. A small sigh escaped her lips. It would be a lovely thing to see the world, and gentlemen, beyond Uckfield. Especially if she could meet more men like this one.

"Where are you going to take me once we reach town? I'm not entirely familiar with this side of Uckfield." She chose not to mention that the vicar forbade all ladies of gentle birth to visit this end of town because of The Griffin.

Michael almost laughed, "I hadn't thought of that. I believe the only public place on this side of town is The Griffin."

Charlotte had been too quick in deciding that light hair was handsome on a gentleman. Mr. Skidmore's brown hair, coupled with his strong chin and dark brows, made him look more distinguished. More masculine and mature.

"Oh, I know for an absolute fact that I should not be in a place like that. I'm sure there is a bench somewhere nearby that I could rest on." Now that they had reached the town proper, they both looked around for seating. That was the exact moment the heavens opened.

"I believe that decides matters for us," Michael said, raising his voice over the pounding rain and hastening their pace. "I'm sure no one will fault you for seeking refuge from this downpour."

There was no way to hide the mischievous look in her eyes. Also raising her voice above the rain, she replied, "I have always wanted to see the inside of The Griffin. I hear the most fascinating stories that always end right when things seem to be getting interesting."

Soon they were practically running, hoping to reach the inn before becoming thoroughly drenched. *On the upside*, thought Charlotte, *at least the rain is washing the mud off my dress.*

Michael laughed as he held The Griffin's door for her. "I doubt that very much shall be happening in here right now. I was taking a ride to explore the land, while I waited for my brother to rise. It is likely the other lodgers from the previous night are also sleeping things off."

Despite his words, Michael worried about taking her into such an establishment, but with the rain, there seemed to be no choice.

However, Michael couldn't help but notice his companion's growing excitement and fascination. But really, what sort of trouble could one young woman get into so early in the morning?

Charlotte felt almost giddy. Surely, no one else would judge her for seeking shelter in the only place available? She really only had to worry about running into the vicar, or anyone else of his particularly elevated moral standing. She nearly laughed. If anyone like the vicar was caught in The Griffin, it would be the talk of Uckfield for years!

Walking into the taproom, the smells of dried, spilled ale, stale smoke, and the beginnings of a hearty stew filled her nose. The combination was somewhat stomach-turning, yet also oddly comforting. This place was incredible.

Charlotte let Mr. Skidmore lead her to a table close to the door. The innkeeper had immediately noticed the presence of the young lady inside his establishment and wasted no time in approaching them. Michael noted the suspicious look on his face.

As the innkeeper neared, Michael saw the two gentlemen sitting in the far corner shoot them curious looks. He recalled them mentioning the previous night to the innkeeper that they were merely traveling through. Michael paused. They may not recognize Charlotte, but others of her acquaintance might still break their fast here.

"Can I bring you anything?" The innkeeper asked Charlotte in a voice laced with disapproval, as he took in her disheveled, sodden appearance.

Michael made a quick decision. Standing, he said, "I'll have the house ale, but bring it to my room."

Charlotte's eyes widened. His room? Would that be at all acceptable? Obviously she should not join him. Michael saw her uncertainty.

"I am concerned about others seeing you in here while we wait for the rain to subside," he told her under his breath. "It might be wise to move to a more concealed location." He held out his hand to draw her out of her seat. Giving her a smile that he intended to be comforting, but Charlotte found temptingly wicked, he added, "I absolutely promise to behave in the most upright manner possible."

Charlotte had never expected to be in a situation where a man would have to say such a thing to her. And exactly why did his promise disappoint her so? Then again, she had never truly encountered a gentleman like him before. He had been so good as to help her after her inordinately embarrassing tumble. He had not made a single inappropriate or rude comment. Most importantly, he had been kind to her horse.

But despite his kindness, what proof did she have that he was a true gentleman? Charlotte had very little experience with men, especially interesting, attractive ones. Her thoughts returned to her dull suitor, Mr. Charles Trivett, who likely never intended to leave Uckfield unless forced.

All of a sudden, she realized she wanted something more in her life. All of the stories of adventure that her father had read to her as a child came to mind. No matter what Mr. Skidmore's intentions were, she made a decision.

"I'll have some ale, too."

# Chapter 2

MICHAEL'S HEAD whipped up in shock. He had only ordered an ale out of concern that the innkeeper would toss Charlotte out if they didn't at least pretend to patronize The Griffin. He had no intention of actually drinking ale this early in the day. To Michael's relief, the innkeeper merely shrugged and left them. Apparently, so long as they put money in his hand, the man would not make an issue of things.

Did she really intend to join him in his room so blithely? Her easy agreement left him a bit disconcerted. Exactly what kind of life did she lead to be unbothered at joining a man in his inn room?

Charlotte could feel her face heat under Mr. Skidmore's curious gaze. But really, how could he blame her? She didn't foresee any future opportunity to converse alone with a man before marriage. This might be the only adventure she would ever have.

The tavern was almost completely empty, except for the two strangers in the corner. No one would know she had asked for ale, she assured herself, as Mr. Skidmore held his arm out for her. She tried to ignore his concerned expression as he led her up the stairs.

After a moment, Michael was forced to say, "I really do not think it's acceptable for me to allow you to drink the ale here. No lady would do so."

Michael opened the door to his room for her, then followed her in. She turned back to him to reply impertinently, "Well, then, lucky for you that it isn't your decision." Goodness, had those words really come from her lips? This was her father's fault. He allowed her to get away with a great deal too much.

Before Michael could reply—likely somewhat censoriously—the innkeeper returned. There was a small table near the single window in the room, where he set the tankards down and hastily left. Michael held the chair out for Charlotte as she sat down in front of the daunting tankard. "Am I really supposed to drink that whole thing?" she asked Michael in astonishment. "I'm not sure I drink that much *tea* in a whole day."

Relieved, Michael laughed. "I don't expect you to finish a quarter of that." He seated himself.

He probably did not mean that as a challenge. Unfortunately, it seemed Mr. Skidmore brought out Charlotte's competitive nature. She gave him a toothy grin. "I'm sure I can manage just fine. My constitution is quite resilient."

Nevertheless, as she looked back to her ale, she couldn't help feeling a bit apprehensive. Michael was looking at her expectantly, a curious gleam in his eyes. She reached out and took a large gulp of the amber liquid, the bitter taste filling her mouth. She swallowed everything down and let out a cough.

Michael contained his laughter, just barely. "I developed the skill of gulping down large quantities of ale in school. It's an acquired talent," Michael said, as he took a large swallow of his own ale. He didn't expect such low quality fare, although perhaps he should have. Michael couldn't hold back a light cough either. At this, Charlotte burst into laughter.

"Ha! You see, I *do* have the stronger constitution!" she boasted gleefully.

Michael cocked his head. "I suppose I deserve that." They both went back to sipping their ale, with a little more care than before.

Finally, Charlotte gave in. "Does all ale taste like this?"

Michael couldn't conceal the look of distaste on his face. "I don't often partake, but no. I would have to say this is unusually atrocious." In mutual agreement, they both put down their tankards and pushed them away.

Now that Charlotte had her chance to converse with someone who was familiar with the world outside of her small village, she had no idea what to ask him. To fill the silence, she found herself telling him about Uckfield's history. After a while, Mr. Skidmore began telling her about his own experiences growing up in Brighton and then London. His words brought the larger cities to life for her in a way that her books never had. She was certain she would never forget the way his green eyes glowed as he described the sunny days in Brighton, when his father would take him to the beach to play. Conversation never lagged, and it surprised Charlotte how comfortable she felt with this man.

After some time, she turned to the window to watch the rain slow. Michael found himself thinking up ways to keep the bright excitement on her face. She had such an alluring smile. His mind wandered to the other things he could do that would please her. Which, of course, led to thoughts about what might please them both. And good Lord, those lips were looking more and more tantalizing.

Blast it all! Following the death of his parents three years ago, he had promised himself to cease engaging in any sort of remotely unsuitable conduct. Briefly, his mind drifted back to the raucous weekend that had led to his decision. Now that was not a story he could share with his new companion. An old school friend had invited a few gentlemen to his estate in the country. On their final morning, Michael had awoken, bleary-eyed on the floor of the stables, accompanied by two lovely women whose names he could not begin to fathom. After standing up, as slowly and carefully as he could, he had ascertained that while asleep one of his friends had thrown all his clothing into the duck pond. On a positive note, despite waking up missing most of his clothing, he had, inexplicably, still been wearing his boots.

The rest of that morning's discoveries had been significantly less pleasant. For example, one of the ladies happened to be his closest friend's secret mistress. While he had not left that gathering with most of his own clothing, he had taken a very black eye with him. Michael had decided to avoid nights that would reach that level of madness from then on. He had been mostly successful.

Yet this particular young lady brought the worst out of him. The images running through his mind no longer just involved her lips meeting his—although they most certainly still involved those lips. Those lips were just more…everywhere.

He shook his head, dissolving an image of her peeling her dress from her shoulders and down her torso. The ale must be getting to him, that's all. Besides, he knew removing a woman's clothing was not nearly so simple.

Charlotte turned back to Mr. Skidmore when she heard him make a strange grumbling sound. The moment her eyes returned to his, her gaze was arrested. She had never seen a man look at her like that before. Somehow, she felt every nerve in her body tingle.

Charlotte heard a door open and slam shut downstairs, jerking her back to reality. The rain had finally ceased. She stood, uncertain. "Perhaps it would be best if I prepared to go. I think I am realizing how this may not be one of my more brilliant ideas."

Michael rose with her. "You're right. Of course." She could not stay any longer without Michael experiencing a great deal of discomfort. His breeches were cut a bit tighter than he was used to and he feared she would have a great many more questions if she stayed. Perhaps standing at this exact moment was not a clever idea…

As she neared the door, Michael called, "Wait!" She stopped, confused. He walked to the door. "I'll check first, to ensure no one will see you leave here."

Charlotte waited behind the door while he leaned out. He stood so close, she could smell him. Right now, he smelled of bad ale and horse. She did not especially mind.

The thought rose in Charlotte's mind that she had never kissed a man before. True, that act ought to be reserved entirely for her husband. But what if Charles didn't kiss well? Shouldn't she have a basis of comparison? Her father had taught her that a single example seldom helped prove an idea or theory. One should always gather as much knowledge and evidence as possible.

Finally Michael leaned back in, "It looks like—"

He had no idea she was standing so close behind the door. Those damned lips were right there. Every one of Michael's muscles tightened. She subconsciously swayed towards him, her lips only inches from his own. He could no longer hold himself back. Slowly, he slid his fingers behind her neck and up into her hair. Looking into her eyes, he gave her a second to change her mind, lean back, and leave. Instead, she stared back at him with that endearing look of surprise and curiosity.

Finally, it wasn't Michael, but Charlotte, who lightly sealed her lips to his. A butterfly touch at first, Michael could barely feel her. Closing his eyes, he leaned down, sliding one hand out of her hair and down her back, carefully drawing her flush against him. Trying to remain gentle, he slowly moved his lips over hers.

Charlotte lightly gasped the moment he drew his lips away, only to press them against hers again at a different angle. Uncertain, Charlotte raised her hands to his shoulders, wanting to get closer. This was her first kiss. And it was incredible. His lips were moving more firmly over hers now, urging her to do the same.

There were footsteps nearing their door. Michael jumped back as the footsteps grew louder, worried that someone would find them in a compromising state.

Ryder swung into the room, nearly knocking the pair over when he pushed the door open.

It was definitely for the best. Their kiss had proven that Charlotte truly was an innocent. Michael was a little bothered that this discovery only excited him more.

Relieved by the interruption, he said to Ryder, "I see you finally decided to grace us with your presence." At Charlotte's questioning look, Michael added, "This is my brother, Mr. Ryder Skidmore." Michael's gaze was arrested by her swollen, reddened lips and the light shallow breaths she was trying to slow. Hopefully she would gain control soon. Michael didn't much care about Ryder discovering their actions, but goodness, it was a challenge to look away as her bosom rose and fell.

Before Michael could complete the introductions, a laughing red-headed young woman followed Ryder into the room. Her dull-toned, unadorned attire certainly indicated a less-than-genteel upbringing, which no doubt explained her presence at the Griffin. However, her face and energy were arresting.

"Ah, Ryder…" Michael tilted his head, indicating Charlotte, who remained partially hidden behind the door.

Charlotte understood that Michael wanted to protect her from anything unpleasant, but she could care for herself. She had just been kissing the man in his room, after all. Besides, this interaction was really quite amusing. Mr. Ryder Skidmore's friend had a lovely time as she tickled and poked him. Charlotte soon found herself giggling along with the other woman.

Michael sighed. "Ryder, would you and your companion mind walking my friend out with me?" Finally, noticing the other lady in the room, the redhead turned to Charlotte and smiled as she stepped back from Ryder.

Before they left the room, Charlotte caught a glimpse of herself in the mirror. She hardly recognized her reflection. Her hair hung loosely all around her face, apart from the bits that stuck up from her head in a frizzy mess, and she could barely see her features. Except her lips, which were redder than she had ever seen them before.

Charlotte was drawn out of her thoughts by the redhead murmuring, "So sorry, Miss," with a teasing gleam in her eye. The girl was so vivacious, it was hard to resist smiling with her as the four of them descended the stairs.

After a moment, Charlotte realized she recognized the red-haired girl. Charlotte was almost certain that she was the maid the vicar had fired. The girl had brought in their tea a few times during Charlotte's visits. What was her name? Sally or Sandy? No that wasn't right.

"*Suzie!*" Oh right, that was her name. Suzie. The shocked voice came from the tavern's entrance. Charlotte turned to their newest arrival.

Her jaw dropped. What was Charles Trivett doing here? She gasped as another question entered her mind. *How did he know Suzie?* Standing behind Mr. Skidmore, frozen, Charlotte could do nothing but watch the scene unfold.

As for Michael, he was quite amused. There seemed to be a woman madly in love with his brother in every town they visited—apparently, little, unknown Uckfield, Sussex was no different. And this pretty redhead likely explained why Ryder had not returned to their room the night before.

Suzie glanced nervously at Charlotte. She carefully stepped in front of their small group. "Charles, what're you doing here?" Her accent had hints of the educated upper classes, but it wasn't too strong. Charlotte considered it likely that the vicar's wife had tried to improve Suzie's speech while she had been in the vicar's employ.

"*Me?* What are you doing with *that* man?" Charles indicated Ryder, whose arm Suzie had recently been hanging from. "Who is he? What's going on? I can't believe this!"

Charlotte had never before seen Charles so passionate about anything.

Amusement slowly fading, Michael realized that now would be a good time to take his companion outside. However, when he turned around to take her arm, she raised a hand to halt him, her gaze riveted on Charles.

Now it was Suzie's turn to look affronted. Hands on hips, she yelled back, "You can't believe what? That I wouldn't wait around fer you? You haven't come to see me fer o'er a week. I just assumed you weren't comin' back, so I decided to stop waitin'." Her cultured accent seemed to give way to a more rural one when angry, Charlotte noted.

Charlotte could not see Charles' face, because Mr. Skidmore blocked her, but she could hear his voice take on a wheedling quality. "But I told you, my mother and sisters were preparing to leave for London and…"

Suzie was having none of that. "And they wanted you to pay court to that other lady," she said as she crossed her arms. "I seen her comin' to visit the vicar's wife. I never expected you to stick around, Charles."

Charles saw no one but his mistress. "So what if I spend time with her? A gentleman needs to marry a woman to give him an heir and manage the house. She would mean nothing to me the way you do. I'll still come to you in the mornings, like I always do."

Charlotte almost did not register his words. When she finally comprehended the manner in which Mr. Charles Trivett spent many of his mornings, she saw red. "Charles!" She practically screeched as she forced her way in front of the Skidmore brothers. "What in the world is going on? And what do you mean, 'like you always do'? How do you know this woman? You're supposed to be a gentleman!"

# Chapter 3

THE ASTONISHMENT IN CHARLES' EYES was almost comical. "Charlotte?" was all he could muster. His mind apparently chose to shut down at that point, although, inexplicably, his lips continued moving.

Michael, meanwhile, realized that he and his brother should not be a part of this dispute. He didn't enjoy the idea of Charlotte being slighted by the other man, but if he defended her, Charles could come to suspect something much more sinister.

Charlotte was clever enough to take care of herself. Michael had discovered that within the short time they had spent together. For a country girl, she was certainly well educated, quite capable of standing up to a man like this Charles. Michael couldn't help but feel some pity for the man. However, he also couldn't suppress a twinge of disappointment. Charlotte was a fascinating young woman. After that kiss, he had wanted to find a way to continue their acquaintance. Alas, it seemed she already had a man for her.

He should leave. He wordlessly motioned to Ryder with his head, indicating the door. Ryder nodded back but pointed up to the ceiling. Damn. Their travel bags were still in their room. He watched his brother turn and head back upstairs, almost going to follow. Something in Charles' face stopped him. Shock had given way to anger.

"What the bloody hell is going on?" Michael almost chastised Charles for such language in a lady's presence. Before he could, Charles continued on, "How often do you come to this place, for heaven's sake, Charlotte? It is highly inappropriate for a lady to be here!"

Charlotte flinched as though he had dealt a physical blow, the memory of Mr. Skidmore's kiss still strong in her mind. But she quickly regained her poise. "You must know I've never been here before, considering you come here *every morning*. I wonder what your father would think of your familiarity with this Suzie person." Not wanting to cause offense to Suzie, she murmured, "Pardon me, Miss." Suzie only shrugged.

Charles was not done. "It is acceptable for a gentleman to come to an establishment like this. Your mere presence here, without anyone to watch out for you, demonstrates that you are barely a lady! Just look at yourself! You look like you've spent the night engaging in completely improper activities." Charles looked triumphant as Charlotte instinctively reached for her hair to smooth it down.

Michael bit his lip in frustration. He knew now what Charles intended to do. Charles hoped to make Charlotte come out of this whole experience worse than him. If he could destroy Charlotte's reputation, his would remain intact. He seemed to be doing a good job of it. Michael reminded himself that it would be much worse for Charlotte if he informed Charles that it was he, a man she had only just met, who chaperoned her. No doubt Charles would then accuse Charlotte of engaging in those improper activities with Michael. Though it nearly killed him, Michael kept silent.

"I was only here to get out of the rain. I fell from my mare and this was the closest establishment I could walk to. That's the reason I'm here, not for some illicit liaison—like you!" Charlotte nearly shook with anger and betrayal.

"I am certain you've been told to avoid this place."

Charlotte couldn't argue with him there. Charles, however, continued as if she had.

"And what are you even doing with these others?"

Michael had been hoping he wouldn't catch onto that.

Charles shook his head. "I do not understand your actions."

"I only wanted to wait for the rain to stop," Charlotte said again, her voice losing its strength as she turned to Michael imploringly. They had only known each other for a morning, but she thought they had developed a friendship of sorts. Why wasn't he supporting her? She opened her mouth to tell Charles that Michael was merely helping her.

Charles cut her off. "There is no way to excuse your behavior. Who is this man, anyway?"

It was definitely the time for Michael to step in. "Viscount Averly. And you are?" He asked in the most supercilious tone he could muster. It was unfortunate how recently he had come into the title; he doubted he sounded at all impressive.

However, he must have pulled it off well enough, judging by Charles' shocked silence. As for Charlotte, Michael watched her mouth form an adorable "O" as she processed Michael's words. Not that he should be trying to impress her.

Charles recovered quickly. "Like hell you are! What would a viscount be doing unannounced in Uckfield? I can assure you my family would already have known of your presence, were you actually someone of importance. You're more likely a thief or charlatan."

Michael tried to insert a, "Now see here," but was drowned out by the rest of Charles' tirade.

"I'm sure my sisters have no idea their friend behaves so improperly," he continued to Charlotte, voice rising, "but I have no choice but to ask you to cease involving yourself with my family. Your behavior could destroy my sisters' reputations. Now, if you'll excuse me—although I can't imagine why I would waste my time on a polite exit." He turned and left the tavern.

⁓

Charlotte was numb. How could Charles treat her like this, when he was in the wrong? What would he tell his family? She knew he would say something to them about her. His words had been too spiteful.

"Well," she heard Suzie say, "he always did act the gormless prat, and that's the truth. Good riddance, I say. We're better off without him, love."

Charlotte turned to her, realization striking. "He is absolutely no gentleman. Oh, but now who will I marry?" Embarrassment flooded her as she realized what she had just said.

Suzie didn't seem to notice. "I don't think it'll be too 'ard to find someone more interestin'. Right boring, 'e was."

"He was quite dull, wasn't he?" Charlotte said, almost with a sense of relief.

Ryder soon returned from upstairs. "I'm ready to leave for London."

Charlotte hadn't thought that far ahead. Mr. Skidmore had been prepared to leave before the rain came, and now nothing kept him from going. Perhaps it was for the best. She wasn't sure how she felt about his lying to protect her. And with such a ridiculously outlandish tale, at that! What would a viscount ever be doing in Uckfield?

But it mattered little now. Her chances for marriage were likely forever halted after this exchange. In fact, she wouldn't put it past Charles to tell every one of his friends about her presence here. She sighed, deciding to worry about that when the time came.

"It was a pleasure to meet you," she said shakily after Mr. Skidmore handed some coins to the innkeeper.

He took in her look of disappointment—or what he could see of it through the hair falling over her eyes and face—before he said, "I really am sorry about what happened. I'm pleased you held your ground so well, even if he did take the easy way out by leaving before you could say anything else. I wish I could have come to your defense without potentially making matters worse." Michael reached for her hand, drawing it to his lips. It was lovely, pressing his lips to such an elegant hand uncovered by gloves. It reminded them both of where his lips had been just minutes before. "You're lucky you discovered how great a fool that man is."

Charlotte barely heard his words once his lips touched her hand. It was such a gentlemanly act. His lips were so soft and warm. All she could utter was a light, "Oh."

"If you are ever in London, and need anything, please come find me," Michael said, releasing her hand.

He doubted he would ever meet her again. London was a large city and, judging by her bedraggled appearance, they certainly didn't travel in similar circles. He could hope to run into her, nevertheless.

Charlotte's mind was still a little muddled after her exchange with Charles, followed by Mr. Skidmore's gallant behavior, but she did manage, "That would be delightful, I'm sure."

Michael nodded. "Are you sure there isn't something I can do here? Perhaps I could speak with that man's family and explain matters. He was coming here to meet his mistress, after all. Pardon me, Miss," he added to Suzie, who only shrugged again.

Not even needing to consider her answer, Charlotte shook her head. No doubt it would make matters even worse, were Mr. Skidmore—a stranger in Uckfield—to defend her to the Trivetts. He wouldn't stand a chance against their snobbery.

Michael nodded, although he was a bit disappointed. It would have been enjoyable to put that foolish boy in his place. Instead, he bowed again and left her, Ryder following behind after giving Suzie a smoldering look.

"Well, there go some lovely men," Suzie said in their wake.

Charlotte turned to her. "I hope you aren't including Mr. Trivett in that analysis." Suzie and Charlotte looked at each other for a moment and then the laughter began. Neither could say why they laughed so hard, but the act relieved Charlotte's anxiety. Perhaps later she would wonder at her lack of disappointment in Charles' behavior, but for now, she enjoyed the moment.

Suzie raised a sly eyebrow as she asked, "Was I mistaken when I thought I saw two tankards of our house ale up in that room?"

Charlotte could only laugh and nod, "But I only managed a little before I coughed."

Suzie let out another amused chuckle. "I can't believe you were tryin' that bloody swill." Charlotte nearly gasped at Suzie's language, but the redhead was going on. "Word to the wise, love, only 'ave the drinks that were bottled far away from 'ere. I'll find us somethin' better." Suzie took Charlotte's arm to lead her to the tavern's private back room. Suzie then left to retrieve a bottle and two snifters.

Charlotte couldn't help but find amusement at life's quirks of fate. Usually, she would visit the vicar's wife for tea on a day so overcast. Instead, Charlotte was sharing a brandy with Suzie, the now ex-mistress of Mr. Charles Trivett.

As Suzie poured Charlotte what appeared to be hardly any brandy at all, she said, "I didn't mean what I said to Charles, implyin' I didn't like you much. I was just mad. I may not be a lady like you, but he didn't need to be so obvious 'bout lookin' fer another woman to marry. Besides that, I didn't e'en recognize you when I said it. You look a tad diff'rent than you do when you come see the vicar's wife—the harridan." Suzie paused. "Was you really goin' after 'im?"

Charlotte took a sip of brandy and managed to suppress another cough. Perhaps it was good that Suzie had given her such a small amount. "Well, I thought I was. I just can't believe he would betray me like that. I've been acquainted with his family for so long. How could he not know by now that I'm not the sort of woman to come to a place like this? Erm, no offense, Miss..." Charlotte realized she had no idea how to address her new companion.

"Perkins. And don't worry. You really are the first lady I've seen in 'ere. We don't even get a lady or two traveling through since most of 'em stop in the bigger towns." Suzie paused again, before adding, "I think I know why he didn't stand up fer you either. His father was makin' it clear that Charles had to do the family proud. Charles weren't even supposed to come to The Griffin, let alone get involved with someone like me."

"He was worried I'd tell his sisters and then his father would find out somehow," Charlotte murmured.

"And then Papa Trivett tightens those purse strings." Suzie rolled her eyes. "That was why he only came to see me in the mornin'. No one would see us meeting at that hour. Let's get a bit o' my puddin' cake too. It's the best in Uckfield." She left for a moment to take a plate from the kitchen. Sitting down, Suzie bit her lip, uncertain if she should say anything else, but clearly wanting to.

"What?" Charlotte gave a bitter smile, as she slipped her spoon into the dessert. "I'm already ruined, Suzie. You won't shock me too greatly if you have any other news about Charles."

"Well, I were thinkin'. You're probably better off without him. He weren't that, erm, *good*, if you catch my meanin'." Suzie couldn't quite meet Charlotte's eyes as she said this.

"Er, actually, I don't catch your meaning. I no longer think Charles was particularly good as a candidate for husband, but I think you're referring to something else," she added slowly.

Suzie looked even more uncomfortable. "Good at those things that go on between a husband and wife, fer example." Her voice lowered to a whisper. "In the bedroom. Some men are better than others at that sort of thing, is all I mean. Charles weren't one of the better ones." Charlotte's eyes widened when she realized what her companion meant.

Suzie couldn't resist adding, "I bet your Mr. Skidmore knows a thing or two about what to do with a woman. When 'e kissed yer hand, I almost sighed out loud, it were so sweet."

Now Charlotte blushed for a different reason. "He was just being a gentleman. Although I don't think I've ever had my hand kissed by another gentleman in Uckfield."

"Well, I 'ear in London, the blokes really know how to treat a woman." Suzie said wistfully, her imagination wandering to the city the Skidmore brothers traveled to. "I certainly wouldn't mind seein' the place."

Charlotte thought about London: Mr. Skidmore's destination. She couldn't deny that she was a little jealous of the Trivett twins for their Season. Now, she could not enjoy any of the Season at all, even if her father could find her a sponsor. Not that she would ever ask him. After seeing Charles' true nature, she wasn't so sure she wanted a husband at all.

Over time, Charlotte's sips of brandy became larger gulps and Suzie was more than happy to keep their glasses full. Charlotte hoped Suzie would not get into any trouble for being so generous with the tavern's libations.

Elbows on the table, Charlotte rested her chin in her hands. "I wish I had given Charles a better dressing down, after all the things he said to me. I can't believe that he had been involved with another woman while trying to court me—not that I don't think you are perfectly lovely. Are most men like that?" Charlotte couldn't resist asking. "I mean, having a wife for one thing and another woman for, er, other things." Charlotte still didn't know specifically what those other things were, but she had an inkling Suzie would divulge at some point.

Suzie just shrugged in response. "As fer me, I don't involve m'self with that many men here in Uckfield. Charles, though, he were just so pretty fer a man, I couldn't resist…I guess that matters little now." Suzie took a sip of her brandy, contemplating. "I 'ear most of Uckfield's men usually look fer companions in other towns nearby. It's so small 'ere that their wives would find out immediately if they dallied with anyone else. I've heard e'en Charles' papa has a lady friend just one town over."

"Marriage is beginning to sound less and less appealing," Charlotte said, more to herself than to Suzie. That was when she remembered her father. "I should probably be getting home. My father might worry." Standing, she giggled as she tried to maintain her balance.

Suzie laughed with her. "I think maybe we should have a bit more to eat before you leave. First time havin' brandy, eh?"

"It's quite wonderful, isn't it?" Charlotte flopped back into her seat, still giggling.

Suzie laughed, "Food or brandy? Yer lucky the stew 'ere is better than the ale."

And so, Charlotte and Suzie continued their morning, and afternoon, together. When she finally left, Charlotte discovered that Michael had ensured Esmerelda was cared for and properly returned to her. After her enlightening conversation with Suzie, she ventured home to her father.

─✦─

Charles sent a note to Charlotte the evening after their little altercation. It seemed that he would be willing to forgive and forget their exchange, so long as she never mentioned it again to anyone.

By then, Charlotte had decided that she never wanted anything to do with Charles Trivett. Instead of replying, she chose to let the man stew. She doubted he would keep his word, had she agreed to his terms in the first place.

Charlotte knew something had changed the following afternoon, when the vicar's wife did not contact her for their weekly tea. Charlotte did not mind. After talking to Suzie, she discovered that the vicar and his wife were apparently dipping into the funds allocated for the poor. Suzie's discovery was, in fact, the true reason for her dismissal.

The same afternoon, after discovering his son's version of events, the elder Mr. Charles Trivett had immediately gone to

Charlotte's father. The experience was quite frustrating. For Mr. Trivett.

When told about the unknown gentleman masquerading as a viscount, Sir Driscoll Henwood had casually removed his round-framed glasses and wiped them on his sleeve. When he saw that Mr. Trivett expected some sort of response, he said, "Well, Charlotte is quite intelligent. I cannot blame a young man for saying whatever he could to engage her attention."

There was no denying Sir Driscoll enjoyed seeing Mr. Trivett's face turn an angry mottled red at his reply. Sir Driscoll had never really liked Mr. Trivett, only maintaining the friendship due to Charlotte's association with Mr. Trivett's twin daughters.

As for Charlotte being exposed to an improper tavern wench, Sir Driscoll raised his eyebrows expectantly. "And? I've heard that you expose yourself to tavern wenches on a regular basis, Mr. Trivett." At this, Mr. Trivett gave up, vowing to never again invite the ungrateful sod to dinner. The man was clearly mad if he allowed his daughter to behave in such a manner.

———

After his conversation with Mr. Trivett, Sir Driscoll called Charlotte into his library. He was not entirely certain how to address recent events with her.

As a girl, Charlotte was always open and forthright in her manner. However, at age four, following the death of her mother, Charlotte had become more reserved. Although it was impossible to hide her overly curious nature, she found that one could discover something new and interesting by quietly observing one's companions. She also got into a great deal less trouble that way. Sir Driscoll knew that the Trivett family enjoyed her quiet, calm nature. No doubt Mrs. Trivett hoped Charlotte would rub off on the more energetic twins.

Charlotte's interactions with her father were the one exception. Sir Driscoll would do his best to answer any question she asked, no matter how odd, and always encouraged her curiosity. He also encouraged Charlotte to express her thoughts on nearly any matter she liked, even if it only involved something as silly as the expletives Mrs. Blakely utilized after dropping a plate of pudding cake. Her father's interest in Charlotte's ideas also led to her developing a biting wit, even if she only shared that wit with him. Sir Driscoll wondered if her experience at The Griffin was a sign that his daughter had finally begun to come out of the shell she had so carefully erected after her mother's death.

Charlotte knew with whom Sir Driscoll had been meeting and expected the worst. She should have told him immediately about what happened, but she had not wished to worry him. Goodness, she had no idea how to even broach the subject of her imminent ruination.

However, as she walked into the room, all he said to her was, "You went to The Griffin without me?"

She had already begun speaking, trying to make her father understand, "Papa, I'm so sorry. It was raining and I needed a place to wait out the downpour—"

He waved his hands to cut her off, "No, no. I mean, why didn't you take me? I haven't been there for ages." He paused to allow the relief to fill her eyes, his own brown ones softening in affection. Relieved that she had not disappointed him, Charlotte threw her arms around her father's slender form. After a moment, he took her shoulders and stepped back. "As for this other man you met there, I'm assuming he was a complete gentleman?" He asked with a meaningful look.

Charlotte smiled. Although she didn't care what Mr. Trivett or the vicar and his wife thought about her behavior, she would never want to hurt her father. "He was, Papa. He was very kind. No need to worry about that." Thinking of Mr. Skidmore, she smiled wistfully. "He took perfect care of me. Up until Charles showed up, that is."

Sir Driscoll had returned to the chair behind his desk. Intrigued, he said, "Now, Mr. Trivett never mentioned that his son was there with you. What was he there for?"

Charlotte smirked. "The improper tavern wench."

Sir Driscoll's eyes narrowed. "I'm going to pretend that you do not seem to know exactly why he was going to see that woman. It will help me sleep at night." Then he smiled, "When given an opportune moment, I may be petty and throw that little fact in Mr. Trivett's face."

Charlotte smiled and walked around the big desk to kiss her father's cheek before turning to go to her room. "I love you, Papa."

"Charlotte." Her father called to her before she left.

She turned back, waiting.

Obviously uncomfortable, her father shifted a bit in his chair. When his spectacles slid down his nose, he pushed then back up. "I wanted to ask you sooner. Did you truly wish to go with the Trivetts to London? Neither Mr. nor Mrs. Trivett broached the subject with me, but I know that you could have joined them nonetheless."

Charlotte was surprised. "I don't need to go to Town. To be quite frank, I doubt I could have competed with them. The twins are quite famous for their exuberance and charm."

"I believe you have quite a few charms of your own. I merely wished you to know that if you did choose to accompany them, it would not be as great a strain on the household as you fear. I want you to be happy."

Charlotte was moved by his sincerity. But she was the one who managed the household accounts and she knew for a fact that this was not true. Putting on a false smile, Charlotte replied, "I'm perfectly happy to spend the summer here with you. No doubt the twins would drive me quite mad after only a week." Her father seemed to accept her words. Nodding to himself, he looked back down to his books.

Although he appeared distracted by his studies, Sir Driscoll instead mulled over the conversation with his usually quiet, perfectly-behaved daughter. He especially recalled the smile that softened his daughter's face when she discussed the gentleman traveling to London. Her eyes never lit up when she mentioned the younger Charles Trivett. Sir Driscoll thought there may be something special about this gentleman. But even if there was not, there were a great many gentlemen in London for Charlotte to meet. With his daughter's best interests at heart, he wrote a letter that he had been avoiding for several years. It was time to call in a very great favor.

# Chapter 4

—◆—

CHARLOTTE WAS BECOMING BORED. Other than her weekly visits to see Suzie at The Griffin, very little happened in her life. She had been forced to alter all of her habits once word of her ruination got out.

Her only other respite was the time she spent teaching a few of the Uckfield children to play the pianoforte. The children's parents, closer to Suzie in station than the lofty Trivetts, made it clear that they were thankful for Charlotte's charity. She appreciated their kindness, but Charlotte had no desire to spend the rest of her life teaching music to other people's children. Besides, if she never married, she would someday be forced to charge for her lessons.

She still found enjoyment assisting her father in his research. Charlotte would always need that intellectual exercise, but she could not escape this ineffable desire for something more; something different.

The only surprise during this time was her father's newfound interest in reading his mail. Usually it took him up to a month to so much as open a letter. Typically, his mail slowly piled up in a corner of his library. Once the pile grew enough for Sir Driscoll to notice it, he would ask Charlotte to respond to certain letters for him.

But now, he requested that Mrs. Blakely bring it directly to him. Charlotte assumed this was an attempt to protect her. If he received all their mail, Charlotte wouldn't notice how little her old friends had sent her.

She was less bothered by the en masse snubbing than she had expected. She had given up on any designs to marry after her experience with Charles, and no longer wished to spend time with ladies whose sole aim in life was to acquire a husband to care for them.

Charlotte couldn't explain why she was so unhurt by the dearth in invitations to tea or supper. Perhaps the time she spent with Suzie Perkins helped fill that void. She no longer had to hide the more bookish aspects of her personality. Instead, Suzie was envious of Charlotte's knowledge; in particular that of European history.

Their difference in social station mattered little to Charlotte. Although Suzie's stories about her family were often amusing and filled with happiness, it was also enlightening to learn how their station in life affected them.

Charlotte thought Suzie and her family deserved more, but a lack of education prevented any chances of social or financial advancement. Meanwhile, it was Charlotte's extensive education that would be her downfall. No gentleman she knew of would want a wife who was better suited to manage the household accounts than he.

—⁂—

Less than a month passed before Charlotte's world was again turned upside down. One day, returning home from another ride to the village, Charlotte discovered an elegant carriage before her front door. As soon as she entered the house, Mrs. Blakely informed Charlotte that her father awaited her in his library.

Charlotte almost giggled. Where else would she find her father? It was the brightest room in the house, with large bay windows on two walls. She found comfort in how it always smelled of pipe smoke, leather, and wood. With its rich mahogany shelves and desk, soft blue overstuffed chairs and chaise longue, it was also the most comfortable and elegant room in the house. Charlotte had caught her father napping on the chaise longue more than a few times. Papa had perhaps caught her doing the same, as well.

Sitting next to her father in one of their overstuffed chairs was a portly, cheerful gentleman. He laughed with Sir Driscoll as she entered the room, bringing out the lines around his eyes.

"Ah, Charlotte, there you are! Come in, come in." Her father and the other gentleman rose as they acknowledged her. Sir Driscoll reached for her hand to lead her in. "This is one of my closest friends from my school days, Mr. Harry Madison."

Mr. Madison bowed. "It's a pleasure, Miss Henwood." His sincere smile compelled her to respond in kind. Mr. Madison continued, "Driscoll knew I was in the area and invited me here. We've been catching up since."

Charlotte was not entirely certain how to respond, never having met the man, but he certainly seemed kind enough. "I am glad you are here to bring my father up for air. He has been making fast progress in his newest project, which means he can be convinced to do little else."

Mr. Madison chuckled. "I know your father all too well on that score. I must confess I am taking a bit of a break, myself. My wife and daughter are in Brighton right now, shopping and seeing the sights. Those ladies have more energy than a pack of racehorses. Luckily, Julia isn't out yet, so we have not yet been subjected to that special brand of terror. At seventeen, my daughter is about two years younger than yourself."

Mr. Madison looked to Charlotte and added, embarrassed, "Not that I have anything against the London Season. I'm just imagining, oh I don't know, the dress fittings, and the requirement that I attend every single ball or soirée. Oh no. *Almacks.*" He pretended to shiver. "I will be required to research the personal and family history of every eligible bachelor in Town. It will be quite an ordeal."

Charlotte didn't believe him for a second. Mr. Madison would likely find the whole experience entertaining, loving an opportunity to catalogue the flaws and foibles of London society. She hadn't known him much longer than a few seconds, but of that she was certain.

They took their seats. As it appeared the gentlemen had already shared some sherry, Charlotte chose not to request that tea be brought in. "Mr. Madison was wondering if perhaps you'd like to join his family in London," her father asked casually, avoiding her eyes. A moment passed before the words registered.

"London?" Charlotte turned to Mr. Madison, uncertain whether to be shocked or excited.

"Your father wrote to me, mentioning that you were unable to travel with your friends to Town for the Season," Mr. Madison answered, his tone matching Sir Driscoll's in casualness. Charlotte met her father's gaze and raised an eyebrow. So this was all his doing. She had not wanted to bankrupt him by trying to keep up with the Trivetts' extravagant lifestyle. How would this be any different? Her acquaintance with the Madison family was nonexistent. What if the wife and daughter heard about The Griffin? What if she ran into the Trivetts while in Town?

"Charlotte," Sir Driscoll addressed his daughter, seeing her gaze become distressed, "there's no need to decide right now. Harry, here, knows you were concerned about the funds we would go through if you went with the Trivetts." Sir Driscoll refrained from mentioning that he had never wanted his daughter to go off with the spoiled Trivett ladies in the first place.

"Papa, that's not something you discuss with just anyone!" Charlotte was appalled that her father had told a man she had never met about their financial shortcomings.

"Charlotte, Harry isn't just anyone. There's no need to be rude."

Mr. Madison cut in, "Miss Henwood, perhaps I should explain all of my reasons for being here today. Although it has been some time since your father and I met in person, I count him as one of my closest friends. While Sir Driscoll spent most of his time after Cambridge pursuing the study of history, I chose to enter the world of business and investing, organizing my own joint stock ventures. There have been quite a few ups and downs, but I have done well for myself, overall." Sir Driscoll cleared his throat, wanting his friend to get on with it. Mr. Madison seemed to catch on. "That is beside the point right now. Years ago, when I began my first truly risky investment, I had the option of inviting your father to invest with me. I didn't ask him to join me because I worried I would have little return profit, if any. But it turned out I did. I feel somewhat responsible now, for not drawing him in at a time when he could have afforded it."

Why in the world were these two talking investment strategies with her? This conversation was becoming quite frustrating and bizarre, she thought, looking from her father to Mr. Madison. Sitting back in her chair, she decided to patiently wait until she learned everything. Mr. Madison went on to mention the dangers of the investment in question and why he feared that he could have bankrupted her father.

One question rose above all the others swimming in her head: Why was Papa sending her away? If he made the effort to contact, well, anyone, then he was quite desperate to get her to London. A painful thought struck. "Papa, are you trying to get rid of me because of what happened at The Griffin?" she accused, shameful of the crack in her voice.

Sir Driscoll looked at his daughter sympathetically. "I'm not getting rid of you. I'm just worried that you aren't going to get a chance to truly experience life while holed up here." A month ago, Charlotte would have had a response to that. But now, she couldn't dismiss the hope that there was more for her outside of Uckfield.

When she had nothing to say, Mr. Madison went on: "Inviting you to London is not my only purpose today. You see, a few years ago I sent a letter, informing Driscoll that I was going to include him in an ironworks in Cornwall that I had recently developed, whether he wanted to be involved or not."

Sir Driscoll put his hands on his hips, which proved to be a bit awkward while sitting in his chair. The image would have made Charlotte giggle on another occasion. "You know that was completely unnecessary," her father said, huffily. "I won't pretend to be unappreciative, but I never expected you to do that."

Mr. Madison said to her father, "If it weren't for you, I would never have survived school. Nor would I have met Imogen." He turned to Charlotte. "Your mother, Miss Henwood, introduced me to my wife. I owe your father a great deal. Along with her being the absolute love of my life, my wife's dowry was enough to begin the joint stock venture I had been planning for some time. Frankly, I would have made very little of my life, were it not for your father." Charlotte was unsure if his eyes watered slightly from thinking about meeting his wife, or about his early money-making strategies.

There was another part of his story that struck Charlotte. Having no real recollection of her mother, it was strange meeting someone else who had known her. Her father had brought Charlotte to Uckfield after her mother's passing, leaving him the only person who could tell Charlotte about her. Charlotte did not always want to make her father recall that happier part of his life, worried that doing so brought him pain.

Finally, her father gave in. "I don't even know why we're arguing about this." Neither did Charlotte. Sir Driscoll addressed his daughter, prepared for further disagreement. "The important thing is that this is your chance to see the world beyond Uckfield. I may be a bit of a...a recluse here, to be frank, but I lived in London and traveled and *did* things before I met your mother. If you stay here, you'll never get a chance to do more than help me with my research and teach the village children to play the pianoforte." As this was exactly what she had been thinking, there was little she could say in response.

Mr. Madison said to her, "Your father told me he doesn't need the money from the mining venture. A man who seldom leaves his library has very little debt. He asked me to instead use what I, well, what *he* has accumulated to sponsor you in Town. Besides, it will be good practice before Julia comes out," he added, a bit too casually.

Charlotte was right; he truly was excited to be involved in London's social scene. She tried to keep her tone innocent, "What about attending all those parties and balls and interviewing eligible bachelors? I could never happily be the source of such acute torture."

Mr. Madison burst out laughing. "You are most definitely your father's daughter. And you're quite right. I do enjoy observing the intricacies of London society. As for the rest, I still refuse to enter the hallowed halls of Almacks."

Well. If the rest of Mr. Madison's family was anything like him, a visit to Town could be quite amusing. Nevertheless, Charlotte was not one to make a decision of such magnitude without weighing all possible benefits and drawbacks. The Madisons also needed to comprehend exactly what they were getting into by sponsoring her.

Taking a calming breath, she turned to Mr. Madison and told him, "I still don't know how well I shall get on with your wife and daughter. I'm practically a ruined woman, here in Uckfield. They may not want to associate with me." There. She had said it.

The disdainful look she expected never filled Mr. Madison's expression.

Unfazed, he replied, "In a week, on our way back from Brighton, we will all stop here to get to know each other. Just make sure you pack your trunks before we arrive. I have the distinct impression you will get on quite well with the ladies."

And so it was decided. Charlotte would pack her trunks and her meeting with Mr. Madison's ladies would help decide whether or not she made her trip.

As they said their goodbyes, a single thought struck Charlotte. "Mr. Madison, is it possible to bring a lady's maid?" There was no masking the mischievous glint in her eyes.

"Charlotte, you don't have a maid," her father told her, suspicion lacing his tone.

Mr. Madison smiled. "I believe that can be arranged." He bowed to Sir Driscoll and Charlotte. "I shall apparently discover what you have up your sleeve in a week, Miss Henwood. Until then…"

A number of questions filled Charlotte's mind, but she hadn't wanted to ask any in front of Mr. Madison. Uncertain what to say, she merely nodded to Mr. Madison as he made his exit. Although she found it impossible to dislike Mr. Madison, she still wanted to hear her father's input before agreeing to anything—her foremost concern being the money.

—⁓—

Sometime later, Charlotte found her father on his back on the chaise longue, one leg up and one hanging off the side, sipping a celebratory glass of champagne. Musing over where in the world he had found a bottle of champagne, she joined him. Obviously expecting her, he sat up and filled an empty flute. They silently toasted their newfound riches.

Her slightly tipsy father began to tell her of all the sights she should be sure to see in Town. It wasn't long before her curiosity became too great. Finally, asking her father if the story was true, Sir Driscoll explained the whole of the matter to her.

"Goodness, you held your tongue for at least fifteen minutes. I'm in shock." At his daughter's stern look, he began, "Now, I should first warn you that I really don't have much understanding of these things. You have always been better with numbers. I believe that Harry used some of his own money, in my name, to develop an ironworks in Cornwall, about four years ago. He likely forged my signature once or twice, but considering the results, I won't be consulting the magistrate. It wasn't a great deal of money, mind you. He tells me it was only about one thousand pounds." Charlotte gasped. Her father didn't have that kind of money lying around. In fact, no one she knew could easily access such an amount. Her father rolled his eyes, clearly agreeing that his friend had been unnecessarily generous.

"I read his letter maybe a year ago, about my recently discovered wealth, not really certain how to reply. At first, I thought that if I never answered him, he could simply keep the money for himself. And then I thought that I could simply save it for you, maybe as a dowry. Perhaps you could finally travel to Italy, like I know you've always wanted. I considered using the unexpected funds for you to go with the Trivetts, even though I can barely stand them, but you never seemed too excited about the prospect. After your little trouble at The Griffin, I finally chose to reply to Madison's letter."

Charlotte supposed this explained Papa's newfound interest in reading his mail. She refrained from mentioning that her disinterest in traveling with the Trivetts stemmed from her wish to protect her father's finances.

He continued, "I don't know what the land was originally intended for—who knows what they do in Cornwall—but it matters little, now. Harry sent some of his men to inspect the land and they found ironstone deposits. After he bought the land, a year was spent using the investment funds to fully develop an ironworks with the necessary forges and foundry. In another year, he made back the money he had invested for me, plus a little interest. Harry is, after all, a businessman. However, he has continued to save up the profits since then. It would have been too expensive for the previous owner to extract the iron in the first place, so Harry refrained from mentioning his discovery to the seller. As I said, he's a businessman first."

When Charlotte tried to cut in and tell him how ridiculous she thought the story, he added, "There has been evidence of iron being found within Cornwall in the not-so-recent past, so it isn't impossible. I believe that Harry's land is currently being mined solely for iron. In addition, the last twenty years have seen impressive improvement in the extraction and manufacture of iron in England. And yes, you're right, I have no clue what I'm talking about, but Harry assures me that everything is on the up-and-up."

He sighed as he took another sip. "I don't believe that Harry owes me anything, but he told me the money would be put in trust for you if I refused it. He just won't keep it, no matter what I say. And so, it's yours."

It was not that Charlotte was unappreciative, but some form of warning before her unexpected encounter would have been convenient. Charlotte began to rise from her chair with the intention of giving her father a good dressing down. She wasn't sure what they could do with the money, but it wasn't right that all of it go to her.

"Now, now, sit down." He waved the flute of champagne. "I know what you're going to say. There really is nothing I need the money for. Nor is there, in all honesty, anything Harry needs the money for. He's richer than Croesus. Don't let his cheerful demeanor fool you. I'm quite certain that the man controls half of London." Her father turned to her, now entirely serious. "The only reason I ever wanted more was for you. And I don't care if you are ruined. There aren't any rules against ruined women going to Astley's Amphitheatre, or touring the British Museum, and joining all the lending libraries they can find. Besides, for now, nobody knows a thing about your past. And honestly, the Trivetts don't travel in the same circles as Harry and his family." Clinking his glass against Charlotte's, he added, "You'll love London, I promise."

---

"We're truly goin' to London, then?" Suzie helped load the better half of Charlotte's wardrobe into an old trunk. Her fingers nimbly folded Charlotte's favorite yellow muslin day dress.

Charlotte ran her fingers over a cotton chemise. She couldn't get over her concern that her taste in attire would not be sufficiently elegant for London. She sighed. Since there was nothing else for it, these garments would have to do.

It was her final night in Uckfield. She had met the Madison ladies a few days ago. After hearing Mr. Madison's tale, they had both refused to wait the week to meet Charlotte. The moment the two cheerfully chattering women walked through her door, it had been love at first sight. Charlotte decided that Julia was the sweetest girl she had ever met, although a little shy. She was a few inches shorter than Charlotte, with adorable light brown ringlets and bright blue eyes—the same shade as Mr. Madison's. Although her figure was a bit on the plump side, Charlotte was certain it would soon turn to her mother's curvaceous form.

The ladies shared tea, while Charlotte listened to the other two tell her everything about London. Her going with them was apparently a foregone conclusion. Charlotte didn't mind their chatter at all. Usually she was more sedate when meeting a new acquaintance, but these two easily drew her into their stories. Before tea was so much as served, she was joining in with their laughter, telling them about her own life in Uckfield.

After hearing about Charlotte's new and somewhat unusual lady's maid, the Madison ladies were quite excited to meet her, insisting that she ride with them to London. As for Charlotte's stories, they were particularly fond of those involving the more rural aspects of Uckfield, having only lived in larger cities. When Mrs. Kingley's pigs escaped their pen the previous week, her neighbor—the vicar, of all people—had been required to chase them down. Charlotte had been happening by when the vicar finally made his way home, covered in more filth than the pigs. Charlotte felt more than a little guilty to have enjoyed the sight so much.

Julia confessed that she wished she could have a pet with her in London. At Charlotte's questioning look, Julia assured her that she would never want a pig. Unfortunately, her papa did not respond well to animal fur.

Finally, Charlotte had to broach a less pleasant subject. Taking a deep breath, she asked them, "Do you both comprehend exactly why I can't find a husband here in Uckfield?"

Mrs. Madison's eyes softened, immediately understanding Charlotte's discomfort. "Harry told us that something had happened that may have damaged your reputation. As for me, I care little. Having conversed with you for well over an hour, I would wager that whatever occurred was not entirely your fault. In fact, most of the time, it isn't the fault of the woman who gets dragged into this sort of trouble. But, of course, she is stuck bearing the brunt of it, isn't she?"

Julia leaned forward, "Besides, Papa's so rich, I doubt anyone will care what happened. As for me," her eyes turned playful, "I think it shall be exciting sharing the same roof as a ruined woman."

At Mrs. Madison's, "Julia!" Charlotte burst into laughter.

By the end of their visit, Charlotte could not wait to go to London with them. The Madisons were more than pleased to take her to the city's various amusements. She would see all of the museums and landmarks she could imagine.

She doubted she'd be able to sleep tonight. Smiling at the memory of her tea with the ladies, Charlotte turned to Suzie. "London is a big city. I wonder what sort of trouble the two of us can cause there?"

---

As the carriage rolled away from the home she had never left for more than a few days at a time, Charlotte felt a wave of regret course through her. She would miss her father sorely. She leaned out the window once more to wave goodbye. She knew he would not go back inside until the carriage disappeared from sight. Her stomach wrenched at the thought of being away for so long.

As Uckfield disappeared from their sights, Suzie broke into her thoughts. "Charlotte, what are you lookin' fer in the perfect gentleman? You'll no doubt meet quite a few in London, so you had better decide what you want now." Charlotte knew that her friend merely intended to provide her with a distraction.

Julia let out a giggle, now that the conversational topic had moved to gentlemen. Charlotte could feel a blush creeping across her face. "I had not thought on it. Perhaps someone honorable, handsome, of course…and intelligent. I could not tolerate a man who was not at all clever." Her thoughts drifted off to a tall, green-eyed stranger whose conversation had entranced her during their brief time together.

Julia was more than happy to fill the silence. "Well I would like a gentleman who is clever too, and strong, like those Greek statues that Mama is so very fond of."

Mrs. Madison cut in, "Julia, really, I cannot imagine what you mean!"

Her daughter was already going on: "He would have to have some hidden depth that I would never expect. Perhaps he plays the violin, or wrestles tigers. Perhaps not that last one. You understand, don't you, Charlotte?"

Charlotte considered this. "I suppose I do, although I would not want him to do something especially strange. Whatever would I do with a man who spent all of his time wrestling unusual creatures? Where would we have to go to find the animals in the first place?" Everyone laughed at that.

By the time they arrived in London, all four of the women chatted as though they had been friends for years. Apparently the Madison ladies enjoyed Suzie's stories as much as Charlotte. Both Charlotte and Mrs. Madison (who now insisted on being called Imogen) appreciated how well Suzie omitted the less proper bits. Nonetheless, it was probably better that Mr. Madison rode outside the carriage, where he could not overhear the four of them.

—⁓—

Nothing could have prepared Charlotte for the Madison family's London home. She took a moment to share a look with Suzie, whose face mirrored her own expression of awe. The Classical white-columned façade was a far-cry from the quaint simplicity of the solid red-brick holding her home in Uckfield together.

Taking a rest after the long carriage ride, Julia and Imogen joined Charlotte in the upstairs family drawing room. Charlotte thought the portrait looking down at her from the mantel might be the work of Joseph Wright.

There was extensive shopping to do before introducing Charlotte to polite society. Conversely, Charlotte did her best to convince the other two that she had no desire to actually partake in a Season. The other two were having none of that.

Imogen told her, "You don't need a Season solely to hunt for a husband."

Julia snorted, "That's not what you told me, Mama."

"Ladies don't snort, Julia," was Imogen's response. "Nor do they roll their eyes."

Julia's eyes widened. "You weren't even looking at me. How do you always do that?"

Charlotte cut in, "I doubt I have enough money for the shopping that you two have in mind." Looking out the window, Charlotte couldn't help imagining herself wearing the same styles as the fashionable ladies out walking, often on the arm of an equally stylish gentleman. Unbidden, she saw herself walking next to an attractive green-eyed stranger with an enticing freckle on his lip.

Charlotte noticed that usually a maid followed these elegant ladies some length behind. She nearly laughed aloud visualizing Suzie carefully following her. Were Charlotte to take a stroll with a gentleman, Suzie would likely decide to hang on his other arm. Charlotte's new maid wasn't one to observe all the fun from a distance.

Just perhaps there was enough money for an elegant dress or two. Thinking it impolite, Charlotte still had not asked exactly how much money she had for her time in Town, but it surely couldn't be as much as they seemed to think.

Imogen quickly dispelled the notion, saying, "Goodness, dear, you have enough money to buy a new carriage and a matching pair of horses." Realizing that Charlotte had never had the full particulars described to her, Imogen added, "Perhaps it would be best to discuss this with Harry. He can explain matters much better than I ever could. Suffice it to say, you need not worry about appearing the drab poor relation when you come out with us."

Slowly, Charlotte nodded. She had best speak with Mr. Madison as soon as possible. Surely funds would run out at some point? Charlotte intended to find out just when that would be. She had no intention of keeping everything for herself, no matter what her father thought.

"You certainly have enough to afford a new wardrobe. Now," said Imogen, "we shall plan on rising early tomorrow to begin our shopping excursion. We have a great deal to do."

—⁂—

Harry had no doubt been expecting her. Charlotte found him in his private study, sitting comfortably at his desk as he read through a rather long letter. While Charlotte already felt close to the ladies of the household, she had only had one brief conversation with Mr. Madison.

Upon spying Charlotte hovering in the doorway, Mr. Madison smiled encouragingly. "You no doubt have more questions running through your head than you can count. Do sit down, Miss Henwood. Hopefully I can alleviate a few of your concerns."

As Charlotte seated herself across from Mr. Madison, she realized she had no idea even how to express her thoughts without potentially seeming the fool. As there was nothing else for it, she asked, "Forgive me for being so forward, but could you possibly tell me what my limitations are pertaining to the Cornwall venture? Mrs. Madison implied that I have enough funds to survive the Season comfortably, but I was wondering how I can ensure that there will be something left over for Papa."

Mr. Madison nodded. "I see the confusion now. You need to understand that you aren't receiving one single sum in return. Your father and I are essentially two investors, along with a few other gentlemen who own shares in the ironworks. Every investor taking part is also sharing in the profits. Now, most of the more time-consuming, costly work is already done. The ironworks needed to extract the iron and the foundries for molding it were completed some time ago. Since then, I have created contracts with several different parties, including the Royal Navy. Britain's maritime efforts have recently required a serious increase in ship production. They primarily use the iron for chains and lining barrels—not to mention weaponry."

Thanks to her father, Charlotte had become quite used to engaging in discussions that most young ladies were expected to avoid. Nonetheless, she knew to appreciate Mr. Madison's willingness to do the same. "Is there anything I need to do to help continue the ironworks' production?"

"Nothing at all," Mr. Madison replied happily. "All we need to do is sit back and let the land in Cornwall continue to produce. Your father said that he wants all of the money to go to you while you reside with us. Sir Driscoll says you have a way with numbers and will need no help managing everything."

In Charlotte's younger years, Sir Driscoll had used the accounts as a means for teaching her mathematics. Upon noticing how much her father disliked the task, she had continued maintaining the accounts.

Charlotte could barely believe her ears. Just a week ago, her life seemed to be spiraling down into a pit of boredom and dissatisfaction. Now, all of a sudden, she had access to more money than her family had ever possessed, and resided in the perfect city in which to spend it.

"Can it really be that simple?" Charlotte asked.

"Can what, my dear?" Mr. Madison's hefty letter was already regaining his interest, but he glanced up at her question.

Charlotte still felt out of her element. "Investing. Does one merely pay a certain amount and then gain more later? If that is all one needs to do, I cannot imagine why everyone does not engage in the practice."

"Ah." Mr. Madison slid the distracting letter aside, rested his elbows on his desk, and linked his fingers. "No. It is not nearly that simple. Take imports, for example. I could organize an expedition to the West Indies with the intention of buying silks that I could later sell in London. However, any number of problems might arise in the process. The ship might need excessive improvements before such a long journey, the crew could mutiny, or the ship might encounter a bad storm. Or the expedition could progress perfectly, but the silks may go out of fashion before it returns. That's not to mention the other investors. Everyone has an idea of how a venture ought to be organized and seldom does everyone agree. A gentleman might abandon the venture to start his own, sometimes taking other investors with him." Again, Mr. Madison's gaze was drawn to that letter. "Anything and everything could go wrong. Investing is a risk."

Instead of deterring her, Charlotte found Mr. Madison's answer fascinating. Investing may be a touch dangerous, but it was certainly exciting.

A thought struck—one that she knew would remain lodged in her brain unless she expressed it. She took a deep breath and sat tall in her seat. "Mr. Madison, could you perhaps tell me if you know of any other investments similar to the Cornwall ironworks?"

Harry Madison was momentarily taken aback by her question, but then he smiled broadly. There was, after all, nothing he liked better than discussing his investment strategies. Finally having a member of his household take a marked interest in such things was more than pleasing. He loved his Imogen dearly, but she cared more for traveling the continent and exploring various ancient Greek and Roman ruins. "Do call me Harry. I know Imogen has already decided that you should be considered a part of the family." Reaching down, he removed several documents from a drawer in his desk. "Tell me, Charlotte, what are your thoughts pertaining to textiles?"

---

It took some time for Imogen and Julia to rescue Charlotte from Harry's clutches, but the ladies had errands to complete before Charlotte could be presented, after all. Charlotte and Harry could begin signing onto whatever ventures they found interesting in a day or two. For now, the Madison ladies were in charge of their new houseguest.

Once again alone in his study, Harry Madison returned to that blasted letter. Sir Driscoll was not the only friend he had brought into the Cornish mine venture. There were a few others, one of whom had repaid Harry's kindness with this letter. It seemed someone had approached Harry's friend in the hopes of pressuring him to sell his shares, and at an appallingly low price.

One of the other investors was making trouble, and Harry could guess who was responsible. The Earl of Tunley had forced his way into the venture when it was first realized, and had made quite the nuisance of himself since. Harry leaned back in his chair in thought. In most instances, Harry could buy out whoever began pulling these tricks. He had a feeling that the Earl would not be so manageable.

—⁓—

As for Charlotte, by the following afternoon, she had selected and been fitted for three morning dresses, two afternoon dresses as well as two walking dresses, three dinner dresses, and a new riding habit. She also bought several silk and cashmere shawls, two spencers and one full-length cloak. The Madison ladies had also helped her select four evening dresses, for attending a ball or the theater. Charlotte had never possessed even one gown that equaled any of her purchases in elegance and quality. All of the dresses were of different fabrics—muslin, silk, it didn't matter. As for the shoes and bonnets...Charlotte had nearly lost her voice trying to assure Mrs. Madison that these items could not all be necessary. But necessary they were. Needless to say, after only two days in London, Charlotte was exhausted and prepared to sleep for a week.

# Chapter 5

C HARLOTTE HAD BEEN ENJOYING the Fortescue ball, her
first foray into the London *ton*. The ballroom out-sized
most homes in Uckfield, requiring three chandeliers to
illuminate the dance floor.

Charlotte did her best to hide how intimidated she felt, but
Mrs. Madison assured her that her fears were allowed. To
comfort her, Imogen promised to stay by her side through the
entire ordeal, but her promise proved unnecessary. Many
admiring looks were sent Charlotte's way. Imogen had
suggested that whenever Charlotte felt uncertain of how she
should behave, that she should keep her statements vague and
perhaps remain a touch detached. Doing so would hopefully
lend Charlotte a mysterious air—one that Imogen did not think
it would be a challenge to cultivate.

In her dark rose silk gown, Charlotte's creamy skin
practically glowed. The dress could not compare to most of the
other elaborate creations worn to the dance, but its simplicity
gave it a delicate, classic look. At first, she thought it would be
inappropriate to wear anything other than white or pastels, but
none of the lighter shades the Madison ladies found suited her
darker features.

Her near-black tresses gleamed in the bright candlelight,
although Charlotte did not enjoy having her hair pulled back so
tightly. Her hair being much too long and heavy to curl with
hot irons, Suzie had decided to ignore the current fashion trend
and not leave any to hang by Charlotte's ears. Suzie had insisted
that the final look brought out Charlotte's cheekbones;

Charlotte couldn't disagree, but she barely recognized herself like this. Still, several handsome gentlemen sought Mr. Madison out, asking about his wife's companion.

Once or twice, Mrs. Madison had needed to insert herself into a conversation in order to keep Charlotte from bringing up her less-than-appropriate experiences in Uckfield. They had agreed that Charlotte's past would remain unknown to the snobbish, bored London *ton* in order to generate interest. Her socializing with the Madisons would be more than enough to attract the fascination of those elevated members of society.

Charlotte had already enjoyed the traditional opening minuet, despite her partner's complaints of it being too old-fashioned for beginning a ball. When she mentioned that she found the dance highly enjoyable, her partner's upturned nose reminded her that her country upbringing did not always fit in well in London.

She resolved to maintain her air of mystery while still—at least secretly—thoroughly enjoying the ball. Her favorite, so far, was the Scottish reel. Perhaps her preference showed just how country-bred she was, for she enjoyed the energetic dance too much to feel embarrassed.

As Mr. Hampstead—her partner from the reel—left to acquire a glass of lemonade for her, Charlotte scanned the crowd. The feathers accenting a few ladies' coiffures swayed here and there above their wearers' heads. Although she was tall enough to see some of the gathering when she stood on her toes, the tops of people's heads were not as fascinating as she would have hoped. Until she saw him.

Mr. Skidmore was taller than most gentlemen attending the ball, making him easy to spot. Charlotte's breath caught. In his formal evening attire, he was the quintessential gentleman. Wearing shades of charcoal and gray, his appearance lacked the frivolity found in many of London's dandies. To whom was he speaking? Would it be completely unacceptable for her to approach him?

"Your lemonade, Miss Henwood," Mr. Hampstead's voice interrupted her thoughts. Startled, she gasped in a lung-full of air, apparently not having taken a breath since seeing Mr. Skidmore. "Goodness, are you alright?" Mr. Hampstead looked at her as though she had just grown horns.

"Erm, yes. I believe it has just become a bit stuffy in here. But I'm fine." Charlotte discreetly looked back out over the crowd, but Mr. Skidmore had disappeared.

She saw a calculating gleam enter Mr. Hampstead's eyes. "Perhaps you would like to tour the gardens, Miss Henwood? Get some fresh air?"

Charlotte smiled to herself. The Madisons had prepared her for this trick. She replied, "I believe I shall first see if Mrs. Madison would also like to join us."

Although Mr. Hampstead was attractive, with his dark gold hair and brownish-gold eyes, he had the air of a playful schoolboy. Beyond attending the necessary social engagements, he likely did as he wished. He needed more discipline in his life, Charlotte thought. But perhaps she was being too hard on the man. Harry Madison had introduced them. Apparently Mr. Hampstead was responsible enough to impress him.

As for Mr. Hampstead, he had not actually believed his ploy would work. Although ascertaining Miss Henwood's interests during a vigorous reel had been a challenge, he had learned enough about his pretty companion to know that she was not easily taken in.

Although not much of a flirt, she could certainly maintain an intelligent conversation. Nevertheless, the ladies who typically held his interest were a bit more playful and saucy. He pretended to suppress a sigh. "Then I suppose I shall lead you to your chaperone."

Taking her arm, he turned Charlotte around, intending to lead her to a cluster of gibbering matrons that likely contained Mrs. Madison. Before he could do so, he heard Charlotte emit a rather awkward squeak. Hampstead followed her eyes to a tall gentleman in polite discussion with Lord Fortescue.

Recognizing the object of her attentions, Mr. Hampstead called, "Lord Averly, a pleasure to see you here." *Well, well, well. Miss Henwood's social aspirations were higher than expected for a sweet little country miss.*

Michael's gaze swung down to the young lady holding Mr. Hampstead's arm. His first thought was, *well done, Hampstead.* The lady was quite attractive. In fact, she seemed familiar. No, her darker, less fashionable looks would never have caught his attention in Town.

Drawn to her expectant expression, he looked closer. *Were* they acquainted? There was something particularly familiar about those luscious lips. She reminded him of...*But that was impossible.* This woman obviously traveled in elevated circles. Michael tried to recall the ladies he had given court to at other balls this Season, but none looked at all like this young woman.

As soon as he had returned to London with his title, he began developing an image of his ideal wife, with the intent of finding her. The time would no doubt come soon when he would have to marry and continue the line. She would be elegant, quiet, composed and proper. He visualized someone petite and perhaps blonde.

This lady would not do at all. There was nothing gentle or angelic in her features. She was much too...sensual. That was the right word. Just looking at her left Michael with the desire to slip his fingers into her perfect coiffure and muss it up. Lord knew, he did not want a wife who left him thinking such things in the middle of a ballroom.

She continued to stare at him expectantly. He could not imagine what she wanted from him. "Mr. Hampstead, please do me the honor of introducing your companion," Michael requested, trying for an attitude of polite interest.

Charlotte could not believe her ears. He had first introduced himself as Mr. Skidmore. Who was this Lord Averly? Those were the same green eyes, and there was the freckle on his lip. It took all of her restraint to keep from demanding how the bloody hell he couldn't recognize her! She remembered every blasted feature on his face! And oh, how Suzie had horridly influenced her language.

Maybe Mr. Skidmore wanted to conceal the fact that they had first met under quite unusual circumstances? No. The curious expression on his face, as though Charlotte were a puzzle he couldn't solve, dispelled that hope. She could not simply tell him they had become acquainted over a tankard of ale in a seedy tavern and then shared a kiss that she would remember for the rest of her life.

"Did you just growl?" Mr. Hampstead asked her in an aside. Charlotte couldn't help but think he found this fiasco entertaining. He did not even comprehend the cause of her frustration. However, if Mr. Hampstead was going to tease her after just meeting her, she felt no qualms in lightly kicking his shin. Which she did.

"Oomph," he grunted. Perhaps her kick was not so light. Also, in the future, she should plan to kick someone while she wore riding boots, or something equally sturdy. Her foot certainly hurt more than Mr. Hampstead's shin.

"May I present Miss Henwood?" Mr. Hampstead continued on, clearly unfazed, "Miss Henwood, Viscount Averly." His formal manner could not hide his amused smirk. Charlotte could have cheerfully murdered the man.

While Charlotte held her hand out to Lord Averly and curtseyed, Mr. Hampstead continued on, "Have you a partner for this dance, Miss Henwood? I'm certain His Lordship would love to oblige." As her eyes shot daggers at him, Mr. Hampstead added, "Or perhaps your feet need a rest? All those *kicks* and jumps from the reel likely have done damage to your toes. How *are* your toes?"

Lord Averly appeared confused. "I'm not certain it is polite to ask a lady that, Mr. Hampstead," he intoned. Charlotte nearly choked. Since when did Mr. Skidmore give a care to the more proper niceties?

Another unfortunate thought dawned. The man now knew her name, yet had no recollection of meeting her. That was the last straw. If their encounter in the countryside and the time they shared at The Griffin meant so little to Lord Averly, then she would simply have nothing to do with him.

Turning to Mr. Hampstead, she said in the smoothest voice she could muster, "I believe we were looking for my chaperone?"

Surprise momentarily filled Mr. Hampstead's expression. *Did this little country nobody nearly give a viscount the cut?* "Of course, Miss Henwood." Mr. Hampstead felt his interest in Miss Henwood grow, as he led her back to Mrs. Madison.

---

As for Michael, the unusual encounter perplexed him. Why had she left? Perhaps he made a bad impression in chastising Mr. Hampstead. Many friends of his teased him for being too rigid when attending these affairs. But he couldn't help that.

Michael worried that polite society somehow found him undeserving of his new title—that he needed to prove his worthiness. Michael—and the rest of the *ton*—knew that the Skidmore brothers were not at all closely related to the original Averly line. His father had no doubt known exactly where the Skidmore family stood, but that knowledge was lost when Michael's parents were both taken by a violent fever three years before. After his third cousin, Percy, passed on four months ago, Michael claimed the title with more than a little trepidation.

In addition to that, Michael found little pleasure in knowing that something was being kept from him. The secretly amused look Mr. Hampstead kept sending Miss Henwood was quite irksome. It was not well done at all. Although, considering the expression on Miss Henwood's face, perhaps he wasn't the only one feeling irritated. If Mr. Hampstead bothered her so, why not continue pressing Michael for a dance? He most certainly would not have objected.

There was nothing Michael could have done to rouse this woman's pique. Well, he had not waited for a formal introduction with her chaperone present, but even Michael did not believe that to be beyond the par. What would cause a woman to dislike him immediately upon their first meeting? Had she expected him to fall at her feet, awed by her beauty? Not that she wasn't attractive.

He did not have time for these musings. His main priorities surrounded learning the management of his new estates and following the previous Lord Averly's investments, which were not as diverse as Michael would have liked. That reminded him: he really ought to make another appointment with his estate manager. An allowance for Ryder needed to be set before he left to tour the Averly estates at the end of the Season.

He set off in the direction of the card room, deliberating sums for Ryder's quarterly allowance. With his brother's current lifestyle, there was a lot of trouble Ryder could get into with too much money. Michael had best be careful.

---

Charlotte arrived back at the Madisons' town house to find Suzie and Julia playing cards on Charlotte's plush bed.

Julia spoke first, as she bounded off the bed, "You're finally back! It feels like we've been waiting for days!" Her exuberance only served to intensify Charlotte's own dismal mood.

"Actually, we came back a bit early," Charlotte answered, trying for a friendly smile.

"You mean I'll have to stay up even later when I go through the same thing?"

Charlotte raised an eyebrow. "Julia, you seem quite awake right now and you did not even have the excitement of a ball to keep you up. Have you really been in here all this time?"

"Suzie and I played cards while we waited. It's not as though I was just sitting here impatiently until you got back."

Suzie burst out laughing, "It's exactly like that! You should 'ave seen the lengths I 'ad to go to keep her attention on the game. I should 'ave made a wager or two while we played. She kept askin' me how many gentlemen would be there, how many dances you'd dance."

"You were the doing the same thing! Asking what sorts of dances there would be at a private ball, what drinks they have and so on—"

"Only because I know 'ow Charlotte 'as trouble holdin' her ale."

"Ladies don't drink ale. What can you mean?"

Suzie had been hoping Julia would ask that. "Well, it all has to do with 'ow she got 'erself ruined…But if she 'asn't told you, I really can't betray her confidence so don't you think any more on it." Suzie shrugged helplessly. "So sorry, love." The sly look on Suzie's face belied her words. In response, Julia grabbed one of Charlotte's pillows and began a relentless attack upon Suzie.

It was not until Suzie cried out for mercy that the two turned expectantly to see what other stories Charlotte could share. They found her sitting, bent over, in an overstuffed chair, laughing hysterically. It was an oddly cathartic experience after her disappointing night.

"I don't think there's much for me to tell you. I mean, you've both created enough scenarios in your minds that my evening is likely quite boring in comparison." Once her laughter fully subsided, Charlotte remembered just how greatly her evening differed. The other two saw the sparkle leave her eyes.

Suzie quickly broke the silence. "Well, it's enough to see you're safe and sound fer now. You can tell us stories tomorrow. You'd best get some rest." Before Julia could protest, Suzie had grabbed her hand and pulled her from the room, murmuring something to the girl as she did so. Charlotte couldn't muster the curiosity to eavesdrop.

Wordlessly, Suzie returned to take apart Charlotte's stays and help her into a nightgown. "Now sleep well. Just give me a ring if you fancy some cheap ale to 'elp you rest. If you ask nicely, I might even bring you brandy." And with a wink, she was out of the room.

Charlotte crawled into bed and snuffed the candles. As she lay, seemingly entranced by the bed-hangings, she forced herself to admit the truth. There had only been one truly appealing reason to try to take part in the London Season. That reason was the man who had entered her daydreams increasingly since her visit to Town began.

Mr. Skidmore.

Charlotte had imagined someone significantly different to the real man. The true Mr. Skidmore—Lord Averly—was no chivalrous knight. Even looking back, he hadn't really rescued her from Charles. When he had finally noticed how badly events had turned for Charlotte, he had interceded. By then, he had been too late to improve the situation.

None of that mattered now. After spending the last few weeks hoping to accidentally encounter him at some function or other, Charlotte now prayed for the opposite. If she subtly questioned Imogen about the guest lists for upcoming parties, it would be to ensure that a certain Mr. Skidmore, or Lord Averly, would not be present.

Nevertheless, Lord Averly's confused, disinterested face appeared unbidden in her mind as she drifted off to sleep.

---

Charlotte awoke the next morning to the sound of window coverings being wrenched open, accompanied by a bright shaft of sunlight shining directly into her eyes.

"Damnit, Suzie, I'm tired," she moaned. "Can't I sleep just a bit longer?"

"Oh, of course, love," her evil and demented maid replied cheerily. "Just as soon as you tell me about what 'appened last night. And if you do it now, I won't tell Mrs. Madison about your use of such unladylike language."

"How is it that my speech is deteriorating, while yours is radically improving? It's not fair," Charlotte moaned again, for good measure. In response, Suzie opened the other half of the window draperies, fully flooding the room with light. "Oh, God, noooooo." Charlotte yanked the covers over her head to escape, but Suzie was ready for her. A desperate tugging match ensued, which Charlotte quickly lost, her fingers too numb from sleep to maintain her grip.

Charlotte's night had been restless in the extreme. Dreams of Lord Averly trying to ask her to dance but unable to recall her name, or Lord Averly standing on a table announcing to the ball that Charlotte was an indecent ale-drinker, left her tossing and turning all night. Charlotte decided not to question why Lord Averly was undressed down to his shirtsleeves each time.

Sometime before dawn, Charlotte had forced herself to admit just how much time she had spent hoping to encounter the kind and helpful Mr. Skidmore. The gentleman would then confess how much he had missed her and beg her to run away with him. Charlotte would, of course, agree to be his wife, but only in a lavish ceremony, attended by all of Uckfield, particularly the vicar, his gossipy wife, and the younger Charles Trivett. Instead, she found the stiffly proper, *apparently blind* Lord Averly. That gentleman would never throw caution to the winds for, well, anything. Charlotte sighed as she piled pillows behind her back.

Suzie pounced on that sound. Eyes wide, she carefully demanded, "Did someone insult you? Don't tell me you saw the Trivetts."

"Everyone I met was perfectly agreeable." Charlotte couldn't suppress a small smile. "Even the gentleman who tried to lure me into the gardens. It's not that." She fingered the bed coverings, hoping Suzie would leave things be, yet also wanting to confess her problems.

"Well you 'ad better tell me what it was, or else I just might forget to bring you your morning chocolate for a week."

"I ran into Mr. Skidmore, except he wasn't Mr. Skidmore, he was someone else, and he didn't remember me," Charlotte said in a rush, as she flopped back against her pillows.

Confounded, Suzie stared at Charlotte. "Well, if it weren't really Mr. Skidmore, why did you expect him to recognize you?"

"No, I mean it was Mr. Skidmore, but he really did have a title."

Suzie cocked a brow. "Perhaps you should begin at the beginning. And don't leave anything out." Suzie sat on the edge of the bed, while Charlotte explained last night's disappointment, even confessing just why Lord Averly's disinterest hurt so much.

Suzie's only answer was, "Perhaps we'll bring you extra morning chocolate for the next few days." Knowing her friend needed some time to herself, Suzie left her alone.

---

Imogen waylaid Charlotte in the upstairs family drawing room shortly after breakfast. Something had brought Charlotte down at the Fortescue ball. Imogen had a feeling it had to do with a man. Could Charlotte already have formed a romantic attachment? If she had, the experience had not been ideal.

Charlotte uncurled from the settee to make room for Imogen to sit next to her. Taking a moment to consider her words, Imogen decided to aim for direct. "Charlotte, you seemed different, perhaps even melancholy, during our trip home last night. I wanted to ensure that no one had…been unkind."

Charlotte stared down at her hands. Lord Averly had not intended to slight her. She could not truly call his behavior an insult. She asked, "Have you ever attempted to attract a gentleman's attention, but failed utterly?"

Imogen reached over to place her hand on Charlotte's knee. "Is there a particular gentleman in question? Harry and I could do whatever possible to ensure his interest is engaged. Undoubtedly, Harry would revel in the opportunity."

Charlotte could not even begin to explain. There was no need, really. She did not want to subject herself to any further disappointment from Lord Averly. She sighed, "No. No, the previous evening was simply more overwhelming than I expected. I worried overmuch about saying or doing the wrong thing and appearing a foolish country nobody."

Now Imogen released a true laugh. "Oh, darling. You are much too clever for that. Perhaps you will not become a paragon after a single night, but more than one gentleman sought Harry out to ask about you. No doubt a few shall pay a visit today."

As if on cue, the knocker sounded throughout the house. Imogen smiled at the sound. "You see. It would seem that we even have a guest or two who are unfashionably early, but we won't fault them for their over-eagerness." When Charlotte did not seem cheered by this news, Imogen continued, "Would you like another day to recuperate? We only want you to enjoy your time here in London, Charlotte. I will happily have any guests informed that you are indisposed for now."

Charlotte appreciated Imogen's thoughtfulness. The Madisons were simply too kind. She would not disappoint them. Rising, she offered Imogen her cheeriest smile. "That will not be necessary. I had better change into something more suitable for callers." Catching Imogen's masked concern, Charlotte added, "So long as you remain with me—and perhaps guide me away from saying anything too graceless—I am certain to enjoy the afternoon."

# Chapter 6

D ESPITE HER UNPLEASANT DEBUT, Charlotte took to Town-life quite well. Most of the friends she made through Imogen were ladies in whose company she took pleasure.

Charlotte's only regrettable moment involved an uncomfortable run-in with the Trivett ladies at a small garden party. Despite the few people invited to the gathering, Mrs. Trivett did everything in her power to keep her daughters away from the tainted Miss Henwood.

At least Charlotte had attended with both Harry and Imogen Madison. Mrs. Trivett would never be so foolish as to directly snub the guest of such influential personages. The only happy moment had been when the Trivetts made their lengthy goodbyes. Caroline Trivett had sneaked away from her mother for a brief moment. She had quickly drawn Charlotte aside and said, "I'm so sorry, Charlotte, about everything. I hope you are well."

Charlotte had done her best to answer kindly. Their conversation had been brief, but Charlotte did glean a few interesting facts from Caroline. It seemed that the Trivetts had greater concerns than the influence of the hoydenish Charlotte Henwood. Mr. Trivett, at his son's suggestion, had decided to try adding sandier soil to their already rich land, in the hopes of developing better-enduring crops. It had not gone over well. After the various conversations Charlotte had shared with Mr. Madison, she could have easily predicted its failure. Adding clay and chalk to courser soil could improve the land's fertility, but doing the reverse was beyond foolish. Caroline expressed a doubt that the ladies would be able to enjoy another Season if their situation did not improve soon.

Charlotte would have liked to have spoken more, but Eleanor had noticed her twin's absence and had immediately alerted Mrs. Trivett. Caroline had hurried away under her mother's reproachful glare.

Despite what the Trivetts thought of her, Charlotte was considered one of the more stolid, mature young ladies in society. Most of her acquaintances sought her out to discuss philosophy or history. She quickly developed quite a reputation for being a well-informed and clever conversationalist.

The only exception to this rule was when Charlotte attended the same gatherings as the illustrious Lord Averly. No matter how she wished to control her actions, she always found herself laughing a bit louder than was polite, or playfully flirting with gentlemen who were known to be a touch rakish. These events were always few and far between; nonetheless Charlotte knew that Lord Averly had taken note of her behavior. She would catch him sending her a curious stare or two. He had even deigned to request a few dances. Charlotte had managed to shock several members of the *ton* when she would stammer an excuse to avoid him. Every time he stiffly walked away, she felt a wrenching pain in her chest.

The two occasions that she could not make an excuse, she simply stared over his shoulder during the set, making only the most basic of conversation. Meanwhile, Lord Averly would stare at her as though she were some bizarre mythical creature. Charlotte hoped he was worried she might bite.

Had Charlotte only known how mad she drove Lord Averly, well, perhaps she would have tried even harder.

---

Ever since that first moment at the Fortescue ball when Miss Henwood had essentially snubbed Michael, his interest had been piqued. What had he done to cause such avid dislike? The *ton* considered him a respectable member of the peerage. His opinion was often sought among members of the House of Lords. Every young woman attempted to engage his interest.

Except for Miss Henwood. A glutton for punishment, Michael could not prevent himself from seeking her company when he saw her. His peers were beginning to talk about it behind their hands, he knew. The woman was making him look a fool and she did not seem to notice or care.

Still, she continued to fascinate him. No one knew where she came from or who her family was, only that she was connected to the Madisons, and therefore a lady of some importance and standing. Michael could not believe he was the only man who wanted to discover more.

The occasions when she could not avoid him proved the worst. The moment he would take her hand to lead her to the dance floor, every muscle in his torso would tighten expectantly. He was appalled that she could have this effect on him. As soon as the set began, he would pray for its end, if only to cease this incomprehensible spark of desire. Yet the next time he would run into her, he would again attempt to engage her attentions. This madness must stop. Perhaps he could flee England for a time? Michael could not wait for the Season to end and Miss Henwood to return to wherever she came from.

---

Happily for Lord Averly, but not as much for Charlotte, the Season finally concluded and it came time to return home. At least Charlotte would be with her father again.

She had every intention of showing off her new clothes, as well as her refined demeanor. Petty, but true. The vicar would likely comment on the negative influences of city-living and how going there might make a person act like they were better than they deserved. In fact, Charlotte almost hoped he would.

Her goodbyes to the Madisons were the hardest. Julia wanted her to remain, even enlisting her parents to convince Charlotte to stay. Harry and Imogen did not object. However, she couldn't allow herself to burden them after the Season ended. They had been so good to her; Charlotte didn't think it would be right. When Julia tried to extract a promise for Charlotte to return the following Season, Charlotte couldn't hide the hope in her eyes. Still, her only response was, "We shall see."

The Madisons lent their traveling coach for Suzie and Charlotte's return journey. Upon Charlotte's first sight of Uckfield, she decided that a little peace and quiet at home would do her some good. More than anything else, Charlotte desperately missed her father. When her home, with its sweet, vibrant flowers and charming red brick came into view, Charlotte could barely sit still. The moment the carriage came to a stop, she flew out the door, leaving the coachman to see to her things.

"Papa, I'm back!" Charlotte called as she swung the door open after their four month separation. Mrs. Blakely caught the door for her. Unlike the Trivetts, they couldn't afford a butler. Charlotte didn't really mind. She liked the solitude and peace of her own home, especially after the excitement and pomp of the Madison household.

She knew exactly where to find her father—the library. "Hello, Papa." Charlotte crossed her arms and leaned against the doorframe, taking in the familiar sight of her father surrounded by his research.

Her father grunted a greeting while he leaned over his desk, squinting at an unpleasantly ill-rendered map. "How is your research progressing?" Charlotte asked. She knew from his letters that he was hoping to find the location of a ship that had disappeared during one of the East India Company's early expeditions.

A pleased gleam entered eyes as rich a brown as her own. His glasses slid down his nose as he shook his head. "I'm telling you, it didn't sink. These records prove that the *Kingston* reached all of the ports it was scheduled to, before it supposedly turned back to England. However, these records here," Sir Driscoll pointed to a pile of loose papers to his right, "contain the names of men who joined the crews of various ships leaving the city of Mumbai after the *Kingston* left its final port. So far, I have found the names of seven members of her crew departing on ships other than the *Kingston*."

Charlotte had not been expecting a heartfelt hello. Her father had a tendency to become a little focused when deep in his research. She smiled as she rounded the desk to get a better look at the map, preparing a counterargument, "So the ship could still have sunk and the surviving crew members maybe swam to the nearest shore, then found their way to Mumbai." She had missed these little debates.

Her father tried, ineffectually, to perch his round-framed glasses farther up his nose. "Ah, but if the ship sank without anyone knowing about it, it could not have been very close to shore. A man can only swim so far, before exhaustion takes hold. Otherwise, the ships leaving the naval dockyard would have seen it go down, and its sinking would have been much better documented."

Charlotte decided to wait to mention the possibility of a rowboat or two being used to escape a more distant sinking ship, instead asking, "So then, what do you think did happen? Perhaps it didn't sink, but is there any evidence that indicates that?" Already she was sifting through the documents on his desk.

"Pirates," was her father's reply.

Charlotte stood straight up, flummoxed. "Pirates? Papa, isn't that a bit outlandish?"

"It's not so uncommon," he protested. "I think that the ship was overtaken by pirates. The surviving crew members joined with the ship that overtook them. Then, they escaped at the first port they could. Look here—none of the ships they joined in Mumbai were from England. And there is evidence of at least one other ship from the East India Company making port at the naval dockyard within two weeks after the *Kingston* disappeared. I think the crew didn't want to face the consequences of losing all that cargo. That's why they didn't immediately return to England and explain what had transpired."

Charlotte considered this. "What if they decided to sell their cargo themselves instead of taking it back to England and only receiving a portion of the profits, if any at all?"

"I didn't consider that possibility." After thinking for a moment, he said, "Had they sold their cargo, they likely would have done it far away from India. In France or another European country the demand for their cargo would have been greater, so the crew would have been found there. Also, after selling everything, they should have had enough money to afford the trip home, instead of signing on as crew members on new ships."

"What if the crew that you found in India were the ones who objected to the scheme?" Charlotte couldn't hide her cheeky grin. "They may have jumped from the ship to escape, but because they allowed the rest of the crew to continue on with the goods, they would be disgraced." After making such a fine point, she decided to retreat, skipping happily to the doorway.

"I can search records from the major ports in Europe to see if there's any evidence the *Kingston's* crew was there," she heard her father say as she left the room. His voice reduced to a low mumble as papers began rustling in earnest.

"Charlotte." She turned at her father's voice. "It is good to have you home."

She smiled and let out a pleased sigh, before leaving to find her room. Returning to the peace and calm of her home was a much-needed reprieve. Perhaps now Charlotte could finally forget Viscount Averly and the man she had once dreamed he could be.

# Chapter 7

---

*London, April, 1811*

"MAMA, THIS DRESS makes me look sallow! I refuse to wear it." Julia attempted to remove said dress without assistance; however she merely succeeded in several awkward jerking motions as she reached for her back. Imogen smiled placidly in response, knowing the dress was not coming off.

Charlotte agreed with Julia, but remained silent. Providing her opinion could result in outright warfare. The off-white muslin patterned with small embroidered yellow flowers was more than appropriate for a young woman about to come out. Nevertheless, the shades somehow leached all of the vibrant color from Julia's face.

A smile slowly spread across Charlotte's lips as she realized how much she had missed the Madisons. Nearly a year had passed since Charlotte's first Season began. Imogen and Harry had almost decided to suspend Julia's debut for another year, concerned about how she would handle the fortune hunters. In Charlotte's opinion, Julia would swiftly learn to manage. She'd know when a man sought her attentions purely because of her dowry.

The last year had seen a marvelous change in Julia's appearance. Now eighteen years old, her figure had become less plump and much more curvaceous. While Suzie spent more than a few minutes every day trying to make more of Charlotte's bosom than there actually was, the reverse was true for Julia.

Charlotte sometimes worried that the weight of the poor girl's front would topple her over. Those assets, combined with her sweet smile and dimples, would have men begging for her hand.

In order to distract Julia, the Madisons had spent most of the last year abroad, particularly in Italy. Imogen had a passion for ancient Roman art. An invitation had been extended to Charlotte, but worry about being so very far from her father had prompted her to regretfully decline. The trip from London to Uckfield was less than a day's journey. But outside England, it might take weeks for word to reach her if anything happened to him.

However, Charlotte had kept herself busy in the meantime. She disliked the idea of the money from the ironworks just wallowing, unused. Upon discovering Charlotte's fascination with numbers and the speculation involved in investing, Mr. Madison quite happily began teaching her everything he knew. Since the beginning of her first Season with the Madisons, she began to reinvest, under Harry Madison's guidance.

Her father certainly didn't object. He would quite happily sign his name to whatever new document or bank draft Charlotte sent his way. Not all of her decisions were immediately profitable, but by now she had found her stride. She preferred looking into various shipping ventures. She loved the idea of traveling to the far-off places her father had taught her so much about. Even though she could never join those particular voyages, knowing she helped bring such beautiful creations from India, or China or even Africa, to England for her countrymen to experience was pleasing enough.

The last few months had seen quite an impressive profit. Enough, in fact, that she decided to rent a small house of her own in London for the Season. Although Charlotte adored the Madisons, she preferred having the peace and quiet of her own space, one of the very few things she missed about her life in the country.

When she had first written to the Madisons, broaching the idea, they had objected. Imogen and Julia had been especially excited about the prospect of having her stay with them again. But they also understood that Charlotte was a private person. Although she enjoyed the lively atmosphere in the Madison family's home, she also enjoyed reading a novel with a cup of tea as her only companion. She had grown up accustomed to relaxed evenings, often spent in quiet reflection with her father.

Charlotte wanted the focus to be on Julia for the girl's first Season. It would be easier for her without another lady in the house competing for attention. In the end, Harry offered to find her a house that would be within walking distance. They would still all see each other regularly, but Charlotte could better relax in the evenings. Mrs. Madison had even asked a female cousin of hers to stay with Charlotte, ensuring things remained proper.

So here Charlotte was, her second Season about to begin.

Charlotte and Suzie had walked over to the Madisons' to prepare for their first outing, a small supper party. Her new chaperone, Frances Harrow, the Countess of Kinsey—having just arrived in London—decided to stay in, leaving Charlotte under Mrs. Madison's supervision. Charlotte's newest evening dress had recently been delivered straight to the Madisons', allowing her to prepare for supper with the other ladies.

In another two nights, they were all to attend a ball, but Julia wanted to start with a simpler occasion before completely coming out. The Season would not begin in full for another few weeks.

Harry had begged off for the supper, surprising everyone. When Imogen noticed his distracted look, she chose not to press him. She could always question her husband later on.

Charlotte watched Suzie step up to adjust the disarray of Julia's dress. Julia crossed her arms and pouted while Suzie did so, apparently giving in to this battle. The ladies completed all final alterations to their ensembles, and then moved downstairs to shuffle into the carriage.

Charlotte paid little attention to Imogen's description of Lord and Lady Pemberly, their hosts for the evening. Tonight was all about Julia and helping her feel comfortable in an adult social setting. Charlotte would finally get her chance to sit aside and observe—something her first Season had never fully allowed. Mostly, she intended to keep an eye on the gentlemen who sought Julia out.

The Pemberly townhouse was a great deal more ostentatious than the Madisons' could ever be. Unable to resist, Charlotte leaned down and whispered in Julia's ear, "I wonder if all this gleaming gold gilt could have a gradual blinding effect." They both stifled a giggle when Lord Pemberly raised a lorgnette to his eye when he greeted them. Apparently, it did.

The drawing room was nearly full when the three of them arrived. During introductions, Julia was all sweet elegance. Any nerves were well-masked.

Towards the beginning of the evening, as the guests mingled, Charlotte overheard a gentleman behind her casually ask another about Julia's dowry. Everyone knew it would be sizable, but the exact amount had never been spread around. Although Charlotte was unsurprised at someone's interest in Julia, she realized the questioner's voice sounded familiar. When she turned, the men had already wandered off.

Once everyone filed into the spacious dining room, Charlotte recognized Lord Averly's younger brother. He sat much closer to the head of the table, but she could see his profile. Was that the voice she had heard before?

Charlotte kept herself amused over supper, despite her tendency to glance towards the honorable Ryder Skidmore. Although she disliked any meal with more courses than fingers on her hand, the conversation was entertaining. An earl's young son had decided to fall in love with some opera singer or other and had recently attempted to learn an Italian aria, serenading her outside her home. To thank him, she sent a maid out to douse him with the wash water. Apparently he should have sought out a better music instructor.

After supper, the ladies all gathered together to chat. Charlotte cared little about which lady expected which gentleman to finally come up to scratch, but she pretended to listen.

Luckily, the gentlemen took less time than usual to rejoin them. While many of the guests sat down to a game of whist or engaged another in conversation, Charlotte watched for Mr. Ryder Skidmore. When she finally located the man in question, she stalked across the room to catch him. Like an arrow finding its target, he had specifically sought Julia out. Worse than that, she appeared to be enjoying the conversation, nodding and smiling sweetly as she listened to Mr. Skidmore.

Although Charlotte had no intention of interrupting, she covertly observed the two. Did Mr. Skidmore stand too close? Was anyone else observing them as she was? In close discussion with Lady Pemberly, Mrs. Madison did not notice Julia and Mr. Skidmore.

Charlotte no longer doubted who she had overheard earlier. Mr. Skidmore was interested in Julia. Unable to decide whether she approved or not, Charlotte bided her time.

When the two parted, Mr. Skidmore requested a glass of port. His quietly self-pleased smirk roused her ire.

Charlotte casually wandered over to where he stood. "Supper was lovely, don't you think?"

Mr. Skidmore's gaze had wandered across the room to settle back on Julia. His smile grew. "The company is exactly what I could have wished for." Finally turning to face his new companion, Mr. Skidmore made a subtle jolt. Surprise filled his eyes. "I could be mad, but you seem vaguely familiar. I hope we met under pleasant circumstances?"

"Actually, we met in a seedy tavern. You had a pretty redhead hanging on your arm."

Comprehension slowly swept across Mr. Skidmore's face. "Ah, yes. You must have been the pretty miss sharing ale with my brother. My, how we have come up in the world." Mr. Skidmore grinned as he looked her over.

Charlotte did not return his smile. "I'm surprised anyone remembers at all." In an attempt to regain control of the situation, she added, "By the bye, Suzie now acts as my lady's maid. She is well."

Not even a blink in response. "A pleasure to hear it. However, I doubt reminding me of an old acquaintance was your objective in approaching me. What topic did you intend to eventually discuss?"

Mr. Skidmore now turned his attention completely on Charlotte. For a moment, she softened; his face so greatly resembled his elder brother's. No. She would avoid going down that road.

Hardening her heart and her voice, she said, "You appear to have taken a particular interest in a close friend of mine. More than that, you appear to have taken a particular interest in her dowry." She gave him a moment to allow that to settle. "I wish to know what your intentions are."

"Isn't it the office of the lady's father to ask such a question?" Despite his attempt at teasing, Ryder Skidmore seemed bothered by her words. "Besides, if I see a lady I find appealing, I am of course going to try to engage her."

Charlotte replied in a low voice, "Typically a gentleman's first question about a lady he has never met does not pertain to her finances, unless he is in desperate straits. Mr. Madison is indeed quite wealthy, as I am sure you know, but he is also quite intelligent. The first thing he will do is look into your own situation, and if he discovers that you are not what you claim, all contact with his daughter will be cut off."

Ryder no longer tried to hide how troubling he found her words. "Are you saying this merely for my own sake? Protecting an old friend, as it were?"

Charlotte shrugged, another habit she had picked up from Suzie. "This has nothing to do with you. Julia is like a sister to me. If something happened that hurt her, I would likely find my own revenge." Across the room, an acquaintance smiled at her. Charlotte nodded in return then gave her attention back to Mr. Skidmore.

"Do you warn off all of your friends' admirers?"

"Only when they have made it clear they are only interested in their money."

"I do not think I have ever had another lady threaten dire consequences were I to cross her friend. Usually it is a jealous lover or angry brother, and so on. This is unexpected." Ryder made a pathetic attempt at a chuckle. "What do you intend to do?"

Charlotte had not planned for the conversation to go this far and frankly, had no real answer. His question left her flummoxed. "I don't know. I originally came over to ask you about your intentions, but we have certainly passed beyond such casual conversation now, haven't we?"

At first she doubted Mr. Skidmore even heard her, trapped in his private thoughts. Watching the amber liquid swirl in his glass, he finally asked, "Would her father really look into the brother of a viscount?"

Gentling her voice, she answered, "I can most certainly assure you that Mr. Madison cares more for his daughter's happiness than the social connection any union would make. I take it an investigation into your own finances would prove problematic?"

This time Ryder did laugh, although Charlotte heard little humor behind it. "I may be in some trouble if I don't come up with additional funds soon. If it helps, I doubt I would have been able to go through with courting a lady purely for her dowry. Miss Madison is a bit too quiet and shy for my tastes. She needs another Season to gain some confidence."

Charlotte considered this. Perhaps she had been too hard on the young man. Perhaps? Ha. She had walked across the room and demanded his intentions. What was it about the Skidmore brothers that caused her to throw all reason aside? It wasn't in her nature to be this confrontational.

One of the few things that Suzie had told her about her encounter with Ryder Skidmore was that he was a considerate and generous man. At the time, Charlotte was under the impression she meant something else. She sighed, "Can you tell me how deep you are in?" Something about the bleak look in his eyes had reached Charlotte.

Ryder again looked down into his glass as he swirled his brandy. "Twelve hundred pounds," he mumbled.

Charlotte gasped, "Good God!" Immediately she looked around the room in hopes that no one heard her outburst.

"I don't really ever gamble, but one night, a friend and I were foxed. The next day, he told me how much I had lost at this gaming den. I don't even remember, but when I went back, they had the note with my vowels to show me. I thought it was a trick, at first, but other friends of mine had seen me playing and losing."

"What of your brother?"

"He had to leave last month for the country—a problem with one of the estates. In Leeds." Charlotte nodded. He was weeks away. "There is no way he could get the money to me in time, even if I did want to involve him. But I don't. I don't think he'll believe that I never gamble like this. It was only the one time." Ryder's eyes widened. "Why in the world am I telling you all this?"

Charlotte had been wondering the same thing. It was one thing to confess that you were penniless, but quite another to tell a lady the entire story behind it.

Her smile turned rueful. "Well, all things considered, you have certainly seen me at my worst. Perhaps this evens the score?" Then she added, her voice less gentle, "Although I really don't know what you were expecting if you intended to pursue a woman for her dowry. Courtship doesn't usually take a week or two." It was not her intention to sound as though she was scolding him, but what else could she say?

"My thinking may have been a tad optimistic," Ryder admitted, staring into his drink, "and irrational."

"Is there no one you can go to?"

"I have a school friend who would likely have the money on hand. But we weren't exceptionally close. He'll charge an exorbitant interest and who knows how long it will be before I can fully pay him back? I have two weeks to decide. As it is, however, I promise to try to leave all innocent young misses out of things."

Charlotte tried to smile for him, "Good luck, Mr. Skidmore."

"Thank you, Miss—Goodness, I seem to have forgotten since we last met."

"Henwood, Charlotte Henwood," she supplied.

"Thank you, Miss Henwood," he said, the sincerity in his voice evident. He began to step away, but halted. "The same Miss Henwood who drove my brother absolutely insane last Season?"

Uncertain how to reply, Charlotte merely offered Mr. Skidmore a mysterious smile, before curtseying and rejoining Mrs. Madison. *Well, Char, this is apparently what occurs when you decide to be quiet for the evening. Perhaps next time you shall be a bit more engaging and avoid getting embroiled in any further messes.*

After Mr. Skidmore left, Charlotte couldn't help but mull over his predicament. She actually did have the money to help him. But for a younger son, whose funds likely came in the form of a quarterly allowance, how long would it be before she got her money back?

Charlotte had been making such great plans, with Harry's help, of course. She certainly didn't want to put those plans on hold. Hopefully things would turn out well for Mr. Skidmore. At least Charlotte could be assured that Julia was safe.

---

A week later, the Madisons attended a ball at the Marquis of Ravencliff's estate. Although the estate was located nearly an hour outside of London, everyone agreed it would be the perfect setting to officially bring Julia out. The ball promised to be a grand affair, society's most important leaders likely to attend. Besides that, the Marquis owed Harry Madison a great deal after Harry helped him out of an uncomfortable fix.

The lavish estate had been fashioned in a Classical style, Greek columns lining the steps leading to the house. White marble statues filled several of the entrance hall's niches once inside. As for the actual ballroom: it was gigantic. The ceiling was so high that Charlotte couldn't imagine how the chandeliers could be lit. Then again, she had never grown up with chandeliers in her own home, so what did she know?

Charlotte did her best to make Julia feel comfortable, while also allowing the girl to do as she pleased. Julia, at least, was not as awed as Charlotte had been at her first ball, having grown up with these people.

Although Julia did not have a harem of men fawning over her, her dance card filled quickly and she managed quite well in conversation. Charlotte or Imogen stepped in a few times, when Julia's shyness took over, but otherwise all went smoothly.

Charlotte finally allowed herself to be distracted. A few gentlemen requested she join them for a set. At one point, her partner brought her to the other side of the room from the Madisons after their set ended. Although she only had one Season behind her, she knew this for the ploy it was, especially when she noticed the open terrace doors a short distance from where she and her companion stood.

Neither Charlotte nor the Madisons had ever felt the need to discuss Charlotte's dowry with the *ton*. Her conversations with

Suzie, hinting at the lascivious activities in which so many married men of the *ton* engaged, had convinced her to avoid marriage at all costs. Bandying her financial standing about would only draw unwanted interest. The drawback was the occasional gentleman who thought her easy prey for a dalliance.

Smiling politely, she informed her companion that she intended to find herself a glass of lemonade. When he insisted on acquiring the glass for her, she acquiesced. Once she could no longer see him, Charlotte began to make her way back to the Madisons. Impolite, yes, but it was always an easy escape without really insulting anyone. She could claim he must have lost her in the crowd.

"Personally, I'm shocked Madison brought her to the ball in the first place," she heard a sly male voice reply over her shoulder.

Charlotte stopped. Who would dare gossip about the Madisons, especially at a ball where they were a personal friend of the host? If the "her" referred to Julia, Charlotte intended to provide a serious set-down. Trying her best to see who was speaking, Charlotte caught glimpses of the back of a slender man with salt and pepper hair and an expertly tailored mauve evening coat.

Another member in the group, this time a woman, asked the question for Charlotte, "Who? You can't mean his daughter? She's certainly old enough to be out, maybe even too old for a first Season, so there is no insult there."

The same man answered her, "No, I mean his mistress. She is right here at the ball. And the worst is Mrs. Madison and their daughter both believe they are her friends!"

The woman and Charlotte gasped at the same time. She refused to believe it; Harry adored his wife and would never dream of betraying her.

This time the woman spoke, "You can't mean…"

"Indeed it's true, that Henwood character!" Charlotte's heart stopped. "She used to live in the same house with them, but *something* happened to require her to find a residence elsewhere this Season. A very elegant, expensive residence in a very popular part of town, and not so far from the Madison estate," the man added meaningfully.

Charlotte could not believe her ears. Dizzy and nauseated all at once, she searched the room for a place to sit down. How could anyone believe such gossip when she was so close to Imogen and Julia?

That vile voice continued on, warming to his story, "According to my head footman, who is acquainted with a maid in the Madisons' household, this young woman and Mr. Madison correspond regularly." The man's voice became even more excited. "And that house she lives in? Mr. Madison is the one who found it and set everything up for her. Everyone says she's some poor little country mouse, but how can some nobody from the country afford her expensive clothes, I ask you?"

Charlotte shook her head in an attempt to clear it. She and Harry wrote to discuss investment opportunities, and Mrs. Madison had chosen the house for her, but naturally a married lady shouldn't set up a house to rent. None of these people listening believed these lies, did they?

Another woman in the group spoke next. "You know, I've actually heard her call him 'Harry.' Can you believe that? And really, the girl ignores any possible suitors. Perhaps there is a man who already holds her affections. A *married* man…"

"Shocking, absolutely shocking."

They believed every word.

It was all too much for Charlotte. She ran away as fast as she could, which in the crush, was not very fast at all. She was going to be sick, she just knew it.

—⁓—

Back with the group he had been spreading his tales to, Lord Tunley smiled to himself. His opportunity had finally come. He had located the original owner of the Cornish mine, a Jeremy

Stowes, ex-boxer. What could be more fortuitous than an ex-boxer to intimidate the other share-holders to sell off their portions? Tunley certainly couldn't be blamed for providing Mr. Stowes with the share-holders' names. Stowes promised there would be no connection between Lord Tunley and himself in whatever attempts he made at intimidation.

Stowes had not taken it at all well to discover just how profitable his land had become. When Tunley offered him a small portion of the profits from the mine in return for a few well-placed threats, Stowes had leapt at the chance. A "discussion" or two had already taken place. Not much later, Tunley had heard rumors of an investor intending to back out.

All Lord Tunley had to do was ingratiate himself to the other investors, making him the perfect person to buy their shares when things turned dicey with Mr. Stowes.

If Stowes ever decided to renege, Tunley could remind the boxer of a little incident involving a member of the peerage and an out of control brawl. Lord Hammond still could not put any weight on his right leg, even two months later.

Best of all, Tunley had found a way to distract that upstart, Madison. He knew exactly who the pretty little miss who spent so much time with the Madisons was. She was the daughter of one of the less important, less influential investors. Perhaps if her father heard about his daughter's possible involvement with Mr. Harry Madison, he would withdraw his money from the venture. One could only hope.

No matter what, the rumors spreading through the *ton* would require a great deal of Mr. Madison's attention if he wanted to protect his family's name. He would have little time to focus on the other gentlemen involved with the Cornish ironworks. Lord Tunley would have ample opportunity to convince the investors to—if not simply sell him their portion—at least allow him to control their shares.

It had taken a great deal of wheedling and cajoling to convince that upstart Madison to even let him invest. Harry

Madison likely enjoyed knowing he had that level of power over a member of the peerage. Madison, whose family began their fortune through trade, could never dream of sharing Tunley's position in society.

Lord Tunley's few other investments would never come close to paying off his debts. Most of them had, in fact, left him worse off than before. But everything would change soon. He just needed more say in how the ironworks was dealt with. Madison, he knew, had opted for using Henry Cort's puddling forge. Tunley may not have been aware of Cort's exact procedures, but he knew they had been used for decades. They were no doubt becoming outdated. And why in the world was Madison bringing in coal to fuel the forges, when he could simply use the surrounding forests? No doubt Cornwall's woods could use some thinning.

Madison was living in the past. In addition, the number of men overseeing the safety and upkeep of the ironworks was outrageous. Tunley cringed each time he was notified of another unnecessary inspection. Those drudges knew they worked in a less-than-safe environment, so why bother trying to improve matters for them?

Tunley needed controlling interest. Upon the death of his father last year, Tunley had finally returned to the family home. Instead of the bustling estate of his memories, he had returned to find a painfully inadequate staff presiding over a depleted estate. Nearly all of the classic artwork and some of the furniture had been sold off to pay the more pressing debts.

If Tunley expected to see any useful profit from that ironworks soon, Mr. Madison, and the men who would side with him, had to be out of the picture. The amount of money they wasted was unconscionable. He doubted Madison's other investors cared whether the mine and foundry produced at all. But for Tunley, this investment was all he had left.

Meanwhile, Charlotte and Lady Kinsey, Mrs. Madison's cousin, made their excuses and borrowed the Madison carriage in order to return home. Charlotte could only feel relief that she had not actually emptied her stomach at the ball.

Charlotte's fear of just how widespread the gossip would become kept her from sleeping nearly at all. However, the lack of sleep had allowed her to think up a counter-attack. She needed a new romantic interest, and she needed him quickly.

# Chapter 8

M ICHAEL HAD FINALLY returned to London. Nearly a
week had passed since he received that damned letter
and immediately ordered his bags packed. Michael had refused
to even wait for a carriage to be brought around for him. His
horse had been readied and, with a few pounds in his pocket
and a change of clothes in his saddle bag, he left. The rest of his
things could damn well follow later. Damn Miss Henwood.
Even across the country, the woman was proving to be the bane
of his existence.

It was bad luck that the one estate he needed to check on
happened to be the farthest from London. He knew the journey
would be long, starting north of Leeds. But he made excellent
time, all things considered. The previous night, unable to sleep,
he arose at near four in the morning to continue his journey.
Now all he needed to do was find his troublesome brother.

After Michael pounded on the front entrance of the family's
London home, his butler Stoome swung the door open. Upon
seeing his master in such a bedraggled state, the man's eyes
widened.

"My lord, we were not expecting you for some time, yet.
Your brother informed us that you would likely be another
month in the country." Michael almost found Stoome's surprise
amusing. Most of the time, their butler was unflappable. Then
again, seldom did Stoome have opportunity to see Lord Averly
with a mud stain on his knee, a smudge of dirt on his cheek,
and the most wrinkled clothing known to man. Not to mention

the state of his boots. Trying to regain his composure, Stoome added, "We will ensure that everything is ready for your return."

"While you do that, could you please inform my brother that I wish to speak with him?"

Stoome appeared taken aback, "My lord, your brother is not at home."

Michael's eyes narrowed. "It is eight in the morning, Stoome. Ryder never leaves the house before noon." He paused. "He is never *awake* before noon, come to think of it."

"Erm, what I meant to say is that he did not come home last night, my lord. I believe he attended a late engagement. He likely stayed at his friend's house." Stoome apparently found the conversation even more nerve-racking than Michael. Was his butler's bald pate beading with sweat? Perhaps Michael ought to give Stoome a reprieve from his newfound temper. Deciding to wait until his brother returned, Michael turned to ascend the staircase.

Before he reached the upper landing, an unpleasant thought struck. Michael froze. "With whom, exactly, was he attending said engagement? It would not happen to be a Miss Henwood, would it?" Judging by the unsightly shade of red his butler's face turned, Michael had guessed correctly. Perhaps now was indeed a good time to seek his brother out.

Stoome stuttered, "I have heard that Mr. Skidmore has been spending a notable amount of time with her, my lord." Were even the servants gossiping about his brother and that woman? Even more disturbing, the servants were usually the ones who got it right.

Considering the letter concealed in his pocket, it appeared that all of London was aware of the pair's involvement. Ryder had a great deal to answer for, indeed he did.

"I believe I have changed my mind, Stoome. Have a fresh horse readied for me. I wish to leave again now."

Heart pounding, Charlotte awoke to loud knocking on her front door. This had better be an emergency. Knowing Suzie was an even sounder sleeper than herself, Charlotte jumped out of bed and put on her dressing robe. The banging continued. What was wrong? Had something happened to the Madisons?

Heart beating wildly, Charlotte ran down the stairs to swing open the front door. She tried, unsuccessfully, to brush her black hair out of her face. She could barely see through it to recognize the man standing there. When her eyes reached his face, she gasped. *He was here*! But, *why* was he here?

The stormy expression in Michael's eyes turned to outright shock. *It was her*! The sweet girl who had shared an ale and a kiss with him so long ago. The mussed black hair and innocent brown eyes were exactly the same. An unexpected desire to smooth those wavy tresses overcame him.

Did she know he had looked for her? Michael had searched for more than one reason to travel to Brighton in the past year. Every time he did so, he passed through that ridiculous small town. He had never found her again, but he did discover why the residents of Uckfield were so famous for their pudding cake. Who knew a man could try so many different recipes of the exact same thing?

He always pretended that he merely took a shortcut as he rode through. Less people traveled the roads through Uckfield, which prevented any chances of Michael being stopped on his way.

Why was she here in London? Upon first meeting her, it was clear that she was not wealthy, but she should not have needed to find employment in Town. Michael had expected that moronic little cretin to eventually request her hand once he got over finding her in that tavern.

If only he had found her sooner. Had she needed the money, he would gladly have done whatever he could to help her.

Finally her full, luscious lips parted. "What are you doing here?"

All of a sudden, Michael felt a little bashful. "I came to speak to your mistress." Really, there was no need for him to feel so nervous. He was a viscount. Women typically begged for his attention. Once he took care of the situation with Ryder, he would speak with the young lady before him.

Miss Henwood had better treat her properly, or there would surely be hell to pay. This girl could do so much better than a maid to another man's mistress. He needed to remain focused on the task at hand.

A thought struck him: if she did not object to working for another man's mistress, then she certainly did not object to the practice. Perhaps he could convince her to take a new residence? One that he paid for...

"My mistress?" *No, my mistress*, he thought. Gracious! What was he thinking? He couldn't take a mistress or anything that might cast aspersions upon the family name.

Michael took a deep breath, pushing these thoughts aside. "Actually, I am looking for my brother, Mr. Ryder Skidmore? I was informed he might be here with Miss Henwood." His words only seemed to confuse the young lady more.

She turned away and started back down the hall. "I can't imagine why he would be here, but why don't you come in? If you will give me a few moments to dress, I can return momentarily."

Now Michael was confused. Did she need to be properly dressed in order to fetch her mistress but not to answer the door? This early-morning disaster was partially of Michael's own making. No, he corrected, this was of Miss Henwood's making.

When she passed the drawing room, she vaguely gestured towards it, still not turning around. He assumed she meant for him to wait for Miss Henwood there. As he cautiously entered the room and took a seat, he couldn't help but think how his lady made a terrible maid. But there were surely other things she was good at. That thought brought to mind a whole slew of other occupations he would like to set her to. Michael shook his head. Such vulgar thoughts were simply due to exhaustion from his travels.

———

While Michael tried his best not to imagine running his hands through her hair and then down her back, Charlotte ran to Suzie's room to wake her.

"Suzie! Mr. Skidmore's here! Wake up, wake up, wake up!" Charlotte had been aiming for a whisper but somehow her words came out more as a screech.

As for Suzie, she wanted none of that. "We're the ones doin' Ryder a favor 'ere. Tell him 'e can come back later. I'm tired." As she pulled the covers back up over her person, Charlotte saw her pause. Suzie's eyes opened a bit more as she sat up. "Wait just a minute. Ryder and I went to the Hawk's Claw last night after you all returned from the Churchill soiree. 'E should be still abed. Hell, he should be unconscious, considering the state he arrived 'ere in. You're speakin' gibberish, you are…" Suzie began mumbling to herself while she drew the covers back over her head.

Charlotte was unsurprised that Ryder spent the night in a guest room. They had agreed that if Ryder was discreet, left very early out the back, and did not awaken anyone in the household, he should stay over when he could not safely return home.

At the moment, however, Charlotte didn't care where Ryder spent the night. If Suzie was right, Ryder was already back at his own home. "It's not Ryder; Lord Averly's here!" That news brought Suzie to sitting straight up in bed while she watched Charlotte pace across her floor. "What am I going to do? He recognized me. I'm sure he did. Oh blast! I look terrible! What does it mean when he only recognizes me when I look terrible?"

"Well, we'll just have to take care of the looking terrible part. Let's go, let's go!" Throwing on her dressing gown, Suzie ushered her mistress back to her room.

Once closeted in Charlotte's bedchamber, the ladies began tearing through her day dresses, hoping to find something particularly eye-catching. Finally, Suzie pulled out a peach silk dress with a green ribbon trim, "You haven't worn this yet. I know you feel a bit leery about wearin' silk in the mornin' but it's such a pretty dress. Ooh, and let's not cover your bosom," she said, as Charlotte reached for a fichu.

"Suzie, that's completely improper! I can't do that at this hour."

"Well, at least wear this instead." Suzie held up a nearly transparent chemisette, decorated with just a touch of white lace down the center and at the neck.

Charlotte's eyes narrowed. "Suzie that is not an improvement. What are you thinking?"

She shrugged. "I merely thought it would be nice to remind this Lord Averly of exactly what he's missed in the last year."

Charlotte stopped. Why was she allowing herself to be so flustered? The man had arrived at her house in an insultingly rumpled state and much too early for a polite social call. She had absolutely no obligation to please her uninvited guest. He could damn well wait for her to dress and fix her hair, she decided, as she put on the chemisette.

Half an hour later, Charlotte descended the stairs, concentrating on maintaining an air of composure. She could have taken longer preparing herself, but her own impatience overcame her desire to irk His Lordship. She finally convinced Suzie to put her hair up in a tight twist, instead of the elaborate style her maid intended, so she could get downstairs.

At the bottom of the stairs, she almost turned around and ran back up. There she was, waiting impatiently to discover the reason for Lord Averly's visit, yet desperately worried about what he would actually have to say. Ryder swore the man was all the way across the country.

Unfortunately, she did live in one of the multitude of narrower town homes in the city, meaning the staircase to the upper floor began almost directly next to the front door and entrance to the drawing room. Lord Averly had likely already heard her come down so there was no turning back now.

She had no need for an enormous home, with only Lady Kinsey and Suzie to share the second floor. They entertained here, although only in small gatherings.

She found His Lordship pacing the drawing room. He didn't even look up when he heard her walk in before he began speaking. "I am perfectly aware that you do not hold me in the highest regard, Miss Henwood. You made that perfectly clear during your first Season in London. However, I would greatly appreciate your hearing me out."

"I'm all ears, Lord Averly." When he heard her voice, Lord Averly finally stopped pacing to address her directly, his stance brought to mind a knight preparing for battle. Several emotions crossed his face upon seeing her, confusion taking the forefront. Charlotte truly tried to hide her self-satisfied smirk, but she knew he could see it.

"Miss Henwood?" *What in the world was going on?* The woman standing before him most certainly was the Miss Henwood who had snubbed him more than once last year. She was also the young woman who had fallen from her horse into an unfortunately-placed mud puddle the first time they met.

After all of this, the final piece of the puzzle fit. "You. You were…But, I don't…How are you the same person?" Well, perhaps the final piece didn't quite fit in all the way.

# Chapter 9

———

"I AM MISS CHARLOTTE HENWOOD. You know, the woman you didn't recognize last Season?" Were a doorway near enough to lean nonchalantly against, Charlotte would happily have done so. As it was, she compromised on slowly crossing her arms as she awaited his response.

"Right. I think I've grasped that now." Michael decided to seat himself, too distracted to wait for her to sit first. Emotions warred within. Elation filled him in discovering she was his social equal. But then he could not make his social equal his mistress. One moment. Mistress...

"But you're Ryder's mistress! Goodness, you're the reason my friend sent me a letter, describing my brother being taken in by some evil temptress." He ran a hand through his hair, slowly accepting that the woman he had been fantasizing about just minutes earlier was sleeping with his younger brother.

As for Charlotte, she quickly lost her lackadaisical pose. He thought she was Ryder's mistress? Her behavior with Ryder should never have led people to reach that conclusion.

"Someone wrote you about my involvement with Ryder? Could you please tell me exactly who it was?" Why did this person have such a vendetta against her? She had wasted the last three weeks trying to find a name. Every time she came close to some kind of answer, it would slip through her fingers. Chasing rumors was like trying to catch the wind.

"What does it matter? It was an old friend of the family. A Mr. Withers, I believe. He spends more time listening to the talk in his club than he does at home." Although the name meant nothing to Charlotte, she filed it away.

"And he informed you that I am Ryder's mistress? How interesting. Did he tell you where he received that particular bit of information? This is certainly the first I am hearing of it," she casually enquired. Charlotte was seething on the inside. How dare Lord Averly immediately believe such an outlandish rumor?

Too restless to continue sitting, Michael rose. "Are you denying it? You live here, alone—no matter that it's the more fashionable side of Town. Who knows what goes on behind these walls?" Michael was desperate to hear that the rumor had no merit. Seeing the place she lived and hearing her call his brother by his first name merely fueled his frustration. The woman had taken his young innocent brother in. Whatever her reasons were, he had to protect Ryder.

Michael took a deep breath. "Perhaps we could come to an agreement. I admit that my brother is perhaps more trusting than he ought to be, but there is no logic behind targeting him. His quarterly allowance is not particularly high."

He heard the woman snort. "Oh, I am perfectly aware as to how limited his allowance is."

Michael ignored that and continued on, "I don't really see your reasons for pursuing him in the first place. Why risk, no, possibly destroy your reputation when there is so little reward?" A woman would have to love a man a great deal to potentially destroy any chances of finding a future husband. Miss Henwood couldn't feel that way for Ryder, she simply couldn't.

Michael recalled her treatment of him during her first Season. She had snubbed him more than once, refusing to dance or even share conversation with him. He once overheard her mocking him in a quiet conversation with her chaperone, calling Michael too stodgy and circumspect. There was nothing wrong with a touch of circumspection. Miss Henwood likely knew nothing about that.

Was her pursuit of Ryder merely another way to flaunt her dislike towards Michael? Perhaps Michael should think himself less important to her, but he preferred that explanation over the possibility of her being madly in love with Ryder. Anything over that.

"Lord Averly, is it not typical for a man to pay for his mistress's lodgings? As well as any other trinkets and items she might enjoy? I believe I have heard this to be true." Her tone reminded him of a schoolteacher giving a lesson to a particularly dimwitted student. "Well, Lord Averly?" Charlotte had a point to make and would brook no distractions.

Trying his best not to snarl, Michael answered, "That is usually the way of things, yes."

"Well, I must tell you, Lord Averly, that this particular townhouse, residing in such an elegant part of Town, is quite expensive. That, combined with the amount I spend on clothing and trinkets...Well, your brother would be completely bankrupt, were he to support me." Charlotte had no desire to add that Ryder was quite close to being bankrupt. That was Ryder's story, and not one she could tell. She continued, "Goodness, I don't even know where he would acquire the funds for keeping me up in such style. Just to remind you, you have been languishing out in the country for quite some time, thereby unable to assist him in paying for my upkeep."

Charlotte understood that someone wished to ruin her reputation. Recalling the Ravencliffs' ball, she knew that people loved to spread gossip about anyone they could find. However, she expected those who knew her to disbelieve such things. Then again, did Lord Averly really know her?

Was it more money that she wanted? Ryder couldn't fully support her lifestyle here, so now she would appeal to the older brother for funds? "Madam, the likelihood of me giving you more money, on top of what my brother provides, is minimal."

Charlotte glared. She felt no compunction to be polite to Lord Averly now. "My lord, I believe you mistake my meaning.

The point I am trying to make, you see, is that Ryder cannot afford my lifestyle. I can, and am, taking excellent care of myself. How many mistresses to gentlemen of the *ton* live in a house in this part of Town? Not only that, but how many mistresses live with an older, well-respected chaperone? Lady Kinsey has attended more than one social gathering with me and is certainly present whenever a gentleman calls on me here."

*Except right now*, Charlotte added to herself.

Hopefully, Lord Averly, with his unusually diminutive brain, would finally be able to catch her meaning. Charlotte watched him intently stare at the wallpaper while he absorbed her words.

After a long pause, Michael looked at her and asked, "If he isn't paying for everything, then why are you his mistress?"

Miss Henwood responded with a particularly unladylike growl. She even went so far as to stomp her foot. Apparently, his ability to logically process information had been damaged at some point. She had best ask Ryder if his brother had been violently thrown from his horse or tripped down the stairs as a child.

Ignoring the rising tide of anger radiating from Miss Henwood, he continued, "Are you in love with him? Is that it? Why not press for marriage?"

Although Michael prepared himself for the worst, he still was not ready for the outburst that followed his question. The usually composed and articulate Miss Henwood screeched, "*Bloody hell!*" Michael was too busy protecting his face and ears to chastise her for her language. "*I am not Ryder's damned mistress! I have never been his mistress, nor will I ever be his mistress! I don't know who started that bloody rumor, but it has absolutely no merit! If you refer to me as his mistress again, I am going to strangle you!*"

Charlotte actually found herself panting, she was so angry. She had been trying to control her temper for so much of their damned conversation that when she finally unleashed it, she saw red.

Goodness, she felt remarkably liberated after that little fit of hers. And considering Michael's shocked, and somewhat chastened expression, she thought she had finally convinced him.

"Not his mistress?" His voice came out as a squeak. Slowly the tension drained from his body. Could it really be true? He had been so thrown to read that the woman who had repudiated him this last year had apparently taken a romantic interest in his own brother. He would be elated to discover that perhaps he had misinterpreted the situation.

Charlotte refused to reply. However, Michael appeared to get the point. Anger and distrust no longer seemed to consume him. His entire demeanor to her appeared to change at this news. The way Lord Averly now looked at her brought an unexpected heat to Charlotte's cheeks.

She heard a door open upstairs. The drawing room door stood wide open. Charlotte sincerely hoped she had not woken Lady Kinsey. Frances Harrow—Lady Kinsey—was a friendly, jubilant woman. However, she simply loved learning everything about everyone. There would be no way to remove the countess once she scented a good story. Luckily for Charlotte, she only shared her discoveries with a select few.

The door opening was probably Suzie. Lady Kinsey was absolutely not a morning person and she slept like the dead. Just in case, Charlotte turned and closed the drawing room door.

"Did you really come all the way to London from Leeds in order to warn your brother against me?"

"How did you know I was in Leeds?"

Charlotte pretended to look out the window, hiding her blush. She certainly didn't want Lord Averly to know just how attentively she listened when people discussed him. "I believe Mr. Skidmore mentioned it when we attended the same gathering at some point or other."

Charlotte finally sat down on the settee, while Michael quickly moved to a chair nearby. It seemed their argument had ended.

Sighing, Michael turned to look steadily into her eyes. Again, like the first time he saw her, he found himself arrested by her beauty. What man would not want to make her his mistress? Hell, he had briefly entertained the notion back in that taproom. And then again only a few minutes before. How could he not have recognized her? But, in a way, he knew.

There was nothing to link this composed, elegant lady before him to the playful country miss he had met over a year ago. The young woman he first met had been sweet and vivacious, her innocence a beacon that drew him like nothing he could comprehend.

But she had been poor. There had been nothing about her appearance or demeanor that indicated she could ever share his place in the *ton*.

The woman sitting before him was her opposite. Usually when she went out in society, like right now, her hair was pulled back in a much more severe style. She was still beautiful, but in a completely different way. He would always associate a powerful sensuality with Miss Henwood—either one—but there was a wildness and excitement in the country miss.

Here and now, she came across as more elegant, but also somewhat detached. Her new position in society had certainly risen profoundly since their first meeting. She associated with the Madisons, after all.

At the moment, he knew she was playing the elegant lady, unlikely to tease or poke fun at the ridiculous situation they had created for themselves. It were as if Miss Henwood's personality transformed, depending on her appearance and dress.

He sighed, "I owe you an apology. Looking back, my friend's letter did not state that you and Ryder were as involved as I had assumed. There were certain implications, but no proof was offered. I may have filled in the rest, assuming the worst."

Charlotte nodded. "I can honestly tell you that I am not involved with Ryder in such a manner. I run this household with the assistance of Lady Kinsey and do my best to ensure that nothing improper occurs here." Charlotte felt the temptation to tell Lord Averly the exact truth about her relationship with Ryder.

After Lord Averly's original hostility this morning, perhaps it would be best to let his brother explain. She was certain Lord Averly would get all his answers from Ryder later on.

"I am relieved to hear that, Miss Henwood." Michael would not yet explore just how relieved. "I suppose I can now understand your immediate dislike of me last year. I must tell you, there was a drastic change in your appearance from the disheveled girl covered in mud to the woman I met later." Gauging the displeasure this description brought, Michael awkwardly hurried on, "I knew you looked familiar, but I would never have put you two together as the same person. I had first assumed you wouldn't have had the means to get to London, let alone share my social circle."

Charlotte at least smiled, although not too warmly. She could not deny hoping that if anyone were to see the resemblance between the ruined girl from Uckfield and the young woman sitting before him, it would be he. "Ryder figured it out quickly enough. I was actually quite surprised. But I do not believe he shares your desire to organize people into such specific slots based on their social position."

Michael crossed his arms and leaned back in his chair. "It would seem the stately dame has returned in full force." There was some disturbing truth to her words. Could he really be such a snob?

Perhaps, now that he had his answers, he ought to make a strategic retreat. "I am relieved at what I learned from our, well," here he stumbled over the most polite way to define his barging into her home to demand answers, "from our conversation. Again, I can only apologize for thinking the worst of you. Looking back, I see that it made absolutely no sense. Mr. Withers, my father's friend, has always been a bit closed-minded. You live comfortably here and are obviously not in need of a protector. Nor, I'm sure, would you want to risk your place in polite society by becoming involved with another man in that manner. Now, if you will excuse me, I will leave you to your morning." They both rose and Miss Henwood led the way to the front door. When she stepped aside to allow him to open it, Michael added, "I also apologize for bringing up such an improper discussion with a lady. I hope you can forgive me at least for that."

He saw a dimple form as she tried not to smile. He refused to hope, especially after botching things so royally. He had finally found his sweet country miss, although perhaps she was not as sweet now, and he had no intention of losing her again.

Charlotte replied, "My lord, if there is anyone who is aware of my less proper side, it is you."

Michael couldn't help but laugh, and Charlotte quickly joined him with relief.

The tension eased a great deal. Standing there by the door, memories of their one kiss filled Charlotte's mind. Her eyes were drawn back to that damned freckle. She looked up into Lord Averly's eyes and her breath caught. He knew exactly what she was thinking. Lord Averly's head lowered a fraction, his breath teasing her lips. As she lowered her lashes, she felt the barest trace of his lips brushing hers.

Another door closed upstairs. A bit distracted, Charlotte turned to see a gentleman reach the upper landing and descend the stairwell.

It was Ryder Skidmore. And he wasn't fully dressed. "Ryder!" Charlotte cried.

"Sorry, Char, love," he said as he concentrated on tucking his shirt into his trousers, "I was so tuckered from last night that I simply decided to stay here. I know I should have left earlier, but I didn't think anyone would be up yet. Usually everyone here except you sleeps late. I'll still sneak out through the back gardens."

When Ryder finally reached the entryway, he looked up to see his elder brother glowering at Miss Henwood. What the hell was Michael doing here? Ryder would have feared his brother had learned about his debt, but if that were the case, Michael would be angrier at Ryder, instead of the girl who had rescued him from that trouble.

Charlotte was so shocked she couldn't think. How much bad luck can a person have in a single month? Slowly she turned to Lord Averly. He was not moving, simply staring steadily into her eyes. She tried to speak, "It's not—"

"Don't," he snarled. "I believe I have heard enough of your lies for one day, madam. I will deal with you later. As for you," Michael turned to his damned brother, "you will go directly home and attend me in my office. Do you understand?" With that he strode outside, not once looking back.

# Chapter 10

———❦———

RYDER SKIDMORE could not even begin to fathom what had gone on between his brother and Miss Henwood. After Michael stormed out of her house, Charlotte completely closed up. She refused to tell Ryder anything, immediately excusing herself to go to her room. Ryder had called out an apology to her as she left, but he had no idea what he was apologizing for.

Unfortunately, that meant he went into the meeting with his brother at quite a loss. When Ryder walked into the office, he found his brother behind the imposing desk, fingers drumming an annoying refrain on the mahogany. The dark blue curtains remained closed, lending the room a particularly ominous air. Before Ryder so much as sat down, Michael said to him, "I assume you know why you are here?"

Ryder nearly laughed. Michael reminded him of dear old Papa, with his doom-filled voice. He just needed to be wearing a smoking jacket and holding an unlit cigar. Ryder couldn't recall their father ever lighting it in front of the family. But this office was nothing like their father's had been. Papa's office had been a touch smaller and certainly not as impressively furnished.

The Skidmore brothers had grown up in Brighton, raised as gentlemen. While most of their peers discussed the other homes their families owned in the country or in London, Michael and Ryder were merely pleased that there was enough extra money to pay for the single family residence in Brighton. They kept up appearances quite well, but there was a bit of debt to repay upon Papa's death. Michael took care of things then, just as he no doubt intended to do now. He sold the Brighton house in exchange for a less expensive one, easily paying off their debts. Ryder never remembered his brother showing any worry about their financial position. Nevertheless, neither brother could deny their shock and relief upon learning of Michael's new title and fortune.

Ryder replied, "I assume you are about to tell me."

Michael leaned back in his chair. "We aren't going to play that game, are we? You're hoping that this is perhaps something trivial? That I might be discussing some insignificant misdemeanor and haven't yet heard about the main crime? If that is your hope, then you are sorely mistaken. I know exactly what has been going on between you and Miss Henwood and I cannot even begin to describe the disappointment I feel in you."

It appeared that Michael did not plan on telling Ryder everything he knew. It was likely part of his master plan. Ryder, however, knew *this* ploy as well. Michael intended to wait for Ryder to list off everything he had done with Miss Henwood in the last month or so, thereby finding more ammunition to use against his younger brother.

Like hell Ryder would let him get away with that.

He turned his face to a surly pout, and then answered in a wheedling voice, "Well smuggling brings in a lot of money and Miss Henwood had some excellent connections. When she proposed a deal, it was hard to resist. What was I supposed to do? Tell her, 'No, thank you, I don't really have any interest in becoming rich.'"

"Smuggling?" Michael choked on the word.

Oh, this was going to be fun. "Hmmm," Ryder murmured noncommittally. "Once we began working together, we got some other ideas. The next step on our list is an elegant, upscale brothel. You know, a place where the *crème de la crème* would come for an absolutely wonderful time. We considered specializing in the kind of place that provides unique…devices. Whips, chains, and the like."

It didn't take too long for Michael to catch on. "All right, Ryder, I don't think you understand the full ramifications of your behavior—"

"And after that we will finally put into motion our plans for overthrowing the monarchy," he continued cheerfully. "Prinny won't even know what's coming. All we need to complete that goal are nine hundred camels, a catapult, and some clotted cream." Ryder finished, one corner of his mouth twitching.

Michael scowled at his brother. Giving in, he said, "The fact that my own brother would dishonor a woman of his own class by taking her as a lover is completely shocking. This could destroy Miss Henwood's reputation! Hell, it *will* destroy her reputation. How could you be so thoughtless?"

No longer did Ryder treat his situation as a joke. None of this had been part of his and Miss Henwood's plan.

"Damn you, Ryder, are you even listening?" Michael stood and began to pace. "Now, I don't know how far word has spread—"

"It hasn't spread at all!" Ryder finally burst out, getting over his astonishment. "No one thinks that Charlotte and I are involved that way. They have absolutely no reason to!"

"Well someone does, or else I would never have received this letter." Michael stalked back to his desk and sat down. He pulled the letter from his pocket and tossed it in front of Ryder, who immediately picked it up. His brows drew together as he read.

"Michael, this Withers person does not specifically say that Charlotte and I are involved. He is concerned that Miss Henwood might draw me into more questionable activities. Considering what people have been saying about her, this is not too surprising. However, she and I are working to prevent any further gossip."

"Perhaps the letter does not state anything directly, but how can you explain spending the night at her house?"

The territory had become a bit treacherous. Ryder answered carefully, "I cannot deny that I spent the night there, but in a guest bedroom." Michael gave him a look of disbelief. "It's true! I swear it. I like to go out on the Town every once in a while, is all. Sometimes when I've come back home, I've been a mite tipsy. Charlotte may have discovered my activities." He failed to mention that she discovered them when he felt compelled to confess to her the events leading up to his present situation.

Ryder laughed self-consciously. "She insisted that if it is ever a closer trip to her home than mine, that I really ought to stop and sleep things off. Apparently she's worried I'll be robbed and murdered by some thief looking for an easy target. That was only the second time I had taken her up on it." There was more to the story, but Ryder doubted his brother would believe it.

"Are you telling me a young woman, living essentially on her own, chose to risk her reputation by asking a man to spend the night in her own home?"

Ryder shrugged helplessly. "Well, she grew up in the country. I gather society is less strict there."

"It's not that much less strict."

Ryder paused, thinking of the various conversations he and Charlotte had shared over the last month. "I don't think Miss Henwood really cares what people think about her. She says she no longer needs a husband. I gather she came into some money recently. She only keeps her reputation clean for the sake of protecting her friends. She wouldn't want them to get into trouble by associating with her."

"What exactly has Miss Henwood been doing to draw so much attention this Season, then?" Michael asked.

"Nothing! That's just it! At her second social engagement this Season, she overheard people discussing her relationship with Mr. Harry Madison. A good friend of her father, Mr. Madison and his wife had taken her in. The gossips were saying that she is *his* mistress, which is why he rented her a house so close to his residence. She doesn't want that sort of gossip to follow the Madisons, so she asked for my assistance."

"How, exactly, are you assisting her?" It was the only pertinent question at this point. Michael was beginning to feel as though events were well out of his control.

"I'm posing as a suitor. Just a suitor," Ryder added, when he saw his brother prepare to comment on that. "I've also promised to help her find the people trying to spread the gossip about her and the Madisons. For the last few weeks, Charlotte and I have attended gatherings together, under the chaperonage of Lady Kinsey—who lives with her, I might add. I believe Lady Kinsey has also been helping rebuild her reputation."

Michael leaned back in his chair, crossing his arms over his chest. "So she has not actually dug her claws into you, the brother of a viscount?" Michael asked dubiously. When Ryder shook his head, Michael said, "This situation could still damage her reputation, if you do not propose marriage after displaying such a marked interest in her." *Unless, you do intend to marry her and don't want to tell me just yet*, Michael thought. What would Michael do were that the case? Could he deny his permission? Probably not, and nor should he. He doubted he would be able to disinherit his own brother for marrying the woman who had occupied his thoughts for most of the previous Season.

Ryder rolled his eyes. "Quite frankly, no one even really believes I'm her suitor. She treats me more like a brother than you do. Besides, she has told me herself that she never intends to marry."

Michael ignored the relief he felt over Miss Henwood's and his brother's relationship. "Why not simply end her contact with the Madisons completely?" Michael asked.

Ryder's eyebrows rose. "Michael, they are her friends. She can't simply give them up, nor should she have to. She never started this."

"So Miss Henwood has requested your assistance in keeping any negative gossip from influencing the Madisons? I see what she gains from your association, but what, I have to ask, are *you* getting out of it?"

Ah, yes, the question Ryder had been hoping to avoid. At least his brother no longer seemed to be spitting fire.

Ryder attempted to sound innocent. "You don't think I'd simply do this out of the goodness of my heart?" No, that idea would not keep Michael distracted. A new tactic was needed.

As he watched Michael's fingers tap on the gleaming wood of the Viscount Averly's desk, an idea slowly dawned. Michael had conveniently moved out to the country at the start of the Season. He probably wanted as little to do with the marriage mart as Ryder.

"Well, by appearing to court her, I don't have to dance attendance on all the other marriage-minded ladies in London." When he saw the doubt in Michael's eyes, Ryder continued, "Once they noticed my marked interest in Miss Henwood, they mostly left me be. I was able to happily enjoy the rest of the engagements the Season had to offer, unfettered."

Michael continued to feel uneasy about his brother's behavior. "You just informed me of how great a failure your performance as the loving suitor was, so I don't buy it. No matter what, I'm not so sure I like the idea of you becoming too involved with that woman. It seems like trouble follows her doggedly." Michael's thoughts drifted to a rainy morning spent in a dingy tavern.

"I'm sure my reputation can withstand the damage," Ryder laughed.

"Fair enough. However, you cannot deny that perhaps you are not the best person to be keeping her out of trouble. Exactly how many evenings have you spent out on the Town since my departure to Leeds?" Michael asked.

"Only three or four times, at the most. And Charlotte cares very little about what I do beyond accompanying her to a few engagements." Neither statement was entirely true. Ryder hoped to keep his friends from discovering exactly how much trouble he was in, carrying on as though nothing had changed. As for Charlotte, ever since that dinner party where they first spoke, Ryder noticed that she kept a careful eye on him whenever she could. She really was as bad as Michael.

Michael thought this over. "You say you're also helping her find out who is threatening the Madisons?"

Ryder sat up in his chair. His brother appeared to believe him. "Yes. Once we find out who is causing these problems, we will break things off, and I'll have paid off..." Blast. "Er..." And he had been doing so well. Ryder usually had little trouble thinking on his feet. Except with his brother. And Michael was not going to let this go.

Michael's fingers ceased drumming on the desk, his whole person motionless. Ryder saw it and knew he was in trouble. Instead of asking, Michael simply waited, green eyes piercing Ryder's like arrows. Fidgeting in his chair, Ryder tried to think of another excuse, but none came.

In the end, Ryder told him everything. Needless to say, his brother was not pleased.

—⁓—

Charlotte was much more prepared for Lord Averly's visit later in the day. She knew he would come back once he'd spoken with Ryder. She and Suzie had deliberated for quite some time on the perfect afternoon dress for his return. For most of the ladies of Charlotte's age, lighter shades added an air of innocence. Charlotte preferred more vibrant colors to highlight her darker features.

The final choice was a light blue batiste skirt draped from just below the bosom, with a darker blue bodice scooped low enough to "show Lord Averly just what he was missing," as Suzie put it. Charlotte still insisted on covering her bosom, so the two compromised on the shockingly transparent chemisette worn that morning. Perhaps Michael would remember it.

Charlotte had a specific goal in mind for this interview and she needed any ploy she could find to distract Lord Averly. Not that her bosom was plentiful enough to be considered even a mild distraction, but every little bit helped.

After being led into Charlotte's drawing room, Michael took a moment to look around. When he had arrived that morning, he had been too angry to take in his surroundings. Now he noticed the exotic gold patterning in the window drapes and carpets. The settee and chairs were upholstered in a deep crimson that well complemented the golden hues. Small objects and figurines that appeared to have come from various parts of the world graced the mantel and shelves. The trinkets lent the room an adventurous air. It suited Miss Henwood perfectly.

Michael assumed that Miss Henwood would take about as long as she had that morning before greeting him, so he sat down to wait. The chairs were clearly designed for a woman's build. Michael felt like a giant in it.

After some uncomfortable fidgeting, Michael leaned back and crossed an ankle over his knee. The moment he did so, Miss Henwood sailed into the room, forcing him to awkwardly untangle his legs and stand.

"Miss Henwood, a pleasure," he said politely, as he stood and bowed. Despite the nature of his previous visit, one should always recall the niceties.

In response, she merely said, "You likely have no more than ten minutes before Lady Kinsley discovers we have a gentleman caller and decides to intrude." Charlotte hoped Lady Kinsey was enjoying her afternoon nap at the moment, but it would be best not to risk anything, as she was quite certain Suzie would be listening outside the open door. Lady Kinsey would easily get everything out of Suzie later. The woman was like a battering ram; she refused to stop attacking you with questions until, exhausted, you gave in.

Apparently they would be skipping the formalities. Well, two could play at that game. Michael paused, momentarily distracted. Why would a lady waste time putting fabric over her bosom if it did not serve to conceal?

Michael stood straight and cleared his throat. "Miss Henwood, I have come with the money my brother owes you, plus any interest that may have been incurred. I merely request you consider his debt cancelled here and now, and look elsewhere for assistance in whatever it is you are doing for the Madisons."

It was Charlotte's turn to be caught off-guard. She honestly had never expected Ryder to come entirely clean. Perhaps Lord Averly possessed more skill in reading his brother than she had originally hoped.

Lord Averly strode to the low table, where he placed a packet of notes. In unison, they sat in the two chairs by the table.

He watched her take up the notes. Her fingers were so delicate, a contrast to the strong personality that had stood up to him that morning. Trapped in his own observations, Michael barely noticed when Miss Henwood began counting through the money.

"Hear now, it's all there."

"That I do not doubt, Lord Averly. You have always been a painfully honest man," she said, as she then removed a few notes from the pile. "However, Ryder and I agreed that the interest for his loan would not be in the form of English pounds." She held the extra out to him.

Michael had been expecting this. Instead of taking the interest back, he said, "By now, your reputation has been quite well-repaired. I see no point in continuing your association with him at all."

"I see." Indeed she did. She and Ryder had spent a great deal of time together in the last month. In that time, she had gleaned many details about Lord Averly's life and personal views. The most pertinent had been Lord Averly's concern with the family name. Apparently he did not want his brother associating with a woman of her caliber. Not that she really knew what her caliber was.

"So you will no longer use him in this scheme of yours?"

"Lord Averly, that is not Ryder's and my agreement," Charlotte answered, in the calmest voice she could muster. "I still need to find out who is working so hard to damage my reputation. I thought that perhaps I had averted disaster when the gossip about Mr. Madison and I ceased. But your presence here proves how wrong I was." She did not want to let Lord Averly off just yet.

Lord Averly did not intend to let go either. "If you are so concerned for your reputation, why allow my brother to stay at your townhouse?"

"Ah yes. I admit that is a strange occurrence," Charlotte answered. "But hopefully I can explain it. At the beginning of our new association, Ryder accompanied Lady Kinsey and me to a small dinner gathering. When we returned home, Ryder and Suzie decided to attend a gathering of an entirely less genteel sort. Apparently over the course of the night, a sailor decided he would stop at nothing to gain Suzie's favors. She was much too overwhelmed by ale to extract herself on her own. Ryder, once he discovered the man's intentions, practically carried Suzie away and home. When I discovered Ryder bringing Suzie through the back kitchen door, I demanded he explain matters. At the time, he was not much better off than Suzie. I insisted that he remain in a guest room for the night as well as any other night that he or Suzie might have gone too far. At the time, I was less worried about any negative rumors circulating pertaining to Ryder and myself and more so about their safety."

Luckily, no one seemed to know where Ryder had spent those two nights. There was still the matter of the rumors pertaining to Mr. Madison. People seemed to have changed their attitudes toward her for the better, after seeing Charlotte with Mr. Skidmore. But Lord Averly did not know that.

"But that is no longer relevant to the matter at hand. If this Mr. Withers believed these rumors, I am still under threat," she continued dramatically. "And until I can be certain this gossiper no longer means me harm, I cannot let your brother out of our agreement. I need the connections his name brings. Your letter, apparently referring to me as some evil hoyden out to entrap your brother, surely proves my point. What if a similar letter is sent to the family of every man who courts me?" Charlotte added. Not that she wanted a great many men pursuing her.

Michael leaned back in his chair, contemplating her. Honestly, what man would object to engaging her affection? She might be painfully stubborn and meddlesome, but Michael doubted any man would immediately believe a strange note defaming her character. Excepting him, of course. Michael cringed, subconsciously.

Ryder had not doubted Miss Henwood. Perhaps he did deserve her. Lord knew, he could be equally mad and meddlesome.

On his own, Ryder could make the strongest man faint with his exploits. When Ryder was eleven, he had convinced the entire household staff that he knew the French had set sail for Brighton and everyone should flee to Ryder and Michael's tree fort. Papa came home to discover an empty household. Everyone was desperately trying to fit into a small fort designed for perhaps five people, while Ryder gorged on every cake and tart he could steal from the kitchen. That occasion took place before Ryder's school days, and before he had discovered the wonders of women.

Meanwhile, Miss Charlotte Henwood drank ale and befriended tavern wenches. She and Ryder together might accidentally bring on the end of the world. Michael could not believe they had been working in tandem for the last day, let alone month. They had to be separated. The future prosperity of England relied on it.

Goodness, there was a thought.

If Michael took Ryder's place, he could keep a closer eye on Miss Henwood and keep her out of trouble. It would also give his brother less reason to see her and become possibly more attached than he already seemed to be.

"Perhaps we could agree to a different arrangement," Michael suggested slowly. "My social contacts are certainly no less significant than Ryder's. Not only that, but a person would certainly think twice to harass a young lady involved with a viscount. I confess to feeling uncomfortable knowing that you and Ryder are going about this on your own. Perhaps if I joined in providing my assistance and protection, we could more quickly find whoever is spreading these tales about you?"

It took all Charlotte possessed not to smile like the cat that got the cream. *Not too fast*, she thought. *It's best if this is entirely his idea from the start.* Charlotte's eyes widened innocently. "Why I believe if I had your help and connections, I would likely have no need for Ryder at all," she replied. Seeing the light flicker behind Lord Averly's eyes, she knew he wanted to hear just that.

"Then perhaps we could agree to work together on this project. If we need Ryder's assistance, I'm sure he can provide it, but otherwise I will do my best to help continue your investigation."

Charlotte knew not to agree too quickly. "But what will people say when Ryder no longer accompanies me in society while his elder brother begins to court me?"

Michael suppressed a smile, certain he had already won. "I gather that most young ladies would prefer to be courted by the sibling holding the title, and not the younger brother. I doubt anyone will say much at all, honestly."

Michael's pompous words annoyed Charlotte, but he never knew it. Did he really think she was that kind of woman? Instead she merely said, "So you are offering yourself in place of your brother in fulfilling the debt?"

She saw him pause. Finally Lord Averly replied, "You may look at it that way. Yes."

*Well*, Charlotte thought, *that was easy*. Oh, these next few weeks were going to be quite amusing, to say the least.

# Chapter 11

L ORD AVERLY, do you see Miss Coleson? I believe she has been making eyes at that particular footman all evening. He may be quite handsome, but what will her dear mama say?" Miss Henwood bounced jubilantly. "Oh, and look there! It seems that Mr. Priestly is removing all of the scones to his coat pocket. I have heard that the Priestly family is in the market for a new cook, but has not yet found a replacement."

No one could overhear her ludicrous comments, but Michael still looked furtively around them. He was not certain how much longer he could withstand this level of stress. The woman would drive him mad with her—wait. Did he just see Miss Coleson slip a note into that footman's pocket?

It was irrelevant. Miss Henwood could not go on discussing society so openly. Michael was certain she wanted to draw everyone's attention with her behavior.

"I believe you actually enjoy having everyone whisper behind their hands about you." Michael slipped a finger under his cravat, as he nervously eyed the various clusters of people surrounding them. He stood next to Charlotte and Lady Kinsey, pretending to enjoy the soirée. This was the first gathering to which he had markedly escorted Miss Henwood. He had called on her once before, during polite visiting hours. Those who had visited Miss Henwood that day had no doubt spread the word.

Michael knew that a few of his acquaintances had noticed the fool he had made of himself over Miss Henwood last Season. What would they say now?

Charlotte tittered as though he had said something clever. Playfully, she tapped his sleeve with her fan, "Oh you!"

Refusing to be drawn in, Michael leaned in and murmured in her ear, "I don't know what goings-on took place while my brother attended these gatherings with you, but must you really behave so outlandishly? I thought you wanted the *ton* to believe you were not acting inappropriately." Despite the reprimand, she could not prevent a shiver as his deep voice rolled over her.

She turned her head up to him with a cheeky grin. "But Ryder never had nearly as much fun as you are having. Why, with the pleasure and joy sweeping across your face when you look into my eyes, how could any woman doubt your intentions?" She concluded by batting her eyelashes up at him. Eyelash batting and fan tapping were new skills she had developed since reentering society under Lady Kinsey's tutelage.

Michael's brows furrowed. "I am here, am I not? Appearing to court you."

"No, you're here appearing to prepare for your execution." Charlotte's teasing smile had disappeared. Her voice remained low. Not even Lady Kinsey could overhear them. "In fact, Lord Averly, I believe you would prefer to be thrown into Newgate, if it would allow you to escape this ordeal. Your *obvious* misery is not part of our arrangement." Now she looked directly into his eyes, challenging him to disagree.

Lady Kinsey, luckily, was doing her part in perpetuating the story that Ryder had been courting Miss Charlotte Henwood in his brother's name. Apparently when Miss Henwood had so obviously snubbed Lord Avery last year, the man's interest had been aroused. How very like a man to want what he can't have. Unable to catch her eye, he had asked his brother to intervene on his behalf. When Mr. Skidmore discovered her objections to his brother were unfounded, Lord Averly felt it best to return to London. Or at least, that was the story they were spreading around Town.

Michael thought it was a bit over-romantic for the *ton* to believe. However, the ladies among Charlotte's set seemed to love hearing it told, giggling and looking at Michael as though he were some romantic hero. It was all he could do to avoid groaning out loud.

Clearing his throat uncomfortably, Michael asked his tormentor, "What is there for me to do? I'm standing here, listening to you and your friends gossip, I fetch you lemonade when you ask, and I have not said a single word in complaint."

A corner of her lips quirked. "You've barely said *any* word at all." Sighing, she turned her gaze to the rest of the room. "You could try dancing with me once or twice, you know. As you are so unhappy, perhaps a bit of exercise shall boost your spirits." She smiled and nodded as she made eye contact with an acquaintance.

"It's more than halfway through the set. We'd look foolish joining in now." Michael tried to convince himself that he was as miserable as she said. His close proximity to her in the last few days had brought to light how much cleverer Miss Henwood's conversation was than that of most ladies of his acquaintance. He seldom took part in those lively discussions with Miss Henwood's friends and Lady Kinsey, but he listened. So long as she wasn't speaking to him, Miss Henwood seemed more and more intelligent and engaging, much to his chagrin. Her conversations with her companions were also a bit less impassioned and ridiculous than those she shared with him.

He discovered that she read *The Times* every day. Michael could not even manage such a feat. Miss Henwood seemed more willing to engage individuals like Mr. Madison's colleagues in conversation than a group of the *ton*'s chattering busybodies. At least Michael did not feel uncomfortable taking part in those exchanges. Earlier this evening, she had found a friendly Portuguese diplomat with whom to converse. They mostly spoke of how maritime trading routes were and were not being affected by the war with France. Even Michael found himself learning a few things. She then went so far as to assert that the tides would change for the better in Portugal. Michael could only commend her outright optimism.

At one point, a Miss Nelson had approached her. Miss Henwood immediately drew the girl aside, where not even Michael could overhear their exchange. He watched the myriad emotions cross Miss Nelson's face, while Miss Henwood listened patiently, never interrupting. Only at the end did she have anything to say to the girl. Whatever Miss Henwood told her was short and simple and somehow managed to release the tension tightening Miss Nelson's slender frame.

Miss Nelson had walked away with new purpose, nodding resolutely to herself after their discussion. But the thoughtful, kind Miss Henwood was not the lady addressing him now. Michael was stuck with the mischievous, troublesome, and somewhat grumpy Miss Henwood.

She went on, "Hmmm. Perhaps we'll be lucky and the next dance will be a waltz. Then you shall have ample opportunity to gaze upon me in abject adoration." She tried to sound teasing, but couldn't deny how sharp her voice sounded.

"Miss Henwood, I do not enjoy dancing the waltz and I doubt Lady Harrington would be so uncouth as to allow such a dance at her ball." Michael nearly winced at his own stodginess.

Charlotte turned away before he could see her growing frustration. Lord Averly must be the dullest, least exciting man she had ever met in her life. "Whatever the next dance will be, I believe that we must join in." Charlotte smiled to herself. There were no rules restricting the dancing of the waltz at such a gathering and the rumor stood that Lady Harrington had approved the dance.

How could a man so devilishly handsome be so painfully boring? It went against nature! Instead of enjoying the prospect of tricking and spying on the *ton*, he continued to furtively look around him, fearful of being caught at his subterfuge. Every time she made one of her playful, outlandish comments, he would wonder out loud how in the world her reputation was not in tatters.

Had Charlotte misremembered Lord Averly's character so greatly? After she saw him at the Fortescue ball the year before, she had been forced to realize that Lord Averly was anything but the rescuing prince she had imagined. Why was she still so fascinated by the man? She must be mad.

Charlotte had been hoping to loosen Lord Averly up since they had made their agreement, but she had since come to the conclusion that doing so would be impossible. Earlier this evening she had teasingly suggested a walk in the garden, but doing so had only managed to make Lord Averly even tenser. Every once in a while, when she behaved in an especially ludicrous manner, Lord Averly would respond beyond an annoyed narrowing of his eyes. He would even sometimes go so far as to chastise her. As if she did not already know how inappropriate her behavior towards him was. Even more irksome was the fact that Lord Averly seemed to bring the worst out in Charlotte. The more circumspect his lordship became, the more Charlotte wanted to annoy and drive him mad. Anything to get a damned reaction from him!

For some inexplicable reason, Charlotte desperately wanted to know what it would take to bring Lord Averly to his breaking point. And what would happen when he got there? She sighed, drawing a confused look from the gentleman in question. She knew he could lighten up; she had seen hints of a kind, yet somewhat rakish personality during their first meeting. And hadn't he nearly kissed her again only days before? Perhaps she had imagined that. In all honesty, his behavior now was even more stodgy and prudish than it had been during her first Season.

But she had not misremembered their kiss at The Griffin. Surely the man who had excited such passion in her was not truly as dull as the one standing stiffly before her? Should she try to kiss him again? Goodness, what was she thinking? She was supremely irritated with the man and had no desire to share that kind of intimacy with him. No, not at all.

―⁓―

As for Michael, he was solely focused on preventing Miss Henwood from doing anything to damage their reputations. Nothing had happened thus far, but he couldn't set aside the feeling that with this woman, disaster could strike at any moment. He was shocked that, after being the subject of such unsavory gossip, Miss Henwood had not become a social pariah. It had happened twice, actually, if he counted that fiasco at The Griffin. How did she do it? She seemed to always find her way exactly to the brink, then make a safe retreat. Neither he nor Ryder had heard anything about her relationship with Mr. Madison since Ryder had begun showing interest in her. In addition, it appeared no one other than Mr. Withers had spoken a word about Miss Henwood and Mr. Ryder Skidmore having an illicit relationship.

One thing was certain: no one would suspect Lord Averly to be anything other than Miss Henwood's suitor. Michael had done his best to represent himself as an upstanding member of society and he would damn well continue to do so. No one would dare begin a story about his seducing or being seduced by Miss Henwood. He was a man thoroughly above such temptation. At least, that was what society believed. Why, it had been years since he had done anything remotely naughty. Not that Michael had been a monk for the last three years, either. But he had developed a skill for discretion.

The next dance set was beginning. Miss Henwood looked up at him expectantly, and an amused gleam lit her eyes when the beginning notes of a waltz drifted to their ears. Resigned that the Fates were set against him, Michael took her hand and led her to the dance floor.

Everywhere Michael placed his hand on Miss Henwood's waist seemed to burn him. He had not had many excuses to touch her in the year of their acquaintance—the few dances they had shared had not been anything like the waltz. Yet somehow, without even looking, he could sense exactly how distant her bosom was from his chest. He knew the distance should be increased ever so slightly for the sake of propriety. Instead, he wanted to pull her even closer.

His fingers tightened imperceptibly against her waist. He must cease thinking these things. She was the current bane of his existence, no matter how beautiful. How could a woman so lovely be so incredibly annoying? In addition, it made Michael nervous when she did not speak; thus far, not a single ill-thought phrase had emerged from her lips. Who knew what plots she was hatching? He tried removing and replacing his hand on her waist, searching for a less searing position. However, the more he did so, the more vivid his mental map of her torso became. Not that he typically visualized her torso, or other parts. Of course he didn't. One should never think of a lady in such a lurid way.

Except that he had been thinking of her like that; and all too often. The first Season he encountered her in London, before he knew who she was, had been simpler. Now he knew the sweet kiss he shared at The Griffin had been with Miss Henwood.

When would the set be over? Now was the perfect time for the woman to open her mouth and remind him exactly why he couldn't stand her. She might make a sarcastic comment on some matron's plumed headdress, or about how the Duke of Neville's nephew could not be kept from overindulging at every gathering he attended with his uncle. Yes, that was the trick. He needed to get her talking. "Is it a bit warm in here?" Clever, Michael, very clever. Because clearly, Miss Henwood would be able to discern his extensive knowledge of European politics and social history through such an inane question. Not that he wanted to impress her. He just needed her to start talking again.

The freckle was moving again. Charlotte loved it when the freckle on Lord Averly's lower lip moved. Although he could have thought up something a bit more engaging to say.

Too warm? Perhaps his cravat was too tight. That usually occurred when a man wore something so very over-starched. No, she remembered seeing him loosening it earlier in response to a comment she had made about the extensive number of plumes in Lady Croffton's coiffure. But really, with her dark turquoise satin dress, the woman looked like a veritable peacock. Besides, Lord Averly always held his chin at that angle. It had nothing to do with the starched cravat. Damned pretentious, snobbish...At the moment, it would be best not to go down that road.

"Perhaps you would prefer a walk in the garden to cool yourself down? There's a lovely fountain at the far end, where barely a patch of light would touch us..." Charlotte smiled innocently when Lord Averly's gaze returned to her face.

Michael attempted to appear unprovoked, but he must have slipped, because there was no hiding her satisfied smirk. That did it. "Perhaps a refreshing walk would be better than finishing the set in this stuffy atmosphere."

Miss Henwood missed a step at his proclamation. Michael smiled. Oh, the pleasure in finally disconcerting *her*. He would be able to remove his hand from her waist if they went outside. Once they were only arm-in-arm, he should be able to forget just how warm and delicate she felt. Because Miss Henwood was proving to be neither warm nor delicate in demeanor. He led Miss Henwood to the edge of the ballroom. Pasting on his most engaging smile, he merely said, "After you."

Charlotte should have given Lord Averly a sickeningly sweet smile as she passed him and went through the terrace doors. However, at the moment she only concentrated on where she placed her feet. She had little desire to stumble and embarrass herself again.

Had Lord Averly changed tactics?

After walking down the path for a few moments, they found the fountain. She had only heard of it from other gentlemen attempting to lure her outside at previous gatherings here. It seemed, however, that Lord Averly knew exactly where to find it. Perhaps he had visited it during the daylight hours. Charlotte couldn't imagine him ever having come here to seduce an innocent lady like herself.

*Now what do I do?* Michael thought as he approached the fountain. A few years ago, he would have been pleased to find his way into a romantic embrace. But now? It would never do for the Viscount Averly to be found with a young woman in the dark recesses of a garden. Such a thing would go against every goal he had set for himself.

A fervid rustling behind a bit of shrubbery beyond the fountain caught his attention. It would seem they were not alone. Had Miss Henwood noticed? Trying to steer her away from the fountain, he murmured, "Perhaps it is too chilly out here, after all. Now that we've had our breath of fresh air, it is best we go inside."

Charlotte was having none of that. She had finally found herself a gentleman by whom she need not fear being accosted at this infamous fountain. "So soon? At least let me rest my feet," she said, as she strode to the fountain's edge and sat.

The rustling stopped. Apparently whoever hid behind those bushes knew they were not alone. But perhaps they did not recognize him and Miss Henwood. It was dark. How else could he make her leave without seeming rude?

Not that he should really care about being rude. The woman was, after all, his adversary. But a man had to have standards. And rudeness was rudeness, no matter at whom it was directed. It appeared, however, that Miss Henwood had no intention of moving. Steeling himself, he sat next to her, but at a discreet distance. If they were being observed, he would do whatever it took to maintain decorum, no matter what Miss Henwood thought up next.

The two sat in silence for a moment or two, not entirely certain if they ought to reengage in their war, or simply enjoy the cool outdoors. However, it didn't take Michael long to realize that whoever hid in the shrubbery had not made an escape. Perhaps he should conjure up a bit of conversation to mask their exit? Would they even take the hint? It would not do to expose Miss Henwood to whatever was occurring behind them.

As luck would have it, she beat him to it. A gentle smile spread across her lips. "I always wondered if my father would be able to enjoy the London Season. On evenings as lovely as this one, I sometimes wish I could share it with him. But he never comes to London, so I only have the Madisons here. And I can't spend too much time with them now, without complicating everything." Goodness, Charlotte had not intended to say so much out loud.

She doubted her father would like anything about the London Season. He always seemed so focused on his studies; there never seemed room for anything else in his life. Except her. Papa had always made room for her. Here, she was on her own, trying to protect the few people she considered the rest of her family.

Startled by her wistful confession, Michael almost couldn't reply. Finally he said, in a low voice, "It's strange how lonely one can feel in a place so filled with people. A few years ago I made the decision to set a solid example for my brother, as well as bring my family's name into a position of respect. Many of my friends found the changes I made dull and unexciting. All of a sudden, I wanted to discuss farming and Parliament, and my standpoint in the House of Lords. My old friends began making excuses instead of meeting me at our club or going shooting."

Charlotte almost felt some guilt over having thought the same things about Lord Averly. She usually only felt annoyed at his disinterest with the things she enjoyed, concluding that meant he had no interests of his own. Perhaps she had little right to judge him. There was something admirable in a man wanting to better himself and his family.

"I know what you mean," she said. "When the gossip surrounding myself and the Madisons began spreading, only a few friends remained in my company, refusing to believe those stories. I felt abandoned. But it also showed me who my true friends were—Miss Nelson, for example, whom you saw me speaking to earlier. In a way, I suppose, I began to feel less lonely because I knew that no matter what happened, these people would stay with me." As soon as Charlotte said it, she knew it to be true. The events of the last month had been a sort of blessing in disguise.

"Over time, I came to discover the same thing," Michael murmured, his deep voice stroking her nerves.

Charlotte was disappointed to realize it was too dark to see the freckle on his lip move while he spoke. Perhaps if she leaned a little closer, she would be able to discern it. Oh, how she loved that freckle.

Michael only noticed Miss Henwood leaning into him, without understanding her motive. Her face was so close now, her full lips curved into a soft smile. Her position also allowed the shadows to play across her bosom in an enticing fashion. Her breasts were such a perfect size. The pert, brazen globes filled her bodice exquisitely. Too late, Michael noticed the effect the focus of his attention created on his person.

Now would be an excellent time to shift his eyes elsewhere. He looked back to her lips. Had they been so close to his only a moment ago? He couldn't avoid breathing in her delicate scent.

Too late, Charlotte realized she had leaned far too close to Lord Averly. Ladies did not do such things, she reminded herself. She still did not draw back. And now he was staring at her lips too. Could he be thinking the same thing she was? Charlotte held her breath, awaiting his next move. When she could hold it in no longer, she parted her lips in a quiet gasp, Lord Averly's eyes remained transfixed upon her every subtle movement.

A rustling in the shrubbery behind the fountain broke the trance. Immediately Lord Averly sat up straight, again achieving the proper distance between the two of them. Charlotte did her best to mask her disappointment by fiddling with her fan. Apparently the perfectly proper Lord Averly was back to his old self.

"Ah, so, do you still ride, Miss Henwood?" he said, after desperately searching his brain for an innocent new conversational topic. Having seen her during his own treks across Hyde Park, Michael knew for a fact that Miss Henwood spent a great deal of her spare time riding.

Charlotte raised her brows at his formal tone. Was the man daft? Of course she still rode! Her voice turned mournful, "Why no, My Lord, ever since so inelegantly tumbling off my mare that day in Uckfield, I have chosen to forgo the sport entirely. The memories of that last ride are too painful. I shall never ride again," she added dramatically, bringing a hand to her bosom.

Surprised at her words, Michael replied immediately, "That is a pity. From what I observed when I saw you ride, you maintained an excellent seat before you, well, before you lost it." Charlotte swung back to facing him at that. "But then again," he went on, "if falling from your mare is a habit of yours, I can certainly understand ceasing the pastime entirely." If she intended to so blatantly mock him, nothing should stop him from doing the same in return.

Charlotte's jaw dropped. Was he teasing her? Shoving the possibility aside, Charlotte was compelled to defend her riding skills. "I will have you know that I have not lost my seat once since that occasion and seldom ever had any troubles before either! I have always been a widely acclaimed rider in—"

"What, in Uckfrond?" Michael replied, deliberately mistaking the name. "That is, most assuredly, a special distinction." He tried to contain his pleasure as Miss Henwood's expression turned to one of complete affront. "Now just a moment," he added in playful surprise, "I thought you had ceased riding after your little interlude with the mud."

Charlotte snorted, a habit she thought she had broken. Really, she lost track of the number of bad habits acquired since Lord Averly's return. "As if a little tumble onto my, erm …"

Michael's amusement only grew at Miss Henwood's discomfiture in the discussion. "Your bum?"

Good heavens, had he just said that? Apparently he had, judging from Miss Henwood's astonishment as well as the snickering from behind the fountain.

For a moment, the two stared upon each other with mirrored looks of incredulity. Charlotte's shock soon gave way to laughter. "And here I thought that you were turning stuffier since I last saw you. Please forgive my mistake."

Michael felt his cheeks warm. This is what became of his trying to tease her. But he had been so desperate to make her forget the weak moment when he nearly kissed her. Oh dear. *Both* weak moments. He had nearly given in to his desires only a few mornings before. He certainly would not make that mistake again. When out with Miss Henwood, at least one of them must focus on adhering to propriety.

Clearing his throat, Michael got to his feet. "I believe we have been outside long enough to raise a question or two unless we return soon."

Charlotte rose as well. "Well, that was certainly a short-lived moment of levity. Nevertheless, I am pleased that it happened at all. Tell me, Lord Averly, what do you think the person hiding in the bushes would have to say about your shocking discussion of my bum?"

Michael raised a hand and drew his fingers through his hair, never even thinking of the picture that it would create when he returned to the soirée. Of course the woman knew someone had been hiding there. He was a fool to think he could protect her from it. Lowering his hand, he accepted that there was truly no way to beat her.

The rustling started again as whoever hid made his way out. Charlotte smiled when she saw who it was, "Why, Mr. Hampstead, it is always an absolute pleasure to see you. What brought you out lurking in the garden?"

Mr. Hampstead made a pointless attempt at removing little sticks and leaves from his hair and clothing. "Why, I was only seeking another opportunity to engage you in conversation. I seem to recall that my first attempt at luring you into the garden was a failure, so I thought it would be cleverer to await you out here."

Michael gave Miss Henwood enough credit to disbelieve the man's courtly words. It was more than likely that some lovely young widow remained hidden in the shrubbery.

However, Miss Henwood's mind had latched onto a different part of his speech. "Mr. Hampstead, I find myself impressed on your ability to remember the night we met. You would be surprised at the events certain men can completely forget. *Especially* first meetings."

Mr. Hampstead gave her a smile that Michael deemed much too engaging. "Madam, I cannot imagine anyone forgetting a single fascinating thing that could involve a lady as charming as yourself."

His scowl deepening, Michael decided he had had enough of that. To Mr. Hampstead, he said, "Sir, it was a pleasure to see you. Perhaps we shall meet again when you are in a less disheveled state. Now, if you will excuse us." He then turned to leave, holding his arm out for Miss Henwood.

Charlotte took his arm, while she turned to shoot a silly face back at Mr. Hampstead, who merely smiled and bowed low as they left.

Charlotte was forced to admit that Lord Averly was right. Although the matrons of society would never judge her for being alone with Lord Averly, it would be best to avoid being alone in the garden with two gentlemen, especially when one of them was Mr. Hampstead. Charlotte chuckled to herself, as Lord Averly led her back inside.

No one ever minded her being in the presence of His Lordship. The man was much too stable and trustworthy by half to do anything improper. But goodness, she wished someone could have seen his face right before he realized the unseemliness of mentioning her bum. His stable and trustworthy demeanor had turned downright wicked. Well, wicked for *him*. Not to mention their almost-kiss. At least she hoped that had been his intention. Otherwise, he was much too concerned for her oral health.

She smiled up at him as they approached Lady Kinsey. Perhaps, just perhaps, her current schemes to drive Lord Averly mad were working. She had enjoyed that dangerous light in his eyes. Maybe, just maybe, that really had been desire she had seen while he leaned down to kiss her.

This settled matters. She had no choice but to remain on her present course. Maybe she would steal a kiss from him after all.

# Chapter 12

***

SIR DRISCOLL was deep in his studies when Mrs. Blakely knocked on the library door. The usually staid and composed housekeeper was practically vibrating with excitement.

"You appear to have a caller, Sir," she informed him, while bouncing on her heels with unexpected youth. Seldom did the Henwood residence have visitors.

Sir Driscoll held his hand out to take the calling card. "An earl? What in the world is an earl doing here?" Entertaining some pompous earl did not seem an enjoyable way to spend his day.

Mrs. Blakely shrugged. "I heard he was staying with Mr. and Mrs. Trivett."

"Even more reason for the Earl of Tunley to avoid this house," Sir Driscoll snorted. "It may be more lax in the country, but I presume that visiting a supposed enemy of your host is frowned upon."

Uncertain how to answer, Mrs. Blakely glanced nervously back towards the entrance to the library and asked, "Should I bring him in, Sir?"

Sir Driscoll seriously considered sending the man on his way, but curiosity finally overcame him. Waving noncommittally, he nodded.

A distinguished man strode into the room shortly after Mrs. Blakely left to retrieve him. As Sir Driscoll made his way around his cluttered desk to offer the newcomer a bow, he was given a moment to look over the earl.

Sir Driscoll wondered if the curl in the earl's upper lip was permanent. As for his choices in apparel, they were equally unfortunate. Even Sir Driscoll knew that the lavender waistcoat should never have been paired with those dark brown breeches. He would otherwise have been quite an attractive man, with his light gray eyes, dark hair peppered with a hint of silver, and slender frame. Then again, perhaps the more stylish English ladies found him quite agreeable.

"Sir Driscoll, what a pleasure to finally make your acquaintance!" While the Earl of Tunley's bow was smooth and graceful, but there was nothing effortless about his smile. The curl in his lip definitely was permanent and it turned any expression the earl attempted into an insulting leer. Perhaps that was what the man was aiming for.

Sir Driscoll nodded as he gestured for Lord Tunley to sit down in one of the plush chairs next to him. "I heard Your Lordship was visiting the Trivett family." Although Sir Driscoll felt certain that the Trivetts made sure every other resident of Uckfield knew of the Earl of Tunley's presence in their home, it was still news to Sir Driscoll. Perhaps he should take Charlotte's advice and at least go on a walk or two each week. Surely someone would call out the latest gossip to him as he passed.

Lord Tunley gave him an engaging smile. "I was merely traveling through your lovely town and came across Mr. Charles Trivett at a local watering hole." Here he gave Sir Driscoll a suggestive wink. "When we became more acquainted, he offered to let me reside in his home for the duration of my stay here. I had only planned on spending a day or two, of course, but I find myself enchanted with Uckfield and its charmingly rustic inhabitants."

Having nothing to say to that, Sir Driscoll asked after the welfare of the Trivetts. Not that he sincerely cared. However, he did seem to recall that some level of casual banter was required in situations such as this; he would have to wait a few minutes before the earl got to the point. Lord knew an earl would need a damned good reason to venture to Sir Driscoll's home, of all places. Briefly, Sir Driscoll wished his daughter was with him to help guide the conversation. Alas, she was happily ensconced in London.

Lord Tunley smiled before answering, no doubt in an attempt to gain his unwilling host's trust. Unfortunately, the action sent the curl in his lip up even more unnaturally high. Sir Driscoll did his best not to cringe. "They are all as pleasant as one would expect. Such a sweet, welcoming family. And the twins are surprisingly accomplished."

While Sir Driscoll was tempted to ask why such a feat was surprising, he felt no need to either defend the Trivetts or argue that Uckfield itself had any merit at all. Except for its pudding cake. The residents of Uckfield certainly knew their pudding cake. Perhaps a trip into town for a quick snack could be added into tomorrow's schedule.

In the silence that followed Lord Tunley's brilliantly flattering comment, Sir Driscoll concluded that it was his turn to speak. "Yes. Well. I seem to recall my daughter enjoying their company." Before the entire family went mad and decided to shun her for consuming some ale. Sir Driscoll knew for a fact that Mr. Charles Trivett, senior, enjoyed a great deal more than a pint several nights a week, at a pub outside of town that was even more questionable than The Griffin. Likely that was where he and Lord Tunley met.

Lord Tunley's tone turned a little flat. "Ah, yes, Miss Henwood is your daughter. I believe I have encountered her once or twice in Town, but we have not been introduced."

Sir Driscoll felt tempted to reply that he and Lord Tunley had also not been introduced, and yet the man felt perfectly comfortable invading Sir Driscoll's library. Instead, Sir Driscoll attempted a smile of his own. Hopefully he was not developing an identical curl in his own lip. What new and sensational topic would most interest an earl? And should Sir Driscoll even care to entertain the man?

Happily, Lord Tunley was already filling the conversational void. They wasted another several minutes discussing the weather in Uckfield and how it compared to London, before the earl finally made his point. "I'm surprised, Sir Driscoll, that you do not join Miss Henwood in London. There are a great many entertainments for a cultured gentleman such as you to enjoy." Was that a hint of sarcasm that Sir Driscoll detected? No. There was definitely nothing subtle in his tone. "In addition, you can keep a more careful eye on your daughter. If you find the prospect of such a large city daunting, I'd be happy to show you around."

The outlandish offer did nothing to improve Sir Driscoll's mood. Here was this irritatingly self-important fool invading his private research, with hints that Charlotte couldn't take care of herself. If only this man knew how well Charlotte managed things.

Quite a bit of time had passed since Sir Driscoll had needed to school his features within a social setting. Luckily, Lord Tunley was too proud of his little speech and the goodwill it conveyed to notice the red staining Sir Driscoll's cheeks.

Through gritted teeth, Sir Driscoll managed to say, "While I appreciate your generous and thoughtful offer, I cannot help but decline."

A flash of irritation flitted across Lord Tunley's face, before being replaced by a strained smile, his lips almost twitching in the effort to maintain it. Sir Driscoll would have expected him to drop the subject. It was, after all, quite an unusual offer to make. However, Tunley continued on. "Surely you have not thought through the benefits of having a knowledgeable guide to show you the excitements a larger city can provide."

Unhappy with having to explain himself, Sir Driscoll answered perhaps more harshly than he intended. "Having spent some time in Town in my earlier years, I have come to the conclusion that the entertainments you are referencing should be left to the young and reckless, or the older and dissipated." The insult, of course, went over the earl's head.

Even without detecting the reproachful undertone of Sir Driscoll's answer, Lord Tunley was unusually put out in hearing this. "But what of your daughter? Surely you worry about how she is faring without your guidance?"

How ridiculous. Sir Driscoll was used to Charlotte guiding him in society, not the opposite. Even without her to help him with certain social mores, Sir Driscoll was well aware of the impertinence in such a question. Now, if only she could be here to help him kindly—or perhaps a touch unkindly—send this bizarre fool on his way. Before Sir Driscoll could suggest the earl enjoy such an unexpectedly sunny day, Mrs. Blakely bustled into the room with a tea tray.

Sir Driscoll turned a mottled shade of red. For goodness' sake, why would Mrs. Blakely decide to bring tea in without it being called for? Did everyone assume that he had no idea how to properly comport himself? If he ever intended to offer a guest in his house a beverage, it would not be a cup of bland tea. But that was beside the point, as he had no desire to share anything with this impertinent, foppish ass.

The impertinent, foppish ass was already raising the cup Mrs. Blakely had poured for him to his lips. Mrs. Blakely practically vibrated with excitement after pouring tea for an earl. Suppressing the urge to bat Lord Tunley's cup out of his hand, Sir Driscoll took his own cup, dismissing Mrs. Blakely from the room with a nod.

As the awkward silence reigned on, Sir Driscoll decided he had no choice but to reply to Lord Tunley's rude question. "I assure you, my daughter is perfectly capable of taking care of herself in such a large, overwhelming city. Besides that, she already has a chaperone, whose experience in London society is far superior to that of a gentleman who has ensconced himself in a small town for most of his life. I gather Lady Kinsey is well recognized as a force to be reckoned with."

Letting out a condescending laugh, Lord Tunley replied, "But she is still only a woman. Surely Lady Kinsey has no desire to prevent Miss Henwood from emptying the family's coffers with endless shopping excursions and trips to the theatre. From the extravagant gowns and jewels I have seen Miss Henwood traipsing about in, I cannot imagine the ladies are assigning much thought to the repercussions of their actions."

Astounding. Why did this man want to come here and make him doubt his daughter's actions? No one had a right to come into Sir Driscoll's home and criticize him, and then his only child. Lord Tunley was taking things a great deal too far and it was time for him to leave.

If there were any concerns to be had, he would undoubtedly hear of them from Harry Madison. There had been no news surrounding Charlotte, except for the fact that a viscount was courting her. Obviously, Sir Driscoll had nothing to worry about.

As for the money, Charlotte was allowed to spend whatever she wanted. He might be the one signing his name to authorize her investments, but she made most of the decisions. Whatever wealth they had today, she had earned. Let the girl wear her jewels and gowns.

Why was the earl noticing her extravagant lifestyle, when he had apparently come across her only once or twice in society? Who the hell was this man?

Trapped in his thoughts, Sir Driscoll did not even at first register that Lord Tunley was still talking. "How can you not see that they need you there to keep them from going too far?"

At that, Sir Driscoll lowered his teacup back into its saucer. If the cup were a sturdier container, he would have slammed it a down more aggressively. At the very least, his answering words conveyed enough anger for even the earl to notice. "Sir, I believe it is you who has gone too far. I can assure you that it is quite impossible for my daughter to shop beyond the family's means. Considering that my daughter's investment strategies have brought the 'family's coffers' to where they are today, she has the right to do whatever she wants with the money." At this, Sir Driscoll rose, preparing to send the earl on his way, even if doing so required a hard boot to the arse.

Irritated, Lord Tunley quickly joined him in rising; inexplicably, he still held his dainty teacup. "You obviously jest. No man would be fool enough to leave a young girl in charge of his finances. There is no need to so blatantly mock me after coming to you in goodwill—" Sir Driscoll snorted at that "—and offering you advice, after seeing how Miss Henwood comports herself in London. Mr. Trivett was so good as to tell me all about the trouble she got into, here in Uckfield. Surely you are at least somewhat concerned about the damage she might further do her reputation." Lord Tunley spent most of his little speech waving his teacup back and forth, tea sloshing over the edges.

Sir Driscoll actually laughed out loud at that. "Ah yes, because the Trivett family knows so much about appropriate behavior. Now, I know it is *you* who is jesting. As for my daughter, she has been managing the family accounts since she turned ten." Not even allowing Lord Tunley to reply, Sir Driscoll strode to the library door. Shooting a hard glare at Lord Tunley, he continued, "I believe you have overstayed your welcome, Lord Tunley. No doubt the charming and *surprisingly* accomplished Misses Trivett are missing their opportunity to entertain a man of your elevated station and wisdom. Good day to you."

Judging by the animosity in Lord Tunley's eyes, Sir Driscoll's treatment of him would not be soon forgotten. In his hurried exit, Lord Tunley blasted past a confused Mrs. Blakely. As she watched him go, she called, "But I brought pudding cake."

Conveniently, the heated discussion seemed to have left Sir Driscoll a bit hungry. Almost cheerful again, he grabbed the abundantly-filled platter and took his seat behind the desk.

Perhaps a less easily-distracted man would have taken a moment to ponder such a strange encounter. Perhaps. He managed to write a short note that he would hopefully remember to have Mrs. Blakely post to Mr. Madison.

Sir Driscoll then got back to work. He had a mythical Greek amphora with impressive healing powers to search for.

A few hours later, Sir Driscoll looked up from his studies. Where in the world had Lord Tunley's teacup gone?

# Chapter 13

APPARENTLY, CHARLOTTE'S THOUGHTS about Lord Averly at the previous week's soirée were a tad optimistic. He no longer seemed to be softening towards her at all. After their brief foray into the social whirl together, His Lordship began avoiding Charlotte entirely. He ceased calling upon her and Lady Kinsey, in no way behaving like a besotted suitor. It was quite unpardonable. Worse, it went against their agreement.

The last time she had seen him was at a small supper party that she requested he attend with her. He had not even picked them up in his carriage. And then the blasted man stammered his excuses and left early!

At least no one else seemed to find his behavior amiss; within three days of their debut soirée, the entire *ton* made sure to include the two of them on their guest lists. So long as Charlotte had entrance to these events, she could weed out any negative gossip. Without Lord Averly's attention, there was little else for her to do.

At least Ryder came to call every few days. In fact, she was just sitting down to tea when he came hustling in, out of a particularly unpleasant downpour.

"Damned miserable outside," he mumbled as he passed Charlotte to take his seat.

"Mr. Skidmore, you will leave that sort of language for the gaming dens and Lord knows what other places you frequent in the evenings, but not here. Do you understand, young man?" Lady Kinsey intoned without even looking up from her book.

Ryder took in Her Ladyship's pleasantly rotund figure as she lounged back in the settee. She was always dressed as though she expected the king to drop in at any moment. Today she wore a stylish dress in vibrant lavender with a darker purple trim. Ryder was tempted to go back out and bring her a matching nosegay.

Instead, Ryder turned to Charlotte. "Does she really hear everything? No wonder the woman knows everything about everyone." Charlotte replied by sticking her tongue out.

"Hardly ladylike, Charlotte," Lady Kinsey added. How *did* the woman know everything? Charlotte was now certain that Mrs. Madison learned all of her tricks with Julia from Lady Kinsey.

"So," Her Ladyship continued to Ryder as she set her book down, "are we likely to see your wayward brother anytime soon, or would it be best for Charlotte to give her other suitors a chance?"

*Well, that was certainly to the point*, thought Charlotte. Lady Kinsey knew that Ryder and now Lord Averly had offered their assistance in stemming the tide of gossip following Charlotte. Indeed, she had asked herself this same question for several days, but did not want to call Lord Averly out on his behavior just yet. Besides, she doubted she ever would force him to truly fulfill his part of their agreement—she hardly knew what would qualify as the agreement being fulfilled, in any case. Would it be until the Season ended? When Julia was safely wedded? When they found the evil gossiper and forced him or her to apologize? None of those possibilities were going to occur anytime soon. It would be unfair to force him to wait so long.

For all Charlotte knew, the man might be searching for a wife himself. She had no right to stand in his way, no matter the odd manner her stomach turned at the thought. Perhaps all she needed was a spot of tea to make things better. No, she thought after a large gulp, the tea wasn't helping. What was it that Lady Kinsey sometimes added to her tea? Brandy? Before

Charlotte could wonder where that particular item hid, Ryder answered Lady Kinsey.

"Has he really not been around at all? I know he has accompanied you two to several gatherings. No one should have commented on his absence as of yet."

Lady Kinsey replied, "His Lordship has attended exactly two and a half gatherings with Charlotte, since his unexpected morning visit two weeks ago. He might as well simply leave her alone at this point."

Charlotte choked on her next gulp of tea. *How had she known about that visit?* Charlotte intended to have a long talk with Suzie in the near future.

"Choking is also unladylike, Charlotte, so do contain yourself. Of course I was aware of his presence here at that ungodly hour. I'm still shocked you didn't throw him out on his rear." Lady Kinsey had a suspicious glint in her eye.

The thought of rear ends put Charlotte into a darker mood. She mumbled into her unlaced tea, "There were things we needed to discuss. I doubt he would have left had I run at him with the fire poker."

Her Ladyship replied, "Well, I do appreciate your restraint in not assaulting a member of the peerage. Nevertheless, the man could have been a tad more polite. All everyone ever hears about is His Lordship's endlessly correct behavior. Personally, I think he's gone a bit too far with it. Now if he slips up at all, the gossips will fall on him like vultures."

"Whereas I," Ryder chimed in, toasting the air with his teacup, "can only improve myself. You see, Lady Kinsey, I am merely the more clever brother. When I reform myself, everyone will be so inordinately pleased and thankful, that they will forgive all my transgressions."

Lady Kinsey's tone turned wry. "First of all, young man, you have a very, very, *very* long way to go in order to reform yourself. The endless work involved in that personal alteration will certainly cancel out any transgressions. However, as I don't foresee any obvious changes within this decade, the point is completely moot. Secondly, your very own brother did, at one point, possess an impressively soiled character himself. He has since made the effort to be the better man, a task I challenge you to take on at some point in the near future, before you are lost to us entirely."

Ryder did appear impressively chastened after this unexpected lecture. Charlotte was as surprised by Lady Kinsey's giving it as she was to hear about Lord Averly's past. Although she knew that Lady Kinsey cared for Ryder, she was not a woman predisposed to trying to change people. Her Ladyship tended to enjoy the flaws of humanity and chose to let people carry on for as long as they provided ample entertainment. Charlotte doubted Ryder would appreciate knowing that Lady Kinsey's singling him out to better himself was actually a sign of affection.

As for this news about Lord Averly's past, she couldn't help but be shocked. His youth had been as troublesome as Ryder's? Knowing what she did about Ryder's exploits, she couldn't imagine that being possible. What had Lord Averly done? And what had caused the complete about-face?

Sighing, Charlotte admitted to herself that she knew very little about Lord Averly. They seldom spoke but to antagonize each other.

But wouldn't it be wonderful if his past truly were a bit spotted? It would certainly explain that kiss they had shared. Charlotte's toes curled just thinking about how close he had come to repeating the experience. The man knew just how to kiss a woman.

Charlotte recalled the playful gleam in his eyes when he had teased her by the fountain. Had the man not been tormenting her at the time, she would have enjoyed that expression.

And he had been charming—up until she had teased him back into his old self. In fact, if Lady Kinsey spoke truth, she had teased him back to his new self. It was certainly something to think on.

"Well, Charlotte?" Lady Kinsey's voice interrupted her thoughts. "Should we still pursue Lord Averly's assistance, or are you done with him?"

Charlotte realized she was not in any way done with Lord Averly. There were too many questions she wanted answered. And she desperately wanted to know what he had been like back in his wicked, younger days.

With as innocent an air as she could manage, Charlotte replied, "It would perhaps be most to my advantage were Lord Averly and I to continue our relationship for the next few weeks. Although I admit that we may never find out who is behind all of this, I cannot deny that his protection appears to have shielded me from any further gossip. I would not mind the opportunity to enjoy that for just a little bit longer."

Lady Kinsey reached across Ryder to pat Charlotte's knee. Charlotte must have imagined the almost victorious light filling Her Ladyship's eyes. "And who could blame you, my dear? No one ought to have such things said about them. It appears we shall continue needing your brother's services, Mr. Skidmore."

And what had that look passing between Ryder and Lady Kinsey meant? Ryder rose and addressed them both in his most formal manner. "I shall go home immediately to inform my brother of just how remiss he has been in his duties to you ladies."

Pleased that Miss Henwood continued to hold his brother prisoner, he prepared to make his way home. Hopefully gadding about with someone a bit cleverer and certainly more attractive than the daughters of Michael's peers would help his brother lighten up a bit.

"Oh no, Mr. Skidmore," Charlotte stopped him. "I would like the pleasure of informing Lord Averly of just how remiss he has been in his duties. Does he still ride by the park in the mornings?"

147

Charlotte had memorized his morning riding schedule during her first Season, in the hopes of encountering him. It was never her intention to approach him; that would have been beyond the par. However, she had hoped he would perhaps notice that her riding skills were not quite as deficient as he had first seen in Uckfield. Or, at least, that had been her intention, back when she expected Lord Averly to eventually recognize her.

Ryder smiled at her, "Intending to ambush him, eh? Can't object to that. Why don't I send over a note tomorrow morning, telling you where to find him?"

"Goodness!" Charlotte answered. "I wouldn't want you to go to the trouble of rising early, Ryder. That would be beyond cruel."

"I believe, dear lady, that the end result will easily make it worth my while. Good day to you two. No doubt I shall see you soon."

---

Things were finally turning around for Lord Tunley. Admittedly, his little chat with Sir Driscoll Henwood did not go as well as he could have hoped, but the rest of Tunley's visit to that miniscule town had proven beneficial.

He was engaged. True, Tunley could have done better. But, for some reason, the concerned papas in Town had a few objections to his reputation. It made his pursuit of the known London heiresses more than a little challenging. However, this particular young lady's papa had no objections to make. For the first time, Tunley's title had proven useful. Although a final sum had not yet been decided upon, her father had agreed to lend him a portion of the dowry early, which had been put to excellent use. Mr. Nigel Withers, Tunley's cousin, and the man who had first introduced him to Mr. Madison, was more than willing to sell off his portion of the Cornish ironworks—at an exorbitant increase in price, of course. Never accused of being a poor businessman, Tunley had at least talked the price down to something reasonable. He was family, after all.

But his greatest stroke of luck had occurred shortly after his return to London. His old school friend, Jacob Davies, was in a bit of a bind. It would seem that when you find yourself in a duel with a marquis, and accidentally win, it becomes a wise decision to leave the country. Possibly Europe. In this case, Davies chose the Americas.

Tunley would never admit that he may have possibly had something to do with instigating the duel in the first place. Being such a good friend, he had immediately offered himself up as Davies' second. He was sure to support his friend when things went horribly wrong. Alas, things went worse than Tunley could have hoped for. As Tunley told Davies, it seemed that the marquis had not been able to get out of bed on his own for days. Worse still, rumor had it that the wound had begun to fester.

Knowing he would need to turn whatever he could into guineas in a short time, Davies had been more than willing to sell off his portion of the ironworks. When the marquis seemed to be coming around, Tunley hastily ushered his dear friend onto a ship sailing for Boston.

Perhaps, Tunley thought, he should celebrate his latest successes. He always had a standing invitation to the charming Madame Ricely's.

---

Ryder had been forced to ask his valet to awaken him as soon as his brother arose the next day. He casually joined his brother in the breakfast room. Although Michael thought it odd for his brother to be out of bed at such an hour, he carelessly answered the questions Ryder posed about his plans for the day. As soon as Michael left the room to prepare his horse, Ryder sent the necessary note off.

Charlotte, however, was none too pleased to rise at such an hour. She knew that Michael rose early, so she did the same. However, Ryder's note still arrived before she was dressed for her ride.

Suzie looked it over. "Well, today he's aiming for the south side of Hyde Park and should be there soon."

"Damn," Charlotte said. "It's a bit of a way for me to go. We had better hurry."

"I 'ope it won't become a habit of his to wake you up early. I don't like the effect it has on my nerves."

"Your nerves? Really, Suzie, you need to cease your daily chats with Lady Kinsey immediately. That woman is a bad influence on everybody."

"She's teachin' me her 'information-gathering skills,' as she puts it. I don't mind. You'd be amazed at the things people tell you when you ask the right questions," Suzie retorted.

Charlotte was again impressed at the improvements in Suzie's accent. However, she was a little less pleased to discover Suzie's intentions of taking after Her Ladyship. Charlotte could not foresee a lady's maid acquiring the level of power that an earl's widow possessed. Perhaps it would be best if she had a chat of her own with Lady Kinsey. She would never want to see Suzie hurt or disappointed. Then again, Charlotte had moved quite a way up in the last year or so. Who was she, to try to hold anyone back from her dreams?

For now, it was high time she embarked on her ride to Hyde Park. Charlotte had sent a message upon waking, requesting the escort of one of the Madisons' grooms for her ride. Tom ought to have arrived by now. Her horse saddled and ready, Charlotte set out to hunt down her quarry.

---

Michael had not slept a full night since that damned soirée. He continued to relive the moment when Miss Henwood leaned in so close to his own lips. Had she really intended to kiss him? Or had he intended to kiss her? No, of course not. That way was madness. Hell, that blasted woman was madness. Somehow, he could not eradicate her from his thoughts. Visions of what could have happened, had he let their lips touch, or of what they could have done had they not been carefully observed by Mr. Hampstead, ran through his head. It was those visions that were keeping him up at night. In more ways than one.

The whole situation was damned uncomfortable. Miss Henwood made him want to do all those activities he had so enjoyed before he received his title. Or at least one of those things.

Seduction.

Michael desperately wanted to seduce Miss Henwood. Never mind the fact that the woman had apparently made it her life's goal to bring him misery. He wanted her on her back beneath him. Now. Every time she made some ridiculous comment, no doubt strategically intended to drive him mad, he wanted to drive her a little bit mad in return.

Michael nearly groaned out loud. If he continued thinking in that vein, his morning ride would go from merely uncomfortable to downright painful.

There was only one solution. He simply *must* cease contact with her. He had worked hard to better himself and he refused to throw everything away, in return for one licentious night.

As he rode on, Michael turned more resolute. These thoughts surrounding Miss Henwood would not compromise his principles. Ryder could go back to assisting her. Michael ignored the nagging thought that called him a coward for taking the easy way out. Not that he expected Miss Henwood to make it easy for him.

No, that wasn't fair to Ryder. Michael had made a commitment and it was his responsibility to keep it. Besides, he had already kissed Miss Henwood. There was no need to repeat the event. He could control himself. All he needed to do was ensure they remained in public together at all times. No more tavern rooms and trips outside to sit by fountains. Perhaps the theatre? There would be an audience surrounding them, forcing them both to be on their absolute best behavior. Miss Henwood only behaved ridiculously when Michael comprised the only audience.

Michael's eye was briefly caught as another rider bounded into the far end of the clearing. Although surprised to see others about at this hour, he continued on, but something compelled him to look back. The newcomer was a hulk of a man, and appeared to be waiting for someone. The man stopped his horse to the side of the path that led into this particular clearing. Michael halted his mount and waited on the other end of the grassy stretch. If nothing happened soon, he would continue on. He simply couldn't shake this uneasy feeling.

Only seconds later, another rider entered: a woman. It was too great a distance to tell anything about her beyond her elegant maroon riding habit and how well she kept her seat. The man immediately cut her off, reaching for her horse's reins by its mouth. Clearly shocked at this man's presence and his daring rudeness, the woman appeared to castigate him. If they did know each other, Michael couldn't imagine how. They didn't seem to share the same circles. Michael shook himself, when he realized Charlotte would have considered his thoughts to be much too snobbish.

All of a sudden the woman kicked her horse into action, forgetting that the man still held her reins. This would certainly not end well for her. Spurring his own ride to a gallop, Michael raced across the field.

—

Charlotte never expected the man to come out of nowhere and grab Esmerelda's reins. Good God, she wasn't about to be kidnapped and shipped off to some foreign harem, was she? Or did that only happen in sensation novels?

"Are ye Miss 'enwood? Sir Driscoll's kid?" The accent of the lower classes was so thick in his voice, she could barely understand him.

"What do you want?" She tried to add a condescending air to her tone, but mostly she sounded as shaky and frightened as she felt. The man was huge, and even from this distance she could catch the scent of stale liquor on his breath.

"I got a message fer ye. You tell yer da' to get rid o' his shares in the mine 'r else 'e'll be real sorry."

"Who are you? And how dare you accost me in such a manner!" Finally, she sounded less terrified. Like hell would she let this ruffian tell her what to do.

The man just snorted in response. "Yer a pretty little thing." He looked her over with a leer. "I'd 'ate to do any 'arm to a lady like ye. I'll be watchin' ye."

Her bravado forgotten, Charlotte could only say in bafflement, "Why does anything that happens with that land matter to you?"

"I got me own interests in it. Jus' remember wot I said. Ye seem a smart 'nough lady."

Charlotte had had enough. She kicked Esmerelda to urge her around the man, but didn't expect his grip on her reins to be so strong. Esmerelda shied, but didn't make any move around him.

Just then, she noticed another rider bearing down on them. *Oh please don't let it be another man like this one*, she thought. She had asked Tom, a groom from the Madisons' residence, to keep his distance during her ride so that she would be able to speak freely with Lord Averly. Without her groom to protect her, she had no chance against two such ruffians.

But it seemed that the bully also didn't expect the other rider. Before speeding away from her and the new arrival, he smacked her mare's rear with a sounding thwack. Esmerelda reared in surprise and Charlotte found herself tumbling from her horse for the second time since her childhood.

The sounds of the approaching horse's hooves grew louder. "Miss! Are you all right?" A gentleman's voice called out to her.

Oh, damn, blast and bloody hell! It was Lord Averly.

Must he see her fall from her mare *again*? Well, this time she would get up on her own. Charlotte rolled to her side to push to her feet. And immediately fell back to her knees in pain. Apparently this time, instead of her bum, it was her ankle that was injured. A hand appeared in her line of sight. Charlotte looked up into his eyes as she took his hand.

"I should have known it was you," Lord Averly mumbled as he tried to ease her to her feet.

Charlotte pulled back on his hand before he could draw her up, "I appear to have twisted my ankle."

Without a word, Lord Averly leaned down to draw one of her arms around his shoulders, while raising them both to a stand. He firmly held his arm around her waist.

Charlotte tried to ignore how secure she felt as he supported her. She also tried her best to ignore the tingling sensation she felt as she was pressed so tightly to his side. She had never allowed another man to hold her so close, her breast brushing his chest with every breath she took. Walking was not an ideal option, so pleasant tingling or not, she had little choice.

"Lord Averly, I'm afraid I cannot go much farther, even with you supporting me. Perhaps I could ride back. You can't carry me and bring the horses."

He knew she was right. He certainly had no desire to cause her further pain. But to hold her against him like this. And with a valid excuse. The woman could hardly support herself, now could she?

Lord Averly sighed. "I suppose you have a point. If I lift you back up onto your mare, you still won't be able to guide her back home with your ankle." He paused, as though forcing himself to say the rest. "But I can take your reins and lead you back, if you would find that acceptable."

"I suppose I could allow your help," she answered begrudgingly.

Immediately another thought struck her. "My groom, Tom! He should have caught up by now. We need to find him."

Lord Averly nodded, before again glancing around the clearing with caution. "But first we need to get you back onto your mare, or else we can't go anywhere."

Charlotte looked around for a bench or stump to stand on, in order to mount Esmerelda. Meanwhile, Lord Averly had stepped up even closer. When she turned back to him, she was looking straight up into his piercing green eyes.

Charlotte's lips parted, but she couldn't think of anything to say. His hands closing around each side of her waist stopped her breath. They stood there, facing each other for what felt like an eternity. Just when Charlotte thought she had the courage to speak, Lord Averly lifted her straight up, to place her on Esmerelda. As he walked away, one hand lingered to run lightly from her waist and down her thigh, sending disturbingly pleasant chills through to her core. He took her mare's reins and mounted his own horse.

When Charlotte recovered, she said, "We came in through that path." She pointed. "He must still be that way."

They found Tom not far from the path's entrance, walking his own mount towards them, rubbing his jaw. Apparently their mystery man had delivered a light tap to the groom's chin on his way out. Although it hadn't been enough to knock him off his ride, he had felt dazed enough to decide that riding might not be ideal.

They agreed that Tom would make his way back to the Madisons' house, which was a shorter distance to travel. Lord Averly insisted on escorting Miss Henwood home.

Too shaken to argue, Charlotte agreed. She wished she could convince herself that this had been a random attack. But for the man to know her groom's identity as well, he must have been following her. And for how long?

She needed to speak with Mr. Madison immediately.

Lord Averly interrupted her thoughts. Unable to contain himself further, he turned around on his mount. "What in the world were you doing riding unaccompanied at this hour? Who knows what could have happened, had you been alone with that man!"

Charlotte decided that "Following you?" was not the most appropriate response, so merely replied, perhaps somewhat stubbornly, "I wasn't alone. Tom was only a short distance behind."

His Lordship answered, unimpressed, "I don't think leaving one's groom behind is the most efficient way to protect oneself. Have times changed in the last year, and ladies are now regularly courting danger for the sake of amusement?"

Charlotte could not think of an acceptable defense to follow Lord Averly's sarcasm.

Lord Averly grew impatient. "Well, Miss Henwood? Does this new adventure top, say, a tankard of ale in some heretofore unmentioned tavern?" Goodness, Michael should not be discussing such things out in the open. He glanced at his surroundings, relieved that the streets were mostly empty. The few shopkeepers opening their doors, or servants heading to market, were not likely to recognize them.

Charlotte's back stiffened. Like hell would she allow Lord Averly to talk to her like this. It was Lord Averly's blasted fault that she was out at this ungodly hour in the first place.

Preparing for another of their battles, Charlotte sweetened her voice in reply. "You know, Your Lordship, I do believe you have it just right. What, with you disappearing for most of the last week, I decided Hyde Park at seven in the morning would be a perfect time to find another gentleman who would be willing to assist me. You have clearly given up on our bargain, and I, therefore, decided to find myself a new man to torture with my company. Perhaps he will be a bit less astoundingly dull than my last victim. So I thought, 'Why not Hyde Park?

Many men ride there for their daily exercise. Perhaps there will even be a petty criminal or two for me to encounter.' Oh, and look, there was!"

Lord Averly turned back to glare at her. "I am relieved that you find this amusing. However, I have a feeling that once I explain to Lady Kinsey what you've done, your reckless disregard for your own safety will immediately be curbed."

Charlotte chose to forgo mentioning that Lady Kinsey had already fully sanctioned today's ride. Thankfully, Michael seemed done with his lecture after that particular threat.

---

Back at Miss Henwood's townhouse, Michael dismounted and strode over to Charlotte, his expression grim. Firmly gripping her waist, he set her down.

Charlotte was unprepared for the jolt to her ankle and stumbled once her feet hit the ground. Instinctively, she reached out and gripped Lord Averly's arms for support, while his hands tightened at her waist. Surprised at the unexpected contact and strength in his arms, Charlotte looked up at Lord Averly. For the first time that day, she caught a look of true concern on his face. For just a moment, his features softened as he asked, "Are you all right? I could send for a physician or—"

"I'm fine," she answered, barely able to find her voice.

Realizing how close they were standing, the two simultaneously released each other. This, of course, led to Charlotte nearly stumbling again. Lord Averly slid under her arm and guided her up the steps to the door.

Although Lady Kinsey was presumably still abed, Lord Averly requested Suzie wake her, so he could explain the morning's adventures to her. As they did not have a groom to attend to Charlotte's mare, Suzie promised to attend to Esmerelda until the Madisons sent someone over.

Lady Kinsey, already dressed for the day, joined Lord Averly before Suzie could fetch her. She calmly took the story His

Lordship delivered and assured him that she would deal with the matter.

After he exited, hardly saying a word to Charlotte, Lady Kinsey turned to her charge. "Well, it seems your morning ride went a bit differently than planned. Personally, I intend to spend the morning in relaxation and calm reflection. You ought to, as well. Best be rested when His Lordship returns this afternoon to check on you."

Charlotte gawked at Her Ladyship, "You cannot be serious. The man will want absolutely nothing to do with me ever again, after this morning. We'll be lucky if he doesn't give me the cut the next time we encounter each other."

Lady Kinsey merely smiled, as though Charlotte had never spoken. "Now, back to bed with you. We'll need to get a compress for that ankle."

# Chapter 14

C HARLOTTE DID GO BACK TO BED. Once she had a
moment to close her mind off from the morning's events,
she slept for several hours. When she awoke, she spent some
time going back over everything. None of it made a great deal of
sense to her. Why would anyone care about her father owning
shares in an ironworks in Cornwall? Not that it mattered.
Charlotte had no intention of asking her father to give those
shares away. A disturbing image rose of that thug cornering her
father in his library, with only his books to protect him. This
ruffian would not go to Uckfield to frighten her father, would
he? Shaking the images from her mind, Charlotte rang for
Suzie.

However, it wasn't Suzie who eventually joined Charlotte
upstairs to help her dress, but the downstairs maid. Lucy came
in most days, to help Mrs. Grayson prepare meals and snacks
for the household, as well as help with the deeper cleaning.
When asked, she answered that Suzie was in the drawing room,
"organizing everything." Upon hearing such a vague, yet
ominous answer, Charlotte hurried to finish dressing.

When she reached the drawing room, her arm thrown over
Lucy's shoulders for support, she found Lady Kinsey among a
throng of chattering ladies. The drawing room was so full, in
fact, that a chair had to be vacated for Charlotte.

She should not be surprised that the events of her ride were
already public knowledge. Likely one of the Madisons' servants
had blabbed to another lady's servant, and so on. Once the
secret escaped the Madisons' home, there was no telling who

knew. Although, judging by the full drawing room, Charlotte would have guessed that all of England knew by now.

At least most of the ladies in the room were women with whom Charlotte was happy to be acquainted. Lady Kinsey had likely already culled the snooping busybodies who cared nothing for Charlotte's welfare.

Looking over the room, she met eyes with Mr. Hampstead and tried not to laugh. Of course the scoundrel would be here on a day guaranteed to have her drawing room filled with her young, attractive friends.

Knowing exactly what she was thinking, Mr. Hampstead raised his teacup to salute her. Finally she did laugh. Ever since his failed attempt to lure Charlotte into the garden so long ago, the man had decided they simply must be friends. And they were. Although the *ton* at first speculated about the nature of their acquaintance, it soon became clear—much to everyone's disappointment—that Mr. Hampstead had no intention of seducing Miss Charlotte Henwood.

Suzie announced another lady to the room. Charlotte missed the name, but turned to look. Shocked, she and Caroline Trivett met eyes. Caroline immediately made a bee-line for Charlotte in her chair. Noticing Charlotte's distraction, the other ladies trying to gain her attention gave up and began conversations with each other.

Caroline came up and attempted a smile, although it came out more as a grimace. Doing her best to lower herself to Charlotte's level, while keeping her dress out of harm's way, she said, "I heard what happened. Although really I assume the part about gypsies kidnapping you and selling you into a harem in Turkey is untrue."

Charlotte laughed as best she could, especially as that possibility had been the first to run through her mind during her ordeal. "Your version is certainly more interesting, but not quite what happened. I've always wanted to run away with gypsies."

Caroline visibly relaxed. Had she truly doubted her welcome? Seeing Charlotte's old childhood friend brought back all of the happy memories of chasing butterflies, pretending to be princesses in disguise, and reenacting whatever stories their young imaginations could create.

Smiling genuinely, Caroline replied, "All I really care to know is if Lord Averly carried you all the way home in his strong, protective arms."

"No, alas, there was nothing so heroic. He led my horse, but that was all." Charlotte tried her best not to think on those moments when his body brushed up against hers. There could only be one explanation for her continuing to dwell on Lord Averly's actions this morning.

Was she possibly still infatuated with him? Was that her true motivation for following him out on his ride at an hour she would normally still be abed? Because she had, heaven help her, *missed* him?

Meanwhile Caroline was trying to appear supportive, "At least you are safe now. I am sure that madman will be found soon and brought to justice."

Charlotte didn't want to think of the man who had accosted her. She attempted to focus her concerns on Lord Averly and what he must have thought of her.

Caroline continued talking, although Charlotte missed most of it. "I just wanted to see for myself that you were well. I can go if you aren't pleased to see me." When had Charlotte and Caroline last spoken in person? Charlotte jolted back into the moment. Certainly, Caroline couldn't intend to leave so soon. Uncertain, Caroline began to rise.

Charlotte almost rose in her concern, but quickly sat back down when the pain became too much. "No! I am so happy you came. I hope you won't be in too much trouble with your mother and sister for coming to see me. But it means a great deal that you came here."

Smiling self-derisively, Caroline answered, "Mama and Ellie may believe I am at the lending library at the moment. We have only just returned to Town, so everyone has been busy making the necessary arrangements. When I heard that you might have been attacked, I decided to come here and see how you were. I had feared that discovering your address might be a challenge, but after this morning's adventure, it seems everyone knows where you live."

Charlotte was not so sure how she felt about that.

"Well," Charlotte answered, still cautious, "everything seems to have ended happily for me. Look at all of the concerned friends filling our drawing room. Clearly curiosity for my well-being has done great things for me, socially."

Caroline let out a light laugh in response to that. Charlotte smiled, but was soon distracted by a tingle down her spine. Before she could reply, Charlotte's eyes were drawn back to the door.

Lord Averly entered the room, confident and prepared to continue their battle.

He had already located Charlotte. Before he could reach her, a group of excited ladies by the door approached him, no doubt to question him about the morning's adventure.

Charlotte smiled to herself. His Lordship was never one to enjoy that kind of attention. Slowly, Lord Averly began to look around the room, unprepared for the horde of ladies now blocking his path. Charlotte nearly laughed out loud. At Caroline's questioning look, she replied, "I doubt Lord Averly will brave the sea of gossiping ladies to reach my side, no matter how desperately he wishes to lecture me."

Caroline looked appalled. "Lecture you? Why would he do such a thing after all you've been through?"

Turning back to Caroline, Charlotte answered, "It would seem that my decision to venture out at such an hour was much too foolhardy for His Lordship. Apparently I should have assumed that hooligans lurk around every corner at seven in the morning in Hyde Park."

It was Caroline's turn to laugh. "One would think that most hooligans would be sleeping late after a night of debauchery."

Charlotte's jaw dropped. "And what would you know about a night of illicit debauchery?"

Blushing, her friend said, "Perhaps very little, but a girl can dream, can't she? I confess to wishing I could have spent a morning or two in The Griffin, myself." Had Caroline just confessed to wishing she had shared the experience that nearly destroyed Charlotte's reputation? Before she could question her, Caroline spoke again. "It appears His Lordship is, indeed, venturing across the drawing room. You know, I've never seen Lord Averly up close before. He is quite handsome." Her voice turned dreamy. "It must be wonderful being courted by such a man."

Wishing she could regale Caroline with all of Lord Averly's imperfections, Charlotte remained silent. There were far too many ears in the drawing room for such a conversation. Instead, she enjoyed the entertainment Lord Averly provided as he traversed the drawing room.

She had never noticed how large his feet were. Compared to the dainty half-boots that most of her visitors were sporting, the man looked painfully graceless. Yet very masculine. Although Charlotte tried to find amusement from his ineffectual movement across the room, her gaze continued to be drawn back to his firm jaw and intent eyes. If only Caroline had not drawn her attention back to how handsome he was. She loved the light wave in his hair and that freckle on his lip. Now would be an excellent time to recall his stodgy demeanor and terrible habit of noticing all of her particularly terrible habits. Instead, she kept recalling the fire in his eyes as he lowered her from her mare that morning.

"I don't know if you have heard, but Ellie is engaged," Caroline said.

Charlotte turned, surprised anyone would want to shackle himself to that girl. "Goodness, to whom? I hope they deserve each other."

Caroline's brow furrowed, confused at Charlotte's tone. Caroline had never noticed Ellie's sometimes vindictive nature. Ellie had never liked sharing Caroline's attention with Charlotte. Caroline began to answer, "Lord Tu—" but stopped, unexpectedly shy, when Lord Averly neared them.

—⁓—

Lord Averly had finally made his way to Miss Henwood, only a little the worse for wear. Although it may have been an accident, when he passed through a clump of gossiping matrons, someone had pinched his bottom. How had the woman reached under his coat in the first place? Needless to say, Michael was not in the best of moods upon arriving at Miss Henwood's side. A lovely blonde woman rose from kneeling next to her. Michael tried his best to focus on the speech he had prepared for Miss Henwood. There was a particularly good bit about drawing even more attention to herself and the Madisons after today, although this was not the wisest place to tell Miss Henwood what he thought of her recklessness. The gossips would practically cry out in joy, were they to see him make a scene.

"Miss Henwood." *Well, that was a start.*

She met his gaze innocently, no doubt well aware of his predicament. "Yes, Lord Averly."

Now what should he say? "I trust you are well?"

"Quite well. Thank you. Although it may be some time before we can share another waltz. I know how you love the waltz," she added, her tone dry.

Michael felt his face redden. He could learn to enjoy the waltz perfectly well, so long as his companion did not drive him completely mad with her improper chatter and uncomfortably appealing figure.

Taking him out of his misery, Miss Henwood gestured to the lady standing next to her, "This is my friend from Uckfield, Miss Caroline Trivett. Miss Trivett, this is Lord Averly."

Charlotte watched Caroline execute a perfect curtsy for Lord Averly while she dimpled, shyly. Charlotte regretted to admit that she still felt some level of envy for Caroline's sweet, effortless charm.

Charlotte added to Lord Averly, "It has been quite some time since Caroline and I visited, so I am very pleased to see her." Caroline shot her a grateful glance. Charlotte continued, mostly to Caroline, "It is unfortunate that we can't have a more private discussion. In a room this filled, I fear that nothing can be said without being overheard."

Michael fully agreed. An evil, yet wonderful, idea dawned.

"Miss Henwood," he said, drawing her gaze from her friend, "perhaps it is not so good for your recovery to entertain so very many people in such a cramped room. I would be mortified to discover that this afternoon prevents you from healing faster."

Charlotte was no fool. The man was up to something. What did he plan to do? Carry her to another room, away from prying eyes in order to deliver his perfectly-worded set-down? Charlotte would not allow him to corner her. "Although there are a great many people here, most of them are claiming the attention of Lady Kinsey and leaving me be. Besides, I am already perfectly comfortable in my chair here."

Lord Averly smiled. Charlotte thought his smile was a bit sly in nature. It sent a surprisingly pleasurable chill down her spine. He replied, "I had no intention of asking you to move."

Before Charlotte could ask him what he *did* intend, Lord Averly was waving to her chaperone, "Lady Kinsey! Lady Kinsey, I must have a moment of your time with Miss Henwood here." Charlotte could not contain her shock. The man had just yelled across a crowded room to demand Lady Kinsey join them. Well, perhaps it was not quite a yell, but he certainly made enough noise to silence their company.

Thankfully, Lady Kinsey immediately made her way over after making her excuses. Charlotte took some pleasure in noting her ease in crossing the room, after Lord Averly's pathetic attempt at doing the same. Then again, the entire crowd had heard his request for Her Ladyship's presence. If they wanted to know what Lord Averly was going to do next, they had best let Lady Kinsey reach him.

"Well, Lord Averly, I am here. What did you wish to discuss?" she enquired politely. No one else in the room spoke. In fact, Charlotte heard several people shush each other into silence. Charlotte had little desire to hear what Lord Averly planned, knowing it would be at her expense. But the die was cast. It would now be much more awkward to send Lady Kinsey away.

Lord Averly immediately leaned down to Lady Kinsey, bowing his head in feigned worry, "I am uncertain that such a boisterous gathering can be good for Miss Henwood's delicate health."

Charlotte, Lady Kinsey, and Caroline Trivett all raised their brows at the word "delicate."

Before Charlotte could tell Lord Averly what she thought of *that*, he continued on, "Although I don't doubt that everyone here is concerned for her well-being, perhaps it would be best to give her some quiet right now? She has, after all, been through a terrible ordeal, and I know how weak her nerves can be." Charlotte almost made to stand at that last bit. Caroline whispering her name was the only thing that stayed her. It would be social suicide to argue with a viscount in front of such a large gathering.

No fool, Lady Kinsey merely nodded and tactfully replied, "Perhaps it would be best for Miss Henwood to rest today. We can have our friends visit later on in the week, perhaps in smaller gatherings, I am sure."

Triumphant, Lord Averly turned to Charlotte, "There, you see? Everyone is perfectly willing to give you a few days to recover you nerves."

But they weren't. Not at all. Although only a few attempted to convince Charlotte that they ought to remain, purely with the intention of helping oversee her recovery, Lord Averly insisted on ushering each of them out.

Charlotte caught Mr. Hampstead's wink before he turned to escort two particularly attractive ladies from the room. She stifled a giggle as he nodded to them sympathetically. At least Lord Averly had allowed Caroline to remain, although Charlotte could not be certain how long that would last.

Meanwhile Lady Kinsey honed in on Lord Averly. "I hope there is a point to all this madness, Lord Averly. I dislike sending all of my friends out of my residence at once." She cocked her head for a moment. "Although I must confess, it was a bit overwhelming having so many people here at one time. There had to have been more than thirty people in our small drawing room."

At just that moment, Suzie entered the room, carrying a tower of cucumber sandwiches. Looking around, she said, "You cannot be serious." Seeing the small gathering by Charlotte's chair, she added, "I hope you four are hungry, otherwise Mrs. Grayson will be more than displeased." And, grabbing a large handful of the sandwiches for herself, Lucy, and Mrs. Grayson, Suzie flounced off, no doubt to eavesdrop outside the door.

Charlotte laughed. "I hope, Lord Averly, you have every intention of apologizing to Mrs. Grayson, our cook." Wryly, she added, "She has a very delicate constitution."

Lord Averly turned to Charlotte with an innocent expression. "I'm sure she will agree that this is all in your best interests." Charlotte heard Suzie's snort issue from somewhere behind the drawing room doorway. She could tell Lord Averly heard the same, but was much too self-satisfied to acknowledge it.

*Remember, Charlotte, murder is never the answer, no matter how you wish it were. And murdering a member of the peerage is generally frowned upon.* Briefly Charlotte wondered at which point in her life this had become her mantra.

The man had no right to make her decisions for her. Oh, how she wished she could tell Lord Averly just how profitable her own ideas were. Knowing his straitlaced ways, the man would be appalled to discover that a woman could make financial decisions all on her own.

She glared at Lord Averly for quite some time while he stared innocently back.

Finally, Caroline broke the awkward silence. "I had best return to Mama. I've already been gone longer than I told her I would." Looking at Charlotte regretfully, she added, "I truly will do my best to write. But only if you promise to write back." Leaning in, she whispered, "Besides, it seems as though your life is currently a great deal more exciting than mine."

Charlotte squeezed her offered hand. "I promise."

After Caroline made her exit, Lady Kinsey addressed Lord Averly. "I trust your desire to have our drawing room vacated had little to do with Charlotte's health. But if you do believe that her nerves are so very weak, allow me to offer you a bit of advice: run. Run fast and far, far away." With that, Lady Kinsey swished out of the room. She did ensure that the door to the drawing room remained entirely open, however.

Lord Averly merely smiled after her. Sitting down on a nearby chaise, he merely held up the overflowing tray of food. "Sandwich? No? Well, I do believe the events of the day have left *me* quite famished."

# Chapter 15

C HARLOTTE WAS NOT PLEASED. The man sends all of
Lady Kinsey's and her acquaintances home, and then
cavalierly nibbles a sandwich. Perhaps she should allow Suzie
and Mrs. Grayson to exact their revenge, after all.

It may not have been the most mature of punishments, but
Charlotte absolutely refused to speak to him, although there
were quite a few things she could say. She could tell him Ryder
would never have been so rude, remind him that his actions
went against his previous stance of avoiding her entirely, or she
could simply dump the entire tray of food in his lap. The last
had the double benefit of allowing her to remain silent, as well
as making His Lordship extremely uncomfortable.

Eventually the pleased smirk left Lord Averly's face. While
Charlotte eyed the sandwich tray with a look akin to maniacal
glee, he said, "Are you ever going to tell me exactly why you
were out riding at that hour today?"

In reply, Charlotte crossed hers arms and looked out the
window, while her mouth settled into a quiet grimace. Like hell
would she admit that she had gone to Hyde Park to find *him*.

She heard Lord Averly sigh. "Please tell me you at least
understand why your actions were so foolhardy. I would
appreciate that false comfort."

There was something about his tone that forced Charlotte to
face him. True, she could see the exasperation and even some
anger in his eyes, but there was something else, too. Worry. The
man had been genuinely worried about her. This was nothing

like the exaggerated shock and concern that her acquaintances had shown her. No, Lord Averly was entirely sincere.

Charlotte uncrossed her arms. "Perhaps I should not have left my groom where he could not see me." When Charlotte saw Lord Averly open his lips to deliver another speech, she added, "But I had no reason to expect that man to accost me. I had no idea that he had been following me in the first place, yet he must have been. He knew my name and spoke about my father." Should she have told him that?

Lord Averly stood and began pacing. He asked, accusingly, "Are you telling me that you knew that man? The man who socked your groom in the face?"

Charlotte was shocked. "No, I have no idea who he is! But he knew of *me*." A chill went down her spine just thinking it.

Although Lord Averly's anger appeared to dissipate with her words, his worry greatly increased. "You think he has been following you? Learning your habits?" As Charlotte sought an answer, Harry Madison strode into the room. His shirt was not carefully tucked in and when he removed his hat, his hair was a mess. Charlotte could not recall ever seeing him so disheveled.

"Good Lord, Charlotte! Are you all right? The ladies and I just got back from Brighton when we heard the news. Tom was practically in tears when we finally arrived. I insisted on coming over first, before Julia and Imogen could bombard you with questions. Are you all right?" Harry took out a handkerchief and mopped his brow.

"I only twisted my ankle. Otherwise, I am perfectly fine, just confused." Charlotte wanted to calm Harry down before she told him everything.

Apparently, Lord Averly had no such tact. Swinging his arm to indicate Charlotte, he said, "She is most certainly *not* fine! I have only just discovered that the man who accosted her may have been following her for some time now. He knows who she is, and, I can only assume, where she lives. This attack was not a random accident."

"Michael!" Charlotte cried. He should have controlled his outburst for Harry's sake.

Hearing Miss Henwood call him by his given name gave Michael pause. The only other time she had done so was back at The Griffin. Back then, however, she had not sounded so distressed. Forcing down his own panic, he finally regarded Mr. Madison, who had gone completely pale at this news.

Walking across the room, Michael poured a generous portion of brandy for Mr. Madison. Holding the snifter, he glanced at Miss Henwood, looking so small in her chair, and promptly poured his own equally generous portion.

Charlotte watched Lord Averly return with the brandy. Had she not been feeling so down, she would have demanded her own glass just to shock him. It certainly attested to her own pitiful state that she didn't.

When Mr. Madison finished his brandy, in only two gulps, Charlotte noted, Lord Averly broached the subject again. "Am I to understand that the news of Miss Henwood being followed today does not come to you as a great surprise?"

Relieved that Lord Averly's tone no longer sounded accusing, she waited for Mr. Madison to answer. Mr. Madison sighed, mopped his brow once more, and said, "No, I suppose not. I merely hoped that her being of the gentler sex, she would be ignored by this man. I had requested a footman keep an eye on Miss Henwood's home, just in case."

Lord Averly raised his brows. "Have you been approached in such a manner?" Mr. Madison shook his head, then continued, "It would seem that a few of the men sharing in our—erm, my investment in Cornwall have had similar, erm, conversations. I believe the man going after them is the same one from whom I bought the land in the first place."

Somehow this news relieved Charlotte. The attack no longer felt so personal. Also, if there were other victims, it might be easier to find and arrest the man. Charlotte was aware that Lord Averly may not be familiar with Harry's ventures, but he clearly understood one thing. She watched any traces of gentleness disappear from Lord Averly's face when he asked, "Are you telling me that you knew there was a chance Miss Henwood could be hurt, yet did not see fit to warn her?"

Uncertain about wanting to hear Mr. Madison's reply, Charlotte prepared to interrupt. Lord Averly, however, noticed her intention and calmly raised a hand to stop her. For some reason, Charlotte acquiesced.

"In the last few weeks, he has approached various investors in a venture of mine, suggesting that they give up their shares. I assumed that Miss Henwood's position as a lady would be enough to protect her. There is no reason for him to think that she has any control over her father's shares. Most ladies do not engage in such activities, you know," Mr. Madison answered, appearing a great deal more nervous under Lord Averly's accusing gaze. Before Lord Averly could ask about Charlotte's exact involvement with her family's investments, Mr. Madison went on, "Mr. Stowes has no logical reason to be going after anyone with those shares in the first place. He can't expect this intimidation to convince everyone to simply hand the shares over without some sort of compensation."

When Charlotte saw Lord Averly prepare another scathing speech, she cut in, "I can understand why you thought I would be safe from this Mr. Stowes. There is nothing gentlemanly about cornering a young lady in the park." Lord Averly wished to insert his opinion, but she went on, as evenly as she could, "I still feel, however, that I should have been apprised of the situation. Even if we don't understand this man's motivation, everyone ought to be prepared for whatever he may do next."

Charlotte understood that many other ladies would need to be protected from these sorts of events. Nonetheless, she liked to think that Mr. Madison thought more highly of her capabilities.

Mr. Madison reached over and took her hand. "I was foolish, Charlotte. No one should have had reason to target a young lady when the major players involved are all gentlemen. Or so I thought. I would never have wanted to endanger you. Your father would skin me alive!"

Charlotte laughed at the image of her father attempting to fight, well, anyone. Sir Driscoll Henwood had to be the least aggressive man she had ever known.

Quirking a smile, Mr. Madison added, "You laugh now, but I assure you, your father can be quite fierce, when given the correct motivation."

Relieved that the mood was less charged, she replied, "Perhaps when defending a particularly important theory of his, but I cannot imagine him in a physical altercation. Would he attempt to beat someone with his books?"

Mr. Madison smiled wryly. "Some of those tomes are quite heavy. Who knows what sort of damage they could do?"

Lord Averly erupted out of his chair, throwing his arms up. "What is wrong with you two? While these reminiscences are entertaining, could we perhaps address the original problem? Miss Henwood was attacked today and there is some chance she will be endangered again."

The blood left Charlotte's face. There was nothing she wanted more in the world than for that morning's ride to be forever erased from her memory. She was being a coward. It was so much simpler to ignore these events and convince herself that nothing was wrong.

Nonetheless, Charlotte compelled herself to forgive Mr. Madison. She should not judge him for responding similarly to the threat of Mr. Stowes. Well, perhaps she should, but only a little. It still bothered her that she had been kept in the dark.

Chastened, Mr. Madison answered, "Of course, you are correct. Come, sit back down and we can decide upon the ideal manner to approach the problem. We have certainly passed the stage of avoiding it."

Lord Averly complied, sitting down next to Charlotte. "Are you certain that it is this Mr. Stowes who is threatening everyone?"

"I am almost positive," Mr. Madison said. "Perhaps a month or two ago, he began pestering a few of my colleagues in the Cornish mine, but not as aggressively as he did with Charlotte today. Not only that, but the timing was absolutely terrible. Nearly all of the investors at once began questioning my choice to use the puddling forge for iron extraction. But the puddling forge has been proven time and again to develop the strongest, purest iron. I gathered that one of the other investors set them up to it. I intend to deal with Mr. Davies' influence later." Lord Averly cleared his throat, momentarily distracting Mr. Madison from his rant. Madison cocked his head. "I digress. Needless to say, I was very surprised that Stowes had even approached Miss Henwood, let alone in such a manner." When Lord Averly raised his brows in reply, Mr. Madison went on, "My colleagues did provide me with a description that greatly resembles Mr. Stowes."

"And you said that Mr. Stowes is the man from whom you bought the land in Cornwall?" Lord Averly asked.

"Yes. At the time, I had no idea that the land could be mined for iron, nor did Mr. Stowes. He had been rewarded the land after a particularly, erm, successful boxing match."

Despite the severity of the situation, Charlotte's curiosity struck again. "'Particularly successful'?"

Mr. Madison coughed self-consciously into his hand. "I believe that certain characters suggested that Stowes lose the match. Stowes did so, with a bit more gusto than was expected. He was knocked out cold for hours and when he woke up, he barely recalled his own name. He was awarded the land in Cornwall as a sort of retirement gift. Anyone could see that his career had ended with that match."

Mr. Madison went on, cutting off any further questions, "I sent one of my men to investigate the area, and he shortly discovered the iron deposits. After evaluating the land's potential for mining, I invited a few of my close friends and acquaintances into the venture. One or two were not even aware they had been brought into the investment. My intention had been to reward the people who had been involved in my riskier ventures and those who had been helpful in my younger years. Instead, I have apparently put them at risk."

Charlotte leaned towards Mr. Madison, as best she could with her ankle raised. "You could never have predicted that this man would begin targeting your friends. I think what we need to discover, now, is exactly what this man wants and to what lengths he'll go to get it."

Brows furrowed, Mr. Madison answered, "If he wants the shares, then he must want control of the ironworks. He clearly doesn't have the funds to buy any of the shares back at their current value. I doubt he has the money to buy the land back at the price he sold it for, let alone to maintain it in the first place."

Lord Averly remarked, "I doubt the man plans on buying anything back, which is why he is using intimidation and threats."

Mr. Madison shook his head. "Then the man is still a fool. None of my friends would simply give their shares away for nothing. They might be pressured into selling them for only a little over their original price, but they would expect some level of profit."

Michael did his best not to demand how Mr. Madison could be so naïve. If these ploys were just beginning, things could only escalate. If Mr. Stowes' threats continued in this vein, eventually Mr. Madison's friends would be begging for someone to take the shares off their hands.

Michael asked, "Are most of your friends sharing in this investment financially stable?"

Shrugging, Mr. Madison replied, "I assume so. The gentlemen I asked to invest with me are all men with whom I have been involved in the past." To Charlotte, he added, "Of course, I never asked Driscoll. I knew he'd never let me do it in the first place."

Miss Henwood rejoined the conversation, "I'm assuming, then, that this ironworks is not like your usual ventures. The only people you allowed to invest were those you are close to and respect? Have you considered the possibility that this man is threatening your friends for more personal reasons? Perhaps discovering the land's success has caused him to lose his head. I mean, it does not seem entirely sane to threaten a young woman in Hyde Park during the day."

Her words in no way soothed Michael. This new vision of Mr. Stowes only made the man seem more terrifying. When he glanced at Mr. Madison, Michael saw his own concern mirrored in the man's face.

When Mr. Madison finally spoke, it was about the subject Charlotte had first broached. "There are a couple of gentlemen," he said slowly, "who approached me during the development of the ironworks. I'm not as familiar with their backgrounds as I am with the other investors. Both of them are men in the forefront of society. One is even an earl."

When Charlotte saw that Lord Averly had more to say to Mr. Madison, she leaned in. "Perhaps we should look into this Mr. Stowes. I think we need to fully understand his motivations before we do anything else." Yes, she was changing the subject. She also hoped to give Mr. Madison a purpose that would alleviate some of his guilt.

She could tell that Lord Averly would not be easily satisfied with her idea. But he was not helping the situation by increasing Mr. Madison's anxiety. For the first time in her life, Charlotte attempted to use a skill she had seen the Trivett twins practice in their youth.

She swooned.

Well, she would have, had she not been already reclining in a chair. However, in order to add dramatic effect, she pressed the back of her hand to her forehead. "Oh dear, I believe the events of the day are catching up with me."

Concerned, Mr. Madison immediately arose and took her hand. "You have had a trying day, my dear. And I am certain my conversation has only added to your strain. When you have had some rest, we will think on what to do about this adventure."

Lord Averly cleared his throat and addressed Mr. Madison. "Perhaps we should take Miss Henwood's advice about looking into Mr. Stowes." Charlotte let out a very odd-sounding whimper, effectively drawing attention back to her before he could go on. Mr. Madison was both a clever and competent man. Having planted the idea of a way to help everyone, he would need no further prodding.

Attempting as innocent and helpless a look as she could muster, she asked, "Lord Averly, could you please assist me back to my room? I'm afraid I cannot manage the stairs on my own." She could tell that Lord Averly believed not a word, although he remained silent. Silent and brooding.

Standing, Mr. Madison recognized this as his cue to leave. "I will certainly hire a man to hunt down Mr. Stowes. In the meantime, allow me to find Lady Kinsey and ask her to look in on you while you rest."

Ignoring the ominous look Lord Averly continued to send her, she thanked Mr. Madison and sent him on his way. His Lordship could lecture her to his heart's content, once Mr. Madison left.

After Mr. Madison was gone, she addressed Lord Averly. "Thank you for not pressing the subject. Mr. Madison is under enough stress right now, as it is. I don't want him to blame himself any further for today's events."

Most of the time, Michael accepted that Miss Henwood had an unhealthy desire to organize everything and everyone around her. But right now, in this case, she needed to stand back and allow the gentlemen to take over. Not that she would ever allow such a thing if he used those exact words.

If he could keep her properly occupied, perhaps she would not get herself into any further trouble. Perhaps, just perhaps, he could drive *her* a bit mad for once.

The stern expression on Lord Averly's face cleared. Before she could wonder at the change, he merely said, "Of course, you are right. Let us not speak of it any further. Like you said, you need your rest."

Not falling for his complacence for a moment, Charlotte began, "What exactly are y—"

Somehow, Lord Averly had reached under her and lifted her up against his chest. Instinctively, she wrapped her arms around his neck to support herself. "Lord Averly! This is not necessary. Surely it cannot be proper!" And she knew how greatly he objected to that which was not proper.

The man was carrying her through the doorway and to the staircase. Could he manage her and the stairs together? Foreseeing disaster, she attempted to dissuade him. "I promise I am perfectly capable of walking up the staircase, so long as you lend me your arm. I'm telling you, this display is completely unnecessary."

Grinning wolfishly, Lord Averly replied, "But I am certain that it is very necessary. Why, only a moment ago, you nearly fainted. Surely, it would be ungentlemanly to merely offer my assistance when you are so very exhausted from the day's trials."

Charlotte was at a complete loss. Here Lord Averly was, carrying her in his arms up the staircase. Goodness, she could smell hints of his shaving soap. Sandalwood and a hint of lemon. It made her want to nibble on his jaw-line. Her eyes widened. Where had that thought come from? Perhaps she was hungry? Hungry and a touch cannibalistic? No. She wanted to know how the edge of his jaw would feel against her lips. Would his stubble tickle? Although he was clearly teasing her for her obvious attempt to distract Mr. Madison, she found she couldn't bring herself to mind.

All too soon, their ascent ended and Lord Averly carried her to the room she pointed out. Instead of setting her on her feet, he continued to carry her to her bed, where he laid her against a mountain of pillows.

"Comfortable?" he asked, with a slight catch in his throat. Admittedly, his original intent in carrying her up to her room had been to shock her, which it had. However, the pleasure he derived from holding her so close against his chest and then laying her out on her bed had nothing to do with amusement.

Sometimes her loveliness overwhelmed him. An irrepressible urge rose up to slowly pull every pin from her hair, allowing him to tenderly run his fingers through every silky tress.

Her voice brought him back. "I should be fine, now, thank you." She barely spoke above a whisper, as though unwilling to break the mood. Uncertainty filled her eyes. Charlotte Henwood was many things, but uncertain had never been one of them. Again he asked himself, as he had numerous times before, just what did she want from him? When the gossip had begun to dissipate, her need for his presence did so as well. Yet she still demanded his assistance.

Another thought, unbidden, came to his mind: Why did he let her? He could easily have talked his way out of helping her, yet he never did. True, he had been avoiding her for the past few days, but that had only been to keep her from so fully occupying his mind. Suddenly shy, leaning over her bed while she merely looked up at him with troubled eyes, he had no idea what to say.

She murmured, "I really should have thanked you for coming to my rescue this morning. I suppose I owe you a favor now."

A faint smile played upon his lips. "I shall endeavor to think of something particularly trying for you to do. It's only fair, after all."

He watched those glorious lips move again. "Fair?" she asked lightly. Finally, they became too tempting. "What exactly do you mean by th—" Unable to stop himself, he leaned in and took them.

There was nothing delicate about this kiss, nothing Miss Henwood could prepare for. Michael plundered, his previous gentleness forgotten. All of his worry over her well-being and all of the frustration that had been building up in him for days now—months, more than a year, even—was poured into that kiss.

Mistaking her moan for protest, he held each side of her face to soothe, yet hold her still, softening his own lips while his thumbs stroked her cheeks and jaw. No longer bombarding her with his desire, he gently moved his lips over hers. Charlotte couldn't decide which was worse. Or better. All she knew was that she wanted more.

When she let a small sigh escape, Michael took the opening to explore her mouth, lightly stroking her tongue with his own.

Charlotte wrapped her arms around his back, pulling his torso down to her. There was an ache in her breasts that could only be appeased when pressed against his chest. Or so she thought. Instead, it became nearly agonizing and heavens, she wanted more.

Michael found himself sprawled next to Miss Henwood as he deepened the kiss. Her breasts pressing into his chest was more than he could bear. Trying to calm himself, desperate for air, he moved his lips to her jaw and neck, sliding his fingers into her hair. Her taste was intoxicating. He needed her whole body against his. When he slid his leg between hers to press his thigh against her mound, she hissed in a breath. Bringing his hand to her breast, he could feel her heart beating erratically, even through her layers of clothing.

He levered himself up to return to her mouth. But when he looked into her eyes, the desire mingling with confusion and surprise stopped him. No man had done this to her before.

Their kiss in The Griffin had been a chaste peck compared to this. He had no right.

When he pulled back a hint farther, she raised her head as if to follow his lips.

Instead of leaning down to again bring his mouth to hers, he moved off the bed entirely, nearly stumbling over his own feet in his haste. He thought he heard Miss Henwood utter a broken, "No," as he pulled himself away.

Staring past the bed and out her window, he waited for his heartbeat and breathing to come back under control. There was another part of him that would take quite some time to come back to normal.

Hopefully the rest of Miss Henwood's staff would not be lurking about in the corridors when he made his exit. It would not be at all appropriate for them to see the Viscount Averly at full mast. Actually, it was not so appropriate for Miss Henwood to see him in such a state, either.

Running his hand through his hair, he turned to face the door. Michael froze in shock. The wide open door. What had he been thinking? Anyone could have walked by and seen him attacking the lady in her own bed.

It was time to apologize. "Miss Henwood, I had no right to force myself on you in such a manner." He still could not face her. "It was not at all appropriate. Please accept my apologies." Running another hand through his mussed hair, he added, "It had only been my intention to invite you to another public engagement when we reached your room. I know I have been neglecting my duty to you for some time and I have not yet had opportunity to use the Averly theatre box."

He knew his excuse sounded weak and perhaps a touch absurd, but it was the best he could muster. Forming complete sentences had become a newly challenging task. Besides, he *had* been considering extending an invitation to the theatre.

When he heard rustling, he turned around to see Miss Henwood move to sit farther up in bed. "I like the theatre."

"Ah. You like the...Ah. Of course you do." What in the world was happening? She should be throwing things at him. Raving. At least issuing a few carefully-phrased set-downs. Instead, she wanted to attend the theatre. "I can bring my carriage by tomorrow evening, if you have no other engagements," he said carefully.

"That would be perfectly acceptable." She smiled tentatively, almost shyly. Miss Henwood. Shy. Not that Michael appeared to be doing much better.

Michael nodded. "Then I shall see you tomorrow. To go to the theatre." He did not even know what was currently being performed. He had best find out. Bowing formally, Michael turned and left the room.

Suzie was waiting for him by the front door with his hat and coat. Not saying a word about His Lordship's mussed state, she merely handed them over and gave him a knowing smile.

# Chapter 16

S HORTLY AFTER WAKING the following morning, Charlotte penned a letter to her father, warning him of the strange Mr. Stowes. She did her best to leave out the more alarming details, while still alerting her father to the possible danger Mr. Stowes represented.

Once she finished, Lady Kinsey invited Charlotte to share a pot of tea—with the requisite brandy, of course.

Just when Charlotte began to wonder why Suzie wasn't present to share the brandy—er, tea—the redhead came bustling through the door, practically vibrating with excitement.

Taking a seat next to Charlotte's elevated ankle, Suzie took the last cup on the tray, poured a generous amount of brandy, and then filled whatever minimal space was left in the cup with tea. Her two companions waited patiently, while Suzie sipped happily from her cup. They both knew the signs. Judging by the energetic bounce of Suzie's foot and her satisfied grin, she had some stirring news to impart.

By the time Suzie made her way through nearly half the cup, Charlotte couldn't take any more. "If you don't tell me what you've been up to all morning, instead of attending to your injured friend, I will hide the rest of the brandy in a place you will never find it."

Suzie snorted. "I clean up after you. There is no hiding place you can think of that I have not already found. But good luck trying." She toasted Charlotte with her cup.

As Charlotte prepared a counter-attack, her troublesome friend went on. "Lady Kinsey sent me out this morning to gather a little information. We thought it odd that the strange Mr. Stowes knew you were riding yesterday and where to find you. You don't usually follow a set schedule, after all, and you almost never ride in Hyde Park."

Sending Charlotte a knowing look, Suzie continued, "Mr. Madison's groom said he had not noticed anything unusual that morning, until Mr. Stowes' fist connected with his face. We thought maybe someone else in the house may have seen something."

"The Madisons do keep an extensive staff," Her Ladyship added.

Alarmed, Charlotte interjected, "I hope you do not believe that anyone in their household is responsible for my attack. The Madison household staff has always been fiercely loyal."

Suzie and Lady Kinsey exchanged a look. Lady Kinsey sighed. "We didn't want to think that, but it was the best direction we could look in."

Quickly, Suzie jumped in. "In this case, it does not seem that anyone working under the Madisons is really at fault."

Properly distracted, Her Ladyship asked, "So you discovered something?"

Giddily, Suzie replied, "Oh yes, I did. I discovered a secret romance, of all things." After pausing just long enough to leave Charlotte and Lady Kinsey on tenterhooks, Suzie went on with her story. "It would seem that one of the downstairs maids recently became acquainted with a footman from the Earl of Tunley's household. Over the last few weeks, he's been bringing her flowers and sweets. It's quite lovely, really." Placing her hands over her heart, Suzie gave a mock sigh.

Charlotte was briefly distracted. There was something important about the Earl of Tunley that she needed to recall.

"Yes, very lovely. Now could you please go on?" Lady Kinsey asked in the politest voice she could muster.

After sending Her Ladyship a fulminating glance, Suzie continued, "It seems that after several visits, he became acquainted with Mr. Madison's household staff, particularly one of the grooms." Suzie waited happily for her story to fully sink in.

Charlotte shook her head. "I do not believe that is enough information to suspect a connection to the Earl of Tunley—a man I have never even met, nor do I know any member of his household."

Putting a finger up in the air, Suzie answered, "I am not finished. Tunley's footman—named Harvey-something, I believe—was invited to a weekly card night held by the Madisons' grooms every week. This card game took place late into the night immediately before your ride. I've seen the shenanigans that ensue over the course of those gatherings. All sorts of news can be exchanged."

Charlotte and Lady Kinsey waited patiently for the other shoe to fall. Observing the expectant expressions on her companions' faces, Suzie admitted, "Well, perhaps that isn't as much to go on as I had originally thought. But I did try."

"Uckfield!" Everyone turned to Charlotte at her outburst. She explained, "Papa mentioned in his last letter that he encountered a Lord Tunley in Uckfield. I thought it was most strange, although not especially relevant. But now...Perhaps we should keep a careful eye on Lord Tunley, to see if he has any interactions with Mr. Stowes."

"Just so, Charlotte," agreed Lady Kinsey. "This information should not be ignored."

Satisfied, Suzie added a touch more tea and well over a touch more brandy to her cup.

―――

They were at The Lyceum Theatre, of that much Charlotte was certain. Were anyone to ask her about the performance, the name of which she could barely remember, she would perhaps answer that there was a great deal of music and laughter.

Hopefully, Lord Averly would not be so cruel as to force a detailed discussion of the show on the carriage ride home.

Charlotte was surprised to be at the theatre at all, having expected Lady Kinsey to object to her leaving the house. Instead, Her Ladyship had practically insisted they go. The *ton* needed to see that Charlotte was none the worse after her ordeal. Showcasing Lord Averly's support was also key.

While Lady Kinsey and Ryder thought Lord Averly's conversation during the ride to the theatre was charming, Charlotte knew that he was not entirely comfortable. The mere fact that he would lead a conversation on something as insignificant as a theatre performance attested to his nervousness. His tone was similar to that which he used when she would intentionally say something that she expected him to find shocking. Admittedly, there was none of his usual censure in the conversation, but she noted how forced and almost stilted he sounded. Perhaps she had been listening for it, hoping that he was not so unaffected by yesterday's embrace as he pretended.

For the entire day, she had continued to think upon his kiss. Could she even classify it as just a kiss? Novels and stories from the faster ladies in her set had never prepared Charlotte for this. Lord Averly made her want. She hadn't the foggiest idea about exactly what it was she wanted, but she knew that she wanted it.

Well, perhaps that was untrue. She knew she wanted more of that kiss, or whatever it was. Just thinking about it, remembering, left her squirming in her seat.

For ages, Charlotte had been waiting for that one moment when Lord Averly would lose all control and do something shocking. She had spent nearly all of their acquaintance attempting to bait him. And now he had done it. What in the world should she do now?

Slumped in her seat, Charlotte let out a desolate sigh.

---

Michael found himself a bit embarrassed. Clearly he should have ascertained exactly what was playing this night. A musical farce was all and good for whiling away a dull evening; but Miss Henwood was an intelligent woman. She needed Shakespeare, or something stimulating and unique to challenge her senses. Every time he glanced over at her, her eyes appeared notably glazed.

Would it be better to merely make their excuses now? He had not intended to take her out for the evening and bore her. However, Ryder and Lady Kinsey seemed to be enjoying themselves. It would be unpardonably rude to leave before the end.

Halfway through the first act, Michael leaned to her and whispered, "Miss Henwood, I believe you have been unusually quiet for most of the performance. I hope you are enjoying yourself?"

Charlotte's fears had come true. He wanted to know what she thought of the play. She had not been able to focus on a single word. Perhaps if she kept things vague, he would not realize her lack of attention? She nodded in response. "It's quite entertaining."

That was all? This was not the Miss Henwood with whom Michael had become familiar in the last few weeks. Raising his brows at her soft response, Michael added, "Have you nothing to say about the male lead's propensity to stand in front of his female counterpart whenever she delivers her lines? What of the chorus' strange chicken-like dance? You must admit that was a bit ludicrous."

Overhearing, no doubt with her unnatural eavesdropping skills, Lady Kinsey said, "Lord Averly, I can assure you that Miss Henwood would never be so unkind to the performers. Ladies do not usually discuss such things so openly."

Abashed, Michael answered as best he could. "I apologize. I believe I have become used to Miss Henwood's banter over the last few weeks. I had expected her to provide some commentary on the performance." Michael did not add that he was becoming accustomed to Miss Henwood's amusing commentary. Goodness, at what point did her ridiculous observations become entertaining to Michael?

Ryder snorted at that. "Michael, I hate to deliver such news, but this is the norm for Miss Henwood. She has always been a thoughtful, careful conversationalist. Why would a lady discuss such things with a gentleman?"

Michael nearly laughed, but then he saw his brother's face. Ryder was completely serious about Miss Henwood. A hint of doubt pertaining to his perception of Miss Charlotte Henwood began to creep into Michael's thoughts.

A while later, Lady Kinsey expressed a desire for lemonade. Forgetting her ankle, Charlotte immediately offered to get her a glass. Charlotte hoped her head would clear a bit once she was no longer in such close proximity to Lord Averly.

Immediately rising, Lord Averly offered to assist Miss Henwood in bringing everyone some lemonade. Charlotte refrained from mentioning that her goal had been to escape him for a moment or two.

Most chaperones would have objected to her charge being alone with another gentleman, but Michael was banking on his impeccable reputation to see him through. Lady Kinsey merely nodded as he left with Miss Henwood leaning heavily on his arm. Had he known Her Ladyship's motives for letting them both go, he would have been quite surprised.

Michael wished to make reparations for yesterday's kiss. There would be no seduction this evening, thank you very much. Running a nervous hand through his hair, he reminded himself that perhaps it would be better for his personal comfort to stop thinking of seduction entirely.

They had not yet reached the main hallway. Still unobserved, Michael stopped their progress. What could he say? The draw to kiss her again was almost insurmountable. Remembering her look of uncertainty after he had practically mauled her, he tried to distance himself while still holding her arm.

Charlotte also wondered over their kiss, just as she had been wondering over it for the entire performance so far. She wanted to ask him if kissing always felt like that. She was almost sure that it didn't, that it couldn't, but she had to know. Their first kiss had not been nearly as exciting. Did this mean it would only get better over time?

Goodness, if kissing always felt that way, it was a shock that people did not spend every waking hour engaging in the act. Then again, if the population of England only spent its time kissing, nothing would ever get done. She ought to commend England's citizens for putting the needs of the nation first.

Clearly Lord Averly did not feel as she did. He had barely spoken to her all evening, and even now avoided standing too close. Had she done something unpardonable in allowing him to kiss her? Would it be uncouth to ask? Oh, hell. The man always expected the worst from her, anyway; why not say something?

He beat her to it. "Are you all right? After yesterday, I mean." Awkwardly shifting his weight from foot to foot, he went on, "It was not my intention to…overwhelm or shock you. Yet I know I must have."

"Oh." Charlotte had never expected Lord Averly to want to discuss the kiss. "No. I'm fine."

Lord Averly nodded. "That's fine then." Excellent. Everything was fine.

"Yes. Thank you for enquiring." How does a lady ask a gentleman to kiss her again? Charlotte reminded herself that ladies did not ask gentlemen to kiss them in the first place. Lady Kinsey would never approve.

No, Charlotte thought, it would not be remotely acceptable to ask His Lordship outright. Could she perhaps trick him into doing it? What if she pretended to trip on her ankle and fell into his arms? No, he was too tall for her to achieve immediate access to his lips. Well, she had the entire second act of the play to come up with something.

Lord Averly studied her face intently. "Are you worried about this Stowes man? Is that why you're so quiet?"

She sighed. Why must he bring up such unpleasant things? She had spent so much of the evening contemplating their kiss that she had not even thought about Mr. Stowes until now. Carefully, she answered, "I confess, I am concerned about Mr. Stowes. Just thinking about what else he might do has left me feeling ill. I hate knowing there is someone out there who wishes to do me harm, when I have done nothing I can think of to cause him unhappiness."

Charlotte let out a frustrated huff as she went on, "I know Mr. Madison will look into the matter as thoroughly as possible, but in the meantime, what can I do? I don't want to lock myself in my room, hiding from the world. I absolutely will not allow this Stowes person to do that to me."

While Charlotte knew she was capable of overseeing her finances, her home, and her role in society, raving madmen were not something for which she was prepared. Their management was covered in neither Mrs. Madison's nor Lady Kinsey's lessons on etiquette and propriety.

After some thought, Michael said, "I do believe it would be best if you avoided being alone for a while." Charlotte did not seem to like that idea. "What I mean to say is you ought to have more than just a servant or maid accompanying you when you go out. I will speak with my brother. I'm sure that between Ryder and me, you should have no reason to go out alone when you leave the house. We will do our best to look after your safety." Despite the circumstances forcing him to do so, Michael found he looked forward to spending more time with Miss Henwood.

Charlotte wanted to argue with Lord Averly, truly she did. But her practical side won out. She allowed a moment of surprise over having to wage an internal debate in the first place.

She typically behaved in a more logical and reasonable manner, but somehow Lord Averly's presence impelled Charlotte to ignore her more rational side.

"I doubt I have any real choice in the matter." Charlotte refrained from mentioning that only a day or two ago, she would have had to threaten Lord Averly bodily harm to make him visit her. Instead, she politely consented to allow the two Skidmore brothers to check in on her.

---

By the time they rejoined everyone in the Averly theatre box, Michael could almost convince himself that everything had returned to normal. Miss Henwood would be looked after, and hopefully protected from this Stowes character. Finally relaxing, he settled in to enjoy the second half of the show.

Lady Kinsey thanked Charlotte for her lemonade, masking her disappointment that Charlotte and Lord Averly had not been gone for very long at all. Something had to be done to spur these two into action.

Perhaps she ought to have another private discussion with Ryder. That boy wanted his brother to be happy as much as she wanted to see Charlotte well-settled. Playing around with textile imports and iron mines was a lovely challenge for the mind, but it did nothing to warm the heart.

# Chapter 17

A S PROMISED, RYDER VISITED Charlotte and Lady Kinsey the following afternoon, arriving shortly after Mrs. Madison dropped in to check on Charlotte. Imogen thought it would be best to leave Julia at home, what with the commotion surrounding Charlotte. Charlotte fully agreed with her.

They spent some time chatting and then listening to Lady Kinsey lecture Ryder on his numerous faults. Charlotte was again distracted from the conversation. While she found Ryder entertaining, Lord Averly was the man she wanted to see.

Not wanting to overtax Charlotte, and perhaps feeling a touch guilty about the predicament she was in, Imogen did not stay too long. Charlotte understood, although she wished she could have spent more time with her friend.

Somehow Lady Kinsey must have convinced their other acquaintances to give Charlotte a few more days to recover, as the house remained almost entirely empty but for the three of them. Well, four. When no one else was present, Suzie typically took tea with the ladies. As Ryder was practically part of the family by now, he never minded.

Currently regaling her companions with the gossip she had gleaned from Mrs. Dayton's lady's maid about Miss Dayton's secret meetings with an inveterate gambler, Suzie did not hear the door sound. In fact everyone was so entranced with the possible scandal that they all jumped upon hearing a *Halloooo* call throughout the house.

At first, Charlotte was excited about the prospect of finally seeing Lord Averly again. However, when Suzie left to lead the gentleman in, Charlotte was forced to bank her disappointment.

Mr. Hampstead cheerfully made his bow and took a seat near Charlotte. Suzie followed behind him and let out a quiet *Humph* while she collected her teacup and flounced out of the room. Although Suzie loved hearing the gossip surrounding London's favorite rake and would certainly be eavesdropping outside the door, she loathed having her stories stopped midway through.

Smiling, Mr. Hampstead poured himself a cup of tea. "Well, Miss Henwood, you seem to be recovering quite nicely. Not that I ever expected any less. You have always been the absolute picture of health and beauty."

In response, Charlotte rolled her eyes. "And you, good sir, continue to be the quintessential charmer. Doesn't it ever become exhausting, thinking up one outlandish compliment after another? Not that you aren't perfectly correct, mind you."

Lady Kinsey and Ryder both leaned back in their seats, enjoying the new entertainment.

"But tell me," Charlotte continued, "what have I done to bring you all the way across Town twice in one week?"

Mr. Hampstead laughed, showing the dimples that he desperately tried to hide. He only lived a short walk away—one that he wished he made more often. Although Miss Henwood had made her lack of romantic interest in him abundantly clear, he found her an intriguing friend.

"I braved such a long and arduous journey in order to ascertain your health and happiness. After all, the last time I saw you, I was being herded out of your drawing room like cattle. My intentions are entirely honorable, I swear it." When she raised her brow at that, he added, "And perhaps I wouldn't object to sharing in a little gossip, if you can stand it. Have you heard that Miss Dayton is not being allowed from her house after she was caught planning an elopement?" Everyone turned towards the door when Suzie let out a disgruntled groan.

Mr. Hampstead gave a broad smile. "If that is my favorite informant hiding behind the door, you might as well come all the way in. Oh look, you even still have your teacup. I'm sure you're parched." When Suzie took her seat, doing her best to appear superior, Mr. Hampstead made a gallant display of filling her cup.

Ryder had become used to Mr. Hampstead's outrageous flirting. He often wondered why Miss Henwood had not originally allowed the man to publicly court her, instead of his brother. While Hampstead's character was not considered spotless, most of the gossip surrounding him was hazy, at best. Then again, Ryder did so very much enjoy the effect Miss Henwood had on Michael—even if Michael didn't. The good and virtuous Lord Averly needed to have his life shaken up just a bit.

Lady Kinsey leaned in to have her cup filled, as well. "You know, Mr. Hampstead, Suzie was just telling us all about the Daytons. I'm sure she would have reached that part eventually. She prefers to have a good build-up first."

Tilting his head to the side in acknowledgement, Mr. Hampstead answered, "Meanwhile I always aim for the shock and awe factor. Both approaches have their merits, I'll give you that. But, now that we have determined our respective gossiping styles, what has Suzie told you of Miss Eleanor Trivett?"

"Ellie?" Charlotte could not contain her outburst.

"Oh, are you acquaintances? I never thought the two of you shared the same circles. Then perhaps you know about her engagement, already. I appear to have failed you again."

So that was what Caroline Trivett had been about to tell her during that brief visit. "No," she said. "We merely grew up in the same town. It was really more of a village than anything," she added, as though that explained things. And perhaps it did. After moving to London, Charlotte discovered the joys of being able to choose one's friends, as opposed to being friends with someone because there was no one else.

Mr. Hampstead continued on with a sigh. "I suppose you ladies already know the intended gentleman, then. And I was so pleased about being the first to tell all."

Charlotte laughed. "I can assure you that this is all news to us." When Suzie smirked at Charlotte, she added, "Well, most of us. Perhaps you would like to tell us who the ever-so-lucky gentleman is?"

"Oh, I wouldn't want to steal Miss Perkins' thunder. Surely she already knows all the details."

Suzie answered by throwing a biscuit at Mr. Hampstead, who laughed. He said, "Oh, I'm so sorry. Does this mean that I just might have actually beat you to a juicy bit of gossip? My, how that must irk you. I do hope you can forgive me."

As Suzie reached for another biscuit, Lady Kinsey chose to put the conversation back on track. "I am sure Miss Perkins will forgive you this once, if you decide to tell us who has asked for Miss Eleanor's hand."

Magnanimously, Mr. Hampstead bowed his head. "The newly affianced gentleman is none other than the illustrious Darren Gregory, Earl of Tunley," he announced.

Charlotte and her companions were shocked into silence. Not one of them had given any thought to the earl until Suzie had uncovered his seemingly tenuous connection to the Madison household. As the silence progressed, Mr. Hampstead seemed less and less pleased with his news, glancing around anxiously.

Finally, Lady Kinsey broke the silence. "I don't actually know very much about Lord Tunley, although his name continues to come up this week. He came into his title perhaps two years ago?" When Mr. Hampstead nodded, she went on, "I never met him, but heard stories. Other boys from his school days called him mean-spirited. Since he became the earl, the stories stopped." Leaning in, she gave Mr. Hampstead an intent look. "How in the world did he meet the Trivetts?"

Mr. Hampstead did not expect those piercing gray eyes to hold him captive. No wonder people spilled all their secrets to this formidable woman.

Nervously, Mr. Hampstead went on. "Well, er, actually, that is the most interesting part of the story. He met the Trivetts in your part of the country," he said to Charlotte, glad to pull his gaze from Lady Kinsey.

It was Charlotte's turn to be on the spot. Unfortunately, all she thought to say was, "Uckfield? Good God! Whoever goes to Uckfield?"

"Unless they are very lost," Ryder added.

"Or love pudding cake," Suzie said.

"Apparently to meet the Trivetts." This from Mr. Hampstead.

"Well, whoever wants to meet the Trivetts?" Charlotte let out a shocked laugh. "I apologize. That was unkind. I didn't mean it." She paused. "My father must have encountered Lord Tunley during the earl's courtship. At least that piece of the puzzle is explained."

Mr. Hampstead merely shrugged at Charlotte's seemingly harsh words. "The Trivetts were not the *ton's* favorite new acquisitions when they first showed up. Too much pretention, combined with overwhelming country manners. It never came across very well."

Charlotte laughed again, "I never knew you to be such a snob, Mr. Hampstead! If that's what you think of the Trivetts, what must you think of me?"

Mr. Hampstead reached over and patted Charlotte's hand. "My dear, in you, it's charming, as always. Besides, you have the impressive gift of always knowing when to remain silent, yet so mysterious. The *ton* cannot resist wanting to know everything about what hides behind those lovely brown eyes."

Forgetting herself, Charlotte rolled her lovely brown eyes at that. If Lord Averly heard Mr. Hampstead refer to her as mysterious, he would call the man out for being a liar. Surprised that Lady Kinsey did not chastise her, she asked, "Why was Lord Tunley in Uckfield at all? You haven't told us that part."

Mr. Hampstead shrugged. "Well that's just it. Nobody entirely knows how they met. I was hoping that you would be able to enlighten us on what exactly Uckfield has to offer. Perhaps the beer is brewed there with magic? Or all the ladies are as breathtaking as you?"

"I cannot say. I have no clue why Lord Tunley would want to go there, unless he is a particular connoisseur of pudding cake. Are you sure he did not already know the Trivetts and plan on visiting them?"

He shook his head. "I believe that is the only part of the story that is confirmed. Miss Eleanor Trivett was extolling the virtues of country living and explained that she met the earl when he decided to seek the same. Nevertheless, the match is quite the *on dit*." With a coy look, he added, "Or at least it was up until your own little escapade a few days ago. Was it truly as shocking as everyone says?"

The mention of Charlotte's attack brought up everyone's back.

Lady Kinsey cut in before anyone else spoke. "We are doing everything in our power to keep Miss Henwood safe. However, if you came here today to glean more information about those events, I'm afraid there isn't much to tell." She sent meaningful looks to Suzie and Ryder, both of whom squirmed in their seats under her direct gaze.

Mr. Hampstead did not miss the exchanged glances. For once, the overwhelming charm left his voice, replaced with a serious tone that Charlotte seldom heard. "I can assure you, Lady Kinsey, that it was not my intention to spread more news about Miss Henwood across Town. I came over only to determine if she was well." Sensing that now was a good time to leave, Mr. Hampstead rose. "Now that I can see that everything is well-managed and that you are healthy, I shall take my leave."

Guilty that he felt unwelcome, Charlotte rose as quickly as she safely could. "Mr. Hampstead, you must forgive us. Everyone is still on edge after what happened. I have even been assigned a personal guard until the smoke clears."

At Mr. Hampstead's confused look, Ryder waved his hand. "Personal guard, at your service. Please don't ask me to carry your packages after visiting the shops."

Mr. Hampstead gave a light smile. "I'm certain there could be no one better to ensure Miss Henwood's protection. However, if you would like a reprieve from your services, I'm more than willing to offer myself for the task." His tone was devoid of its usual playful gallantry. Mr. Hampstead truly meant to help.

As Ryder prepared to inform him that he had things under control, Charlotte cut him off. "I'm certain that would be excellent, Mr. Hampstead. Feel free to come visit us whenever you like. You are always welcome."

Relieved, Mr. Hampstead nodded and took his leave. Charlotte knew Mr. Hampstead well enough to trust that his intentions in visiting today had been good. Hopefully the man would feel welcome to return soon. Charlotte refused to allow the happening with Mr. Stowes to set her friends so greatly on edge that they could no longer trust each other.

# Chapter 18

MICHAEL DID NOT VISIT Miss Henwood that day because he intended to observe the townhouse at night. He had decided to conquer her fear that Stowes might be waiting outside her home during the hours when she was less protected.

Unfortunately, he had failed to prepare for just how uneventful those hours would be. It had been just over an hour, in fact, and already Michael was wondering if he ought to leave.

Did anyone even live in the surrounding houses? A few streets away, he could hear a carriage or two pass by, but he had only seen one go through Miss Henwood's street.

The moon was bright enough to reflect across the dark gray cobblestones. It would be hard to miss anyone sneaking around from his position, in a dim doorway across the road. But then again, he could not see the back of the house.

Michael had already learned everything he could from Ryder about his overnight stays in the Henwood town home. It would not do at all for anyone to have seen Ryder entering her house in the middle of the night.

Michael now knew there was a small garden to the rear of her house, with an entrance into the kitchen. It was the way Ryder sneaked in following his more eventful evenings. There was apparently a key hidden under a cheerful flower pot near the kitchen doorway.

Making his way around the back, Michael stepped over a low fence that provided the only barrier between the front of the house and the small garden at the back. Although it was night, he was able to appreciate the carefully tended shrubs and rosebushes. There was no doubt in his mind that Miss Henwood was responsible. Perhaps it was her way of bringing the country with her to London.

Seeing no criminals hiding in the bushes, Michael prepared to make his way back around the front. As he turned, he saw a candle flame flicker back and forth through the kitchen window. According to Ryder, Lady Kinsey and Suzie slept like the dead, so they were unlikely to be wandering the kitchen at night. As for Miss Henwood, although she had insisted that her ankle was fine back at the theatre, she still ought to be keeping off it whenever possible. It could be a housemaid. He knew they had at least one more in the household beyond Suzie.

A low-lying shrub crunched under his foot as he made his way to the kitchen window. Cringing at the unexpected sound, Michael hopped sideways to avoid damaging any further greenery. No doubt Miss Henwood would not take kindly to the destruction of her well-loved garden.

Michael stood on his toes and peeked in through the kitchen window. Unfortunately, even with his above-average height, he could not get a proper view inside. He made his way up the steps to the kitchen door, carefully stepping around a multitude of pots filled with various blooms as he went. There was barely any room for his feet. The small window in the door should be just the ticket.

When he finally had a view into the room and the face lit by a single flickering candle, Michael let out a relieved breath. The lady of the house had her hair bound in a loose braid and had not even bothered to put a wrap over her night shift as she rooted through cupboards searching for who knew what. He was unused to seeing her in such a sweetly domestic scene. Michael forced down the memory of her hair unbound and wild after a ride across the countryside.

It would be perhaps unwise to be caught watching her through the window. Apparently Miss Henwood's household was safe from any intruders tonight. To avoid disturbing anyone else in the house, he turned to make his way back.

—⁓—

Despite her knowledge that Ryder and Lord Averly were keeping their eyes on her, Charlotte could not sleep. She tossed, she turned, she beat her pillows, but still no rest came. She would relive the scene with Mr. Stowes, turning it into a nightmare, as she obsessed over the threats he had made.

When she forced herself to think of something else, her thoughts immediately turned to the kiss she had shared with Lord Averly in this very bed. The fear was then replaced with a burning desire so acute, she could not bear to simply lie there with her lips tingling and her breasts and other parts aching to be touched.

Finally, after tossing back and forth, desperately praying for sleep, she rolled out of bed. Lighting a candle, she took herself downstairs to the library. She briefly thought about reviewing her personal accounts and correspondence, but knew she might not get any sleep at all if she came across something new and exciting.

Perhaps a book and some warm milk would do the trick. Recalling how uncomfortable she had been just a few minutes before, she decided something stronger than warm milk would be required. Charlotte felt a soothing glass of wine would do the trick. Knowing that nothing too intellectually demanding would help her sleep, she selected an unusually vapid sensation novel from the drawing room.

The moon was close to full that night, and sent pale light through the windows and onto the carpet. Making a game of stepping only in the darker areas to avoid disturbing the pools of light, she made her way to the kitchen.

These types of night trips were not common for Charlotte, so it took her a moment to find a glass, and even longer to find the wine. She had no idea that her trips back and forth across the room with her single candle would give an outside viewer the impression of a furtive search.

She whirled around in fright at the sound of a pot falling over outside, dropping her candle. The flame went out as it hit the floor. She couldn't easily see outside the kitchen windows, but she could certainly hear the string of creative curses that followed the first sound. Her heart nearly beating out of her chest, she decided to make a run for Lady Kinsey's room. Just as she turned on her bare heel, she recognized the voice, although the curses were certainly something new to be heard from those lips.

Amused, Charlotte made her way to the door and opened it. "What was that part about hammers and the hairs of my arse? It seemed particularly creative."

Michael froze mid-creep when her call reached him. Embarrassed that it had been Miss Henwood and not a villainous intruder that drew him to the kitchen door earlier, Michael uttered one more heartfelt curse as he turned around.

"Don't think I didn't hear that one too!" she called.

"Ladies are not supposed to repeat curses that they overhear. It is not seemly."

"Nor is cursing in the presence of a lady in the first place, Lord Averly," Charlotte replied. "For shame." Amused, she leaned against the doorframe as he made his way back to her. "And what, pray tell, were you doing in my garden in the middle of the night?"

"I felt that it would be wise to see if anyone was watching your house at night. Just in case." Best to admit it, before she discovered his reasons for circling her house. Miss Charlotte Henwood was not one who would appreciate being patronized for the sake of protecting her nerves. He went on quickly, hoping to ease any concern she might have, "No one was. I saw neither hide nor hair of anyone, until I noticed your candle flame."

Charlotte did not enjoy knowing that he felt compelled to keep watch on her house. At least he seemed to think she was safe for the night. Calm enough to offer him a fractured smile, she teased, "Don't tell me you thought I was an intruder in my own home."

Shaking his head in answer, he said, "Now that I can see that you are perfectly safe, I'll just make my way home."

"But—" Charlotte didn't want him to leave so soon. Not when she finally had him to herself. What should she say? "Wouldn't you like some tea after standing out there in the cold? You must be freezing." According to Mrs. Madison and Lady Kinsey, tea solved all afflictions man could ever possess. Not that Charlotte thought Lord Averly was afflicted with anything. Still, it was the best offer she could think to make.

Michael merely shook his head, still too embarrassed to notice that perhaps Miss Henwood's motives had less to do with casual politeness than he assumed. "We are almost fully into summer, so the night is actually quite refreshing and not at all cold. I will certainly see you tomorrow, Miss Henwood." With that he made his bow and turned.

Was the man daft? Of course the night was not too cold. She was merely desperate for an excuse to make him stay. Except she really should not be trying to lure Lord Averly back into her house in the dead of night; it simply wasn't done. What had possessed her? "Oh dear."

Michael immediately halted and made his way back to her. "Is everything well?" Leaving her feeling nervous or unsafe after all she had been through would be unpardonable.

"Erm. Well? Oh, I-I thought that I heard something. I am sure it was just the wind. I wouldn't want you to concern yourself. After all, you said you had not seen anyone near the house." *Charlotte! You naughty girl. It is not at all correct to make up excuses to draw an unsuspecting man into your home. Shame on you!* "I believe it was coming from the drawing room, but I could be mistaken." *Could be? You're not just mistaken, you're inventing the whole thing.* "Quiet," she whispered to the voices.

"Sorry?" Lord Averly said, as he passed her to stride into the drawing room. He kept his left arm out, making it clear that she was meant to stay behind him. Seeing his alertness at the possibility of a threat that she knew didn't actually exist, Charlotte felt even worse.

She merely watched as he made a careful circuit of the darkened room. He then moved to the mantel, where he lit a few candles.

No longer searching the room for anything odd, Michael was able to again take in Miss Henwood's appearance. He wasn't certain, but he believed he could see her nipples through the thin fabric of her shift. Perhaps he merely wanted to. The burn of desire that so seldom left him in Miss Henwood's presence erupted into flames. Shocked at his immediate physical response, he resolved to leave right away. Hurriedly, he said, "The room seems empty enough. You should be fine for the night. Do you think you'll be able to sleep now?" Did his voice sound as strained as it felt?

Charlotte almost laughed. If only he knew what else was keeping her up, beyond things that went bump in the night. "I had only come downstairs to pour a glass of wine. I confess I had already been having trouble sleeping before finding you knocking over my flower pots."

Entranced by the way the yellow candle flames caressed her face, he found he could no more look away from her than stop breathing. God, how he wanted to take her into his arms and draw her upstairs. To comfort her. He wanted to comfort her. "Yes. Well. I hear that can work very well for sleeping troubles." Finally, recognizing that if he continued to stare, he would put action to the fantasy spinning in his mind, he looked away. Pretending to carefully inspect the ormolu clock on the mantel, he went on, "Now that everything appears to be in order—"

"Perhaps you would like a glass of wine, as well, Lord Averly. If you are up and about this late, you must be having trouble resting too," Charlotte interrupted.

Although she knew it shocked him, Charlotte walked to him to remove his coat. After all, she was dressed only in her nightgown. It was only fair that they even the score. In addition, the act of putting his coat back on would slow down a hasty retreat. Bewildered by the entire situation, Lord Averly actually allowed her to take it off.

Before he could utter a polite objection, she placed his coat over the back of a chair. "Come, sit down," she said as she gestured to the settee. Her tone may have been warm and inviting, but there was a hint of steel underneath.

"I'm not sure that would be entirely appro—"

But Miss Henwood was already making her way out of the room. "I won't be long. I just need to pour the glasses. Do make yourself comfortable."

Dazed, Michael made his way to the settee and sat down, only to immediately come to his feet in shock. "I'm being seduced!" Luckily, his outburst came out more as a hoarse whisper. Too confused to sit still, he began to pace.

Michael knew all the tricks in order to convince a woman to sit down with him and share a drink and...so on. Surely Miss Henwood had no intention of allowing such things to happen. She may sometimes be the bane of his existence—although he had to admit that she had been on excellent behavior recently—but she was a thoughtful and kind woman, as well. He had seen that clearly in the last two weeks. She was always willing to listen closely and intently to any story, good or bad, from a close friend. People trusted her. Trustworthy women simply did not lure men into their homes and seduce them. She was probably frightened of being left alone. Michael ceased pacing and sat back down on the settee, resolved to alleviate her fears.

Charlotte had no idea what she was doing. Yes, she wanted to share another kiss with Lord Averly, but beyond getting him into the house, she had no plan. Having wasted enough time fretting in the kitchen, Charlotte returned to the drawing room with two glasses of red wine.

She had needed to slip the stems of the two glasses between the fingers of the same hand in order to take the candle with her from the kitchen. Her hands, therefore, were much too full when she stumbled on a rug after coming back into the drawing room. Although she caught herself from falling entirely and only a bit of wine sloshed onto the floor, she could not easily disentangle her feet from the blasted rug. She would have the rug removed first thing tomorrow morning and burned, that's what she would do. Embarrassed, she looked up as Lord Averly rose to take the glasses and candle from her and place them on the table.

Taking her hand to lead her to the settee, he said, "No doubt your ankle still bothers you, despite what you told me at the theatre."

Charlotte merely smiled nervously. A moment passed where they neither spoke nor looked at each other. Finally, uncertain what to say, Charlotte leaned forward to take up her wine.

Michael watched her slowly raise her glass to her full lips. It was torture. The woman must know the uncomfortable effect she had on him. How could she not? In but a few moments the evidence would be more than noticeable. Now would be a good time to look elsewhere. Taking a deep breath, Michael did just that. Unfortunately the elsewhere his eyes were drawn to was Miss Henwood's bosom. Good Lord, what was he to do? "Miss Henwood, are not you concerned about catching a chill? Would you like me to fetch you a shawl?" *And for the sake of all that is holy, cover your bosom?*

Would it not have been childish, Charlotte would have stomped her foot. Here she was, doing her very best to engage in just one more kiss with Lord Averly, and the man was concerned about her catching a chill. In the middle of June?

"Like you said before," she replied, "it is quite warm tonight. I should be fine."

Damn. Now what? A strategic retreat was in order. "That is good. Now that I can see that everything is well, I should perhaps make my way home. It is late, after all."

Before he could rise, Charlotte leaned forward and took his glass of wine up from the table, saying, "At least have a sip before you go. To help settle your nerves," she teased. She handed him his glass.

Looking her in the eyes, and not at her lips or that blasted transparent night shift, Michael took a sip. Maybe the wine would help dampen his raging desire for this woman. Desperate, Michael practically upended the glass of wine as he gulped it down.

Setting the empty glass back down, he turned to Miss Henwood to make his excuses. Her mouth was shaped in a perfect "O" of surprise and uncertainty. Had he insulted her with his haste?

Flustered, Charlotte rose to lead him out. She could not keep her unwilling guest any longer. It was only a kiss, after all. Surely, there were many other men in the city who would have no qualms with kissing her. Only, Charlotte wanted that kiss from Lord Averly, and to hell with everyone else. Still standing, she took up her own glass and gulped the remaining wine down before setting it back. Hopefully, it would help firm her resolve.

Michael stood as well, wanting to apologize, "Miss Henwoo—"

He was never given a chance to finish because her gorgeous, incredible lips were firmly pressed against his. Michael's last coherent thought for some time was the realization that she was, in fact, trying to seduce him.

How wonderful.

# Chapter 19

———◆◆◆———

CHARLOTTE WAS SHOCKED at her own actions, truly. Not that she had any intention of stopping. Oh no. Although she had nearly needed to stand on Lord Averly's boots to reach him, she would take her kiss and ignore any of his protestations.

Michael, however, had no protestations to make. He nearly burst his breeches when Miss Henwood had the audacity to slide her tongue into his mouth. Caught up in the whirlwind that Miss Henwood created, Michael wrapped his arms around her waist and pulled her body tightly against his. When this proved not enough to satisfy, he bent down to slide his thigh between her legs.

Charlotte may not have known exactly what pressed against her hip or what it meant, but she did know that the pressure of His Lordship's thigh nearly made her go mad. Warnings flashed through her mind, telling her that she needed to end things before she lost her sense of self, but she refused to heed them.

Wanting to feel more of her against him, Michael lowered them both to the settee. Miss Henwood acquiesced, instinctively pulling him down to cover her. He stretched out over her slender frame. This time when he slid his leg between hers, she gasped in pleasure.

This was quite a bit more than the mere kiss Charlotte had so greatly craved. Charlotte did not care. Tonight she intended to discover just what it was about Lord Averly that so fascinated her. She would not stop until she had all of her answers. Unknowingly, she raised her pelvis to press her torso more firmly against Lord Averly. She had an ache there that only made her more desperate.

Although she had no idea how to appease her raging needs, Lord Averly seemed to have some clue. As he ran his lips up her neck and rained kisses across her cheek, she felt his hand sliding up the outside of her leg, raising her gown with it. Finally he was caressing her abdomen and side, his palms gliding over her skin.

Her body surged against his as he grasped her waist in one hand and took her breast in the other. Charlotte was so lost in the alien sensations, she had not even felt him lower the neck of her gown. Only in the far, far recesses of her mind was there any thought that ladies ought not to be doing such things.

Michael heard himself groan. She felt even more incredible than he could ever imagine. And God, how she wanted him. Finally, he gave in to his own desires and brought his fingers delicately to her mound. That little voice in the back of his mind reminded him that his actions had firmly passed beyond the realm of gentlemanly. He almost hoped Miss Henwood would throw him off her. Well, perhaps that was not entirely true. Instead of the shock and affront that he expected, she dug her fingers into his hair, pulling hard and forcing him to kiss her even deeper.

He began to stroke her, working her into a madness that brought her only pleasure, combined with a sort of desperation. Despite her innocence, Charlotte moved against his hand, increasing the pressure and speed. Soon she was writhing against him. Michael nearly came as he felt her frenzy, it was so unexpected and satisfying.

Charlotte had never imagined that the feelings beginning at the apex of her thighs and coursing through her body could be so overpowering. The muscles in her upper thighs twitched uncontrollably, making her frantic. Heaven was only so far away. Finally, Lord Averly found the exact spot that she never even knew demanded his attention. Breaking their kiss,

Charlotte cried out as the waves began pouring over her, her body rocking to its own rhythm against Lord Averly's hand.

Michael looked down upon her in shock. He had not even needed to slide his fingers into her passage to bring about her release. He had never known a woman to come so fast and beautifully before. The mere thought left him nearly shaking in need and arousal. Would she be even more responsive with him inside her? He absolutely had to know.

He had to have her. And it must be now.

But perhaps not on the settee.

Michael looked behind him to see his knees bent awkwardly, ankles in the air, in an unconscious attempt to fit on the settee. Miss Henwood was not doing much better. One leg was bent between his thighs and the other hung off the side. This would never do.

Slowly Miss Henwood's eyes blinked open, revealing a lazy smile. While she regained some semblance of self, Michael raised himself off her and carefully brought her to her feet with him. Although still wobbly, she went quite willingly. To prevent any further distractions, he raised the shoulders of her night dress.

Although there were not a great many coherent thoughts floating through his mind, Michael did note that he really should have discovered this trick of turning Miss Henwood so pliant and complacent much sooner. It would have relieved a great deal of the stress in his life.

After clearing his throat, he began, "Miss Henwood, perhaps now would be an appropriate time to take you to your room."

Still a bit dazed, she answered, "'Miss Henwood.' How very formal that sounds now. Perhaps you should switch to calling me Charlotte. Don't you like Charlotte?"

He smiled. "I believe Charlotte is a perfect name."

Giving him a slightly loopier smile in return, she smoothed her hands up his chest and behind his neck. "May I now call you Michael? I think Michael is also perfect."

Although it pained him—he was in quite a bad way—Michael gave a mock sigh and answered that he would tolerate her calling him by his given name. Michael did allow himself to slide his hands around her waist and pull her close for a brief kiss, even though that mere touching of lips left him even worse off. "But, for now, we really must adjourn upstairs."

Charlotte nodded and allowed him to lead her up the staircase. They both knew which room was hers and quietly went in, Michael firmly closing the door behind him. He would not make that mistake again. Before the door closed, he thought he heard some shuffling coming from the room across the hall. Which room was Lady Kinsey's and which was Suzie's? He knew the maid was allowed a guest room upstairs. The practice was quite unusual, but Michael knew that Charlotte considered the girl more of a friend than a servant.

In addition to the disquieting noise, the short walk up the stairwell had given him time to consider his actions. Miss Charlotte Henwood deserved to be treated like the lady she was. It would not be remotely appropriate for him to take her before marriage.

Soon, that terrifying word "marriage" began floating through his head. Usually the idea made him cringe, and perhaps not too long ago, the idea of marriage to Miss Henwood would have seemed even worse.

But now? After seeing the effect he had on her, the various expressions crossing her face as she came for him? Quite frankly if marriage was a way to ensure that he could do such things again, perhaps he would tolerate it.

There was no denying he had always wanted her. First, he had met Charlotte, the sweet, playful, talkative country miss and had desperately desired to make her his mistress. And then he had encountered the elegant Miss Henwood, refined lady of the *ton*, who had both fascinated him…and made him want to throttle her.

But this Charlotte Henwood, the one standing before him and the one he had come much closer to in the last fortnight, was now both of those women at once. He was fascinated by, sometimes wanted to throttle, and desperately desired her. Yet he did not mind the contradictory sensations one bit.

He was now mostly in control of his agonizing need for her. He could wait. So long as he went home soon, to at least take his desire to hand—he needed to go home very soon.

Before he could prepare a little speech to make his excuses, as one should always be polite, even in a lady's bedroom, Charlotte had something to say. He could see her turning a question over and over, trying to work it out.

Michael sighed, "Yes, Miss Henwood?"

"Charlotte," she replied, distracted.

He teasingly cocked his head, hoping his attempt at nonchalance would keep her from noticing just how much pain he was in. "Yes, Charlotte?"

He watched her nod to herself before clearing her throat. "I am almost certain, for I am an avid student and read nearly everything I can find." This was no surprise to Michael, so he merely waited. "I am quite certain that...Well, what I mean to say is, am I still actually a...well, a virgin?" The last bit came out more as a whisper than anything else. In fact, after saying "virgin," Charlotte looked suspiciously about the room, as though Lady Kinsey was possibly hiding in the armoire, ready to jump out.

"Yes, damn it. You're still a bloody virgin." Michael turned from her as he reached up to run his fingers through his hair. He wanted to laugh and cry at the same time. Nervously, he tried pulling at his hair in an attempt to regain some semblance of control. But not even the pain distracted him.

Had he really just spoken to her in that manner? The tension was getting to him. Even though the physical evidence of his arousal had lessened, that did not mean he felt any better.

Bloody hell, he felt worse, especially knowing that he could have taken her on that damned settee.

Blast. He had no right to blame Charlotte for his own decision, even if that decision was entirely for her own benefit and not at all for his.

"I apologize," he said, turning back to her. "What I meant is that nothing happened that would have, erm, rendered you a non-virgin. I did not completely, that is to say, I didn't do everything that there is to be done." *How very specific, Michael. Knowing Miss Henwood, she would certainly have no awkward questions to ask after that brilliant statement.*

Charlotte only had one more question to ask, as she stepped closer and looked up at him. Even in the moonlight, Michael knew her eyes glowered with new feminine power.

"So there's more?"

All of the blood drained from his head, pooling somewhere farther south. Images flashed through his mind of all the "more" they could engage in. His hands were shaking, he wanted her so strongly.

He may have been in a physical agony more acute than he had ever imagined in his worst nightmares, but he had to leave that very second. Charlotte Henwood deserved better than some hasty tumble in the dark of the night. If he remained any longer he could not be held responsible for his actions. God, how he wanted to sink his fingers back into her thick black hair. "No, no, no." He couldn't.

Charlotte was confused. "No?"

Michael shook his head, vehemently. "No, there's more, but I really ought to go. Not that I wouldn't love to show you the more. But right now is probably not the best time. Or place. Or time." Oh, Lord. He had to make a quick escape. "Er, sleep well." He touched her face and considered how terrible just one more kiss would be for him.

He leaned in, watched her eyes slowly slide closed. He was losing himself. He stopped just before his lips touched hers and pulled back. It would definitely be too much.

Only an inch away, his breath lightly teased her lips. "I will see you tomorrow," he whispered, then turned and made a hasty retreat. At least he had enough self-control to remember to leave carefully through the kitchen door. He would, above all else, protect her reputation.

—⁓—

Charlotte spent a great deal of her morning cursing her idea to go to the kitchen last night for a glass of wine. After Lord Averly had left her, she had not achieved a second of sleep. How could the man have left her in such a state? It just wasn't fair.

There she was, finally given a chance to know exactly what that magical thing shared between men and women is, and the man abandons her before her questions were answered.

Desperately wishing her mind would latch onto something else to ponder, Charlotte rose from bed early and put on a morning dress. Suzie likely had only just risen. Charlotte smiled at the thought of her maid, who was really just more of a nosey friend than anything else. Suzie had been enjoying the night life that London offered and loved telling Charlotte her—carefully worded—stories the next day.

Charlotte almost couldn't contain her surprise in finding the playful redhead in the drawing room. As Charlotte walked in, Suzie turned around and slowly waved two wine-glasses from side to side, cocking her head in silent question. Charlotte covered her face in embarrassment, never catching the giddily pleased look that crossed Suzie's face.

"Well," Suzie said, "I had best get these cleaned before Lady Kinsey comes down. Lucky for me I woke up early today." In fact, ever since Lady Kinsey woke her up after a mysterious man below Her Ladyship's window broke half of their flower pots, Suzie had been impatiently waiting for day to come.

Concentrating hard on not giving anything away, Charlotte merely asked if Suzie knew whether breakfast was prepared. Suzie was a very clever interrogator. Charlotte would have to be well-guarded.

———

Lady Kinsey had already served herself breakfast, but remained in her seat in the dining room, sipping her now-tepid tea, while patiently awaiting her young charge's arrival. She had the look of a queen preparing to pass judgment over a misbegotten subject. Charlotte avoided Lady Kinsey's eyes when she entered the room with Suzie right behind her.

Lady Kinsey maintained her air of nonchalance quite masterfully. Charlotte Henwood had been up to no good last night, and Lady Kinsey intended to find out just what that "no good" was.

"Good morning, Frances." As with Suzie, Charlotte intended to use short sentences in addressing Her Ladyship. The less words spoken, the less information they could glean. She merely gave Her Ladyship the most convincing smile she could and then went to fill a plate.

"Good morning, Charlotte. How did you sleep last night? Did you have pleasant dreams? I hope your sleep wasn't interrupted, like mine." Lady Kinsey paused to give Charlotte a chance to respond, but Charlotte merely looked at her plate with what felt like an expression akin to abject terror. Lady Kinsey turned to Suzie. "What about you, Suzie? Was your sleep at all bothered? You know, it's funny. There I was, drifting off into a pleasant, relaxing slumber when all of a sudden, I hear a strange crashing sound outside my window. My window, as you know, Charlotte, looks down onto our sweet little garden. I've always loved the smell of the flowers wafting in through my open window." Charlotte was blushing now, she could feel it.

Her Ladyship went on. "And then after this crashing sound, I heard a jumble of curses from a readily identifiable masculine voice." Charlotte's blush was practically burning her face at that point. "But, of course, that must have just been a dream. Because if I were awake, I simply know my charge would not have opened the door and allowed that gentleman into the house for who knows what sorts of activities."

Charlotte thought hard for some sort of explanation that would free her from that direct stare. There was none. She let out a shaky breath and sat down. "Good thing it was just a dream, then." She had no idea where the nerve came from, but she managed to elegantly pick up her fork, and begin her meal.

Impressed, Lady Kinsey snorted. Most people would have caved under her intent glare, but not Charlotte Henwood. The girl was certainly learning. Well, she would let her have this small victory. Lady Kinsey doubted that anything unpardonable had taken place the previous night. Lord Averly was not the sort of man to readily take advantage of a young woman. If he did so, he would know the consequences of his actions.

Frances Harrow, Lady Kinsey, rose elegantly, shook her skirt out and prepared to leave the room. In the doorway, she paused and said softly, "Charlotte, I want you to know that I do trust you and, in all honesty, am not entirely certain I wish to know exactly what transpired last night. However, if anything irreparable did occur, it is your duty to tell me, just as it is my duty to take care of you. Do you understand?"

Charlotte had been too nervous to taste any of the breakfast she was forcing herself to eat, but now the bite filling her mouth had an odd, sawdust-like flavor. She really had no reason to feel guilty. No matter how much "more" she wanted from Lord Averly—Michael—he had proved himself a true gentleman. She swallowed the sawdust. "I do, Lady Kinsey, and I promise that I will always keep you informed. When necessary."

She watched Lady Kinsey nod and promptly leave the room. Although her appetite had been soundly destroyed, Charlotte waited a few minutes before leaving as well.

True, Michael had not ruined her in the only sense that should matter to a potential husband. However, Charlotte was quite certain he had ruined any other man for *her*.

# Chapter 20

DESPITE HER EFFORTS, CHARLOTTE could not find distraction in her favorite morning pursuits. Usually she enjoyed the few sweet hours before the *ton* rose and began making the social rounds. Enough time had passed since the day Michael had sent everyone from her drawing room for her friends to begin visiting her again.

Already a few notes indicating an intention to drop by in the afternoon for tea had arrived. A few other acquaintances sent well-wishes and their apologies. She assumed their families did not want them visiting her, if doing so could endanger them. It was almost a relief to know that people were no longer avoiding her due to something they thought she had done, even if they were avoiding her, nonetheless.

At this very moment, Charlotte could not find anything enjoyable to do. She listlessly attempted to learn a new tune on the pianoforte. She then picked up the sensation novel she had sought the previous night, but could not concentrate on a single word. She spent a bit of her time in the garden, mostly fixing up the mess Michael had made. Each of these activities felt more like a duty than the usual joy it was.

None of her current investments had any recent news so she could not add anything to her notes. Maybe it was better that business had become boring, while she had so many other concerns.

There was simply nothing to do to distract her from last night's memories. Never in her wildest dreams had she imagined that a man could have such an effect on her. She had read Shakespeare (her father had never forced her to read the editions edited for a lady's gentler disposition) and a great many Greek plays, and seen prints representing less than properly clothed Greek statues. She had assumed she was prepared.

However, last night had been a complete shock to her system in a remarkably satisfying way. Sadly, Michael could not simply knock on her back door every night, come in, and pleasure her. That would certainly not meet with Lady Kinsey's approval.

At that thought there was a knock on the front door. Charlotte could hear Suzie make her way to the front hall from the kitchen and let the newcomer in. It was a surprise that anyone would venture to her place of residence so early in the morning, until Charlotte heard Suzie say, in an obviously loud voice, "Why, Lord Averly, what a pleasure. Shall I see if Miss Henwood is in?"

Michael's response was somewhat quieter than Suzie's outburst, so Charlotte was forced to wait for Suzie to find her in the drawing room. Suzie was practically quivering in excitement. "It looks like our favorite viscount is here. Should I give you a moment to compose yourself? Oh goodness, you are only wearing your morning dress. That just isn't done."

Charlotte looked down at her dress in surprise. Suzie was correct; she had to change. Yet she didn't want to wait so long to speak with Michael. Besides, he had already seen her in her nightdress, although Lady Kinsey and Suzie were pretending that they did not already know that. She couldn't actually allow him to see her undressed without raising questions.

Oh dear. It was time to improvise. "My yellow and rose pelisse. It should be enough to make everything proper." Not fashionable, perhaps, but she would be appropriately covered.

Making a dash for Charlotte's room, Suzie was back in less than a minute with the pelisse. After all, the sooner Charlotte was properly dressed, the sooner she could listen in on what would likely be a very intriguing conversation.

Charlotte opted to allow for the single braid she had pinned around her crown that morning to suffice. Lord Averly had seen her in disarray on too many occasions to comment on just one more.

Shortly thereafter, Suzie led Michael into the room. He looked so well-rested that Charlotte nearly wanted to shoot him. He also appeared a bit uncertain, looking nervously from Charlotte to Suzie, who had quietly remained in the doorway, looking on as though she belonged there.

"That will be all, Suzie," Charlotte said in the most formal voice she could muster. Suzie had the gall to look insulted and even made a face at Charlotte behind Michael's back. Nevertheless she turned on her heel and stalked from the room.

As soon as she left, Michael made his way up to Charlotte, taking her hands from her sides and squeezing them. "Good morning, Charlotte." His deep voice flowed smoothly over her. She almost closed her eyes in pleasure.

Michael had not, in fact, shared in the same sleepless night as Charlotte. Although he had at first tossed and turned, reliving those kisses and caresses, he had found a couple of ways to relieve his stress. One of those had been the making of a firm decision on his part.

As he had lain on his side, watching the shadows of the moon reflect on the walls, he thought further on the subject of marriage. Just perhaps his bachelor friends had no idea what they were talking about when they exhorted the single life. Perhaps they had not yet met a woman who practically made them burst through their trousers at the mere thought of her delicate body.

Well perhaps they had—they were still men, after all—but perhaps that woman had not been a virginal unwedded lady. As for him, he had to confess that Miss Charlotte Henwood had been making him horribly uncomfortable in that particular manner for weeks now.

She never bored him. Sometimes she terrified him, but she certainly never bored him. She was beautiful, kind, and intelligent, if a little irresponsible with her reputation, although if she married him that would no longer be a problem. And good Lord, how he wanted her. Or had he mentioned that already?

Yes, marriage was becoming a more and more appealing idea. As soon as that thought took solid root in his mind, he drifted peacefully off to sleep, with the intention of seeing her as soon as he could the following day.

So here he was.

Charlotte was happy to see him, but perhaps a bit wary; he could read it in her eyes. He was also nervous, but for different reasons. How did one go about proposing marriage? He had certainly never tried *that* before. In fact, the closest he had ever come to such a thing had been when he had considered making Charlotte his mistress.

Here she was, looking up at him sweetly. There may have also been a little heat in her gaze. Good.

"Miss Henwood. Charlotte. You must know why I'm here." He pulled her in by her hands for a kiss. Only a small one to help him continue. Her lips were even already moving. She wanted his kiss. Or she was actually saying something...

He leaned in, giving her his ear instead of his lips. "The door." No. No, he wasn't here for the door. Perhaps she was still tired from the previous evening's exertions? She said it again, this time a little louder, adding an obvious head-jerk in the direction of the entrance to the drawing room. "The door."

Shocked, he swung around. Not again. He immediately stalked to the drawing room door and closed it. As he made his way back to her, he was certain he overheard a muffled curse from outside the room.

Now he could kiss her all he wanted. Taking her waist in his hands, he drew her flush against him and took her mouth. Because he only intended to give himself a few moments to indulge, he poured all of the passion he felt for her into it. When she ran her hands up his back, he forced himself to pull back. He could not go too deep right now.

"Miss Henwood." When that came out a touch raspy, he cleared his throat and focused on regaining his composure. "As you know, I find you an attractive, intelligent woman."

He took a deep breath. That wasn't so terrible. She was a practical, reasonable—currently somewhat confused—woman. Surely she would understand that his proposal would be mutually beneficial for them both. "I was hoping you would do me the honor of becoming my wife." Usually in plays and stories that exact phrase elicited positive results.

Charlotte did not answer.

Had he rushed too quickly to the actual proposal? Standing here now, he realized that he had not even brought flowers, or discussed his intentions with Lady Kinsey or Mr. Madison. Did Charlotte consider his approach completely uncouth?

In fact, Charlotte had not remotely expected this conversation. True, she had remained wide awake most of the night, thinking about and reliving what she and Michael had shared. Yes, she had fretted over what their relationship meant now, but she had not truly thought over their future. A brief wave of euphoria swept through her, but she forced it down. The manner in which he presented himself gave her pause. How could the man simply walk into her home and have the first words out of his mouth be a marriage proposal?

Most ladies grew accustomed to a man through a courtship and came to expect a proposal after a certain period of time. This courtship, however, was all a sham in the first place. Bloody hell. What did a woman usually do with, "Hello, you seem clever, let's get married"?

Her silence adding to his apprehension, Michael said, "I know that you get on well enough here, on your own." His voice lost its formality in his hopes to convince her. "But if we marry, no longer will the *ton* scrutinize your every move. You won't have to worry about harming the Madisons. They will no doubt obtain even greater social clout, due to their association with a viscountess."

He watched her eyes narrow. Could a woman's eyes narrow in joy? Probably not. He needed a new tactic. What else did she need? Perhaps a bit desperate, he went on, "We'll combine finances. My estates are varied after becoming the viscount. We can go to any one of them, until this whole situation calms down. You'll be safe and out of harm's way."

Charlotte was not pleased that almost all of his reasons surrounded protecting her from the Madison debacle. This should be any woman's dream. Goodness, her friends would have a fit if Charlotte rejected him. But money and safety? She didn't care about those things as much as she should, although she did care a little more after that ride in Hyde Park.

She looked into his eyes, trying to determine his true feelings, but saw nothing other than an uneasy, guarded look. There was none of the heat and passion she found in his kisses. Here and now, he was so contained and unexciting. Had he rehearsed his words before coming to her? "I don't want to go to one of your properties, like some secret mistress. I have no wish to hide myself away like that."

Now was probably not the time to mention that only a few weeks ago, Michael had desperately wanted to make her his mistress. The idea of taking her far away from London and locking her away, where only he could be with her, was unexpectedly exciting. And not something he should tell her.

None of these thoughts registered on his face. One of the first skills he had been forced to develop after becoming the Viscount Averly was the ability to mask his thoughts. All of a sudden, the *ton* wanted to know everything about him, his interests and habits. He had developed a more standoffish demeanor as a form of self-preservation. Here and now, her response would likely change his life. He needed that mask more than anything right now.

She went on. "I don't want to leave London at all, until everything here is resolved. Harry gave us a new direction to investigate. I refuse to give up."

Michael was already shaking his head before she finished. "I don't see why you cannot allow Mr. Madison to manage this. Everything that is happening to you seems to have been caused by his business decisions."

How could he say that after everything the Madisons had done for her? Michael may not know her very well, but he should know how important her friendship with them was. "No. I was a part of those decisions and I refuse to leave them alone in this. If you do not understand that, then perhaps you do not know me at all. I appreciate your concern for my safety, but marriage should not be the only solution."

Charlotte needed time to process everything and at this hour, after so little sleep, she had not a clue what to do about anything. She hoped her panic did not register on her face. Not while he managed to be so dignified and controlled.

She did not intend for her statement to come out as a rejection, but Michael took it that way. With forced calm, he said, "Need I remind you that our acquaintance grew because you needed my brother and me to provide you with some semblance of security, both socially and physically?"

Why did the man continue to argue with her? "There is clearly something you do not understand, Your Lordship." Charlotte bit her words out to keep from yelling. "The only protection I need from you is the kind that I have already specifically requested. A proposal of marriage is carrying that duty a touch too far."

Michael began pacing. "But surely you can see that things have changed. Stowes could come after you again at any time. We still don't understand why he wants your father to give up the ironworks. It could take longer than we would like for Mr. Madison or your father to take action."

"My *father* to take action?" she repeated in a flat voice.

"Surely he will release the shares after he is fully apprised of the situation?" Michael's question was intended to comfort Charlotte. Instead of relieved, she appeared incensed.

Charlotte had thought Michael respected her ability to make her own decisions. She could damn well protect herself without her father's intervention.

After a moment, she smiled. Michael took no comfort in the expression. "Lord Averly, I feel it has become necessary to inform you that I am the one who manages the Henwood finances—or do you think I read *The Times* purely for the scintillating gossip and entertainment? In case it has not already been made clear: I have no intention of letting this man intimidate me into relinquishing my shares."

Baffled, Michael went silent. How was this possible? What woman could easily access the information needed to make the sorts of decisions necessary to invest wisely? Charlotte might have Mr. Madison to help her learn. At first. But the Madisons had spent a large portion of the previous year abroad. Charlotte would have had to do a great deal of reinvesting on her own. According to Ryder, the Henwood investments had grown exponentially in the last year. He had not indicated that Charlotte was solely responsible. If this were true, Miss Henwood had certainly done well for herself and her father.

The more Michael considered this news and the many things he had learned about Miss Henwood in the previous weeks, his amazement lessened. Charlotte was, without a doubt, incredibly competent, perhaps even brilliant.

Unfortunately for Michael, it took him a bit longer than Charlotte liked for him to reach this conclusion. "Lord Averly, I am coming to the realization that you may not understand me at all. I do not believe there is anything more to be said."

Snapping back to the moment, Michael refused to give up so easily. "Miss Henwood, I understand that you are not one to always choose the more conventional method, but—"

"Lord Averly! This has nothing to do with conventionality! We are discussing my entire future. Despite what you seem to think of my intellect, I am not one to make a decision of this magnitude without thinking everything through."

Michael had a feeling that reminding Charlotte of her many impulsive moments would be unwise. Instead he said, perhaps equally unwisely, "You must realize that marriage is the only acceptable option after the night we shared. It is the right thing to do."

Could Michael actually see her pulse beating violently in her neck? For some indefinable reason, he doubted her response had a thing to do with romantic passion. That was his last thought before the explosion hit.

"*The right thing?*" Charlotte cried. Flinging her arms up in exasperation, she went on, "Why must you always do the bloody right thing? How can you stand being so perfect? To hell with you and your bloody good intentions!"

Bewildered, Michael had no idea how to answer her. He had spent years working to become the man he was today. Of everyone, he expected Charlotte to accept that. After all, she was not the same person he remembered from his time in Uckfield. The Miss Henwood before him possessed a strength and confidence he did not recall from that first meeting. It pained him to discover that while Charlotte had improved her own person and situation, she could not appreciate the efforts he had made to truly earn his position as a member of the peerage. She refused to accept the man he was today.

There was nothing else he could think of to change her mind. He couldn't threaten her reputation. She only wished to avoid causing the Madisons any embarrassment. Besides that, she would know he was bluffing if he threatened to divulge last night's events to the *ton*.

No. There was nothing else to say to persuade her. Instead he gave her as formal a bow as he could muster and left the room, too angry and confused to so much as offer a good-bye.

On his way out, even Suzie avoided eye contact as she handed him his hat and greatcoat. He opened the door for himself and left.

---

Suzie managed to impress Charlotte with her silence. It would have been too much to expect Suzie to leave her be entirely. But there, also, Suzie impressed her. While Charlotte moped around the house, again trying to find any activity to occupy her thoughts, Suzie drew a heavily-scented bath. Usually Charlotte would have found lavender overpowering, but today, the floral aromas helped distract and soothe her.

How could Michael not recognize her need to support the Madisons? If not for them, she would never have come to London and escaped her small town of Uckfield. They had taught her how to achieve financial security, thus preventing her from having to throw herself at the first man who would have her. They were a second family, filled with love and kindness. She had a duty to do everything she could to repay them. Not only that, she *wanted* to repay their kindness.

She thought Michael had understood that, especially after seeing everything she had already endeavored to help them. Ending the rumors would have been good for her, but it was more important that the Madisons remain protected.

While she did not doubt the correctness of her decision, she wished she had been more prepared for it. Goodness, this was her first marriage proposal. Probably her last, as well.

She ought to have expected it after last night. Michael Skidmore was a man of honor. He would never abandon a woman like her after the sort of activities they had engaged in. Had he seemed more enthusiastic at the prospect of sharing his life with her, Charlotte honestly had no clue how she would have answered him. Instead, he listed all of the reasonable benefits of their potential union, most of which involved her protection. She could damn well look after herself, thank you very much.

Feeling oddly resolved to go out and discover which of the Cornish mine's investors was plotting against her and the Madisons, she quickly dressed and went back downstairs to look through her personal files. She needed to get the names of each and every investor.

Enjoying her new purpose—a purpose that did not require the assistance of one particular viscount—she ordered tea service from Suzie and awaited the guests who would likely begin pouring through the front door in just a few hours. It might even be less, considering how curious the *ton* could be.

However, before the tea tray ever arrived, a knock sounded on the door. Lord Averly would not come back after such a tepid proposal, would he? Before she could wonder what Michael had been thinking, she overheard a cheerful male voice engage Suzie in conversation. She could tell it wasn't Ryder, which left Mr. Hampstead. Oddly pleased that he was the first to arrive, Charlotte leaned back against the cushioned settee and sipped her tea.

A moment later, Mr. Hampstead burst into the room, an excited glint in his eye. "I have news." Instead of taking offense at her relaxed pose, Mr. Hampstead poured himself a cup and curled into the opposite end of the settee.

Charlotte merely raised a brow and waited patiently. Mr. Hampstead would need no further urging to start his story.

He began, "You gained my interest when you raised questions about Lord Tunley going to Uckfield. I must confess, it is a place that, had I even heard of it, I still would not wish to visit. Just the name makes a man cringe."

"Clearly you have never tried our pudding cake," Charlotte replied drily. "I'm sure after you have extolled the many virtues of my birthplace, you will get to the point."

"Well," he willingly went on, "I decided to discover what exactly transpired during his visit." He paused, waiting for some sort of encouragement from Charlotte.

Instead she said, "You know, we really ought to bring Suzie and Lady Kinsey in on this now. They are likely just as curious as I am."

Suzie called from the hallway, "I'll go get Her Ladyship straight away!"

Charlotte smiled at the excitement in her friend's voice. "It always impresses me how silent she can be. I mean, I know she is there, but I have no idea how she could be."

While they waited, Mr. Hampstead enquired about her ankle and health. Charlotte asked about his meddlesome, but sweet, mother. The woman was apparently traveling again. Hampstead thought it might be Scotland this time.

Lady Kinsey prepared herself surprisingly quickly. "Well, Mr. Hampstead," she said as she strode into the room, "I gather you have some interesting discoveries to reveal."

Unwinding himself, he sat up on the edge of the settee. "I think it would be better to say that I found more questions than answers. But I could not resist digging just a little bit deeper into Miss Eleanor Trivett's engagement. It wasn't that difficult," he went on. "Most ladies—you are apparently not included," he added teasingly, "find me to be a particularly pleasing catch, as do their mamas."

Mr. Hampstead paused, perhaps expecting the ladies to agree. When no one spoke, he rolled his eyes, but still continued. "I discovered that Mrs. Trivett was no exception to the rule. In fact, she was unusually excited when I began questioning her about her girls. Typically, most mamas do not appear so very anxious to rid themselves of their daughters."

Charlotte was surprised at Mrs. Trivett's lack of tact. The woman had always given the impression of supreme refinement and calm. But that was before Charlotte had traveled to London. Mrs. Trivett was a pale comparison to the women here. Besides, Ellie was already engaged. Caroline was the bluestocking of the two, much shyer and more reserved compared to Ellie. Perhaps Mrs. Trivett despaired of finding Caroline a husband. She shouldn't. Charlotte had no doubt that her friend would find herself someone perfect when she was ready. Caroline was patient and thoughtful and certainly attractive enough to catch the eye of most London gentlemen.

Charlotte felt that now was a good time to satisfy Mr. Hampstead's ego. "I'm sure the *ton* would agree that you are a *somewhat* impressive specimen of manhood, Mr. Hampstead," she teased.

Hampstead nodded regally at the compliment, and then continued, "Mrs. Trivett did not even seem to notice that I mostly led the discussion towards the engaged daughter instead of the unengaged one."

Lady Kinsey suppressed a chuckle as she said, "I'm sure you were inordinately clever."

Nodding, Mr. Hampstead went on. "Mrs. Trivett was quite pleased to have hosted such an impressive personage. She waxed on about how Lord Tunley absolutely adored country living. And of course, it was love at first sight with her sweet little Eleanor. Not that the Trivett girls aren't lovely, but I always thought Tunley would aim a bit higher."

When he rose and began to pace, they could tell he must be getting to the good bits. "I gather that Tunley encountered Mr. Trivett on his way to Uckfield and the gentleman invited Tunley to reside in his household. Tunley was more than happy to join him. The Trivetts are the most influential family in those parts—just ask Mrs. Trivett."

Finally, Suzie cut in. "You know, Mr. Hampstead, you are an excellent gossip and I do love the way you tell your stories. Nonetheless, I much prefer the way you tell us the shocking end first and then explain how it all happened."

Pretending not to hear, he continued, "It would seem that, while he thoroughly enjoyed his time with the Trivetts, Lord

Tunley desperately wanted to meet another resident of your sweet little town. In fact, the entire purpose of his visit was to meet a Sir Driscoll Henwood." Mr. Hampstead paused to allow his companions to take this news in.

Charlotte found her voice first. "I knew my father had run into the earl, but I did not realize Lord Tunley had specifically sought him out. I can't imagine why. The only connections I know of my father possessing here in London are Mr. Madison and a few other friends from his school days. He obviously is well acquainted with several gentlemen from Oxford and Cambridge, but none of those men occupy Lord Tunley's level in society. This is too great a mystery to resist," she added, leaning forward in her seat.

Mr. Hampstead replied, "The real mystery, in my opinion, was why Sir Driscoll Henwood had no desire to meet with such a noble personage as the Earl of Tunley." Charlotte could not contain her shocked expression. "Oh, did I not mention that? According to Mrs. Trivett, Lord Tunley was forced to venture uninvited to your home in order to meet your father, who had been patently ignoring him. I gather the earl returned a short time later in a foul mood. By then, I believe, he had found himself engaged to Miss Eleanor Trivett."

Charlotte suspected that her father had avoided Lord Tunley due to his association with the Trivetts. Although she trusted Mr. Hampstead, she did not want to tell him why the Trivetts and Henwoods were not close. No doubt, the challenge of trying to find out would be good for him. Mr. Hampstead needed something more to do with his time.

At that thought, a bubbly flurry in a rose spencer and ivory dress burst into the room, passed Mr. Hampstead, and made her way straight to Charlotte.

# Chapter 21

C HARLOTTE! I'M SO GLAD TO SEE YOU! I know I'm not supposed to be here, but I wanted to check on you for myself. I had hoped that arriving sometime before luncheon would beat your other callers here. Mama and Papa said you were fine and healthy, but I had to see for certain."

Miss Julia Madison had not stopped moving since bursting into the room. Goodness, she must have burst into the house as well, since Suzie was not available to open the front door. Charlotte really ought to chastise Julia for the excessive amount of bursting that she seemed to be doing, but it was such a joy to finally see her sweet friend.

Julia vibrated with excitement as she walked the room, waving her hands this way and that as she spoke. "I don't understand why Mama was so worried about me coming here. Honestly, I can't imagine that ruffian would come after you in your own home. And it really is my duty, as your friend, to ensure your safety, despite what Mama says. Besides, you would not believe the things people are saying. I've heard stories, ranging from you going out to the theatre as if nothing happened, to you taking to your bed, at death's door. Surely you can understand why I had to come for myself, can't you?"

Looking to Lady Kinsey first, Charlotte answered, "I can perfectly understand your concern. I know firsthand how fast interesting gossip can spread through Town. However, I don't want to be the one to get into trouble with your mother for your being here. She can be quite formidable."

Julia waved that away. "Oh, don't worry about Mama. She'll blame me entirely. But how are you? Does your ankle still hurt terribly?"

As Charlotte laughed at her friend's energy, she noticed another occupant of the room remaining as still as Julia was mobile. Arrested, she watched Mr. Hampstead, feeling a devilish smile creep onto her lips. Lady Kinsey and Suzie both noticed Charlotte's pause and turned to see what caught her eye.

Lady Kinsey's voice, even more booming than usual, knocked Mr. Hampstead out of his reverie. "Julia, perhaps you have not yet met our other guest?"

Although she hid it well, Julia was clearly mortified to discover another visitor. Flustered, she gave a delicate curtsey, avoiding eye contact with everyone, especially Mr. Hampstead. The flurry that was Julia Madison appeared to have calmed. Mr. Hampstead executed a perfect bow, again finding that charming smile of his and pasting it on his face. If the smile looked a bit more distracted than usual, no one commented.

While Lady Kinsey made the introductions, a slow blush spread across Julia's cheeks. Charlotte could relate. Not many women could withstand the onslaught of Mr. Hampstead's charm. "I am sure no one will find fault with Miss Madison checking upon the health of her friend," Mr. Hampstead gallantly announced to the room at large. His words were enough to ease Miss Madison's embarrassment. Charlotte, however, was forced to give Mr. Hampstead a second look. While certainly not a shy man, Mr. Hampstead tended to ignore innocent girls like Julia, preferring sultrier, more experienced women.

Still somewhat frazzled, Julia took a seat at the politest distance possible from Mr. Hampstead. Clearly, his words were not enough to fully gain her trust. "Well," she said. "I did not mean to interrupt your conversation. What were you all discussing before I intruded?"

The ladies each provided Julia with a different answer at once. While Charlotte answered "flowers" and Lady Kinsey said "parasols," Suzie said something about wanting to buy a miniature poodle. Shockingly, Mr. Hampstead remained silent.

At Julia's confused look, Charlotte went on, albeit a bit stiltedly, "I went shopping for a flowered parasol yesterday, er, during which we saw a woman walking her poodle. Suzie wondered if one could easily find miniature poodles for a companion. They are usually so large, after all."

As Lady Kinsey appeared to choke at her statement, Charlotte merely remained thankful that Mr. Hampstead had not also added something to the mix. The man could be diabolical if given the right incentive. Goodness, why hadn't he spoken up? No matter how awkward or inappropriate his words might be, he still felt no qualms in voicing his thoughts. That unique habit of his was one of the reasons the *ton* adored inviting him to their parties.

Charlotte sent him another look. When their eyes met, he made a show of examining his nails, feigning disinterest in the proceedings. Well, if he wanted to let the ladies take over, so be it.

Shortly thereafter, Charlotte ensured the conversation focused entirely on the latest fashion trends, particularly shawls. She had once overheard Mr. Hampstead complain about the invention of shawls. Charlotte assumed his opinion had to do with that garment's unfortunate habit of covering bosoms.

Exactly as Charlotte expected, Mrs. Madison arrived a short while later. While she said she would "discuss things later" with Julia, there was little heat in the threat. Instead, the ladies continued their discussion, thankfully taking Charlotte's mind off her current troubles. Mr. Hampstead made his excuses as soon as was politely possible. His parting smile seemed a bit more strained than usual.

Before they left, the two Madison ladies promised to return together, when the excitement had died down a bit.

Not too much later, the drawing room began filling with guests, well-wishers, and the occasional curiosity-seeker. Most of their visitors were polite, but every once in a while someone would begin asking a few too many questions. Lady Kinsey oversaw everything, managing to intercede whenever Charlotte appeared close to losing her temper.

There was quite a bit of interceding, as Charlotte's temper was unusually short today. Everyone else seemed content to blame such things on her fraught nerves, which merely fanned the flames.

It was not her nerves that bothered her, but Lord Averly. When he had first delivered his proposal, she had felt so angered by the reasons he had provided that she had not thought about what accepting him would mean. It was true that she would no longer be a subject of the gossip mills, but that should not be the only reason to marry someone.

They surely had to have some things in common, similar interests that could be discussed over the table at supper. So far, Charlotte knew she enjoyed making him uncomfortable in social situations and that they enjoyed the more carnal aspect of their natures. She supposed he was sometimes quite intelligent and responsible. And his teasing could make her laugh. Not to mention the enjoyment she derived from his kisses and so on, which could easily be lumped in with enjoying their carnal natures together.

A Miss Priestly interrupted her thoughts to enquire if she intended to attend the Ashton ball, or whether her injuries were still too severe. As Her Ladyship had been doing all afternoon, she smoothly answered for Charlotte that they would be there. The ball was the following night, so that was a bit of news. "In fact," Lady Kinsey went on, "I believe we ought to give Miss Henwood more time to rest her ankle before a night of dancing."

Still trapped in her thoughts, Charlotte barely noticed the room clearing. Lady Kinsey, on her way out, paused, as though considering whether to say something to Charlotte. Her eyes softened as she took in her obviously distracted charge, before she silently continued out of the room.

—⁓—

The Ashton ball was quite a crush, much to the hosts' pleasure. However, they would have been less pleased had they overheard the murmurings circulating. It would seem the Ashtons had invited a few less-than-noteworthy characters in order to fill the space.

Charlotte felt as though she were being slowly suffocated. Bodies pressed into her from all sides and she had to strain to hear her companions, let alone the music. She was not in the best of moods and perhaps viewed the gathering with more disdain than she usually would have. At first she had thought that going out would take her mind off her concerns. Too late, she realized that she would have felt better had she allowed herself to fully analyze her feelings regarding Lord Averly.

Despite the crush, her acquaintances managed to find her quickly enough. Nothing new and exciting had yet distracted the *ton* from their interest in her. It had become quite the thing to be seen in the company of Miss Charlotte Henwood. Lady Kinsey and the Madisons were serving as her guards for the evening, keeping the gossip-mongers at bay.

Currently she was in deep discussion with Miss Nelson. Charlotte seldom saw the shy young woman, but whenever she did, she enjoyed their talks. They primarily corresponded by letter. Miss Nelson could have put Charlotte's father to shame, with her knowledge of ancient Greek philosophy. It was a pity the girl's guardian was so protective of her, rarely letting her leave their house without her particularly dowdy chaperone in attendance.

Mr. Hampstead claimed Charlotte for their dance, although how he could hear the musicians over the chatter, she would never know. She was forced to observe her fellow dancers, especially those closest to the orchestra, to know when to move.

Judging by the large number of times she ran into the other dancers, it would seem almost everyone shared the same plan. Considering the amount of jostling, Charlotte was relieved that Suzie had insisted on wrapping a sturdy fabric around her ankle to lend her some support. Nevertheless, Charlotte avoided the usual bounces and kicks that most of her dances required.

Lucky for Charlotte, Miss Nelson danced to her left. Her partner had arrived with Mr. Hampstead, allowing the ladies to position themselves next to each other for the set. Miss Nelson would giggle each time they missed a step. Despite the growing soreness in her ankle, it was probably the first time Charlotte had fully enjoyed herself since the night before last.

Wishing she had not recalled that night and the following morning, Charlotte vowed to enjoy the rest of her evening, assuring herself that because the ballroom was so full, even if by some chance Lord Averly was in attendance, they would not cross paths.

---

After that miserable proposal, Michael had gone straight to Ryder and demanded his brother find a particularly depraved location where Michael could get searing drunk. For once curbing his curiosity, Ryder sat at a rickety table in a smoke-filled room and simply watched Michael get so smashed he could barely walk. Ryder then took Michael home and put him to bed. At four in the afternoon.

Upon rising late the next day, with a slightly unpleasant headache, Michael resolved to avoid Miss Charlotte Henwood as though she carried the plague. For the rest of his life. To hell with their agreement.

His plans for the evening included having supper at his club, then going over his accounts. If he was feeling especially adventurous, he might go out with Ryder again. He would not diverge from these plans in the slightest. No, not at all. Miss Henwood could slip and sprain her other ankle at the Ashton ball, for all he cared.

When he unconsciously found himself dressing in formal attire, Michael gave in and called for his valet to tie a stylishly intricate cravat and help him on with his greatcoat. Perhaps the plague would not be such a very miserable way to go, all things considered.

———

Michael was almost relieved to discover the crowded ballroom. Perhaps he could avoid Miss Henwood entirely if she had decided to attend. He should have expected her rejection. All that tied them together was essentially a form of blackmail; no matter that he had begun to enjoy their association. He must face the truth: Miss Henwood merely tolerated him because she needed him.

He must remind himself that he had no need for a woman who got herself into as much trouble as Miss Henwood did. The ideal Lady Averly would be a quietly elegant woman, capable of controlling her less than exemplary urges and ideas. At least in public. She would never consider using extortion to force a peer of the realm to take her out in society. But his perfect woman would also have the strength and intelligence to rebuild her family's finances from practically nothing. She would possess a kindness and willingness to listen to and help her fellow man.

Perhaps he should leave. The more he thought of all she had done—practically on her own, according to Ryder—the more she impressed him.

What seemed to be a cotillion came to a close and the dancers began making their way back to chaperones and friends. Of course, Miss Henwood would be the first person he saw. She had partnered Mr. Hampstead, at that. Surely she had not so easily fallen for his charm? At least she had not yet noticed

Michael. In fact, she appeared to be distracted by another party. Did he recognize the young woman with whom Miss Henwood spoke? It seemed he ought to. Ah yes, that was the young lady he had met in Miss Henwood's drawing room after her accident. The pretty blonde was shortly thereafter joined by another young lady on the arm of a dapper gentleman. When she turned enough for Michael to see her profile, he realized she was the near mirror image of the first pretty blonde.

He watched as the pleased smile on Miss Henwood's face faded into a mask of politeness. Michael really ought to stop staring at her. He could hardly even see her, after all, yet he could not bring himself to look away.

Now an older woman joined their party, distinctly aligning herself with the other three, seeming to want nothing to do with Charlotte. Judging by the set of Charlotte's shoulders, she was agitated. Not that it was any of his business, of course. Mr. Hampstead seemed perfectly capable of protecting Miss Henwood and, in fact, appeared to be delivering an impressive set-down. The crowd forming around the group certainly found it amusing. Why didn't the crowd disperse, then? Damn it all, it was none of Michael's business anymore. Charlotte had made it abundantly clear that she no longer wanted his assistance. Even as he talked himself out of it, he found his feet carrying him over to the group.

———

Charlotte was quickly coming to regret her impulse to approach Caroline Trivett, but this being the first time Charlotte encountered her old friend at a ball, she wished to give her regards. Everything had certainly begun well. Quietly conversing with a kind-looking young man, Caroline appeared to have been left to her own devices. Although Charlotte would have felt a touch ridiculous searching the crowd for Ellie and Mrs. Trivett, she did note that neither lady was present before saying her hellos.

Pleased to see Charlotte, Caroline enquired after her ankle and overall health. Caroline was describing her latest trip to Tattersall's, when Eleanor Trivett and another gentleman approached. Before Charlotte could wonder how she recognized Ellie's companion, Mrs. Trivett quickly made her way over as well. Squaring her shoulders, Charlotte reminded herself that it would be unlikely for the Trivetts to cause a scene. Mrs. Trivett had spent many hours drumming the need to appear dignified and composed into her daughters' heads—at least when they were in public. How convenient that they were all in a very public place.

Despite striding up to Charlotte as though prepared to declare war, Mrs. Trivett managed to utter a polite "Miss Henwood," upon reaching her and curtseying. She then introduced the unknown gentleman staring on in feigned ennui as the Earl of Tunley. Charlotte took in the slender gentleman with the silvered hair. So she was finally meeting the elusive Lord Tunley.

Mrs. Trivett went on, "And have you not yet heard that he and Miss Eleanor are engaged to be married?" Although the question was posed in a sugary-sweet tone of voice, there was no denying the pleased sneer on the woman's lips. Charlotte would never have taken Mrs. Trivett for a sneerer.

Resigning herself to the unpleasant encounter, Charlotte took a calming breath and offered her congratulations. Ellie stiffly accepted them. Charlotte wondered how rude it would be to remind the girl that she was not yet married to the earl. But no, they had once been friends. Besides, she could see how strained Caroline was.

Meanwhile, Ellie's earl was looking at Charlotte as though she were some fascinating imaginary creature, pretend boredom gone. When Charlotte sent him a curious look, he finally spoke. "It is no doubt a pleasure to meet you, Miss Henwood. I've heard so much about you." At that, Ellie sniggered. He went on, "If only Charles were here to share in this little reunion."

When he and Ellie met eyes, they appeared to be sharing in their own private joke.

Appalled, Charlotte realized that the Trivetts had revealed their version of the events at The Griffin to Lord Tunley. While the Trivetts avoided spreading their story among the *ton*, Tunley felt no such compunction.

Well, thought Charlotte, it would seem Lady Kinsey and Mr. Hampstead were spot on. The Earl of Tunley was not a remotely interesting or respectable man, and she wanted nothing more to do with him.

As Charlotte prepared to excuse herself, Ellie said, "You do remember my dear brother, don't you, Charlotte? After your last encounter, I am certain he shall never forget *you*."

At the mention of Charles, Charlotte's fingers tightened on Mr. Hampstead's arm. He sent her a commiserating look. A soon as possible, she knew he would extricate them from the Trivetts.

Glancing around, Charlotte noticed that some of the surrounding groups of people were avidly listening in on their exchange. The *ton's* ability to scent out disaster never failed to impress her.

Tunley patted Ellie's hand where it rested on his arm. "Come now, dearest. Now is not the time to spread unsavory...news." His announcement drew even more guests out of their conversations. Too late, Charlotte realized that Ellie and the earl had every intention of causing a scene.

Even if she did leave now, the curious gossip-mongers would spend the rest of the night drawing the story out of them. Her usually agile mind could not rest on an easy way to escape the potentially disastrous confrontation.

Good fortune continued to demonstrate its absence. Upon spotting Charlotte, Julia Madison stopped her previous dance partner as he escorted her to her mother. Quickly assessing the tone of the situation, she took a place to Charlotte's left, grasping her friend's hand in support. While she felt invariably less tense, Charlotte still wished Julia would not have to witness this.

What could she do? Deliver some clever set-down? Try her best to mar Charles Trivett's character before his story could sully hers? That method had certainly worked well for him back in Uckfield.

Mr. Hampstead shook his head as he said, "Tunley, I believe, by now, that people have learned to disbelieve whatever story you decide to concoct. Why, I remember just a year ago, you tried to convince everyone that Colonel Jones-Wright's mother was a French spy. Good Lord, man! The woman was seventy if she was a day!" This elicited several laughs from the growing crowd. "Not only that, but wasn't she Scottish? Not French, of that I am certain. If I recall correctly, you owed the colonel more than just a few guineas after making a particularly foolish wager." All laughter ceased. Not only had Mr. Hampstead discredited whatever story Lord Tunley intended to tell, he had also managed to imply that the earl was not entirely a gentleman.

Tunley sputtered before finally answering, "How dare you, sir! I will have you know that my charges were thoroughly investigated, as people *do* listen when I have something to say. I do my best to maintain what connections I can, unlike some people I could mention." Tunley paused theatrically before adding, "At least I can say that I have not been barred from my ancestral estate."

Several members of their audience gasped at that. The statement certainly gave Charlotte pause. Had she been so caught up in her own troubles that she missed the important and sometimes unfortunate happenings in her friends' lives? Although he hid it well, Charlotte could detect a hint of pain in Mr. Hampstead's eyes.

She was certainly more than prepared to defend Mr. Hampstead, as he had her, but it was not necessary. Julia spoke first. Thrusting her shoulders back and staring the earl straight in the eye, she said, "Do not pretend to have even a basic understanding of familial duty or responsibility, Lord Tunley. I believe everyone here can agree that Mr. Hampstead is a man worth respecting."

*Well said, Julia,* Charlotte thought as her lips quirked up at the corners. Several gentlemen in the crowd nodded in response to her forceful statement.

Finally recovered from Tunley's slander, Hampstead managed a mocking smile. "True to form, once again, Lord Tunley. Not only do you have the facts almost entirely reversed, but you've no doubt made up an entire scenario that has nothing to do with reality."

Mrs. Trivett and Caroline had remained silent during the entirety of the altercation, but at this they both stepped forward. No fool, Mrs. Trivett knew her daughter's future husband would carry things irreparably far if left to his own devices. She made a valiant effort to begin a new conversation about the earl's newest acquisition in horseflesh. Meanwhile, Caroline gently took her sister's arm. "Come, Ellie. I believe I would like a glass of lemonade." Charlotte sent her a look of thanks.

It was not to be. Before Caroline could lead her away, Ellie spotted something behind Charlotte's right shoulder.

"Charles!" she cried. "Look who is here. It is Miss Henwood! I know you have been avidly awaiting a chance to speak to her again after your last, most unusual, encounter."

# Chapter 22

IT SEEMED THAT MICHAEL was a touch too late. Why was that always the case when it came to rescuing Miss Henwood? Not that he had any intention of rescuing her. He simply wanted to ensure that she was well.

He would remain behind the dozens of people pretending not to listen in on her conversation. The woman was no longer his blasted responsibility, after all. Why, just look at the negative influence she had over his language, internal monologue or not.

No, he would remain here, where Charlotte would not notice him. Michael watched the man he vaguely recognized as Charles Trivett join the three ladies and the Earl of Tunley. He seldom encountered Tunley in the House of Lords, however whenever he did, he and the earl tended to firmly disagree on most issues at hand. This was especially true when it came to how Tunley believed the lower classes—particularly poor laborers—should be treated under English law.

One of the younger blonde ladies spoke, her voice turning shrill as it reached an unpleasantly high volume. "Where was it you said you last saw our dear Charlotte before she ran off to Town last year? I can't quite remember, but I seem to recall thinking it a bit odd," the voice whined.

Pleased to receive such a large audience's rapt attention, Mr. Charles Trivett answered, "Oh, Ellie, it was so long ago, I can hardly recall. Besides, it truly isn't a tale for a polite audience." His mother sent him a look of warning, but the polite audience in question was clearly enthralled; Mr. Trivett could not decide whether he ought to go on or remain silent.

Tunley did not feel as compelled to silence. "Oh, but I remember what you mean, Eleanor. Charles finally told us when I was visiting you in Uckfield. You had all been keeping it from everyone in the hopes of protecting the young lady's reputation. But, goodness, if a lady behaves as *this* one did, there really is only so much a gentleman can do." Tunley sent Charlotte a triumphant sneer at that.

Michael had heard enough, disgusted with the man's mocking tone. Although he wished he could hold himself apart, no one had a right to treat Charlotte Henwood in such a manner.

He paused in his forward movement. Would she resent him if he intervened? She had changed since they first met at The Griffin. She was prouder now. And stronger. There was a good chance she would object to him speaking on her behalf.

Before he could push his way to the front, Miss Henwood laughed. "Well, Charles, you may as well come out with the whole sordid tale, now! I certainly shan't stop you." When Mr. Trivett stared on in shock, she continued, "Well, go on, tell everyone—" Here she flicked out her wrist to include their audience, who promptly pretended to look somewhere else. "—how you found me waiting out a torrential rainstorm in a public house. In the morning, of all unsavory hours! It was quite a shock to the forward-thinking town of Uckfield, I can assure you," she added to the crowd.

Well, that certainly explained things. Miss Charlotte Henwood had gone daft. But then Michael swept a glance at the surrounding faces. One primary emotion ruled: disappointment. But not disappointment in Miss Henwood. No, everyone seemed displeased that Mr. Charles Trivett had built up their excitement for such a dull tale. Why should it really matter that Miss Henwood did what she could to shield herself from a rainstorm?

Charlotte had taken his story and practically ridiculed the man with it. Michael beamed with pride. Of course she could thwart the horrid Charles Trivett, son of a country squire, and his partner in evil, Lord Tunley. The woman was incredible. Trivett would be a fool to try to continue with his story.

Unfortunately, Mr. Charles Trivett was a fool. "Well!" he snarled at her in a desperate attempt to regain their audience's attention. "You seem to be leaving out the most intriguing part! Miss Henwood was not alone at that tavern. There was another gentleman present. Well, I use the word loosely, as he clearly possessed a questionable character."

Sensing new disaster, Michael began pushing his way to the front. The task proved more challenging than expected. Despite demonstrating a general disinterest in the proceedings, members of the crowd certainly were loathe to give up their positions.

Miss Henwood rolled her eyes at Charles. Michael looked behind him, expecting Lady Kinsey to be near enough to catch the gesture. "That man was more of a gentleman than you can ever dream of being, Charles Trivett."

Michael snorted. Trivett had not been a gentleman at all during their little interlude at The Griffin. Then her defense of him registered. Oddly pleased, Michael again slowed his forward progression.

Charlotte's reply left Mr. Trivett a bit red-faced. "So you do admit there was a man with you!" Not comprehending the effect her concession had on the audience, Miss Henwood merely glared in reply. People began whispering behind their hands and amused faces turned to ones of censure.

Perhaps she would forgive him just a little, were he to step in and help her. Michael certainly hoped so, because it would be a cold day in hell before he would let Charles Trivett destroy Charlotte's reputation again!

As Michael continued to push his way forward, some elderly woman began beating his foot with her cane. Evidently, she objected to his attempt to move in front of her.

While Lord Averly took a moment for the pain to recede, Charles Trivett proudly went on. "I cannot imagine how you could call that man a gentleman. He had the gall to claim to be a peer of the realm, when anyone could see he was dressed like the commonest ruffian!" Michael thought his dress was always quite smart, if perhaps a bit less colorful than fashion allowed.

But that was beside the point.

By now, both Miss Madison and Mr. Hampstead were voicing their objections to Trivett's story. However, the audience did not seem to care what they had to say.

Seeing the audience was firmly on their side again, Lord Tunley rejoined the dialogue. Speaking over Charlotte's friends, he said, "He claimed to be a peer? You never mentioned that part. You can't be serious!"

"A viscount, actually." Michael stepped forward. It was more of a limp than a step, but he preferred to believe his entrance was a touch more gallant. "And I am sorry you don't approve of my traveling attire, but I must confess to never understanding why a gentleman must wear his best if he intends to sit astride a horse all day."

Michael tried to contain his grin when faced with Charlotte's look of complete shock. A wise man, Mr. Hampstead released Charlotte's arm and stepped aside to allow Michael to take his place. When Michael raised her hand for a kiss, he sent her a playful wink, as well. In response, she made a sound that was somewhere between a laugh and incredulous huff.

Michael turned to Mr. Trivett and Lord Tunley. "Come now, Trivett, you're leaving some bits out, as well. Miss Henwood had been out riding that morning and promptly fell from her horse the moment I rode onto the scene. It was quite tragic." He briefly paused to give Charlotte's hand another soft kiss. "You really must try to break that habit of yours. Falling from your horse so often cannot be good for your health." Several people laughed. Reluctantly, Michael turned back to the crowd. "When the downpour began, I insisted we go into the nearest place we could find to get dry, which happened to be The Griffin. Come now, Mr. Trivett, you must remember me. Shortly after our arrival, you came barging into the tavern in search of your mistr—"

"Yes, yes, I remember now." Michael watched the foolish boy pull at his cravat. Charles Trivett looked around nervously, no doubt hoping his mother and sisters had not understood where Michael's story was leading. The suspicious glint in Mrs. Trivett's eye implied that there would be an interesting conversation later on.

"I thought that might jog your memory," Michael murmured, as Mr. Trivett made his excuses and wandered aimlessly away. The rest of his party followed shortly thereafter, although Lord Tunley sent Charlotte a vicious snarl before turning.

---

Charlotte's mind was reeling. Where in the world had Michael even come from? This whole encounter brought to mind her previous exchange with Mr. Charles Trivett at The Griffin. The man she had then known as Mr. Skidmore had attempted to defend her, but as she had stood waiting for his assistance, he had been slow to find his voice and perhaps less than effective.

Now here she was, neither wanting nor expecting his help. Yet he had been perfect. Charlotte knew, perhaps better than anyone else, how greatly Lord Averly detested being the center of attention. Despite that, he had delivered his short speech in such a manner as to leave a giddy smile on the face of anyone with even the smallest of romantic inclinations.

It all became crystal-clear at once: why she had allowed a complete stranger to lure her into his inn-room; why she had been so broken-hearted to discover that that stranger had not been the man she thought he was, but instead a lofty viscount;

and why, when she had the right hold over him, she had practically blackmailed the man into attending to her. Honestly, her actions had been a touch juvenile, but she still would have done whatever she could think of to bring Lord Averly closer to her. Looking up into his teasing eyes, she felt the knowledge wash over her. She was absolutely and unequivocally in love with Michael Skidmore, Viscount Averly. She most likely had been since that first day at The Griffin. Even then, she had known he was a man of honor. In the last weeks, she had discovered that he was responsible and clever too, if a bit more reserved than a gentleman like Mr. Hampstead. Just maybe she loved the quiet in him as well, even if it did make him appear a touch stodgy.

Oh Lord. After this little scene, the *ton* would expect them to soon become engaged. Would he be angry? True, he had already issued a proposal just yesterday. But she had refused in a less-than-gracious manner. However, she had been perfectly justified in her reaction. That proposal had so little to do with love and affection. Gracious, it had not even had much to do with basic lust. Could Charlotte bear to be with a man who did not feel those things for her? Of course not.

If they did not marry now, they would both be ruined. True, Michael would come out of things better than she. But even a gentleman would lose his standing in the *ton's* eyes, were he not to wed a woman after confessing to having been alone with her in a tavern. Charlotte knew how important his reputation was to him. When viewed in that light, she had no choice but to marry him and save his good name. She would simply have to convince Lord Averly that he did, or at least could, feel everything for her that she felt for him. Starting with desire. It was a new feeling that Charlotte found she quite enjoyed. Hopefully, Lord Averly did as well.

Perfectly timed to her new decision, the strains of a waltz drew several couples to the floor. Although she vaguely recalled having a partner for the dance, she looked up at Lord Averly expectantly. Without hesitation, he led her out.

---

For the first time since they met, Michael had no desire to ignore his feelings for Miss Charlotte Henwood. Only days ago, he would have spent their entire waltz wishing he could hold her at as great a distance as possible. Tonight, for this dance, he drew her nearly flush against him. She may not want to admit it, but she was now entirely his. There would be no excuses or wild accusations to get her out of this one.

Neither spoke for almost the entirety of the dance. Instead, Michael concentrated on how smoothly they moved together, enjoying the brush of her forehead against his cheek and how delicately her hand rested on his shoulder. True, he had needed to provide her with some extra strength and support, due to her ankle; happily, that gave him an excuse to hold her even tighter.

As their dance drew to a close, Charlotte pulled back to look up at him. Michael almost laughed aloud. This was likely the first time he had seen such uncertainty and bashfulness in those sweet brown eyes. If she were only now realizing that they had no choice but to marry, Michael felt no qualms in informing her that she was well and truly caught.

He watched her take a steadying breath. "Lord Averly." She spoke just above a whisper, forcing him to lean in. "Do you not think it would be wise to check on my house again soon?" Michael's eyes narrowed. After everything that had just happened, she wanted to discuss his role as her personal guard? Damn it all, he could do a damn better job of protecting her if they were damn well married! He did not want to discuss her protection right now. She went on, "Tonight, maybe? When everyone is asleep? Like the last time?"

*Wait, what now?*

Before Michael could fully regain his sanity, a voice boomed from not too far away. "There you are!" It would seem that during his dance with Charlotte, Miss Madison and Mr. Hampstead had fetched Lady Kinsey.

"Hello, Lady Kinsey." Goodness, she could move fast when she needed to.

Her Ladyship gave a quick curtsey. "It is a pleasure to see you again so soon after your visit yesterday morning." Michael swung his gaze to Charlotte, who widened her eyes in innocence. How *did* Lady Kinsey do that? "No doubt you must be prepared to make your excuses after tonight's strange turn of events."

Not one to miss such a subtle hint, Michael nodded in answer. "I was going to do just that."

Looking back and forth between Lady Kinsey and Michael, Charlotte announced, "Perhaps we should make our way home, as well. I believe we have all had enough excitement for one night."

Her Ladyship snorted derisively. "Yes, let's allow your old friends to dig themselves deeper in your absence. I am not entirely certain they realize just how greatly they have allied the *ton* with you two." Charlotte, Michael, Julia, and Mr. Hampstead all nodded. "Well? What are you all waiting for? Mr. Hampstead, return Miss Madison to her parents, Charlotte, come with me, and Lord Averly, you do whatever it is you were planning on doing."

As everyone broke apart, Michael wondered why no one saluted after being given their orders. Instead he bowed, then he walked the ladies out of the ballroom, saying, "I shall see you soon, Miss Henwood. Lady Kinsey, good night."

Once in the carriage, Michael allowed himself the broad grin he had been holding back for much too long. Miss Charlotte Henwood would be his wife. And damned soon, if he had anything to say about it. Well, he thought, as he slouched back and threw a hand behind his head, if matters progressed nicely tonight, he could insist on a quick wedding.

———

Charlotte was glad to be rid of Lady Kinsey. The woman had forced her to retell the entire story of her encounter with the Trivetts in exacting detail. Some parts she had been forced to repeat several times. Exhausted by the time she arrived back home, Charlotte took to her room. Hopefully she had worn Her Ladyship out as well.

By the time Suzie came in to take down Charlotte's hair and help remove her gown, Charlotte could barely stand. While Suzie made great efforts to get her friend to recount the evening for her, Charlotte recommended Suzie ask Lady Kinsey. Likely the woman knew more than Charlotte did by now. Realizing that Charlotte was much too distracted to regale her with any exciting tidbits, Suzie left her friend be.

———

Concerned that Lady Kinsey or Suzie might hear his arrival, Michael arrived a few hours after the ladies should have retired. He had even gone so far as to borrow Ryder's less remarkable carriage and left it at a nearby inn.

This time, when he made his way to the back door, Michael avoided the various ceramic pots lining the short stairway. Although he did not seem to have awoken the household on his last late-night visit, one could never be too careful.

However, now that he finally reached the door, Michael realized that he had no idea how Charlotte intended for him to get in. A quick try proved that the door was locked and he could not see any glimmering candles through the kitchen door's window. If he knocked, there would be a higher chance of waking someone. Could she have left a key? Or had something gone wrong, forcing her to change her mind about tonight?

Torn between pounding down the door to discover what had happened and giving up entirely, Michael recalled Ryder mentioning a hidden key. It was cleverly covered by a pot.

With only the soft moonlight to guide him, Michael began lifting the various pots, starting at the bottom of the steps and making his way up. Of course, no experienced intruder would dream of searching under the pot closest to the door. Michael would need to have a conversation about Charlotte's security precautions.

That could be done later, he thought, locking the door behind him and pocketing the key. For the moment, Michael had something entirely different on his agenda.

By some miracle, Michael managed to not make a sound as he crept through the kitchen and up the stairs in the dark. After the ruckus he made during his previous late-night visit, he tripled his efforts to remain silent. When he reached Charlotte's room, he felt a moment of concern at finding no light flickering under her door. Hopefully it was a precaution against alerting Lady Kinsey to their plans.

Michael froze, uncertain what to do next. He couldn't knock to make his presence known. There was no other option but to simply go in. Nearly holding his breath, he turned the knob and did just that.

Even after he softly closed the door behind him, he could not hear any movement or sound from within Charlotte's room. Wait. No, he could hear Miss Henwood's even breathing. Blast it all, was she asleep?

The moonlight filtering in from her large window allowed him to see her form lying flat on her back. Michael approached her nightstand, where he knew candles should be, managing to trip over a small carpet and then banging his shin on the nightstand, on the way.

When he lit a flickering candle, her eyes did not flinch. Should he leave her to her rest, despite his traveling here in the middle of the night? He could tamp down on his desperate need for her for another day or two, surely? He really ought to let her rest after such a hellish evening, he thought as he bent down to get a closer look at her face.

So close to her now, he could not resist pressing his lips gently to hers. If he couldn't have her for the night, he would at least steal a kiss. He was immediately rewarded with a muffled shriek and a pillow sent so forcefully into his face, he staggered back several steps.

Convenient for Michael, Charlotte was too tired and hoarse to provide a decent scream or two. Most of the sounds she made came out as a series of quiet but high-pitched screeches.

Michael cut her off in a hushed voice, "By all that's holy, woman! It's Michael. Don't wake up the whole house!"

Soon Charlotte's strange shrieks gave way to a few choked breaths and then quieted entirely. Once she appeared to have regained her composure, Michael thought it safe to approach her bed. By then, she was sitting up with her legs hanging over the side, while she shot him what he assumed was an icy glare. He opened his mouth to speak. "I'm sorry—"

The pillow, still tightly gripped in her hands, once again smashed into his face. "Your method of waking a person leaves much to be desired."

A mite embarrassed, he answered, "I thought I was being romantic. I seem to recall you being the one to invite me here, in the first place. The least you could have done was remain awake."

Had she been remotely aware of just how long Michael had waited before coming over, she would certainly have defended herself. As it was, she felt a little guilty.

Michael went on. "I did not intend to keep you from your rest, if the evening's events exhausted you." Well, actually, that had been his entire intent. However, seeing her so tired and disheveled—and grumpy—he thought his plans might be better suited for another time. Clearly, Miss Henwood did not share in his excitement for the night to come. "I should go. I wouldn't want to further risk waking Her Ladyship. May I still call on you on the morrow?" Michael hated how formal his voice had become.

"Goodness, no!"

Michael felt the blood leave his face. Did she still refuse to marry him? How could she be so foolish? Michael tried to guard his expression, but for once he could not find his calm. He had always thought her better than that.

Apparently Charlotte quickly understood her mistake. "I mean don't leave! I am sorry I was asleep and I'm always awful when I'm woken suddenly." Standing, she reached her hand out to him. "But I want you to stay." Excitement, tinged with a touch of nervousness, filled her eyes. Her nightdress hung loosely from her subtle curves, while her unbound hair cascaded down her back, reflecting the candlelight.

Michael could not imagine a more beautiful woman in all of creation.

Backing towards her bedroom door, he said, "I really should not hold you to your invitation. No doubt it was issued in reaction to the evening's stresses." He knew how greatly she objected to anyone calling her nerves into question. "There is no need to feel any form of obligation to me. I shall let myself out."

He held her baffled face in his mind's eyes while he turned and made his way to the door. No longer facing her, he replaced his somber expression with a jaunty smile.

As Michael reached for the doorknob, an unexpected weight landed on his shoulders. It would seem the elegant and unflappable Miss Charlotte Henwood had launched herself onto his back to stop his progress.

Her breath warm against his ear, she murmured, "I do wish you would cease looking for excuses to leave my room. I find this an unpleasant habit, if you must know."

His ego happily restored, Michael turned himself around in her arms, wrapping his own around her waist. When she saw his face, she gasped. "You were teasing me! You never intended to leave!"

Shrugging, he answered, "Had you truly wished me to leave, I would have. Mind you, I may have been exceedingly disappointed."

Michael allowed himself another moment to enjoy her embrace. The knowledge that she still wanted him sent delight coursing through him...and blood pooling in his groin.

"Lord Averly. Michael." Charlotte reminded herself that there was no need to address him so formally. This was not even their first encounter in her bedroom. Straightening her spine, she went on. "I seem to recall you mentioning that there were a great many more things that a woman and a man can share beyond what we did...before." His tongue a lead weight in his mouth, Michael nodded carefully. "Well," she went on slowly, unable to keep the nerves entirely from her voice, "I was wondering if you would like to show me those other things now."

Her fascinated, excited expression was his undoing. Hands nearly shaking with need, Michael reached for and took her waist, pulling her to him. "Very much." His voice was hoarse, but he couldn't help it. He brought his mouth to her eager lips, savoring their feel, before drawing back. "I can show you. God, how I want to show you."

His hands slowly stroked the length of her spine, sliding down to the small of her back, then drawing her up against his arousal. He gently ran his lips over her neck as he spoke. "But if I do..." *Don't tell her, just be quiet,* his mind screamed. He forced himself to lean away and look directly into her eyes. "If I do, there will be consequences," he finally ground out.

"Consequences?" she said with the most enchanting smile he had ever seen. "How exciting."

# Chapter 23

MICHAEL WAS CERTAIN he misunderstood; she couldn't have just given him the go-ahead already. Perhaps she didn't know what she was agreeing to? Should he explain? Could he even manage that discussion without losing his mind?

Looking down at those incredible lips, he decided he had been honorable enough for one day. She had made up her mind when she invited him into her home in the dead of night. Leaning down, he took her mouth.

Slowly, not wanting to pull his lips from hers unless the world was ending, and maybe not even then, Michael carefully led them to the bed. When they reached it, he picked her up and laid her out across the sheets. Unable to resist, he took a moment to just enjoy the look of Charlotte gazing entreatingly up at him, her lips swollen and her eyes bright and excited.

But what to do now? She was a virgin—at the moment—and Michael was not entirely certain how she ought to be treated. Should he explain, in detail, exactly what they were about to do, in order to prevent her from feeling nervous? Not that she appeared nervous or frightened.

Again, Charlotte surprised him. "Are you not a little uncomfortable in your formal attire? You have been wearing it all evening, after all. Besides, it is hardly fair that you are still so overdressed. I very much want to know what a man looks like under his shirtsleeves."

He found himself laughing. Was he even surprised at her forthrightness? Tonight Michael would appease any curiosity she might have, once and for all. He smiled to himself as he unbuttoned his waistcoat and threw it over a chair. Sitting in that same chair, he pulled off his soft leather shoes. "Is this an improvement?"

Charlotte cocked her head to the side. "It is better, I suppose, but now I can barely make out your frame, your shirt billows out so much. How do you men ever manage to put your sleeves into your fitted coats?"

In his knee breeches and shirt, Michael made his way over to the bed and spread out next to her on his side. "You have my permission to remove any articles of clothing you feel are hampering your exploration of the male form," he teased. But quickly his tone turned serious. "Charlotte, do you truly realize what you are asking of me? And what the consequences of our actions will be? I don't want you to misunderstand what will have to happen tomorrow."

He watched her brows furrow. "Lord Averly...Michael. Are you perchance proposing to me?"

Charlotte knew most gentlemen would have gladly enjoyed a consequence-free night with a lady. However, Michael was not like most gentlemen.

Michael pulled back. "Charlotte, I would not engage in this particular act with you if I did not intend to ask for your hand. Again."

She did not answer him.

Although it was torture, Michael drew back and prepared to leave the bed, and her, for good. She had rejected him once. He did not want to risk the misery that followed it ever again. Charlotte reached out before he could leave her, taking his hand.

"Lord Averly, I did not accept your proposal, because I objected to the reasons you provided for accepting your suit. You must understand that I need neither your money nor your protection."

Michael took a moment to consider that. After their scene, he had begun to see Charlotte in a whole new light. Taking a deep breath—*Lord, she smelled incredible*—he told her, "I can accept that. I will need you to accept that I still intend to do everything in my power to protect you, nonetheless. It has nothing to do with doubting your capabilities and everything to do with the instincts you instill in me. If we marry, that will only increase."

Charlotte considered his words. "I shall happily discuss marriage with you tomorrow. Now may we please continue?"

Michael froze. She must be joking. In his current state, it was a challenge to focus on anything she said, but he was quite certain that he was getting a bargain. "Is that all?" Michael didn't care how ridiculous he sounded. He primarily concentrated on containing the unexpected excitement coursing through his veins.

Instead of answering, Charlotte pulled him back to her. He might change his mind, but for now, she would have this entire night with him to enjoy. The man she loved was in her bed. What else could she do?

Michael finally allowed himself to unleash the desire pulsing through him. He stretched out over her, straddling Charlotte's thighs, his member pressing against her hip as he leaned down to take her mouth.

This time, when he kissed her, he started out gently, slowly running his lips back and forth across hers, until her own parted. Then he took more, slipping his tongue into her mouth, but still keeping the pace from becoming too frenzied.

Almost of their own volition, her hands began stroking his back. She wanted to touch all of him, but had no idea where to start. Although, on second thought, his rear end proved to be a particularly interesting bit of terrain. It was one of many regions she intended to explore on Lord Averly. He felt so firm and strong under her hands. When she dug her fingers in for a sound squeeze, Michael groaned in pleasure, thrusting his pelvis against her. His kiss turned from gentle to demanding in a split second.

Slowly, he pulled the fabric of her nightdress upwards. The gentle, almost imperceptible, brush of the hem sent a tingle through her as it made its progress up her legs. Michael couldn't resist running the backs of his fingers over her thigh as it was exposed to him. Charlotte took his chin to draw his mouth back to hers.

Resisting the temptation to pause between her tender thighs, Michael slid his palm across her abdomen. Charlotte arched her back in the hope of increasing the pressure of his hands. Just the glide of his palm over her stomach was enough to send warmth flowing through her. When his hand closed around her breast, Charlotte could not hold back her moan.

Michael smiled against her lips as he gently squeezed her nipple between two fingers. Charlotte tightened her arms around his back. When he made the most delicate twisting motion, she couldn't help but dig her nails in.

Meanwhile, Michael's exploring fingers ran back down her torso and found her delicate folds. At first touch, she tensed. However, when he began gently stroking her, she seemed to recall how well this went for her the last time. Of their own volition, her eyes slipped shut as her head fell back on a gasp.

As her body relaxed, Michael took his chance to slowly slide a finger into her warm passage. When her legs parted to allow him better access, he realized that he still straddled them. Not only that, but looking down, he noticed that he was still partially dressed.

Unexpectedly, Michael slipped his wonderfully torturous finger out of her and leapt from the bed.

"What the...?" Charlotte murmured as he was wrenched from her arms. Was he leaving? Had she done something wrong? When she heard Michael chuckle, she looked up to see him pull his shirt over his head. That explained things.

When his hands reached for the front of his breeches, Charlotte's excitement grew to a new level. Although the room was lit only by the single candle, she could not wait to see her first, and only, naked man in the flesh. And what exquisite flesh it was, judging by the solid chest and broad shoulders now almost fully revealed to her.

Should she help? More likely than not, she would just get in the way. But if he was undressing, she should do the same, shouldn't she? She believed these sorts of things tended to be better facilitated when both parties were fully nude.

Unfortunately for Michael, Charlotte chose the moment in which he was removing his first ankle from his breeches to pull her shift over her head. Her action left him completely arrested in shock as he took in her sinuous form. Most importantly, it rendered him completely frozen, with one foot raised, yet still trapped in his breeches. Before he could regain his senses, he had already begun to overbalance. By then, it was too late to free his foot and catch himself, sending Michael into an awkward tumble to the floor.

Charlotte leapt off her bed to kneel at his side. "Are you all right?" He had better not be too injured to finish what they started. "You didn't hit your head or anything important, did you?"

In her concern, Charlotte gently ran her fingers over his chest. When her hand slid lower down his torso through the crisp hair on his chest, she felt him tense. She watched her fingers, almost of their own accord, glide toward his rigid member. What would it feel like? Her curiosity was quite engaged now.

"They don't usually look like this on the Greek statues," she murmured. "You didn't perhaps injure this part of you when you fell and that's why it's so unusually...swollen?"

What could Michael really say? Of course he wasn't a statue. He was entirely flesh and blood, even if most of that blood was concentrated within a specific part of his body. Finally, his mind began functioning enough to allow him to speak. "Actually I believe my current state is a good indication that everything is perfectly healthy."

"Huh." Her fingers continued to near his member, then shied away before doing anything especially interesting. Michael thought he might die as he watched her kneeling beside him, staring at his "unusually swollen" flesh like it was a puzzle she could not solve.

A lock of her hair slid from behind her ear to fall before her eye. Did she know how beautiful she was? He realized two things at once: first, if she kept stroking him in this bizarre teasing dance, there was a chance he might find himself unmanned, and second, Miss Charlotte Henwood did not belong on the floor.

---

"Do you really think he'll come?"

Lady Kinsey very nearly gave in to a moment of rudeness and snorted. But she refrained. One should always lead one's charges by example. And she did consider Suzie to be in her charge. Perhaps Lady Kinsey did not intend to teach Suzie how to flirt with a duke while dancing the quadrille. Nevertheless, Suzie was learning several vitally important skills—skills which Her Ladyship fully intended to suggest her charge put to good use on the morrow.

Despite this being nearly the hundredth time Suzie had asked her, Lady Kinsey replied, "More than likely. We know he has been here at least once before in the dark of the night. Judging by the cow-eyes Charlotte was sending him tonight, I would be quite surprised if he doesn't appear."

They had been playing cards for three hours now and were running out of ideas for new games. Lady Kinsey looked down at her unimpressive hand while Suzie took her turn. She absolutely hated piquet, but was concerned that there was nothing left for two people to play. Not at any point within those three hours had there been any violent crashes or loud eruptions of profanity to alert them to His Lordship's presence.

Not that Lady Kinsey intended to stop him. Lord Averly would not sneak into a lady's room unless he intended to marry her. Well, he wouldn't do it twice. Her intention was merely to hurry things along.

The interest that that madman had in Charlotte concerned everyone more than they let on. Lady Kinsey simply wanted to provide the lovers with a reason to rush the wedding, possibly even obtain a special license. A viscountess was a great deal more challenging to harm than a young lady living with her older chaperone and a devilish maid for protection.

Suzie continued, "What I don't understand is why we must lie in wait for Lord Averly if we have no intention of stopping him. Not that I mind beating you shamelessly at cards. But please remind me once more why we cannot get just a little rest."

"I have no intention of letting Lord Averly slip past me a second time." It still rankled that His Lordship had not remained long enough the last time for her to catch him in the act. By the time she had run down the hall to wake Suzie, waited for Suzie to dress, and then waited for Suzie to help Her Ladyship dress, Lord Averly had already sneaked out.

Ignoring Suzie's arguments for the contrary, Lady Kinsey refused to meet with any gentleman in a state of undress. It was simply not done. Therefore Lady Kinsey and Suzie found themselves playing cards in Her Ladyship's room while clothed in a manner perfectly appropriate for activities ranging from taking a casual walk outside to catching a viscount in flagrante delicto.

"Once we hear his entrance, we shall wait an acceptable amount of time for...whatever we must wait for." Her Ladyship still shied away from admitting exactly what she was allowing her charge to do under her nose. "After that, we shall make our presences known and demand Lord Averly do the right thing."

Suzie seemed to accept Her Ladyship's instructions. Mostly.

"Why couldn't we perhaps take turns sleeping?"

Unluckily for Lady Kinsey, Lord Averly's use of the hidden key allowed for a relatively silent entrance. While Suzie trumped Lady Kinsey's last good card, Michael lifted the very unclothed Charlotte Henwood back onto her bed and stretched out over her.

As Michael again moved his fingers down her torso to slide between her thighs, he gently brought his mouth to her breast, flicking his tongue over her nipple.

Charlotte never could have prepared herself for something that so overpowered all of her senses. Languid, she wondered if she would slowly melt into the mattress.

Unexpectedly, Lord Averly changed from slowly stroking her to a slightly more fervid pace, forcing her to again arch her back away from the bed. No longer soothed by his attentions, the muscles in her abdomen and inner thighs began to tighten, leaving her shaking in a foreign state of desperation. Her fingers curled into the sheets and mattress.

Instead of gentling his pace to again calm her, he slid a finger into her. Waves coursed through her body, while he caught her surprised cries in his mouth. Watching Charlotte with her head thrown back and torso bowed as she rocked against his hand nearly brought Michael to the breaking point right then. Damn it all, he would finish this the way he intended.

Before her climax reached its end, Michael knelt between her legs. Tense and throbbing, he used every last vestige of self-control he possessed to carefully, slowly, enter her slick sheath. His arms shook when she tightened all around him. He looked down into her sensual, trusting eyes. She wanted him and she was ready.

Lowering his head, he took her mouth while one gentle thrust broke through her maidenly barrier. Unconsciously, she bit his lip in response to the unexpected pain.

Reminded that this particular part may not be pleasant for a virgin, he waited a moment for her body to grow accustomed to him. Michael then sought out the sensitive nubbin between her legs with his thumb while he slowly thrust in…and then out.

Although she disliked the pain, Charlotte trusted Michael. She concentrated on the teasing, flicking movements of his fingers. Soon, the magic he worked with his hand completely overshadowed any discomfort she may have had. After a while, his careful, controlled thrusts were not enough to satisfy her. She began moving with him, even speeding the pace.

Enjoying herself thoroughly, Charlotte took advantage of exploring his form with her hands as he moved within her. The combination of Michael filling her so completely and the pressure and motion of his fingers brought her again to a point of insanity. A second release began to overtake her.

No longer able to maintain a gentle pace, Michael nearly cried out a benediction as he felt her tighten around his member. As she came, he buried his face in her neck and exploded with her.

Before he succumbed to a sleep, he had one single thought. *She was his.*

---

Charlotte hadn't a clue as to how long they both lay there, asleep and unmoving. Something jolted her awake, but she could not recall exactly what it had been. Mostly, she focused on how she felt with a good portion of Lord Averly's weight pressing down on her. While she found it oddly comforting and maybe even a little arousing, the experience also seemed to be a touch stifling. It was time he moved so she could fully breathe in again.

But how does a lady easily move a full-grown man who is sprawled over her? First, she tried jostling back and forth until her right shoulder was freed from under his arm. She then made a valiant attempt to push off from her right side, hoping to roll Michael off her.

All attempts were unsuccessful. Collapsing back into the mattress, she decided she had no choice but to wake him.

---

Michael awoke squirming and laughing hysterically. What in the blazes was happening? He had been having such a lovely dream involving a certain dark-haired beauty stroking his hair and feeding him grapes from her lips. While that part was lovely, it did nothing to explain why the scene took place in the crow's nest of a ship rocking gently in the middle of an unrecognizable ballroom. Least explicable, however, was his being woken in such a violent and cruel manner.

"Holy hell! Are we on fire?" He speedily rolled off the woman beneath him and jumped out of bed. Where was he? The guttering candle on the bedside table displayed a surprised but amused Charlotte Henwood. "You! You tickled me! What kind of evil heartless creature wakes a man up by tickling him?"

Stifling the impulse to cover her eyes as a very naked viscount waved his arms and accused her of foul deeds, she replied, "You wouldn't wake up from anything else. It was an act of desperation. One moment longer and I may have suffocated to death." He might have believed in the level of her desperation a touch more had she not delivered her little speech between giggles. "Who knew you were such a sound sleeper?"

"Me? You're the one who went to sleep instead of waiting for the man you had so plainly invited into your bed." The ludicrousness of the situation was setting in, as was his state of complete undress. Quickly, he snatched his breeches and put them on. He should probably prepare to leave in order to preserve Charlotte's reputation.

As Michael continued to dress, Charlotte decided she ought to do the same. Spotting her nightdress on the floor, she donned it while smiling serenely at Michael's complaints.

Despite his grouchy demeanor, he clearly was pleased with the night's recent events.

Michael proved it by returning to the bed and delivering a soft kiss to her lips. Unused to such displays, or really being kissed regularly at all, Charlotte could not contain an embarrassed blush.

Oddly pleased with Charlotte's bashfulness, Michael leaned back to take in the moment. Finally, perhaps for the first time since he met her, she could not seem to come up with a single thing to say. Hoping to prolong the moment, he moved back in for another kiss.

Before his lips met hers, enraged feminine shrieks coupled with a great deal of noisy clattering across the hall filled the house's silence.

---

Jeremy Stowes was not entirely certain how he felt about his latest task. Having "conversations" with several stuffy, priggish fools about what to do with their money was one thing. Sneaking into a lady's house was quite another.

The earl had said that it needed to be done. This girl and her father wouldn't give up their shares. Stowes was a little fuzzy on why a woman would have any say over those shares in the first place, but he had a feeling the earl knew more about these things than he.

Besides, it wasn't as though he had much choice. A man gets into one little fight with the bastard son of some rich snobbish cove and he's marked for life. Tunley had promised Stowes his protection. If the authorities ever became involved, the word of an earl should keep him out of Newgate. He hoped.

Conversely, if Stowes ever crossed Tunley, he was certain the man would pass his knowledge to a less than convenient source. Stowes wished he hadn't needed to tell Tunley exactly why he required the man's protection. The Earl of Tunley now owned him.

So here he was, sneaking around to the back of Miss Henwood's townhouse. Stowes was not one to notice the quaintly arranged plants and flowers surrounding him as he climbed the stairs to the back door. Looking through the small window there, he didn't see any movement or light.

Before attempting to break the door in, Stowes lifted a few pots surrounding the house. You never knew if the gentry was foolish enough to leave a key out for the average housebreaker to use.

When he found nothing, he went back to the door. Stowes had the foresight to realize that breaking the glass would be pointless; he would never fit through the opening in the first place. Shrugging to himself, he gave the door a good kick and walked straight in. Foresight did not prepare Stowes for the crack the door made when the lock broke.

Making his way through the kitchen as quickly as he could, he shook off the sense that something wasn't quite right. His apprehension no doubt helped him get soundly lost in his search for the living quarters. By the time he found the staircase and reached the top floor, the strange feeling was making him a mite jittery. He needed to find Miss Henwood, complete his assigned task, and then get the hell out of there.

So which bloody room was hers? There were two rooms that had light flickering from under the door. Stowes thought he remembered the earl saying that only one other woman lived with the girl. Neither man worried much about any servants in the house. They'd likely be sleeping on the third floor, anyway.

The light from the room on the left was much brighter than that from the one on his right, where it looked like someone had left a candle burning before falling asleep—not very safe and a bit of a waste, really.

Well, he couldn't imagine an old woman still awake at this hour. Therefore, the room on the right likely belonged to Miss Henwood's chaperone. Just like some soft-in-the-head crone to drift off with a candle burning.

Seeing nothing else for it, he turned the knob on the left door and strode in.

When everything went dark and his ears were filled with a series of terrifying war-cries, he realized what had been bothering him so much. Usually kicking a door in makes enough noise to wake at least one member of a household. Until this particular moment, the house had remained perfectly silent. Why had no one come to investigate the sound?

However, he had more pressing concerns at the moment. For example: what, exactly, was hitting him on the head over and over again?

# Chapter 24

———❦———

MICHAEL RAN OUT OF THE ROOM and across the hall, with Charlotte fast on his heels. What they found in Her Ladyship's room certainly gave the pair of half-dressed lovers pause.

A very large entity was making a desperately futile attempt to escape Lady Kinsey's bedroom. Perhaps it would have been easier for the poor creature had it not been covered in layers of various fabrics with a curtain tie wrapped tightly around his middle.

Charlotte recognized Lady Kinsey's curtains as well as Her Ladyship's quilt. And goodness, was that flowered pastel on his head from a night wrap? It was hard to be sure, as both Lady Kinsey and Suzie were busy attacking the draped mountain. Charlotte decided that now would not be the best time to inform the ladies that hairbrushes and feather dusters did not make for the most effective weapons.

Michael, bless him, immediately pulled Lady Kinsey off the behemoth and took her hairbrush from her hands. Charlotte decided to focus on Suzie, who did not stop when Her Ladyship was pulled aside. No amount of yelling managed to distract her friend so, in the end, Charlotte ran at Suzie from behind and wrapped her arms around her before Suzie could deliver any further blows.

When the mountain realized it was no longer under attack, it ceased making pained whimpering sounds and instead made a run for it. Its plan may have warranted better results had it been able to see. As it was, the hulk ran head-first into Lady Kinsey's wall, promptly knocking itself to the ground.

Silent now, the four of them spent several seconds merely staring at the unconscious mound of fabric lying on the floor.

In the most casual tone he could muster, Michael asked, "Perhaps you ladies would like to explain exactly why there appears to be an unconscious man on the floor of Lady Kinsey's bedroom."

Her Ladyship and Suzie exchanged looks, but neither spoke. Nervously, Suzie rubbed the back of her neck. Her Ladyship cocked her head, as though considering a safe way to explain this particular scene. Her following shrug indicated that nothing came to mind. Neither made eye contact with Charlotte or Michael.

While she awaited a response, Charlotte took in the rest of Lady Kinsey's room. Playing cards were strewn everywhere and a curtain rod leaned up against the wall. Lastly, Charlotte took in Her Ladyship's state of dress. The woman looked prepared for a walk down Mayfair. Even her hair had been styled, although it appeared a bit worse for wear after her altercation.

Charlotte raised a finger to point accusingly at Her Ladyship while her jaw worked in shock. "You were waiting for *Michael*!"

Again, neither lady answered, but Suzie developed a telltale blush. "Bloody blasted hell!" Charlotte cried. "Were you planning on catching him in the act?"

Unable to hold back, Michael murmured, "Charlotte, your language."

Michael stared on, while Charlotte continued her rant. "Oh for cripes' sake, Michael! They were going to try to catch you with me! Of all the sneaky, underhanded tricks!" Never had he imagined she could throw such a fit. And on his behalf. The arm-waving and foot-stomping was actually quite adorable.

Michael's calm was really starting to irritate Charlotte. At his, "Now, let's not get too carried away," she nearly threw Suzie's feather duster at his head.

Taking in Michael's more relaxed attitude, Lady Kinsey finally said, "We were only acting in your best interest, Charlotte. Truly."

This did not soothe her charge's rage. "I can act in my own bloody best interest, thank you very much!" When she went on about over-officious meddling and the negative repercussions such actions could have on her future endeavors, Michael leaned back against the wall until she wound down.

Although he knew he should soothe Charlotte, Michael instead took a look around the room. It really was a mess. The only thing that looked tidy was the curtain rod leaning carefully up against the wall. One would almost think that the curtain and its accompanying tie had been removed from the wall well before any of the action took place. Michael's eyes narrowed as he looked from the curtain rod to Lady Kinsey's innocent face.

"I have a question, Your Ladyship," he said. Charlotte quieted at his thoughtful tone. Lady Kinsey nodded for him to continue. "Were you somehow aware that a ruffian intended to break into your home today?"

Her Ladyship's back went up. "Of course not! I can assure you that had I thought we were in any danger at all, I would have requested protection of some kind."

"Ah." Charlotte watched his brows lower in concentration before he met her eyes. "And Charlotte seems to believe you intended to catch me here, at least before I made my way back home."

He had to give her credit. Lady Kinsey neither blushed, nor gave any other sign that she might be a touch embarrassed over her actions. Crossing her arms and looking him straight in the eye, she said, "We only hoped to help hurry things along with you two. I'm guessing from your presence here that you wouldn't *mind*." He heard Charlotte let out a frustrated huff.

"No, I wouldn't say that I mind that part," he went on, slowly. "It is only that you seemed very prepared to defend yourselves, even before this man came into your home. I can

277

only surmise that you intended to truss *me* up in your curtains and quilt and then tie me with the curtain cord. I hope that you did not also plan to beat me with your hairbrush and feather duster."

Before either lady could answer, the pile of fabric on the floor groaned. "One guess as to the identity of your assailant," Michael said as he removed the quilt and Lady Kinsey's wrap from the man's head.

No one was surprised to find Mr. Stowes blinking up at everyone. When that did not seem to explain his circumstances, he gave his head a shake or two. Michael pulled him to his feet, where Stowes wobbled for a moment before gaining his balance.

It was time to ask their intruder a few questions. Charlotte doubted that Michael's ingrained politeness would allow for a thorough interrogation. Therefore, she decided to take the task upon herself.

Lady Kinsey beat her to it. Giving Stowes several harsh pokes in the chest, she demanded, "Just what did you intend to do in a house full of such kind, gentle ladies as us? I warrant you didn't expect this welcome, now, did you?"

Stowes shook his head again in an attempt to clear it. "I was only supposed to deliver a message to Miss Henwood. That's all, honest." His head jerked in Charlotte's direction. Stowes winced at the motion. He thought he might deserve the painful twinge. After all, the earl had *not* ordered Stowes to merely deliver a message.

Charlotte raised a brow. "The ironworks, again, no doubt. You are proving badly repetitive, Mr. Stowes. And I simply must inform you that after seeing Lady Kinsey's, er, apparel wrapped around your head, I may not ever again find you intimidating. I am sorry, but there you have it."

Her announcement appeared to put Stowes into an even greater funk, which Charlotte certainly did not object to. She wanted to deliver a few blows to the man too, after all that he had put her through. And she would have, if she wasn't certain doing so would hurt her more than him. But before they damaged his confidence even further, there was one thing Michael needed to clarify.

Michael cleared his throat, and then asked, "Do you even know what those shares are worth, Mr. Stowes? Knowing what I do of Miss Henwood's investments, I would warrant that they are much too valuable to just hand over to anyone. No doubt someone much more influential than you is pulling the strings and, I am certain, reaping the real rewards. Does that not bother you?" Although Stowes continued his silence, Michael could tell his words were raising a concern or two.

Stowes sent Charlotte a steady glare. Perhaps Charlotte should have been scared, but after seeing him ram his head into a wall, she was hard-pressed to take him seriously. Hands on hips, she said, "Well, it doesn't matter because you chose the wrong side, Mr. Stowes. Mr. Madison, the head of the mining investment, can afford a great deal more than whoever is pretending to support you. In the end, he shall do whatever it takes to find whoever is controlling you and end this."

A grain of doubt seemed to be growing in Stowes as he looked back and forth between Michael and Charlotte. Michael seized on it. "It may go better for you in the end to give your employer up now. I wouldn't be surprised if Miss Henwood or even Mr. Madison would reward you for your help."

Betraying his employer was apparently not Stowes' preference. "It'll be a cold day in hell before I 'elp another stodgy cove like you! One irritating arse telling me what to do is bloody well enough!" While his point was made perfectly clear already, Stowes decided to accent his decision by tossing off the remaining bits of fabric and throwing his fist into Michael's face.

Michael moved reflexively but the man still managed to get a good swipe at his cheek. Even the glancing blow hurt like the devil, the force of it throwing him back a few steps.

Immediately all three ladies began shrieking at Stowes, which only made the pain seem worse.

In the midst of the yelling and chaos, Stowes tried to make his escape. Michael knew exactly what would happen next. He watched Charlotte, who stood closest to the door, prepare to pounce. Acting only on instinct, Michael lunged, but not for Stowes. For a moment, Charlotte struggled against him as he wrapped an arm around her waist. Tightening that arm while using his other to ward off her swinging fists, he yelled, "You are not running after that madman!"

It only took a moment for Charlotte to cease struggling against him. At least she seemed to understand that she could not give chase to an enormous ex-boxer. Michael carefully released her. One of her fists had connected with his cheek, close to where Stowes had socked him. He was going to have a bloody miserable headache soon, he thought as he raised his fingers to his cheekbone.

A new furor erupted over Michael's injured chin. Immediately ushering a confused and wobbly Lord Averly downstairs, the ladies poured him a snifter of brandy and pressed some cold, clammy concoction that may have once been a living creature against his face.

The ladies spoke so fast and moved so quickly, Michael felt as though he had been thrown inside a tornado. He could hear them all cry out and chatter even more when they discovered the broken-in kitchen door, but the ringing in his head kept him from understanding most of their discussion. Hopefully, Mr. Stowes would likely think twice about entering their home again after his first welcome.

Only after Michael was fully settled on the settee with a brandy, a cold meat slab, and innumerable blankets and pillows, did the three Furies pour themselves a brandy and each sit down.

Even when everyone stopped chattering and moving, his headache did not dissipate. Of late, his life had become a touch more stressful than he would have liked. Whoever controlled Mr. Stowes needed to be caught as soon as possible.

When no one else spoke, Michael broke the silence. "Events appear to be escalating." Although Michael could not see everyone in the dim candlelight, he knew they all shared the same apprehensive look. "It's time for us to take action."

Charlotte finally looked up from her brandy to meet his eyes. She was scared and Michael did not know if he and Ryder were enough to protect her any longer.

Still no one answered. It seemed that the ladies were willing to allow him to guide events for the moment. How long that would last, he couldn't say. He had best take advantage of the lapse. "In the morning, I intend to enlist a Bow Street runner to investigate this Mr. Stowes and discover his whereabouts. While threatening well-established members of society is already an act that the proper authorities frown upon, breaking into the home of unprotected single women simply cannot be ignored." Michael would have sought out a runner right away, had he not been concerned about leaving the ladies alone in a house with a broken door.

For a while, no one else spoke, but finally Her Ladyship nodded in agreement. "What we need is a plan of action." *Oh dear.* "While I am certain your runner will be able to find and capture this Mr. Stowes—the man has proven to be a bit thick—I feel we also need to discover his employer. It is puzzling that whoever controls Stowes continues to take greater and greater risks. We should take it upon ourselves to unmask him," she announced.

Damn. This was not at all what Michael intended. "Perhaps we should not be so hasty—"

"Do not worry, Your Lordship." Now Suzie decided to join in. His headache was definitely worsening. "We will do everything we can to make Charlotte safe again."

Charlotte also shook her head in denial, but the other ladies did not seem to notice. Before Charlotte could convince them to cease their planning, Lady Kinsey went on, "In fact, I have already been thinking of ways to discover more about Mr. Stowes' puppeteer. Come, Suzie." The other two rose, holding a hushed discussion as they prepared to leave the room.

Lost, Michael turned to Charlotte, who only continued shaking her head, a pained but accepting look in her eyes. She leaned in to him, "When those two begin scheming, nothing short of Napoleon riding naked into London can stop them."

There was nothing more terrifying than Her Ladyship transforming into an army general. He called to them as they reached the doorway, "My lady, I believe we really must avoid direct contact with anyone who may turn out to be a villain."

In unison, the two ladies turned and raised an eyebrow. Apparently the general had already begun amassing her army. Suzie spoke first, "Lord Averly, I hope you do not doubt our skills in discretion. After all, time is of the essence. Even you must admit that in order to catch Mr. Stowes, we must act quickly. The more chances we give him to prepare for us, the more opportunities he will have to either finish what he started, or make his escape."

Michael could not be certain, but he thought he could actually hear Lady Kinsey's voice in that short speech. Those two needed to be separated, perhaps permanently.

And why did Charlotte remain silent? Surely she could at least make an attempt to dissuade those two?

Lady Kinsey came back into the drawing room to hover over him, hands on her hips. "Lord Averly," she announced, "perhaps you would prefer us to investigate your presence here tonight instead? I'm sure we have a great many questions to ask, particularly those surrounding what your intentions are now."

Michael's eyes narrowed. Apparently blackmail was a skill Charlotte had learned from Lady Kinsey. It was his turn to be affronted. "I can assure you, Your Ladyship, there is no need to feel concern over my intentions towards Miss Henwood." He tried to rise, but any movement only worsened his headache.

He heard Charlotte murmur, "So formal now, Lord Averly?" under her breath as she hid a smile. Her teasing almost put him in a better mood. Almost.

As he fell back against the settee from his sitting position, Her Ladyship addressed him. "If that is the case, then I recommend you remain here for the night." Michael was surprised. He had planned on remaining within the vicinity in order to keep watch over the house, but it would be a great deal easier, and certainly more comfortable, if he could stay inside. "Now, please excuse me while we ladies return to our beds. Alone," she added, giving Charlotte a stern look.

Charlotte nodded in acquiescence but remained seated next to Michael. When it became clear that Lady Kinsey had every intention of waiting the two lovers out, Charlotte sighed and joined Her Ladyship as they all went upstairs.

Stretching awkwardly out on the unpleasantly small settee, Michael prepared to spend the next few hours in sleepless discomfort. Perhaps ten minutes later, he thought he heard a door softly open upstairs. No wonder Charlotte had been so willing to follow the ladies to bed. Perhaps he would not be spending the night alone, after all.

"Don't even think about it." Lady Kinsey. How did that woman do that? After he heard an exasperated huff and then two doors close, Michael blew out his candles and leaned back. It seemed he *would* be spending the night alone. Pity.

# Chapter 25

———

**M**ICHAEL AWOKE to a heavy pounding. At first he thought the pounding was limited only to his head, but once he gained some level of consciousness, he decided that was not at all the case. There was a door somewhere being soundly attacked. But the front door to the Averly's London house was quite a way from his bedroom. His valet would never pound so hard on his bedroom door and Ryder would simply barge in and pour water over Michael's face or jump on his mattress. At least Ryder was never so evil as to tickle Michael awake.

*Charlotte.* Michael opened his eyes to Charlotte's drawing room, remembering how he had spent the previous night. It would seem that despite his attempts to remain awake and keep watch, he had nodded off. Not for long enough to feel rested, but his headache had somewhat improved.

Why was no one answering the door? He remembered Charlotte having to come to the door during his eventful early-morning visit. The ladies of the household could probably sleep through a horse race. Damn it all, someone needed to answer the door, if only to end the pounding.

Perhaps if Michael were a touch more awake, he would have gone upstairs and brought Suzie or Charlotte down to answer the door for him. Instead, Michael rolled awkwardly off the settee, tripped over a table, and finally made his way to the front door.

He swung Charlotte's town home door wide open in a desperate attempt to prevent another agonizing headache. The cool breeze ruffling his shirtsleeves drew his gaze down. He wasn't even wearing shoes, let alone a waistcoat. This may not have been one of his better ideas.

The visitor cleared his throat. "I do apologize. It has been some time since I last visited the city." Michael met the confused eyes of a slender, tall, older man who seemed more than a little agitated. His salt-and-pepper hair and round-framed glasses gave the impression of a kind-hearted, gentle character. However, the intelligence in those eyes told a different story. They also reminded Michael of something. "Am I not at least somewhat near Miss Charlotte Henwood's residence?" The visitor stepped back to steal another glance at the house number.

"Oh. Ah." Instinctively, Michael reached up to rub his morning stubble, accidentally brushing his new bruise. Wincing, he answered the stranger, "No, no. I mean, yes. You found the correct address. Allow me to awake the household and fetch her."

The man reached out to catch Michael's arm. "She is well, then? Perfectly fine?" he asked.

Michael nodded. "She is home and in perfect health. I'll just go and fetch her." He thought the visitor's obvious relief was a bit odd, but he refrained from commenting.

Michael turned around before he could catch the look on the man's face turn to suspicion before the visitor murmured, "Dress for household staff has certainly become lax since I was last in London."

When he reached the staircase, some semblance of reason reached Michael's mind. With all the problems surrounding Charlotte, he really ought to better ensure her safety. Letting a complete stranger into her home did not fall into that category. Should he ask the man to wait outside? No, if he were a threat, he would already know to simply go to the back and use the broken door to gain entrance.

At the foot of the stairs, Michael turned. "Might I enquire as to your name?" Perhaps that might not be the most effective defense strategy. Polite introductions did not tend to instill insurmountable fear into a possible threat.

"Sir Driscoll. Now could you please see to Miss Henwood?"

Why was that name so familiar? "Erm. Please excuse me." Michael hoped Sir Driscoll did not notice the slight catch in his voice.

---

A soft creak roused Charlotte from a fitful sleep. Memories from the previous night came rushing back. Gasping, she sat up in bed, preparing for the newest danger.

The spots cleared from her eyes to reveal Michael standing in her doorway, in only his shirt and formal breeches. Letting out a relieved breath, Charlotte smiled. Not all of the previous night's memories were bad.

"I thought Lady Kinsey was quite clear about staying downstairs. Don't you care about protecting my maidenly honor?" she asked while stretching her arms slowly above her head. Distracted by the way her chest thrust forward with the motion, Michael couldn't avoid his own satisfied smile. This beautiful, interesting, clever woman was finally his. Now what in the world would he do with her? While a great many immensely satisfying images swirled through his mind, his primary concern was keeping her out of trouble—a heroic task indeed.

Leaning against the doorframe, he said, "It was, of course, my every intention to leave you safely ensconced in your room. However, you have an early visitor." Glancing at the clock on the mantel, he added, "Well, an only somewhat early visitor. A Sir Driscoll?"

More than a moment passed for Charlotte to fully process this information in her sleepy state. What reason would bring her father out of his quiet library to the busy streets of London? Another horrific thought struck. "Michael! Did my father see you dressed like-like-like *that*?"

"Well, my shoes and coat are in here. What else could I have done?" Cocking his head, Michael realized he had never before heard Charlotte stutter. While he had a special talent for bringing out her more fiery nature, she was usually an impressively composed woman. Wait. Her father? "Your *father*? You said he never left Uckfield!"

Appalled, Michael immediately took up his discarded clothing and began frantically dressing. Perhaps they had been lucky and Sir Driscoll had been too intent on finding his daughter to notice Michael's state of partial undress. And perhaps Michael would one day overthrow the monarchy. Actually, with Charlotte and Ryder's assistance, such a thing could come to pass.

Charlotte took the first day dress she could find from her wardrobe. It was a burnt orange gown with a dark blue trim. Charlotte nearly dressed faster than Michael. However, at one or two points, his assistance was required to hurry things along. On her way out, Charlotte drew a slip of paper from a drawer in her bedside table. Before Michael could question it, Charlotte rushed out of the room and down the stairs.

She did not stop until she ran into her father's arms. "Papa! I can't believe you are here!" Her voice was muffled against his coat.

A soft smile on his face, Sir Driscoll Henwood murmured, "Well, my reason for being here is certainly a story, I can assure you." The smile slowly left his face as he again took in the elegantly dressed, if slightly rumpled, gentleman who stood uncertainly at the foot of the stairs.

Sir Driscoll did not believe the black knee breeches and coat with the matching soft leather shoes had recently become the rage in London society's day wear. Likely the man's attire had been put to use at a previous evening's entertainment. Sir Driscoll's eyes narrowed. "I seem to recall you wearing a great deal less apparel when you first came to the door."

Sir Driscoll gently released his daughter, even going so far as to offer her a quiet smile as he stepped around her to approach Michael. Michael felt his face heat as Sir Driscoll's smile transformed into a hard scowl. Although he had no idea what to say in his defense, Michael took in a breath, intending to try.

As Charlotte's irate father slammed his fist into Michael's face, Michael decided there was probably nothing he could have said. But goodness, why was everyone so inclined to immediately resort to violence? Even a man that Michael had taken to be quite the scholar was turning to his fists. It was a most disturbing trend.

Even worse, Michael discovered that, unlike Mr. Stowes, Sir Driscoll was left-handed. What would people say when they saw the Viscount Averly with a wicked bruise on each side of his face? Michael was not a vain man, but he was a touch bothered by how ridiculous he would look in a day or two, when the bruises fully darkened.

As Sir Driscoll raised his fist for another go, Charlotte called out, "Papa, stop! He's a viscount!"

That was her defense? Michael had a feeling her news would not improve his situation. In fact, this new bit of information appeared to make matters worse.

Her father sent her a fulminating look over his shoulder before he brought his fist back. "We're engaged!" Michael yelled as he desperately held his hands in front of his face. The plea in his voice was a touch embarrassing, but what could he really do if Sir Driscoll continued to pummel him? It would be beyond the par to return a blow to a man of Sir Driscoll's age.

Sir Driscoll stepped back and looked to his daughter, whose eyes were now wide in shock. "Is this true, Charlotte?"

Michael waited for her to confirm his announcement. And waited. Then waited some more.

She did not seem to be avoiding an answer. Far from it, she appeared to be staring at Michael as expectantly as he was staring at her. The longer she took, the more agitated Michael became.

Was she all of a sudden unsure? Had last night changed her mind? Damn it all, it had not exactly been a terrible experience for either of them.

Before Michael could fully question his ability to comprehend the female of the species, a set of footsteps descended the stairs. Michael looked up to see Her Ladyship stop halfway down the staircase, fully dressed for the day, her hair in a complicated twist that must have taken hours to create. Had she slept at all?

Upon taking in the scene before her, Lady Kinsey regally announced, "Charlotte, we really must find you friends who are aware of exactly what constitutes polite visiting hours. It is much too early for us to engage in another unnecessary brawl in this household," she added, noticing Sir Driscoll's boxer-like stance and raised fists. Michael decided to refrain from mentioning that everyone had slept until well after ten. Lady Kinsey did not brook disagreement. In anything.

Charlotte called up to Lady Kinsey, "Lady Kinsey, may I introduce my father, Sir Driscoll Henwood. Papa, this is my chaperone, Lady Kinsey." She added to Her Ladyship, still addressing Sir Driscoll's primary question, "Papa is currently defending my honor from the possibly insidious Lord Averly. I think it's quite sweet. Pray continue, father."

*Why, that mischievous little minx!* "Charlotte, you know damn well that we're engaged. Do be so good as to tell your father to stand down before I am forced to fight back!"

"Oh I don't know, Michael. Whether or not I do that depends on whether or not we are actually engaged. I would never want to lie to my father, after all."

"What are you talking about?" Flabbergasted, Michael watched as Sir Driscoll made another swing at his head. At least this time he was prepared to jump back in time. But with Sir Driscoll continuing to close in on him, there were only so many steps back he could take before hitting the wall. Feeling like a cornered fox, Michael tried another tactic. "Lady Kinsey, could you please explain to Charlotte's father that I was left to believe that she and I are engaged?"

Still standing halfway up the staircase, Lady Kinsey clasped her hands in front of herself and serenely declared, "Sir Driscoll, I have no doubt that Lord Averly speaks the truth about believing him and your daughter to be engaged."

Relief flooded into Michael and he relaxed. "Thank you."

"That does not mean that the engagement is official."

"What? Oof!" Sir Driscoll's fist connected with Michael's now unprotected midsection. Why were the women of the house suddenly so bent on his destruction? Just because the bans had not been read, it did not mean they were not engaged. After last night, how could they not be?

Desperate, Michael threw his hands up. "Wait, wait, wait! Let me discover what is going on here, then you can pummel me all you like."

Sir Driscoll eyed him suspiciously, but in a moment stepped back. "Perhaps we should allow the ladies to explain themselves. Charlotte sometimes takes perverse pleasure in leaving everyone in the dark."

Michael snorted. "Sometimes?"

"You should know that I can hear you right now, Michael," Charlotte called from the entryway.

"Well if you can hear everything, then why not join the conversation? Perhaps you could explain what is happening in that demented mind of yours," he called as he rubbed his abdomen.

Eyes slit from temper, Charlotte began crossing the hall to them. Michael discovered that Charlotte developed an alluring little sashay when especially irritated. She said, "Oh, I will gladly tell you exactly what is happening in this demented mind, Lord Averly."

Sir Driscoll had become more than a little irked by their interchange. "Charlotte Euphedora Henwood!" Charlotte did not like the way that Michael perked up, upon hearing her heinous middle name. Her father went on, "I've spent the last day worried sick that you were in some kind of danger or worse. Now is not the time to get caught up in meaningless arguments."

Michael cut Charlotte off before she could answer. "Perhaps Lady Kinsey will be a safer source for us to question," he said to Sir Driscoll.

Recognizing the seldom-seen glint in his daughter's eye, Sir Driscoll nodded his agreement. "Yes, you're right. Lady Kinsey, would you be so good as to explain? Why does my daughter dispute the claim that she and Lord Averly are engaged after he appears to have spent the night in her home?"

Her Ladyship practically preened with the opportunity to share her knowledge. "Certainly, Sir Driscoll. And may I say your fist was quite expertly delivered to Lord Averly's belly. No doubt His Lordship shall be quite uncomfortable for the next few days." After emitting an awkward choking sound, Michael tried to interrupt, but Lady Kinsey went on. "I believe your daughter is referring to the fact that, in the midst of last evening's chaos—we did have an eventful break-in last night— Lord Averly no doubt forgot to make a formal request for Miss Henwood's hand."

"Ah—wait. Someone broke into your home? Blast it all, Charlotte, you assured me that this was the absolute safest part of Town!"

Charlotte groaned in frustration. "Papa, it was nothing like that!" When her father put his hands on his hips, Charlotte threw her arms up in exasperation and turned to Her Ladyship.

While Lady Kinsey explained the details to Sir Driscoll, at the same time trying to reassure him, Michael closed the distance to Charlotte. "That's what this is all about? You allowed your father to attack me, because I never got down on bended knee and begged for your hand? I assumed our being engaged was simply a given, or else I would never have checked on your townhouse last night. Damn it, Charlotte, the entire *ton* believes we are engaged. There's no way you could get out of it anyway."

Satisfaction replaced anger in her brown eyes. "Lord Averly, I think you should know that I have no intention of marrying you, unless you get down on that bloody knee and ask me." She wagged a finger at him, "Last night, we agreed we would *discuss* our future and the possibility of marriage. Nothing was decided on at that time."

After all they had been through, Michael was infuriated that she still wanted to put him through hell. "Why is it so blasted important that I formally propose? I would think that marrying me in the first place would bloody well be enough!" Why did he only curse in Miss Henwood's presence? "Isn't it?" Michael had an uneasy feeling that that had not come out as he intended.

Michael guessed that the red staining her cheeks after his proclamation had more to do with newfound rage than romantic passion. Best to escape now. What were Lady Kinsey and Sir Driscoll doing? Perhaps they could draw away his hopeful fiancée's ire. Turning to join them, Michael found the two staring at him with somewhat dumbfounded expressions. There was even a hint of pity in Sir Driscoll's eyes.

"Well." As a change of subject, Lady Kinsey's one word was a bit unimpressive. Another awkward silence filled the room. No one seemed prepared to fill it.

Michael decided it was up to him to distract everyone. "So." The time had come to move beyond these single-worded sentences. "Sir Driscoll." Charlotte's father raised his brows. "Erm, what particular occurrence instigated your unexpected visit to London?"

A slight upward quirk in Sir Driscoll's cheek acknowledged Michael's attempt at a diversion as he answered. "You are perfectly right, Lord Averly, in thinking that something beyond an overwhelming desire to see my daughter brought me here. Not that I did not wish to visit Charlotte," he added quickly. "But my presence here has a great deal to do with an unexpected visit from an irritatingly odd man followed by a few equally odd anonymous letters, not to mention the one from my daughter describing a worrisome occurrence in Hyde Park. Most of these letters suggested I back out of the mining venture. The last letter was quite short but the meaning was clear. It demanded I come to London immediately as my daughter had been kidnapped." Everyone's jaws dropped at this news.

Charlotte turned to Michael. "Do you think that is what Stowes was up to last night? To kidnap me?" Michael could only shake his head helplessly in answer. "Papa, is there anything else you can tell us about this letter?"

"Not exactly. It was short and to the point...But what do you know of the Earl of Tunley?"

Charlotte was momentarily awestruck. "Lord Tunley claimed to have kidnapped me?"

Sir Driscoll shook his head. "No, no," he said. "It is only that Lord Tunley happened to pay me a strange visit in the midst of all this."

"You sent me a letter mentioning Tunley's visit to Uckfield, but went into little detail," Charlotte interrupted. "I've been desperate to discover why he went there in the first place."

Her father sent her a wry look, which appeared to be enough to quiet his daughter. Michael briefly wished that he could find a way to duplicate that expression. Likely such a look was only perfected after years of parenting. Sir Driscoll continued on as though she had not spoken. "I certainly cannot blame a Londoner for visiting our lovely little town. Uckfield is, after all, quite famous for its pudding cake."

Charlotte interjected. "Papa, I doubt that Lord Tunley visited Uckfield to experience its pudding cake firsthand. Just what exactly did you and Lord Tunley discuss when he dropped in on you? From my experience, he seldom has anything interesting to say—or at least nothing that I would want to hear—the odious little man," she added under her breath.

Instead of answering, Sir Driscoll eyed the group surrounding him. Charlotte watched him briefly glance towards the drawing room. It would be polite to offer him a place to sit, but there were so many things to do, starting with a visit to the Madisons. Sitting down for tea would not fit into their schedule at all.

Recognizing that a rest time would not be forthcoming, Sir Driscoll answered, "He primarily wanted me to visit London with him. Apparently, His Lordship thought I should bring myself to Town so that my troublesome daughter would cease depleting the family coffers. He seemed to think Charlotte was in great need of my guidance."

Turning to face his daughter, Sir Driscoll added, "Whatever his motivation, the earl seems to have certainly taken an interest in your actions. From a father's perspective, I cannot say I like him. I even contacted Harry about it. We had hoped to take care of the matter without worrying you. Once I learned about this Mr. Stowes character, I began making plans to come to London. Harry's letter was much more forthcoming about your encounter than you were, my dear. When I received the last anonymous letter, I came straight away."

Affronted, Charlotte returned, "Papa, I assure you, I can take perfect care of myself without Harry and Imogen checking in on me. Besides that, I have been trying so very hard to keep them from all the trouble surrounding me."

The baronet nodded. "Harry wrote to tell me that you, young lady, have been avoiding him and the rest of the family. I had a feeling that something must be wrong."

As Michael watched Charlotte's eyes narrow in that special way of hers, no doubt in preparation for a carefully worded response, he decided that silence could only be a virtue for so long. It was time to cut in, before a family tiff began. Michael said, "Charlotte, I hope you realize we have greater concerns than the reasons behind your father's visit. We need to consider what to do about Lord Tunley after the appalling things he said last night."

"Oh, so you've also had the pleasure of his company? Charming, isn't he?" Sir Driscoll asked cheerfully. "He certainly seemed to dislike you, dear darling daughter. The aspersions he cast upon your character were most impressive. Whatever did you do to the poor man?"

"I really haven't a clue," Charlotte said curtly. "You may have a point, Lord Averly. He seems to be connected to quite a few of the problems we have been facing for the last few months. This is quite remarkable."

Several moments passed as everyone in the hallway pondered just why an earl would spend so much of his time attempting to defame Miss Charlotte Henwood, a woman he had seldom ever encountered in society. Judging by the faces surrounding him, Michael could tell everyone was drawing a blank.

Although he had been more than pleased to be ignored by an angry potential fiancée, her disgruntled father, and her diabolical chaperone, Michael again felt compelled to speak. Perhaps he was going mad. "Is it possible that none of this really has to do with Charlotte?"

While Lady Kinsey and Sir Driscoll appeared to consider the possibility, Charlotte seemed a bit put out. Lady Kinsey answered first. "You may have picked up on something important. Just who else is affected by these attacks on Charlotte?"

Sir Driscoll replied, "Other than myself, you mean? Well I should think the answer is obvious." Here he looked directly at his daughter, brows raised in expectation.

Charlotte groaned in understanding. "The Madisons."

# Chapter 26

———◦◦◦———

O F COURSE, this was all about the Madisons.
Charlotte said, "I've been so focused on protecting them
from the attacks on me; I never thought that they were the
desired victims."

Shaking his head, her father said, "My dear, Harry is a great
deal better guarded than a young unmarried woman with only a
female chaperone and lady's maid as protection. I doubt anyone
would be able to break into Harry's home in the middle of the
night without alerting several members of the household.
Harry's extensive staff is much better equipped to fend off
unruly intruders."

Why must Charlotte's father support every statement with
irrefutable logic? Surely that was not necessary for every
occasion.

Cutting into Charlotte's thoughts, Lady Kinsey said, "We'll
never have the complete story until we speak with Mr.
Madison."

Charlotte felt apprehensive about bringing the Madisons
into this debacle. After the weeks she spent protecting them, it
almost seemed like doing so would signal defeat. She had been
so hopeful that she would be able to end the gossip on her own.
Now she realized that the idea was foolish and perhaps a touch
optimistic. Blast it all! She had almost managed to bring
everything back to normal. Things only became troublesome
again when that man accosted her in Hyde Park.

Before Charlotte could think up another protest, she noticed
Lady Kinsey begin donning her outerwear. It was too late now.

On a sigh, Charlotte said, "We had best try to arrive before the Madisons leave to go calling."

As everyone put on their coats, Michael offered to find a hackney. Charlotte immediately replied that it was far faster for everyone to walk, the Madisons lived so close. "But you, Lord Averly, should consider going home. Your formal evening attire will likely draw unwanted attention," she said as she donned a dark blue spencer.

Lady Kinsey opened a concealed drawer in the entryway's table and withdrew several pins. It took only a few expert twists and loops on Lady Kinsey's part to pin Charlotte's hair into a surprisingly formal, if simple, style. Her hair was then covered with a bonnet, the ribbons of which perfectly matched the dark blue ribbons in her dress. The whole transformation was quite impressive.

Sir Driscoll slowed his exit to wait for Michael. "Charlotte has always been a well-prepared young woman. No doubt it is due to her natural curiosity, combined with her education. I must say, I hope you have an extensive library, Lord Averly, else my daughter will likely turn you out of pocket in building one up." At that, Sir Driscoll jogged a little to catch up with the ladies.

Well, now what should Michael do? He really could not be seen with the Henwoods dressed as he was. Everyone would know his apparel was from the previous evening's engagement.

Apparently, he must make his way home to change. If Charlotte thought she could get rid of him so easily, she had best be prepared for a surprise. As soon as he changed out of his formal evening clothes, he had every intention of joining them at the Madisons'. By the time he drew in a breath to inform everyone that he would be seeing them again soon, the trio had turned a corner and were out of sight.

It was only after he found his brother's carriage to ride home that he realized Sir Driscoll might have just given Michael his blessing. Trust a Henwood to do so over a brief conversation covering Charlotte's unpredictability and her need for well-stocked libraries.

---

When Charlotte turned back to ask Michael if he would meet them at the Madisons', she discovered him gone. Had she been so hard on him that he no longer wanted anything to do with her? Considering what she had put him through for the last few weeks, she greatly doubted he would give up now.

Truly, why couldn't the man be so good as to formally request her hand in marriage? Every woman at least wanted to be given the choice. Charlotte sighed again, thinking of her friends in London. Perhaps that wasn't true. Most of her peers would not be given such an option, as the gentleman in question would simply go to the lady's father. She supposed she should have been shocked when Michael announced their engagement to dear Papa without first requesting his permission—not that Papa had much choice. Yet no one had expressed any particular outrage at Michael's comment, nor would Charlotte have expected them to.

Well, that was not entirely true. There had been quite a bit of ire on Charlotte's side. That had more to do with wounded pride. She ought to be impressed that Michael had at least skipped the tradition of first speaking with the father. The man was so bloody straight-laced in everything else he did; she should commend him for those few moments in which he unbent, if only a little.

Charlotte stopped walking, momentarily awestruck. She was unusually lucky in her friends and family. She was lucky to have a group of people who accepted that she did not always live her life the traditional way. She was certainly lucky to have a father who did not believe in the standard education for a young lady. Not only that, but what other girl had a father who trusted her skills and intelligence so greatly that he would happily sign his name to whatever new investment Charlotte found for him?

She was lucky to have friends who did not think it odd for a young woman to wish to learn all she could about the process of investing. Those same friends were more than willing to guide her in an elevated world—one she had only ever read of in novels.

With all the trouble she had fallen into, Michael had expressed wonder that she had not completely ruined herself. Charlotte finally understood exactly why she always remained just clear of impending disaster. Her friends and family helped and protected her. More than that, they taught her how to protect herself.

Perhaps she had had the greatest luck of all in finding a kind, intelligent man who cared for her, despite her habit of pressing against so very many social boundaries. Certainly, at first, Michael had expended quite a bit of effort keeping Charlotte out of trouble. But look at him now, causing a bit of his own trouble, by sneaking into bedrooms in the dead of night and confronting an earl in the middle of a ballroom.

Hadn't that been her greatest objection to that pathetic proposal of his? He always acted too bloody proper. She couldn't resist a soft smile. Should she concern herself with the fact that she had turned one of London's perfect gentlemen into just a bit of a scoundrel?

Lady Kinsey and Sir Driscoll soon realized Charlotte stood alone on the corner of the street. Patient as always, her father simply placed his hands behind his back, while Lady Kinsey cocked her head and raised a brow.

When Charlotte continued to stare off into the middle of nowhere, Lady Kinsey decided it was time to break the girl's reverie. "If you want to stand on a street corner and take in the sights, instead of find out what the devil is going on, you're welcome to. However, I do wish to continue on, if you are ready."

Speaking of Charlotte's friends...

"Where in the world is Suzie?" she asked.

Lady Kinsey's lips compressed, as though she were suppressing a smile. "She's pursuing another avenue in our investigation."

Charlotte could only shrug. She doubted Her Ladyship would volunteer any more information. Returning to the task at hand, Charlotte strode up to and between her two companions. Taking their arms, she said, "No need to dilly-dally, let's go and see the Madisons." She would have time later to think on Michael Skidmore, Viscount Averly, and all of his qualities. At the moment, they had a villain to unmask. Goodness, to think only a year ago her excitements involved teaching the children of Uckfield music, and riding Esmerelda across the countryside.

Smiling to herself, she set a brisker pace. For just a moment, she wondered what direction her life would have taken, had she not accepted a stranger's invitation to join him in his tavern room.

---

The moment Michael strode through his front door, Stoome waylaid him. "My lord, you have a visitor."

Michael did not have time for this. "If it is one of Ryder's creditors, tell the bloody man that I will meet with him another day. Now I need the carriage to be kept ready and please send my valet to my room."

Already striding up the wide staircase, Michael missed Stoome's seldom-seen look of dismay. "My lord."

The strain in his butler's voice gave Michael pause. He leaned over the banister to call, "What is it? If Marlowe has not yet arisen, I can certainly dress myself, but I need my brother's carriage to be kept ready." Michael would have preferred to simply take his horse, but he had a feeling he should not expect to be traveling alone for the day.

Before the Skidmore family's harried butler could again appeal to his equally harried employer, a door below Michael's vantage point opened. While Michael only felt irritation at the interruption, Stoome appeared relieved. Perhaps Michael ought to take a moment and discover just what new event needed his attention.

"Lord Averly, is that you?" An unusually unkempt Mr. Hampstead strode nervously into the entryway. Then again, Michael had little right to judge Hampstead on the man's appearance. At least Hampstead was not still wearing the previous evening's formal attire.

"Good Lord, Hampstead, whatever are you doing here at this hour?" Had something changed in their friendship to justify the man coming over to share breakfast? Hampstead was a good friend to Charlotte, but Michael always considered him to be a bit of a rival because of that.

Michael had at least won the lady. Well, mostly. Then Michael noticed the bouquet of especially sad posies clutched firmly in Hampstead's hand.

All of a sudden, an unpleasant scenario unwound itself in Michael's mind. He could imagine Hampstead deciding to woo Charlotte in the middle of the night, but discovering that another gentleman had beaten him to the punch. Michael felt an oddly primitive emotion sweep through him: possessiveness. If Hampstead did not already know that Charlotte belonged to Michael, Michael would happily tell him right now.

Before Michael could do any such thing, Hampstead began talking. "I'm truly sorry, Lord Averly. I simply couldn't think where else to go. I doubt Miss Henwood would even understand. And I certainly cannot discuss such a delicate matter with my usual friends. But you have always seemed the height of discretion. Besides that, she's Charlotte's friend and I just know Charlotte would chastise me for arriving so early to visit with anyone. I planned on waiting." While Hampstead rambled on, he began to wave his arms in his agitation, scattering pink and red petals across the entryway. Stoome did not look pleased. "I planned on waiting until a better hour before visiting, but since I could not sleep, I left much sooner than I intended. But I was going to wait until a polite hour to call, I swear it."

Oh dear. How long had Hampstead been outside of Charlotte's town home?

He continued, "I simply thought it would be wise to be the absolute first caller of the day, you understand. To make a sound impression. There is nothing wrong with doing my waiting outside the Madisons' home instead of inside my own. I was going to have to wait somewhere, after all. I admit it is a bit unorthodox, but I'm sure no one saw me."

Michael's mind latched onto one specific point. "The Madisons? What in the world were you doing at their home at this hour?"

Exasperated, Hampstead slammed his fistful of flowers onto a side table. "Why I was there is beside the point now. I have something more important to tell you." Nonetheless, both men's eyes traveled to the wilted posies resting so pathetically next to Hampstead.

"Something more important than the fact that you appear to have stood on the London streets for several hours, waiting for an appropriate time to call on Miss Julia Madison?"

Already shaking his head, Hampstead broke in, "That doesn't matter now. It would appear I don't stand a chance, seeing as how Miss Madison has eloped."

Michael was shocked. "You can't be serious. Miss Madison would never do that to her family." Michael had seen enough of the Madison family to know that their daughter was incredibly loyal and honest.

Hampstead waved that off, as he began to pace in the entryway. "You must be wrong. Perhaps it is because the man in question clearly was not her social equal. They were both in an obvious hurry to leave. I could see how nervous Miss Madison was, by the way she continued to glance back at the house. I can only assume she was making certain no one saw their furtive exit." Hampstead's anxiety over the newest turn of events seemed to be a touch extreme for a man barely acquainted with the Madisons. What had Michael missed during his distracting association with Miss Henwood?

However, after the events of the previous evening, Michael was willing to warrant that things were not quite as they seemed. On any other occasion, Michael would have invited his unexpected guest to join him for refreshments, or perhaps a cigar. Instead, he looked for Stoome to reenter the room from the service door. As though on cue, Stoome returned and nodded discreetly at Michael. Michael turned back to the agitated Mr. Hampstead. "I am already on my way to the Madisons'. Why don't you join me, so we can try to sort everything out?"

Hampstead instinctively shook his head in denial. Michael said, "I think Miss Madison is more of an innocent in this than you think."

Hampstead seemed unprepared for the possibility of actually confronting the Madisons. Finally, he nodded. Michael sprinted up the stairs to change as quickly as possible.

As he returned downstairs, he waved for Hampstead to follow. Hampstead found his horse already tied onto the carriage.

"Now," Michael said as they seated themselves inside, "tell me exactly what you saw today, starting with a description of the man you saw with Miss Madison."

―⁓―

Charlotte, Sir Driscoll, and Lady Kinsey arrived to absolute chaos at the Madison townhouse. The front door was wide open. They could see the entire staff running back and forth, tearing the house apart.

Mrs. Madison bustled into the entry, stopping short when she saw the visitors. Instead of Imogen's usual cheerful welcome, the woman's face fell. "She isn't with you?" she cried.

"I just sent a footman over to see if she was there. Perhaps you've been out and missed her?"

"Who? What is going on here?" Charlotte asked, but she was starting to get the idea. There was only one lady who could send the house into such turmoil.

Hearing their voices, Mr. Madison emerged from somewhere in the direction of his study. "Julia is missing. There is no note. We haven't a clue where to even look." The announcement was enough to send Mrs. Madison over the edge. The woman erupted into tears.

Offering soothing words and comfort, Lady Kinsey ushered Mr. and Mrs. Madison up to their private family drawing room. "Here, sit down." She set them onto a chaise longue. "Now, I must tell you that none of us have seen Julia since the Ashton ball. When was the last time you saw her?"

Harry answered. "It was also last night, directly before we retired. One of our downstairs maids saw her this morning. We had not yet risen, but apparently Julia did not sleep well, so she requested tea and a few biscuits, until breakfast could be prepared. The maid said she was already in her morning dress, but certainly not prepared to leave the house."

Charlotte, and no doubt Lady Kinsey as well, tried to think of some offer of reassurance. Before anything truly insightful or helpful came to her, Mrs. Madison burst out, "Oh, I just know it must be that estate manager of yours, Harry! You should not have hired someone so young and attractive, with a sweet girl like our Julia in the house. No doubt he has convinced the poor girl to run off with him."

Charlotte had never before heard Imogen leap to such a dramatic conclusion. The woman Charlotte had come to think of as a second mother always seemed so very cheerful and unflappable. Harry quickly replied, "I highly doubt the young Mr. Stratton would risk his new position in such a way."

"Harry, how can you be so naïve? What is an estate manager's pay, compared to Julia's dowry?"

While Mrs. Madison had an excellent point, Charlotte knew for a fact that Harry Madison paid everyone in his employ exceptionally well. His previous estate manager had retired after only seven years in his service. With that in mind, Charlotte would have been shocked to discover any man would risk his position in order to abscond with his employer's daughter. One could not be certain he would actually get his hands on Julia's dowry. Not only that, Mr. Madison was not a man that one should cross. If Mr. Stratton did take Julia, there was really only one reason he would do so—a reason that Sir Driscoll foolishly voiced.

"Perhaps this Stratton fellow is in love with Julia?"

As expected, mayhem erupted within the drawing room. Lady Kinsey tried to offer some comfort to the Madisons—who were now engaged in a full-blown argument about Stratton—while Charlotte chastised her father for not thinking before saying such a thing. The Madisons could not care less about their employee's feelings where their daughter was concerned. Running off with him would result in Julia's immediate social suicide.

It was in such a state that Lord Averly and Mr. Hampstead arrived at the Madison household. Amongst the frantic staff, they found their own way to the drawing room, only to discover the occupants in a raving panic.

---

Perfectly content to see Charlotte's ire focused elsewhere, Michael chose to refrain from joining the others for a moment. Hampstead also remained near the entrance, no doubt drawing on Michael for support. Michael could understand his reticence; the Madisons and Henwoods did not seem especially welcoming at the moment. If Hampstead were surrounded by an army of the *ton's* most charming widows, doubtless he would have been perfectly in his element. Instead, he was about to face the parents of a young unmarried lady. Michael wondered if

Hampstead had ever spoken with such a young woman's parents—without attempting to seduce the mother, of course.

The dainty floral and pastel décor of the room was at odds with the intense group occupying it. But now was not the time to take interest in the design standards of the day.

As the various arguments in the room reached an alarming crescendo, Michael decided he had best intervene. Stepping into the center of the room, everyone's heads swung to face him.

Now he had no choice but to speak. Blast. "I assume this furor involves the disappearance of Miss Madison." He watched Charlotte's brows draw together, no doubt preparing another tirade. Michael turned to Hampstead, who remained in the doorway.

Hastily, he said, "Mr. Hampstead saw what happened." Michael quickly strode across the room to stand in front of the window. The bright sun shining in from behind obscured his features to everyone else in the room, allowing him to safely observe the proceedings. He might as well let Hampstead deliver the latest news.

Judging by the look Hampstead sent him, Michael felt certain the man would have preferred setting himself on fire than face this group of worried people. But, if he wanted anything to do with Miss Madison, he had best get used to dealing with whatever new disaster the Madisons and Henwoods became embroiled in.

Mrs. Madison had quieted enough to again sit next to her husband on the chaise longue. Her Ladyship sat nearby, prepared to calm the Madisons if necessary. Sir Driscoll paced behind them.

When Hampstead began to explain what he had seen earlier that morning, Michael realized that staying on the outskirts was no longer an option. Lady Kinsey murmured comforting words to Mrs. Madison as Hampstead delivered his news, but there was another lady who needed his comfort and support. He took an empty seat next to Charlotte.

Clearing his throat in discomfort, Hampstead contended that he just happened to be wandering by, when he saw Miss Madison alight into an unfamiliar carriage with a strange man. Michael avoided adding just why Hampstead happened to be in the area.

Michael reached over and took Charlotte's hand. It was a risk. Instead of pulling her hand back, she turned and offered him a small smile, concern still crinkling her forehead. Michael squeezed her fingers in support.

Mr. Hampstead finished, "I wouldn't have noted her departure at all, had it not been so early. This all took place close to eight this morning."

Mrs. Madison cried out, "You see, Harry? Julia has clearly eloped! You call on Mr. Stratton and demand he return our dear daughter to us. Dear Lord! Eight in the morning! They could be halfway to Gretna Green by now!"

Michael chose not to correct Mrs. Madison's skewed understanding of the relationship between distance and time. If Mr. Stratton was truly on his way to Gretna, it would be quite the challenge to call on him. Lady Kinsey murmured something soothing in Mrs. Madison's direction, but it seemed to have little effect.

Instead of answering Mrs. Madison, Mr. Madison leaned back, pinching the bridge of his nose. Before Mrs. Madison could add to her terrifying scenario, Hampstead said, "I do not believe Miss Madison has eloped."

This news managed to quiet Mrs. Madison. Michael had a feeling it wouldn't be for long. Mr. Hampstead went on; "After speaking with Lord Averly, I believe she may have been kidnapped."

Oh, so now Hampstead decided to draw Michael back into the conversation. *Well done. Well done, indeed.*

# Chapter 27

**M**ICHAEL WAS PREPARED for the outburst that followed. Sir Driscoll and Mr. Madison both began demanding more information from Hampstead, while Mrs. Madison let out some sort of eerie, keening wail that Michael prayed he would never again have to experience. Lady Kinsey waved her arms vigorously and called for everyone to quiet down.

As for Charlotte, she remained separate. Silent, she stared fixedly at the mantel, deep in thought, before turning to Michael. Worry and confusion filled eyes that begged for his support. Despite the untenable situation, Michael felt warmed. He may not know just how and when to deliver a perfect proposal, but when things turned sour, Charlotte trusted him to help her.

When Lady Kinsey finally managed to silence the room, Michael gave Charlotte's hand one more squeeze before speaking. "When I spoke with Mr. Hampstead earlier, he was able to describe the gentleman with Miss Madison in relative detail to me. I believe the man with her now is a Mr. Stowes, the same man who paid a visit to Miss Henwood and Lady Kinsey last night. Most likely, when things did not go well there, he concocted a new plan."

By now everyone was listening intently. Mr. Madison enquired exactly what had transpired the previous night. Michael briefly explained, trying his best not to upset the Madisons further.

As Michael went over the events of the last few hours, Charlotte was impressed by the calming effect he had on everyone. As he went on, somehow without alarming his audience too greatly, Charlotte realized something important. No matter what challenges or tragedies life offered, Michael was the only man she would want to stand by her side.

Holding his hand, here and now, Charlotte forgave everything. Michael had every reason to believe they would marry after last night. The poor man had not grown up reading every romantic story he could get his hands on like she had, after all. How could he understand that the young girl in her, who was so far removed from the woman she had become, would dream of an outrageously romantic proposal?

Charlotte resolved to speak with Michael as soon as they rescued Julia. It was strange, but Charlotte felt certain they would find her.

Michael concluded his short iteration of their strange visit last night. "I do not believe that Julia is in any physical danger from Stowes. His primary focus throughout this whole ordeal has been those mining shares."

With forced calm, Mr. Madison spoke. "If I could give him complete control over the ironworks and its shares, I damn well would. But that is impossible. It was simple to buy that land *from* Stowes, but now that we've begun mining it and extracting such large amounts of iron, no one could possibly be convinced to sell their shares back. Maybe a few friends would do so as a kindness to me, but not everyone. I certainly cannot convince anyone to do that in the time it will take for people to begin noticing Julia's absence."

Michael refused to offer false hope. Mr. Madison was right. If that was Stowes' demand, Madison would certainly have a problem on his hands. But Michael did have something to add. "We need to keep something else in mind. There is no longer any doubt that Mr. Stowes is acting at the behest of someone else. Stowes made it clear last night that a man who is clearly his social superior controls him." Should Michael go on? If he told Mr. Madison about his suspicions, what would the repercussions be? Worried that Madison might react precipitously, Michael looked briefly to Lady Kinsey. At her supportive nod, he went on, "Perhaps the solution seems too obvious, but we should seriously consider the possibility of—"

"Tunley," Mr. Madison nearly spat out the name.

Surprised at Mr. Madison's insight, Michael answered, "Well, yes. After his actions at the ball last night, coupled with the information Sir Driscoll provided this morning, I am nearly certain Tunley is responsible for sending Stowes after Miss Henwood both last night and that morning in Hyde Park." Michael decided to avoid mentioning his suspicion that Lord Tunley was also responsible for the vitriolic gossip surrounding Charlotte.

Mr. Madison nodded slowly in resignation. "He has also been demanding more power in the ironworks' management. But he started in on that nearly two years ago, a short while after I first allowed him to invest in it. After his inappropriate actions back then, I chose to disallow him access to any other ventures I oversaw. Since then, I believe he has acquired shares from several other investors. I still cannot imagine how he convinced those gentlemen to sell them."

Charlotte, who had remained silent for most of the conversation, replied, "Easy. Stowes." Charlotte had been coming to think of him as a comical figure after seeing him trussed up in Lady Kinsey's curtains, but now his name resonated through the room like a bad omen.

If Harry Madison had to give control of the ironworks over to Tunley, the results could be drastic. Not too long after mining officially commenced, a small village had developed to support its laborers and their families. Mr. Madison would never forgive himself if Lord Tunley chose to ignore the various safety measures he had implemented. And what would happen to those men and their families if their wages were significantly lowered? There was little doubt that Tunley would happily leave everyone quite destitute in order to acquire a few extra pounds.

Lady Kinsey leaned forward. "Speaking of Stowes, are we just going to wait for him to contact us with information about Julia? I do not know how else to approach the situation."

For a moment no one spoke. Charlotte was surprised to hear her father offer a suggestion. "If we are so certain that Tunley is behind all of the trouble that has been plaguing us, why not confront him now? From what I've seen of the man, I doubt he realizes that we suspect him of anything. The foolish sod likely is congratulating himself at this very moment." *Goodness, apparently Lord Tunley had made a notable impression on dear Papa.*

Once again, unfortunately, Charlotte had to agree with her father. Lord Tunley was undoubtedly mean-spirited, but not especially bright. "Well. Why don't we surprise him, then?"

Charlotte stood, preparing to rally the troops. It would seem that she was learning a few things from Lady Kinsey after all. When she turned to face everyone, she noticed none of her audience was rising. That certainly would not do. However, the raising of her two delicate brows was enough to spur everyone into action.

As the group shuffled through the drawing room door ahead of her, Charlotte realized that Michael still held her hand. She took a moment to tighten her grip and offer a small smile. It was the most she could muster in the circumstances.

While everyone's back was turned, Michael took a moment to lean in and kiss her forehead, ever so softly. If she could have, Charlotte would have melted into his chest, letting him hold her up for a moment. But Julia was the priority now.

Once they all made it to the entry, the recently reviled estate manager arrived. Mr. Madison took a few precious moments to apprise the man of the situation at hand, especially detailing Lord Tunley's expected involvement. Mr. Madison led Mr. Stratton into his office, to find Lord Tunley's address as well as deliver further instructions, all the while leaving out his wife's previous demands that he and Stratton duel.

While Mr. Madison engaged Mr. Stratton's attention, Mr. Hampstead pulled Michael aside for a brief conversation. As she was helping Mrs. Madison don her pelisse, Charlotte only caught snippets of it. There was something about a hunting lodge and cheap brandy. Charlotte did not think this was the time to discuss the latest fête, but Michael seemed to be listening quite intently.

Soon, everyone was ready, hastily spilling outside to alight into Michael's carriage. It was not until they crammed inside, that Charlotte realized Mr. Hampstead was missing. Craning her head sideways within the two inches of spare space the carriage would allow, Charlotte decided that Mr. Hampstead would not have fit comfortably in the first place. Six people stuffed into a carriage designed for four certainly allowed for everyone to become better acquainted.

Just as the carriage began rolling down the drive, everyone heard a distant, "Wait! Stop!"

Suzie had apparently made it back to the Madisons' house. Lady Kinsey had been a touch too evasive when Charlotte had asked about her maid. It would seem that Charlotte was about to discover what her friend had been up to all morning.

To Charlotte's dismay, when the carriage stopped, Suzie leaned through the door to speak with Mr. Madison. Charlotte had hoped she would speak with Lady Kinsey, who sat close enough for Charlotte to potentially overhear.

Whatever Suzie said to Harry was only loud enough for Charlotte to hear the words "rice" and "riding crop." They exchanged a few more words, and then Suzie leaned back out the carriage door, shooting Lady Kinsey a quick wink.

Charlotte expected her to object to remaining behind; instead, Suzie promised to wait at home, in case Julia made her way back. She tapped the outside of the carriage, signaling that everyone could go on.

None of it made a bit of sense. First Mr. Hampstead, and now Suzie was keeping things from her. Well, perhaps they were not doing so intentionally; nonetheless, Charlotte preferred being kept informed.

Perhaps Mr. Hampstead was following on his horse? When Charlotte asked Michael, whose lap she was practically sitting on, he simply replied that Mr. Hampstead had something else to look into. She could not blame Hampstead; the man was only connected to the Madisons through her.

So why was she bothered? She must have been imagining Mr. Hampstead's interest in Julia.

---

On the outside, Lord Tunley's home had an air of elegance and sophistication. But no immaculate butler or housekeeper opened the door. Instead, they were welcomed—not so warmly—by an obviously tired and disheveled footman. Briefly, Charlotte wondered if he was the same footman who had romanced the Madisons' maid. If so, she felt compelled to question the maid's tastes.

"His Lordship is not currently home. If you wish to leave a card, I can deliver it for you upon his return." The greeting seemed as if it had been delivered by rote. Michael had a feeling that very few were allowed through the heavy, beautifully-carved front doors.

The polite, proper thing to do would have been to leave the requested card and return at a later time. When he sneaked a glance at Sir Driscoll and Charlotte, Michael knew that that would not be happening. As one, their party pushed their way into the house. The poor lone footman did not stand a chance against the jabbering, frantic horde that the group created.

When they made their way inside, the classic opulence of the façade of the Tunley London residence fell away. There were lighter rectangles on the wallpaper, where expensive paintings and old mirrors had been removed. Within the rectangles, one could see that the walls had originally been of a light green, with a pattern of small, blue flowers. Except for those small spaces, the walls were mostly a dark, grimy, gray color.

Michael ignored the protestations of the harassed footman. He was primarily concerned that if the footman attempted to manhandle Sir Driscoll, Sir Driscoll would lay the man flat.

Perhaps they should all have had a discussion about better ways to maintain the element of surprise. The Madisons were arguing with Lady Kinsey about which rooms to search first, while the footman continued issuing objections to everyone's presence. Charlotte and Sir Driscoll were calmly discussing everything they could see in Tunley's home and what it could mean for his current financial situation.

Tunley's home had a wide stairwell that curved around the outside of the entry. It would have been considered lovely, had the dark wood been polished sometime in the last ten years.

Lord Tunley himself also made for an interesting picture as he descended it, loosely wearing a silk dressing robe and clutching his head with one hand, fingers digging into his hair. Issuing a groan, Tunley stopped half way down the stairs, gripping the banister to steady himself. It would seem that he had spent the previous night celebrating on the town.

Half of Michael's party did not even notice the man, until he spoke. "What the hell is this infernal noise? What do you people want?" By now, Tunley had seen the faces of his early visitors, although their identities took a moment to register. Upon seeing Charlotte Henwood's discouragingly cheerful smile, Tunley went pale. "Oh blast."

Quite illogically, Tunley turned and ran back up the stairs. Michael wondered if the installation of an upper-floor escape plan had become the new architectural style.

Michael immediately ran up and after Tunley. It seemed that being socked in the face in front of the woman Michael loved had turned him into a man of action. Michael stumbled on the stairs at his revelation. He was in love with Charlotte Henwood.

Of course he was. He would have to think further on that later. At the moment he had a villain to corner.

Vaulting to the top of the stairs, Michael saw Tunley stumble into a room at the end of a short hallway, slamming the door behind him. Michael reached the door at a dead run, no doubt bruising his shoulder as he rammed into it. It was no surprise to discover it locked. Rattling the knob a few more times, Michael turned to see Charlotte, her father, and Mr. Madison reach the top of the stairs, Charlotte leading the troops. Perhaps the other ladies were searching the house. He could either waste the time of finding the footman and demanding a key to the room or he could...

Hopefully the door would go down after the first kick or two; the alternative would be a touch embarrassing.

It took precisely two kicks for the door to swing wide and slam against the wall. Lord Tunley made a kind of high-pitched squeal in shock, dropping whatever documents were on their way to a wall-safe. No doubt the only painting left in the house covered it. Glancing around him, Michael noticed the room to be a sort of smaller study, with similar worn floral wallpaper to that found in the rest of the house, this room in a faded puce-like shade. How unfortunate.

Tunley first glanced desperately around the room for an exit. When he saw there was nothing else for it, he steeled himself and confronted the group. His signature snarl quavered a bit when he spoke. "Lord Averly, Mr. Madison. To what do I owe this pleasure?" Tunley's obvious skipping over the rest of his unexpected guests did not go unnoticed. Then again, no one curtsied or bowed.

Mr. Madison forced his way to the front of the group. "Lord Tunley, you can have little doubt as to what has brought us here. I do not know what induced you to send a man to intimidate Miss Henwood in the middle of the night. Don't deny it!" Madison raised a hand to silence the fiend before going on. "The fact that you would then threaten the daughter of a well-known member of society—I do not believe you fully comprehend the myriad ways I could destroy you with one little note to the right person."

Tunley didn't respond, but he stared on in mute shock.

Mr. Madison scoffed in disgust. "Is there no line you will not cross? Heaven's sake man, where is your head?"

Michael watched Tunley's snarl tremble again. The earl tried for a placating tone. Barely able to find his voice, he said, "I have no idea to what you are referring. Of course, I have nothing but the most profound respect for you and your friends and would never wish anyone the least bit of harm."

No one believed him, of course. Michael joined Madison at the front. "Lord Tunley, we would like to make our visit as brief as possible. At this point, we care little for those papers you so desperately want to hide from us."

Mr. Madison added, "If, for some obscure reason, you don't think I am aware of the Cornish venture's shares you currently possess, allow me to allay you of your misconception. It must be rankling to still not have complete control over the ironworks. You've exerted so much effort and time, not to mention what it must have taken to bring Mr. Stowes under your thumb."

Tunley, despite his original trepidation upon discovering his guests, had again gained some semblance of calm. Face turning almost impassive, Tunley replied, "I have no idea who this Stowes person is. As for those shares, I acquired them in the most acceptable manner possible. The largest portion was from family, and maybe a friend or two. Another portion was from a gentleman who wanted to leave England for a spell."

Michael expected that the events precipitating his friend leaving were orchestrated by Tunley. At the moment, Tunley was not exactly at his best, and might even be a touch inebriated. He certainly did not appear the great mastermind.

Tunley went on. "I do not appreciate having several people with whom I am barely associated barging into my home and making rash accusations. This sort of treatment is beyond the par."

By some miracle, everyone had been willing to allow Tunley to go on, hopefully with the intention of letting him bury himself. When Michael sensed that Mr. Madison intended to reply to Tunley, likely with a particularly cutting remark, Michael subtly shifted his foot to put some weight on Madison's toes. Although Madison understood, he sent a scowl in Michael's direction.

Tunley continued with his monologue, "I know several people who would be very interested to hear about this unannounced visit. I am not at all surprised to see the Henwoods here, but I cannot believe that you, Lord Averly, continue to include yourself with such an unruly bunch."

That appeared to be the end of Tunley's little speech. Now that Tunley had said his part, Michael asked, ever so politely, "Just what is it that you hold over Stowes to keep him at your bidding? You obviously can't pay the man." Here Michael looked around the room with obvious disdain. "One would think it would be below a man of your station to know such a character."

Tunley turned a bit red as he replied, "I have already told you that I have nothing to do with this street thug who appears to be harassing Miss Henwood. No doubt she has become involved in some highly improper dealings to have engaged the interests of such a man."

Michael was becoming a bit concerned that the lack of planning behind their surprise visit would be their downfall. Tunley could remain as tight-lipped as he wanted. After all, they were the ones who had forced their way into his home, making so many accusations that Tunley never had to focus on answering to a single one.

Unfortunately for Michael, he was not close enough to Charlotte to step on her toes. His almost-fiancée called from somewhere behind Mr. Madison, "Have you not yet realized that you've lost, Lord Tunley?" Charlotte nearly spat the man's title.

Tunley's cheeks turned a mottled red at her words. The earl attempted a scoff at her words before saying, "My dear girl, do people actually continue to take you seriously? What will Lord Averly do when he realizes that he should not be the only reason society treats you with respect?"

Charlotte paused, but quickly rallied. "My lord, no one cares what *you* have to say. You've spent too much time creating gossip and stories that have all been proven false. In addition to those wasted efforts, you still do not have controlling interest in the ironworks. Had you remained content with the shares you already possessed, you likely would not be in such a miserable position, now."

Michael watched as a change came over Tunley. No longer was he the slightly drunk yet still carefully polite roué. Tunley's flush appeared to spread through his entire person and Michael would have sworn he started shaking in anger. "Why couldn't I leave well enough alone? The answer is *you*, Miss Henwood— you and your newfound wealth. I come back to London after years away to find my home bare and rotting. My father had to sell most of his properties, as well as every single piece of art and most of the furniture in this house, after his finances went awry. There was nothing left but the family name. So I kept up appearances and convinced a friend to put in a good word for me with Madison, here. Finally, thanks to that ironworks, things seemed to be turning around."

Tunley began pacing, gesticulating as he did so. Michael was not sure if Tunley even remembered that there were more people in the room beyond Charlotte.

The earl went on, "I had tried to invest in shipping, but nothing brought back as much as that land in Cornwall. I managed to increase my shares—"

"Through intimidation and deceit!" Charlotte cut in.

At her words, Tunley faced her again. "But then I discovered how many people Madison had working in the ironworks and how much he was paying those drudges. That money should have been *mine*. Clearly Madison is going soft if he cares so much for the conditions of such filth as those commoners." His eyes narrowed to slits as he continued to glare at Charlotte. "After having Stowes question a few of the other investors for me, I discovered that Miss Henwood—the newly arrived heiress in Town—was the daughter of the man who could give me exactly what I wanted. You and your father possessed the most shares, second only to Madison, here. I needed you out of London, Miss Henwood, and away from Mr. Madison's influence. But you refused to leave and instead began to draw the attention of a viscount, of all people. No matter what I did or said, nothing seemed to drive you from London."

When Tunley paused for a breath, Charlotte added, "Forgive me if I don't apologize."

Tunley took a step toward Charlotte, rage in his eyes, but Michael and Mr. Madison moved to block him. "After last evening, I finally recognized that my original methods of sending you back to that God-forsaken Uckfield had failed."

Michael, calm despite his growing hatred for this vindictive man, asked, "Was that when you sent Stowes to the home of two unprotected ladies?" Tunley refused to answer; instead he stared angrily at Charlotte. Michael asked again, "What did you hope to accomplish in doing such a thing?"

Tunley finally dragged his eyes from Charlotte. No longer looking at the source of his vitriol, Tunley sounded almost eerily calm. "A conversation. On my terms." No one interrupted, now. "As Mr. Stowes has proven incapable of convincing Miss Henwood of the dangers of keeping those shares, I thought it was my turn to have a go at filling my coffers. It was a simple plan. Stowes was to remove Miss Henwood as delicately as possible from her residence in Town and bring her to a secluded location. I had already written to Sir Driscoll to inform him that his daughter had been taken. I intended to then demand that Sir Driscoll here pay for her safe return or risk her ruination. I don't care about the shares in the ironworks anymore. I just want to pay back my debts and I need a guinea or two to make that happen. I simply would prefer those guineas to belong to Sir Driscoll and Miss Henwood. They have done nothing to deserve their wealth—Miss Henwood is a nobody, damn you all!" Tunley looked down at his hands in resignation. "How could I expect Stowes to fail at such a simple task?"

Although Michael did not see it, he could practically feel Charlotte shrug noncommittally before she spoke. "I've been nearly ruined once or twice before—no thanks to you, Tunley, I might add—but for some reason I've managed to get along just fine. I doubt our 'conversation' would have gone as well as you expected."

Part of Tunley's story caught Michael's attention. Even though the question might not seem important to the earl, Michael asked, "Did you plan on having Stowes bring Charlotte here? Wouldn't there be the risk of your staff seeing her?"

Raising a brow, Lord Tunley replied, "This may shock you, but I had already thought of that. While the staff here is currently comprised of a very busy housekeeper and a single lazy footman, I still can't trust them to ignore a kidnapped heiress. No, one of the few properties entailed to the earldom is a hunting lodge just ten miles out of Town. I would have been there already, had Stowes not sent me a note describing his failure to remove Miss Henwood to that location."

For the first time during their visit, Michael smiled, "A hunting lodge, you say? Well, isn't that convenient?" Michael turned to Mr. Madison, "I believe we can be on our way now. Unless you have anything final to say?"

Confused, Madison said, "But what about—"

"That particular matter is, I believe, being remedied at this very moment."

Michael could see that Madison was torn between trusting him, or throttling Lord Tunley until the man told him where his daughter was. Hopefully Madison would realize what Michael already knew—that Lord Tunley seemed to know nothing about the disappearance of Julia Madison and it would be best if he never did. "Trust me." Michael knew he was asking for a great deal when the safety of the man's only daughter was at stake, but finally Madison nodded.

"Well," Tunley said in an unpleasantly cheerful tone, "it would seem that everything is resolved. I bid you all good day. Please excuse me while I prepare to visit my betrothed. It would seem that one good thing has come from this disaster. I have engaged myself to a lady with nearly enough of a dowry to pay off my father's debts."

Now it was Mr. Madison's turn to smile, although there was nothing cheerful about it. Charlotte had never before seen him look so very pleased and yet so very feral. "Ah, about that, Lord Tunley. I should have you know that I am such a successful man of business primarily due to the level of research I devote to every investment I make. This also includes the gentlemen with whom I invest. Before I agreed to allow you to partake in the Cornish venture, I had my man of affairs discover just how much money you owe in London, as well as to whom. Had your cousin not been so very persistent, I would never have allowed you into the venture, after I learned how desperate you are. As of this very moment, my estate manager is buying every single one of your debts on my behalf." Madison allowed Tunley a moment to absorb that before adding, "After this enlightening interlude, I've decided to demand payment. Immediately."

Tunley's smile disappeared like it had never been there. Nearly trembling, he answered, "You cannot do that." Trying to regain his composure, he added, "I'm sure the courts would agree."

"They might," Madison replied. "They might also be interested in just how many pounds you owe to a certain

Madam Ricely." Charlotte perked up. Suzie's previous comment pertaining to "rice" and "riding crops" no longer seemed like such a strange combination. Well, actually, they still seemed a bit outlandish.

Harry went on. "I've never met the woman personally, but I have heard that she does not like having the unique services she provides brought to the attention of the public. Just think how many new and powerful enemies you could make with one careless decision." Madison shook his head in mock sympathy. Charlotte remained uncertain how any of this related to riding crops, but perhaps Michael would tell her later on.

Too angry to speak, Tunley simply waited. Madison was certainly not done. "From what I have gathered, pertaining to your financial situation, I am aware that you are not currently able to repay me. No doubt most of your funds have gone directly to the slightly more frightening gentlemen you owe. But perhaps we can come to another arrangement."

By now Lady Kinsey and Mrs. Madison had returned, after searching the house for Julia. Mrs. Madison had clearly become quite frantic in her growing fear for Julia's safety. Out of the corner of his eye, Michael saw Charlotte whisper softly to the other two ladies, hopefully ordering neither to mention Julia to Lord Tunley.

Tunley shifted into a slightly more relaxed pose as he faced the group across the room. "I'm willing to listen to your proposal, Mr. Madison."

Madison nodded regally. "In return for ignoring the existence of your debts, I will accept all of the mining shares you possess. You see, I have decided that I do not enjoy engaging in business with you, my lord."

"*All* of them? You cannot possibly be serious."

"Indeed I am. I would not be surprised to discover that you are actually the one benefitting from this transaction. However, because I have always been considered a generous man, I will add something else into the bargain." Everyone waited for Madison to finish. "Two thousand pounds."

Mrs. Madison burst out, "Harry, you cannot possibly be willing to give this man any money after all that he's done! He doesn't deserve anything more than your foot in his arse!" Charlotte's jaw dropped.

Tunley smirked. "It would seem the inability to control one's women is not limited to Sir Driscoll or Lord Averly."

By some miracle, Mr. Madison remained calm. Ignoring Tunley's comment, he went on in a pleasantly reasonable tone, "There is a catch, of course. In two days' time, the *Windsong* sets sail for the Americas. You will have a cabin with a view, and inside that cabin will be your two thousand pounds. As I own that particular ship, I promise that it will not set sail without you. There are several ports of call on the register and you may take your pick. My only demand is that you do not return to England. I will hold your vowels in safekeeping, in case you do. How does that sound, Your Lordship?"

When Tunley did not answer, Charlotte added, "I'm sure you are thinking that perhaps your dowry from Miss Trivett will carry you over. From what I have gathered from my friend, Miss Caroline Trivett, it likely won't. Apparently the Trivetts are facing their own troubles, after implementing some unsuccessful changes to their farmland's soil. No doubt they expected *you* to save *them* from impending disaster. Considering your lifestyle in London, you will go through the few pounds you receive upon your wedding in days. It might be wisest to move to a city where you are not immediately aware of the location of every gaming den and brothel. Who knows? Perhaps you will find another way to occupy your time."

Tunley continued to glare, but finally answered. "Three thousand and I will start packing this second."

"Done."

When no one left the room, Tunley added, "Forgive me if I don't see you out."

Madison replied, "Of course, you will likely be busy making arrangements. However, I still need those papers in your safe."

Jaw clenched, Tunley turned to the still-open safe and retrieved the requested documents.

"You will allow me to take a moment to ensure everything is in order."

While Madison took an insultingly long time to go through everything, Michael faced Tunley. "I really must extend my gratitude, Lord Tunley. Had it not been for your convoluted machinations, I would never have come to know Miss Henwood." At the lady in question's cleared throat, he added, "Again."

Tunley raised a brow, "Yes, that woman is certainly your responsibility now. I wish you all the luck in the world," he added drily. When Michael didn't move to join the others, Tunley asked, his snarl even more prevalent than usual, "Did you require anything else, Lord Averly?"

Brows together in thought, Michael nodded, "I believe there is one more thing that I have been meaning to do for some time." And at that, Michael drew back his closed fist and swung out. Watching Tunley's head jerk back before his body followed, slamming him into the wall, was surprisingly satisfying.

*Who knew? Resorting to violence had its pleasant moments too.*

Grinning rather broadly, he turned back to the rest of his party. "Ready to leave this miserable place?"

Charlotte could not decide whether to be appalled or impressed. Trying to regain her composure, she replied, "Only if you are certain you are done?"

"I do believe so. No sport in kicking a man when he's down, after all. Shall we?" Offering his arm to Charlotte, who could only shake her head, they led the way downstairs, and back to the carriage.

Once everyone was settled awkwardly upon each other's laps, Mr. Madison asked, "Lord Averly, could you please explain just why you seem so very unconcerned for my daughter's safety?"

"Of course. I did not want to say anything before, because it seemed unlikely, but when Mr. Hampstead was with us earlier, he mentioned Tunley's hunting lodge. Apparently Hampstead was invited to a gathering, of sorts, at Tunley's lodge a few years ago. He seemed to think that if Julia was not here in Town, the lodge could be a good possibility. I have a feeling that when things did not go as planned with Miss Henwood, Mr. Stowes decided to take matters into his own hands. He no doubt kept the same plan, but chose a different victim."

Madison burst out, "Why the bloody hell aren't we on the way to that lodge right now?"

No one corrected his language.

Carefully, Michael answered, "Because he could still be wrong, and if Julia is somewhere in Town, you should remain here in case a note of some sort arrives." Although Madison seemed ready to argue, Michael went on, "Hampstead took one of your stablemen with him to the lodge. If Julia is found, the man will immediately return with news. Your stableman probably chose to ride one of your better steeds, for which I am sure you will forgive him. By now, Hampstead should just be arriving at the lodge. There is little we can do but wait for news."

While the carriage's occupants considered this, Mrs. Madison poked her husband in the shoulder. "I cannot believe you agreed to give that man an entire three thousand pounds. He does not deserve a shilling from us."

Mr. Madison shook his head. "He will go through it in a week, my dear. Men like Tunley have no concept of temperance. I only wish I could be present the moment he realizes how little import his title will have across the sea."

# Chapter 28

ONLY SLIGHTLY LESS WORRIED than when they had left to see Lord Tunley, everyone filed back into the Madison family's drawing room. They had less than an hour before society would begin making its rounds.

Tea was brought in. Charlotte poured, but no one actually drank any. The room mostly remained silent, except when Lady Kinsey observed that they should really think of an excuse for Julia's absence. It was agreed that were anyone to ask, Julia was visiting a cousin just outside of the city.

Perhaps it was just her nerves, but Charlotte felt certain that the room was unusually chill for such a sunny day. Although her anxiety primarily surrounded Julia's safety, one other concern pulled at her. What would the Trivetts do once they discovered Tunley's absence? Ellie and, by proximity, Caroline could be ruined by his abandonment.

Charlotte resolved to send off a note at once to warn them of Tunley's new situation. Perhaps they could contrive a story in which Ellie chose to reject the earl. If she and Lord Averly married, no doubt an invitation to visit at one of His Lordship's estates would go a long way to preserve the Trivetts' position in society as well. Despite Charles Trivett's role in nearly ruining her, Charlotte would never wish for Caroline, or even Eleanor, to suffer. They had all once been friends.

Then she met Michael's eyes and all of a sudden the room felt too warm, her worries gone. Just when she thought she would go mad from the silence, the pounding of a horse's hooves resounded up the drive. Charlotte was the first to reach the window overlooking the Madison drive. "The stableman's returned."

At that news, everyone rose unceremoniously and ran down to the entry. The stableman was out of breath, but there was no doubt of the relief on his face. "She's fine. Hampstead has her." Mrs. Madison, bursting into tears, threw herself into her husband's arms.

Still catching his breath, the man went on, "Miss Madison was certainly in a mood once we got to her. Mr. Hampstead only has the one horse and was not certain of the most proper way to return Miss Madison. He said he would send a note once they found an inn outside London. I hope I have done everything I could, Mr. Madison, but Mr. Hampstead seemed to have everything well in hand. In fact, he appeared to be enjoying himself immensely."

Charlotte did not doubt it. Hampstead always had the most ludicrous sense of humor. Now Hampstead was resigning everyone to wait again. They all returned to the drawing room. This time, instead of tea, they would have brandy. Mr. Madison sent a man out for champagne. No doubt Julia would be quite thirsty after her adventures today.

Everyone's relief, mixed with a little brandy, sent the group into high spirits. Charlotte laughed at the stories Harry shared about her father's younger years. Her father managed to cut him off before he got too carried away, which only made Charlotte laugh harder.

Perhaps an hour or two after the groom arrived with his news, Mr. Hampstead's promised note arrived. Charlotte saw Harry's slight concern as he passed the note to Imogen. Sir Driscoll and Lady Kinsey were engaged in a very energetic discussion about pirates, so they did not notice the exchange. Suzie was regaling Michael with Ryder's last night on the town. Charlotte could tell that Michael could not decide between being amused or appalled at his younger brother's behavior.

After nodding to his wife, Harry went to the door to speak with a footman. However, when he came back into the room, he raised another toast to Julia's safety. Charlotte decided to think nothing else of it. Harry and Imogen's worry already seemed to have dissipated.

In everyone's exuberance, Michael found her hand. Slowly he drew her to the doorway. "Miss Henwood, if I might have a moment?" he murmured in her ear.

---

Mr. and Mrs. Madison watched as Lord Averly drew Miss Henwood from the room. Mr. Madison leaned in to attract Lady Kinsey's attention. "Your Ladyship, I did not wish to distress Miss Henwood, not while she and Lord Averly seem to have matters to discuss. It seems that Julia will not be returning to London straight away, as expected."

At Lady Kinsey's look of alarm, Mrs. Madison cut in, "Julia is perfectly safe and healthy. It is only that when Mr. Hampstead found a place to stop on his way back to Town, they may have been discovered. He writes to mention his crossing paths with a Mrs. Priestly, who we all know is an inveterate gossip. We must come up with a reason for Julia to be traveling north of London, and practically in her underclothes, no less."

Lady Kinsey attempted to contain her excited smile. Her adventures were not nearly done, after all. "It would seem, my friends, that what you are in need of, at the moment, is a well-seasoned chaperone to make everything proper."

---

Charlotte watched Michael nervously look up and down the hallway, no doubt uncertain where to take her. Taking pity on him, Charlotte pulled Michael deeper down the hall. "My old room is just this way. It may be…quieter in there."

"Quieter is good."

Although they had started at a walk, they were practically running by the time they both reached Charlotte's old room.

Had they not been so nervous, they would no doubt have been laughing by the time they reached her door.

Charlotte's room was primarily dark wood and white fabric. There was a chair and writing desk by the window. Wisely avoiding the bed, Michael brought Charlotte to the chair. But she wouldn't sit. She couldn't.

Now that they finally had the privacy to speak openly to one another, neither knew what to say. Charlotte watched Michael with fascination as he took a deep breath, his eyes resolute. At the last moment, he just let the breath out in what seemed to Charlotte a sort of agitated sigh.

All of a sudden, Charlotte felt supremely guilty. She had practically demanded a proposal from him this morning. After such a harrowing day, Michael had no time to prepare anything especially moving and romantic.

She took his hands, "Michael." He looked down at her, a touch of apprehension in his eyes. "I should not have been so harsh this morning. Considering the manner in which we spent last night, you had every reason to wake with certain expectations. All I wanted was the chance to discuss our future before making any announcements. Both of our lives will change. You must understand that I was never raised to be the wife of a viscount. My father taught me mathematics and history, and a whole number of other things, in the hopes that I would not have to marry if I did not want to. And I've been doing quite well, if I may say so, without anyone to support me."

Michael's lips turned up at the corners. "That you have. You know, except for the gossip that seems to follow you wherever you go, a retired boxer who seems to continually want to attack your person, and a mad earl who considers you the root of all evil."

Charlotte's brows knit. "Are you possibly teasing me, Lord Averly? Because I think you should know that I have brought quite a bit of much-needed excitement into your life. Were it not for me, you would be contentedly going on with your dull, stodgy ways."

"Dull and stodgy? Were I not a gentleman, I would ask just how dull and stodgy you found me to be last night," he drawled.

Charlotte reddened just a little bit, but did not back down. "What I am trying to say," she bit out, "is that I never truly had time to seriously consider what our union would mean. Will I have to put everything aside to care for our home and family? Because I will have you know that if anyone should oversee the family's investments and finances, it should be me."

"This may come as a shock to you, but I have been doing just fine on my own as well."

"I have been doing better than just fine." Charlotte crossed her arms, ready to stand toe-to-toe with Michael.

After holding his stern look for just a moment longer, Michael burst into laughter. As the unexpected sound rolled over her, Charlotte also relaxed. Before she could uncross her arms, Michael slid his hands around her waist. Leaning down, he said softly in her ear, "You are the most strong-willed, stubborn woman I have ever had the pleasure to meet. But you are also brilliant, clever, and perhaps the most beautiful creature I have ever laid eyes on. I don't care that you were not educated from birth in the finer points of fashion, or how to plan the perfect fête." Charlotte relaxed even more, as she felt his deep voice whisper down her spine. Slowly, she uncrossed her arms and brought them around his neck. "Perhaps we could agree to a compromise. I will manage the Averly estates and finances, no doubt with quite a bit of your meddling, while you continue doing exactly what you are doing already."

Charlotte stood on her toes so as to fully embrace him. "Perhaps I can set funds aside for our daughters' educations. We can send them on their own European tours. I was always so jealous of the gentlemen who traveled on their own before coming back to England to settle down."

Michael chuckled softly in her ear. "Now that, my dear Charlotte, sounds perfectly acceptable. You should know that I will now take you wherever you wish to go."

"Do you absolutely promise to let me continue my investments?"

"Quite frankly, I would be a fool not to." There was a great deal of pride in his voice.

"Is there some way we could have that as a part of the settlement?"

"I do not believe such a thing would stand up in court, but we can certainly put it in there. No, my dear Charlotte, you are simply going to have to trust me."

"That, my dear Michael, is something I believe I can quite easily do. I love you, you know."

Michael gave her a final squeeze before standing back. "And I love you." Taking her hand, he knelt. "Charlotte Euphedora Henwood—" her jaw dropped at his use of that odious middle name "—would you do me the honor of becoming my wife?"

Before answering, Charlotte asked, "Is there any chance you have an equally vile middle name?"

"James."

"No! That will not do at all."

"Charlotte, would you please be so kind as to answer me. A man can only wait so long before nerves begin to take hold of him."

"Well, you were the one who so foolishly decided to use my middle name. But yes, I do believe I shall relieve your delicate nerves and agree to marry you."

Laughing, Michael rose and engulfed her in an embrace that ended in a passionate kiss. As he nibbled his way along her jaw line, Charlotte could just barely hear Lady Kinsey call from the hallway into the drawing room, "They're getting married! Isn't it wonderful?"

She could just make out Mrs. Madison say, "What, Julia and Mr. Hampstead? What can you mean?"